To my wife, Moira

Best Wishes
Bill Yates

Formerly titled: The Russian Rocks

Bill Yeates

=========================

Treasure Of The Tzars

(The Rob Blackstock series – Book 1)

Copyright © Bill Yeates 2024

The right of Bill Yeates to be identified as author of this work has been asserted by the author in accordance with sections 77 and 78 of the Copyright, Designs and Patents Act 1988.

All rights reserved. No part of this publication may be reproduced, stored in a retrieval system, or transmitted in any form or by any means, electronic, mechanical, photocopying, recording, or otherwise, without the prior permission of the author.

Any person who commits any unauthorised act in relation to this publication may be liable to criminal prosecution and civil claims for damages.

This is a work of fiction. Names, characters, businesses, places, events, locales, and incidents are either the products of the author's imagination or used in a fictitious manner. Any resemblance to actual persons, living or dead, or actual events is purely coincidental.

Treasure Of The Tzars

Millionaire Rob Blackstock, widowed father of two, is drawn into a world totally alien to him when his son is witness to the murder of a young Russian girl. Events lead Rob into dark times as he tries to protect his family from a chain of corrupt Metropolitan police officers, London street gangs and the Russian Mafia.

A stolen gemstone, stories of long-lost jewels and untold wealth can turn even the most law-abiding person to a life of crime. As Rob uncovers things he'd rather not know about on a path that leads him from London to the salt pans of Astrakhan in Russia, he exposes some powerful people for who they really are.

His help comes from one of the few people he can totally trust, a former military police woman with Russian ancestry. Together they unravel the mystery of what happened to the Russian Royal Family's riches but can they beat the mystery person known only as The Inspector to the ultimate prize.

As the body count rises, they find themselves working with MI-6 in Russia tracking down The Inspector and being watched every step of the way by the mafia.

Chapter 1

"The plan is simple. Pete and I are booked in at 9:45 to see some gems in a private showing in a side room. Harry you've got an appointment at 10:00 to see some engagement rings, you'll be in the main gallery. When we arrive, we have to go through a security check before the door is unlocked for us to go in and then it's locked behind us. Jameson and Rebecca will arrive slightly after us to view the new security system. Harry you wait five minutes after you see Jameson go into the back office then you shout for everyone to pay attention. That is our signal to burst out of the side room. Pete you go to the door and secure the guard and I go into the back office. We all must make sure our guns can be seen."

"Whatever you do, don't shoot Jameson or Rebecca. She'll be carrying out the diamond. Harry you get as many gems into the rucksack as you can. We leave when the cops arrive. I carry the rucksack out and as soon as we're challenged by the cops we put our hands up and I drop the rucksack so that it spills. We'll be taken into custody and charged with armed robbery, but The Inspector will see to it we serve no more than twelve months inside and we'll each get half a million pounds. OK!"

****

Two raindrops raced down the car window gathering speed as they merged with small droplets clinging to the glass. They raced on until they joined the stream disappearing over the curve of the door panel and splashing down into the stream running forty yards down the road to the drain.

Looking out at the rain, but not actually seeing it, was Justin Brian SilverlyBlackstock, JB to everyone except his grandmother to whom he will always be Justin or Justin Brian when she was unhappy with him and that was more often than either of them was happy with.

JB was a thirteen-year-old, bored son of a millionaire looking for adventure. At least that was the description he put against his name on his new Facebook account that he was finally allowed to create two days ago, the day of his thirteenth birthday. All of JB's friends had been on Facebook for several months but his father had said many times that, "Using social media creates bad habits that impact on proper communications. Abbreviated words used do nothing to improve a person's spelling nor does it help them in learning how to construct sentences. Only once the person has learnt how to use the English language properly should they then start to use social media. Certainly they should not be using it for direct communication with people outside of their local community until they are at least thirteen, when he would hope they would have enough about them not to be drawn into communications with strangers." JB thought this was a bit of outdated thinking but had been stuck with it until now.

    JB was sitting in the back of his father's six-month-old Jag at the A1 motorway services at Peterborough. He had shaken his coat hard to get rid of the worst of the rain then draped it over one of the bags in the boot. He knew that there was no hope of it drying but spreading it out would not do it any harm. He opened the rear door of the Jag and climbed into the seat behind the driver's seat as quickly as he could trying his best to get undercover out of the rain, before his clothes got too wet and uncomfortable. He eased off his soaked trainers and pushed them under the seat in front of him. His socks remarkably were still dry but his jeans were damp all over, the bottoms of the legs were particularly wet, having trailed through puddles in the carpark. JB followed the fashion for wearing his jeans low on his hips so there was a lot of material around the ankles and this was now wet and wouldn't dry very quickly. All he'd done was run from the car to the building to go to the loo. Now he wished he hadn't done so. He hadn't really needed to go but his father had suggested it as a good idea, as they still had a long way to go and he didn't want to have to stop again.

He turned the radio on for the latest weather report and caught the news.

He had missed most of the first item, something about a politician who had been found to have submitted a false expenses claim, but he listened carefully to the remaining items.

"Metropolitan police have issued a statement confirming that an armed robber was shot dead this morning and two others detained in custody after a foiled robbery attempt on a London diamond merchant. A police spokesman said that the gunmen burst out of a side room on the ground floor and held everyone at gunpoint. A member of staff had been able to trigger a new silent alarm that also opened a series of hidden microphones that allowed the police to listen in and determine that the robbers were well armed and dispatched an armed unit to the scene. In attempting to escape, the police shot the robber carrying the stolen gems, causing him to drop the bag and spill its contents. All but one of the gems have since been recovered. The missing diamond was quite a famous gem referred to as 'The Rose of Russia' and was said to be worth between £250-300,000..."

Having missed the weather, he turned the radio off again without listening to the rest of the bulletin. He sat back and thought what he would do if he found that diamond. There was bound to be a reward, perhaps as much as ten percent. He dreamt of how £25,000 would change his life. And there had been a shootout in the streets of London. Maybe this trip would be fun after all.

JB and his dad were on route to his dad's London flat from North Yorkshire where JB now lived with his grandparents, or more correctly lived when not away at school in Edinburgh. Edinburgh had been JB's choice out of the three options offered him by his dad, when he had been ten, and his dad wanted him to have the best chance of being successful in life. Ski lessons in the Scottish highlands during the winter term had been the ultimate decider for JB, there being nothing between what was being offered academically by the three establishments, in his opinion. He had loved skiing since he'd first hit the mountain slopes of Austria, aged five, on a family trip. There had been five of them then. Dad (Robert 'Rob' Blackstock), mum (Jayne Silverly), JB and seven year old twins Michael and Lucinda. It was rare for dad to be there with them. He was normally too busy with work to be able to spare the time, so this had been something special for all of them.

As it turned out, that had been their last family holiday before mum and Michael were killed in a car crash just three weeks after their return home. Run off the road by a drunk driver, moments after she had collected Michael from his Wednesday football practice at Villa Park. Jayne's car had been pushed into the central reservation of the dual carriageway, causing it to spin back into the path of a fast-moving lorry, heavy with its load of building materials. They didn't stand a chance. The lorry hit them broadside and pushed them sideways some two hundred feet. The collision had split the fuel tank causing it to leak petrol across the carriageway. Friction of metal on the road surface had generated sparks which ignited the petrol. A cone of flames backtracked along the stream of escaping fuel and when it reached the split tank the remaining petrol exploded engulfing both the car and the cab of the lorry, resulting in Jayne and Michael's death and the death of the young lorry driver.

At the inquest held two months later, Coroner Louise Potter concluded all three died as a result of a road traffic collision. She added that Christopher Blunt had been the undoubtable cause of the accident, whilst he had been driving under the influence of alcohol.

The inquest had heard that Blunt had been three times over the amount of alcohol in his system than was considered to be a safe legal limit. In her summing up Louise Potter instructed that Blunt should be remanded in custody until he can face trial and she would also be recommending he be charged with manslaughter which carried a maximum sentence of life imprisonment, whereas causing death whilst under the influence of alcohol only carries a maximum of fourteen years.

Christopher Blunt actually received a sentence of only two years less the three and a half months already served while waiting for the case to reach court. His expensive legal team had used the time well.

Back in those days, the family had lived in a large house in the northern outskirts of Birmingham in the district of Aston. Jayne had always taken responsibility for running the household, doing everything from doing the weekly shopping to buying the children's school uniforms, making sure that the children got to school on time, nursing them when they were ill and entertaining them during weekends and school holidays. She was always where the children needed her to be. She was also Rob's best friend and lover. One of a kind, she could never be replaced. When she had met Rob she had totally given her life to him. No more dreams of becoming a big screen star but a supportive role as wife and mother.

Rob was a successful business man earning big money. His work took him away from home on a regular basis, often for several days at a time. Now that Jayne had gone there was no way he could look after two young children and run the house. Even if he gave up work he couldn't do it. He didn't know how Jayne had managed to juggle everything all the time. He engaged a housekeeper and a live in governess but even the two between them couldn't do everything. Bills didn't get paid because neither the housekeeper nor the governess could be expected to have control of the household finances and when Rob was at home, there were so many demands on him that he simply overlooked things or just didn't have enough time to do everything he needed to do. After just six months he realised the situation was hopeless and the children were the ones suffering the most. He had to find an alternative that would work for all of them.

To give everyone a break he took time off work and drove the children up to North Yorkshire for a holiday at his father Eric's racing stable. The children loved having their dad around all the time and not being tired and grumpy. They loved the open space of the country side and Rob's mother, Rose, loved having people about, keeping her busy doing all the little jobs that are necessary to keep a family running. For a few days she had purpose in her life again. It was an obvious solution. The children should relocate to North Yorkshire to live with granny and gramps, Rose and Eric Blackstock, at their horse stables near Tadcaster.

Eric Blackstock, like his father George Barclay Blackstock before him, and his father Barclay Fredrick Blackstock before him, was a racehorse trainer. George had been quite successful and had had two classic winners in the 1960s, but George had died young and Eric was only nineteen, with very little business experience, when he took over the family businesses. George had very much been in charge of the business not allowing anyone to help him. He was the total manager. His wife was just that, his wife and his staff were only the hired help. So when Eric took control there was no one he could turn to for help. The closest that Eric had got to winning a big race was a second in the 1992 National. However he knew a lot about horses, having lived with them all his life and was proud to say he could ride any horse.

Although his small racing successes around the country gave the family a steady income, it was his second business he had built his fortune on and which he was happier being involved in, although he enjoyed nothing more than race day. He was torn between the two businesses. Luckily help came when he found a manager for the day to day running of the racing stables. Phil had worked his way up through the ranks at a stable in Newmarket and the vacancy at Eric's stable had come at the right time. His career had reached a plateau and his wife had just walked out on him leaving him with a small son to raise.

It had all started with Barclay Blackstock, Rob's great-great-grandfather, who had by all accounts been a bit of a rogue. At nearly nineteen had joined a cavalry regiment to escape the wrath of the husband of one of the many ladies he was frequently bedding.

He had only been in London for four months, coming up from his family home in the Cotswolds near Cirencester, where his fondness for the fair sex had put him in trouble on many occasions. From the age of fourteen or fifteen he had been a magnet to all women of any age. He didn't have to do anything, women just swarmed over him and much of the trouble came from women physically fighting over him. His latest trouble came when a husband caught him actually in the marital bed and Barclay had been lucky to get away without a beating or worse.

Soon after completing a short period of basic training and joining his regiment, they were called to action to fight the Boers in South Africa. He learnt how to play poker on the long boat transfer south and long before he disembarked at the Cape he had become a very accomplished player.

He was a very likeable person, so quickly established himself and was well in with his senior officers. There were very few women about and almost no opportunity to meet any of them, so his past troubles did not follow him.

He had lived all his life in the country. His family ate whatever they could find in the hedgerows or shoot in the woods, so he was more than comfortable riding and shooting both rifle and pistol, skills that helped him rise through the ranks and at the end of his two years in Africa, he held the rank of captain.

Playing poker with his fellow officers had built him a reputation and a large enough cash pile to buy himself out of the army and secure passage to America at the end of hostilities.

After time in the Caribbean, he eventually landed in New York in the autumn of 1905 and then spent the following years working his way across the country moving from job to job and state to state doing whatever work he could find, warehouse night-watchman, restaurant pot washer, ranch hand, road sweeper and park attendant, anything to allow him to eat and regularly move on. He finally ends up in the small village of Hollywood in the spring of 1923 where he immediately stepped into a job caring for the horses being used in one of the very first motion picture westerns.

Some days he had to have as many as twenty horses on set at one time. Delays because animals were not ready were costly and not acceptable. Distinctive markings had to be avoided so that one animal could be used for a role in multiple scenes. Barclay's skill with horses made him a natural in this job so, when at the end of filming when the horses were to be sold off, Barclay took them in lieu of outstanding wages. He used the last of his savings to buy property with stables in the nearby district and to retain two of the stable boys to help care for the horses.

It took several years for the film industry to recognise the value of letting someone else manage the horse flesh but slowly more and more movie makers came to Barclay with their requirements for horses in their filming.

Barclay's business grew alongside the rapidly growing film industry and Barclay soon established himself as the sole supplier of horses to the movie makers of California but also he was training riders as stunt men and hiring them out to the movie makers. By the time war broke out in Europe, Barclay's business was a multi-million dollar concern and he was personally a millionaire with a massive reputation.

At the end of the war in 1945, he made the decision to move himself and his wife back to England, leaving his twenty one year old son, George, in control of the American business.

On arrival in England, Barclay sought out the key people from the British film industry and made himself known. Within a few months he had located and purchased a suitable property and set about creating a replica of his US business. The property he had purchased was an established racing stable on the outskirts of London at Esher, only a mile or so from Sandon Park racecourse and within easy reach of the courses at Kempton Park and Epsom. The stables were surrounded by miles of open countryside on which the race horses could be exercised and the stable buildings were very suitable for housing and training the horses to be used in films. There was also domestic accommodation where stunt riders could stay whilst training. It's only failing was it was south of the Thames and the main film studios were some distance north of the Thames, but as more and more filming was being done 'on location' this was no real issue.

Most of the staff of the racing stables were happy to stay on with the new owner, there were just a couple of places that had to be filled. But the movie side of things needed both horses, staff to look after and train them, plus men and women who wanted to train as stunt riders. The first few years were very slow, so to fill his time Barclay took a growing interest in horse racing and started to attend big race meetings. The British film industry did not try to compete against the big block busting westerns and war dramas being produced in America, but was producing gentler, romantic movies to lighten the peoples mood after the violence and upheaval of six years of war. Barclay was just happy that George was doing so well in America with his horses and stunt riders permanently in demand.

The big break for the British company came in 1948 with the making of Bonnie Prince Charlie, a movie starring David Niven and Margaret Leighton. George supplied over one hundred horses and twenty stunt riders for that movie and as part of the contract his company name appeared in big letters in the rolling credits.

On the course during the 1951 Epsom Derby, Barclay suffered a massive stroke leaving him wheelchair bound. George, wanting to support his father, came over to England with his new bride and took control of both the racing stables and the movie connected business, running these and the US business from his new built home in Buckinghamshire. Over the next couple of years he acquired land near his house and built racing stables with a private race track on which to exercise the horses. He also built a separate complex to support a stunt riding business, with its own large indoor training arena, a mini cinema and what looked like a hotel block to house up to twenty four training stunt riders. Both projects were funded by selling the Epsom stables to property developers who built housing for what was being called London Overspill.

The racing stables became very successful, attracting significant new owners, bringing in several high quality horses and leading to even greater successes. He expanded by buying a second racing stable in

North Yorkshire near Tadcaster. George was recognised through the 1950s and 1960s as one of Britain's top trainers averaging more than one hundred and fifty winners each year and winning two classics.

The heavy demand of running two businesses, one in Britain and one in US took its toll and George suffered a fatal heart attack at the age of forty eight, leaving an estate valued at more than one hundred million pounds to his only son Eric. Eric, now a very rich and eligible bachelor, turned his back on society and married his childhood sweetheart Rose Littleton and in 1976 Rob was born.

As Rob grew, he showed little interest in the horse businesses even though he had become a very accomplished rider. However, he proved to be a great academic and was the first member of the family to go to University. At twenty one he left Oxford with a first class honours degree in mathematics and was snapped up by a major accounting firm in London. With his family connections to the US and British film industries he joined the firm's movie support team. He soon held a significant position in that section and was regularly crossing the Atlantic dealing with the finances of several movie companies, bringing in to the company many millions each year, whilst retaining a considerable percentage for himself to boost his already indecently high salary.

At this time JB's mother, Jayne Silverly, a former child model and budding actress, was being recognised and cast in increasingly more important roles. Rob and Jayne met at a party, hosted by movie director Brice Williams looking to finance a new project. Jayne had been invited to add a little glamour to the occasion and having been in the last film directed by Williams, was hopeful of being included in the next. Rob was there to represent his firm and to spot potential investors, so that they could be checked out as being financially sound.

Rob had noticed Jayne early in the evening when they had both arrived and he'd followed her up the eighteen steps into the hotel. His eyes being drawn to her extremely attractive rear end, as it moved seductively under a figure hugging ivory full length gown. His thoughts were drawn to wondering what the body beneath looked like and fantasised that this gorgeous creature in front of him wore nothing under the rags that he saw.

He did not see her again until they literally bumped into one another at the buffet bar. Jayne was moving along selecting a few nice titbits, when the strap of her elegant shoulder bag wrapped around the neck of a champagne bottle causing it to over balance and fall from the table emptying its contents across the polished floor. Jayne instantly spun about and bent to retrieve the bottle, not noticing that Rob who stood just second in the queue behind her, was also attempting to rescue the bottle before it emptied all of its contents.

They met head to head.

Bouncing off one another, they sat up holding their heads, looked at one another, then down at the now empty bottle and burst into laughter. Totally ignored by those around them who were more interested in avoiding the growing puddle of French fizz.

To Rob she was even more beautiful up close than he had thought, when he had seen her on the steps outside earlier. He felt a very strong attraction to her, even before they shared their first words. Jayne too felt an instant tingle deep inside as she looked at this slender, tall, and by his suit obviously very rich man. He stood first and offered to help her up. Taking both of his offered hands, she allowed him to pull her to her feet. He then took a handful of napkins from the table and began to brush her down, taking more care when he brushed across her rear. He couldn't help but smile to himself thinking he had been right earlier about what she wore under that gown. Now standing, Jayne turned to face him and began to thank him, but before she had spoken more than two words, they again burst out laughing and she lent in towards him. Briefly resting her head on his shoulder before placing a gentle kiss on his cheek and whispering, "Thank you," in his ear, then turning and walking slowly away.

Immediately Rob's attention was draw to the damp patch across the back of her dress and realised the seat of his trousers was similarly wet. He quickly followed her, taking hold of her arm to stop her and in a low tone said, "That dress must be terribly uncomfortable. I know my trousers are. We should get into some dry things. I'll get you a taxi so you can get back to your hotel." She smiled, nodded agreement and they walk towards the lifts. No one saw them leave or missed them once they'd left.

They exited the hotel and the doorman hailed two taxis to the curb side. As she entered the taxi she called her destination hotel through to the driver, Rob reacted quickly, grabbing to door to stop it closing, "Hey, I'm staying there too! We could share." Again she smiled and nodded her agreement, then slid across to make room, leaving a damp mark on the seat where she had been sitting. Both of them saw it, made eye contact and smiled as he climbed aboard.

As they passed through the empty streets Rob decided to take a chance.

"You know it's only just 9 o'clock! We should get cleaned up, put on dry clothes and go down for dinner, my treat. Maybe share a bottle of wine and laugh over this evening's incident."

"That's a great idea! That party was beginning to bore me anyway," she said as she placed her hand on top of his on the seat between them and at the same time turning her head towards the window and smiling, knowing he couldn't see her face.

On arriving at the hotel they collected their keys from reception, walked across the deserted foyer and into an empty lift. She flashed her key at him, ten twelve; he pressed for floor ten then floor twelve and flashed his key back at her. Twelve-twelve.

"Well, who'd have guessed we'd be sleeping less than twenty feet apart tonight," he said smiling at the suggestion as to what 'less than' meant.

She in turn simply blew him a kiss and turned away. The door opened and she walked out. He called after her.

"See you downstairs in fifteen."

"Make it ten. I'm hungry!" She called back over her shoulder, without turning her head.

As the doors closed he said out loud "SHIT—I didn't get her name. What if she doesn't come down in ten or fifteen."

As the doors opened again, he ran to his room peeled off his suit, splashed quickly though the shower, not waiting for it to reach temperature, pulled on his jeans and a company branded t-shirt. He was still pulling on his shoes as he left the room. A quick glance at his watch, six and a half minutes, three and a half minutes should be plenty of time. The lift had returned to the ground floor, so he took the stairs down two floors and knocked on the door bearing the number ten twelve.

A female voice from behind the door responded with, "Who's there?"

"Your escort to dinner, madam," he replied trying to disguise his voice with an obvious false French accent.

The response, when the door opened came as a real shock that left him speechless and mouth open. There standing in the space where the door had been, was his dinner date, framed by light from the room. She had changed from that stunning gown and now wore simple black leggings and an oversized printed t-shirt pulled down low off her right shoulder. He could easily make out the shape of her nipples through the soft printed shirt fabric, indicating she was bra less and her auburn hair that had previously been piled high on her head was now loose and cascaded some three inches below her neck line and shone as if freshly washed. He could have easily pushed her back into the room and had his way with her there and then. But, this girl, no! This lady already meant something special to him and worth far more than a quick romp on a hotel bed to satisfy his lust. He offered his arm, closed the door behind her and they took the lift to the restaurant floor.

It was now almost 9:30 and their appetite for food had faded. Rob ordered two Caesar salads and a bottle of champagne. They ate slowly, talking continuously, telling one another their entire life stories and not taking notice of their surroundings or the fact that the restaurant was slowly emptying. By 11:30 they were still at their table finishing their champagne and the head waiter suggested they might be more comfortable moving to the lounge. Looking around, the restaurant was empty and the other tables had been laid for breakfast. They quickly draining the remains of their glasses then moved to a quiet corner of the lounge and continued talking. The barman saw them as they settled down and walked across to their table, to take their orders and instructions to repeat every forty five minutes. Time for them flew by and when 3:00 came round they decided to call it a night and let the barman go off duty.

In the lift Jayne invited Rob to join her for a last nightcap from her mini bar. He accepted and followed her into her room. "Brandy with ice please. I need the bathroom for a minute. Pour yourself a drink," she said as she left the room.

Rob scanned the room for the mini bar. On the floor in a heap was her dress from earlier but no sign of underwear. The mini bar was just behind it. He picked up the dress and draped it over the nearest chair, opened the bar and poured two brandies. As he placed the drinks on the side table next to the two seater sofa, the bathroom door slowly opened. His jaw dropped for the second time that evening because walking through the open door was the perfect shape of Jayne's totally naked body. As she crossed the floor towards Rob and into the light of the bedroom, he noticed she had no body hair at all which added to the appeal.

No words passed between them, they weren't needed. She tugged at his shirt and he helped her pull it over his head. She ran her hands down his chest, dragging her nails across his nipples and on down to his belt. They kissed for the first time as she undid his trouser fastenings and push them and underpants down together and freeing his stiffening flesh. She dropped to her knees, now using one hand to pull his trousers to his ankles. With her other hand she guided his growing flesh into her wet mouth and to the back of her throat. She had lost her virginity at fifteen and had many lovers since. She knew how to act the role of high class whore, giving her man exactly what he fantasied about, so that he in turn would satisfy her needs.

He lifted her to her feet again and to kiss her and she breathed heavily into his mouth. Their tongues entwined, as did their bodies. Locked together.

They made love for several hours before falling into an exhausted sleep.

They woke at 9:15. As an actress between parts, Jayne had nothing urgent to get up for and a lunch date with her mother could be easily rescheduled. Rob was never expected in the office on the day after a director's party. So they ordered room service breakfast for two and made plans for the day.

It only took a few minutes for the breakfast to arrive, almost as if it had already been prepared. Jayne slipped on her baggy tee-shirt to answer the door and let in a very attractive maid, who set the tray down on the side table and left, closing the door behind her.

"I see you thought her very attractive," Jayne said looking at the bulge in the bed cover.

"Jealous?"

"Should I be?" she said as she peeled the tee-shirt off and slid into bed.

They kept their romance under covers, not telling anyone. But the girls in the office could see he was getting good sex somewhere, by the perpetual grin on his face. Three months after that first evening, they were married in a backstreet Soho hotel, witnessed by two maids. Two days later they left for a four week honeymoon. Rob was sent to Los Angeles for a series of business meetings, so took Jayne with him and while he worked she visited all the sights she had hoped her career would take her to. They spent the time he was not working together.

On their return to London, she confirmed she was four months pregnant with twins. Conceived on that first night. They were born in the February and named Michael after the hotel barman and Lucinda after the maid who had delivered their breakfast. JB was born just over two years later.

At the end of that first 6 months Rob's parents had agreed to provide a home for the children and Rob made some life changing decision. He ploughed a large sum of money into his father's businesses, modernising and expanding both. He left his job and took over running the stunt man business where he could use his network of contacts to further expand. Eric would focus on racing. Rob's house north of Birmingham was sold and he bought a large London flat. To give the children some security, they went to stay with Eric and Rose on a permanent basis and Rob joined them as often as he could.

When Luci and JB arrived at Eric's estate, they were introduced to housekeeper Madge Little. "Welcome to Yorkshire, call me Madge. You both must be tired, come into the kitchen for a drink and a slice of chocolate cake." The children instantly took a liking to Madge. Not a replacement for their mother, more a substitute.

Madge lived in the gatehouse at the end of the main drive to the house. Its proximity to the main house meant she was available twenty four seven, but the Blackstock's never took advantage and gave her more time off than she really wanted. Reg Little, Madge's husband, was also a Blackstock employee. He maintained the buildings and kept the garden tidy. He liked to be known as the maintenance man rather than gardener/handyman. He was also the Blackstock's occasional Chauffeur.

The two children had suffered a lot in the months since Jayne had been killed but they were always there for one another. The bonds grew even stronger now they had moved to their new home. Rob got to see them as often as work would allow and made sure he was in Yorkshire for at least 1 night each week.

And so the years went on until JB realised that Luci was beginning to take less interest in the things he wanted to do. Instead she liked to go down to the local village and watch the boys' schools football team, he was also aware of her getting moody every three or four weeks and when she was 'on one', as he referred to her moods, she didn't want anything to do with him. Thinking she might be ill or something he shared his concerns with Gramps. Eric gave a chuckle.

"That's just women's trouble. Luci is growing up," he said.

Even more confused JB went to the kitchen and asked Madge what she thought. She sat down at the kitchen table with him and proceeded to explain what was happening to Luci's body and that it was totally normal. Afterwards, she thought she had said too much, but his questions had led her on and after all he was ten going on eleven.

With Luci's interests moving towards other things, JB was at a loose end most days. He spent a lot of time with Eric, keenly learning the business of race horse training. He impressed his grandad as to how quickly he learnt. Then one day in early spring when he found his grandad in the stable block. He saw a very worried man talking on his mobile phone.

"Thanks Phil, as soon as you can it looks bad!" he heard Eric say. "Oh JB we've got a real mess here. One of the yearlings has broken one of the fence rails and sliced his flank open on the jagged timber. It really looks bad, blood everywhere," Eric explained to his grandson.

JB responded sounding shocked, "What can we do? Can I help? Will he die?"

"I certainly hope not, he's very valuable, a future champion. That call was to Phil Parsons, it's his day off but he's coming over as quickly as he can. He manages the stables for me and I don't think there is anyone who knows more about horses than Phil. Now, you can help me calm this animal. Just hold his head and stroke his neck to his hand gently like I showed you how to do the other day. I'll get some warm water to wash some of this blood off him, so we can see what we're really dealing with."

The water didn't help much because the blood was still pumping out. Phil Parsons arrived within ten minutes. He was possibly the blackest skinned man JB had ever seen. Coming in alongside Phil was a second person, a smaller version of Phil in every way but not as tall. Like

JB he came up to the big black man's shoulder. JB deduced he was Phil's son, perhaps the same age as himself.

"Hi Eric, let's have a look at the damage. I've brought Jake with me, thought we might need an extra pair of hands. Jake come and say hello to the boss. Your grandson you were telling me about then?" Phil asked.

JB and Jake became firm friends from that meeting. JB discover that Jake was a fantastic mechanic. By the time he was ten he had been able to strip down an engine and re-build it again just a quickly. Now at twelve, eighteen months older than JB, he would often be seen lay under one of the estates' vehicles, sorting out some problem or other.

Soon after meeting Jake, JB began his first term at his Edinburgh school, but he saw Jake whenever he could during school holidays. Luci was all too often away doing things that girls do. Jake was no academic, in fact he was barely able to read. Whereas JB excelled academically at school. So there was no competition between them, they knew one another's strengths and played to them.

Chapter 2

"We've really got our work cut out Phil. This bank loan is by no means a certainty. We need to really build a strong business plan. It's going to take us a couple of weeks and the boys will have to be on their own most days. We need to make sure they stay out of trouble. I'll get some sandwiches you get back to the car."

****

The rain was getting harder and the dark clouds overhead showed no sign of breaking. JB hoped that Luci wasn't getting this weather. She had left the previous day, for a camping trip in North Wales, with school friends. If she was being washed out now the rest of her week would be hell. Camping was becoming a regular thing with her, she had a close bunch of friends that seemed to enjoy one another's company and camping gave them the opportunity to get away and have some fun. There were four of them and with an adult to drive them, generally one of the parents who was prepared to stay with them, the group fitted nicely in a five seater car or four by four and their kit, comprising Rachael's four man tent and gazebo for daytime, Amy's dad's two man tent for the driver, a crate of food, a stove and a rucksack each for clothes, the car boot was always full. JB has often thought about what his grandpa would do when it was his turn to drive and spend time with four fifteen year old girls.

It was raining too hard for droplets to race down the window any more, instead the water ran like a river blurring the image of the service station buildings that JB was looking at. They had been on the road for almost four hours and possibly another three hours to go. The weather was certainly slowing their progress. They had left the stables at 7:00, straight after one of granny's full English breakfasts expecting to be in London for lunch, anticipating a total journey time close to four hours. But that plan was out of the window and Rob had gone into the services to buy some sandwiches to keep them going, this preferable to sitting in the services and having to stop again later for a hot meal and then being even further behind schedule.

There were two other people travelling with them. The horse expert Phil Parsons sat in the front and his son Jake joined JB in the back. Rob was planning to expand his business and open a horse stunt rider training ranch in India to supply the Bollywood film industry and had invited Phil to go out to India to help set it up and see it through the first year or two as manager. Phil would be responsible for recruiting staff to care for the horses and finding both men and women to train as stunt riders. Quite a step up for him in terms of responsibility and he jumped at the chance.

The basic plan was to establish a company modelled on the American and the British set-ups. Only local labour would be employed and instead of raking off all the profits, the Blackstocks would take an annual dividend and the profits, after the loan had been paid off, would be ploughed back into the Bollywood film industry. This trip to London was to present a business plan to the bank and try and obtain finance for the project, £5.2 million. Rob or Eric could each afford to fund it themselves from their own fortunes, but that would be personal money and would be a last resort if the bank refused their loan request.

JB had been told this trip was a birthday treat for him, to spend five weeks in London with his dad and plenty of opportunity to get out and about to see all the sights. Jake was coming as companion for JB. Rob didn't like the thought of JB out and about in London on his own, two boys together could look out for one another.

The final decision about the trip had only been made three days ago and JB wasn't sure whether it really was a birthday treat or if it was a ruse by his dad to get him to London to meet his latest girlfriend. In the last three years there had been a steady flow of ladies passing through Rob's life and bed sheets. The latest had been announced in a phone call to his mother interrupting the family evening meal on Wednesday three weeks ago. After ending the call and placing the handset back on the charger she announces to the family around the table "He's got a new girlfriend."

Eric responded with, "Bet she's blonde."

"Course she is gramps!" Luci butted in with "You know mummy was a brunette and he loved her so much that he doesn't want anyone to cloud the image he has of her."

Eric nodded and asked, "Is this another actress or singer?"

"No," said Rose "Apparently she is 31, divorced twice and senior cabin crew for British Airways doing the trans-Atlantic routes. He's spoken with her on several of his trips to the States and when he eventually asked her out they clicked and are dating regularly. Oh, yes she is blonde, with green eyes."

So JB didn't expect too much from the trip. He and Jake would just have to make the most of things. He was also aware that this was a business trip for his dad and Phil, so for several days they would be working in the London office, preparing for their meeting at the bank. Then after that, if the bank said no, they would be chasing down alternatives, and if the bank agreed they would be putting together plans to get the project started.

Rob returned to the car with a plastic carrier bag bulging with sandwiches, crisps, chocolate and drinks for four. He'd also bought a collapsible umbrella which he held above his head, while he climbed into the driver seat. He shook the umbrella violently to rid it of most of the water, then collapsed it and laid it in the foot well of the passenger seat.

"Roast chicken or Tuna mayo, Son?" Rob said as he looked for JB in the rear view mirror. "And I got you cheese and onion crisps and an orange tango. Okay?"

"Thanks. Tuna mayo please."

Rob passed back the requested food, took out a pack of Roast chicken sandwiches and a tango for himself and dropped the bag on top of the umbrella in the foot well.

Phil and Jake returned together just a few minutes later. Both were as wet as JB had been, but neither had worn a coat so would have to sit for the rest of the journey in sodden tee-shirts.

"The great British weather! Hey Phil?" Rob said.

"The forecast said occasional showers, not a bloody downpour like this," came Phil's reply "We're absolutely soaked through. What did you get us for lunch Rob?"

"In the bag down by your feet. Roast chicken or tuna," Rob replied. "There's also crisps and drink. Help yourselves."

They were back on the move again just before mid-day and were at last making good progress heading towards the M25, when Rob called out loudly, "Quiet everyone. It's the mid-day news." He pressed the button on the steering wheel several times to increase the volume.

The first item was again about a politician who had been found to have submitted a false expenses claim. Phil made a comment about politicians thinking they are above the law.

The second item was about the raid on the jewellers and a diamond that was missing. Exactly as JB had heard when they had been at the service station.

"Phew!" exclaimed Phil, "Bet there's a lot of folk on their knees around that place looking for that famous rock, hoping there is a sizeable reward for its return."

"I heard that on the last bulletin," JB said "Makes London sound like an exciting place to be with street battles and armed robberies."

"Or a dangerous place to be," Phil added "We don't want you two getting involved in anything like that."

The next report was of a strike by French Air Traffic Controllers causing serious delays to holiday flights and leaving hundreds of holiday makers stranded at several resorts.

The final report was about the bad weather affecting the North of England.

The news having ended, Rob turned the volume down again.

"There you go, those useless weather people still saying a chance of showers.

Why don't they look out of their bloody window?" Phil proclaimed.

"I hope Luci and her friends are not getting that bad weather," Rob added.

"That diamond thing sounds very strange. If the robbers were knowledgeable enough to take a diamond like that, why didn't they know about the new alarm system? All sounds a bit fishy to me," Rob concluded.

"One of the gang dead and two others in custody, is a bit of a mess for them. I wonder how many in the gang?" Phil queried.

"I wouldn't be surprised if there wasn't someone on the inside. But they would have known about that alarm. It doesn't make any sense," Phil added.

As they reached the M25, the rain suddenly stopped and the Friday afternoon traffic was moving quite quickly. They had no further hold ups and with a clear road they did make up a little of the lost time. By the time they arrived at the flat, the sun was out and there was no sign of rain at all. Roads and pavements were all bone dry and there were no puddles. If it had rained here it was some hours ago.

As they approached the apartment block that contained Rob's city home, Rob spoke a six digit number into the car media system. The sequence automatically connected with the apartment block's security system and the up and over door entrance to the underground car park lifted and they drove straight in.

"Neat!" Exclaimed Jake.

The door closed behind them, securing the car park from the outside world again. Rob manoeuvred the Jag into a parking space clearly labelled as Apt: Eighteen.

"If each of us takes a bag now. I'll come back down for the rest later," said Phil as he opened the car boot. "Should only need one trip."

They each grabbed a bag as suggested and walked towards the lift. The building housed four apartments on each floor, two two-bedroom apartments and two three bedroom apartments. Apartment eighteen was on floor four but the lift buttons were labelled with apartment numbers, so there was no need to know what floor you wanted. There were twelve buttons, two columns of six. The bottom two were labelled 'open' and 'close' for the doors, immediately above those was a button labelled 'Park' and one labelled 'Emergency'. The remaining eight buttons were labelled with the apartment numbers, four per button.

Once they were all in the lift, Rob pressed the button for apartment eighteen, triggering a ring around the button to glow red. The ring around the 'Park' button was glowing green. The doors closed and the lift started to ascend. As it passed each floor, the light around the corresponding floor lit green until the lift had passed that floor. When they reached floor four for apartment eighteen, the red glow around the button changed to a green glow. A bell announced their arrival and the door opened. Apartment eighteen was directly ahead of them. Rob pushed past the boys and entered another six digit code into the keypad on the wall, next to the door and the door opened.

"The system can hold twelve numbers, currently only three are used. My cleaner, the maintenance man and myself, so I'll set you all up later," Rob explained and walked into the entrance hall.

"Welcome home, Rob," an unknown voice said. "Since you were last here your cleaner has entered ten days ago and stayed for forty seven minutes and three days ago and stayed for twelve minutes. You have three new messages on your phone."

"She's called Jackie. I had her installed six months ago. At the time she was the very latest thing in home security, but the speed at which things advance these days, she is probably way out of date now. It's all done through facial recognition," Rob explained. "Come on in."

Phil crossed the threshold.

"Good afternoon, sir. I'm afraid I do not recognise you. Please tell me your name," the voice said.

"Phil Parsons."

"Welcome Phil." Jake was next.

"Good afternoon, young sir. I'm afraid I do not recognise you. Please tell me your name," the voice said.

"Jake Parsons."

"Welcome Jake."

Finally JB entered.

"Good afternoon young sir. I'm afraid I do not recognise you. Please tell me your name."

"JB."

"Welcome JB."

"That's very impressive Dad," JB said.

"Not bad is it?" Rob replied. "It will greet you like that every time you enter the apartment, providing you left more than 30 minutes prior. If someone knocks on the door and you let them in, they won't have to announce themselves and the system will record them as Visitor 15:30 20/08/18. Then another time if they enter, as you just did, it will say 'Welcome visitor, please give your name'. If you don't expect them to return, they can easily be deleted. It has so many features. I don't make anywhere near enough use of it."

"JB, you and Jake will be in there and Phil that one is yours," Rob pointed to two closed bedroom doors.

JB and Jake found theirs to be a twin room, Phil had a single. After dropping their bags in their room, the boys got out a list they had made of the sights they wanted to see and were now search a tourism magazine to find anything they had missed, while Phil brought the remaining stuff from the car. Rob was on the phone trying to book a table in a restaurant somewhere near to the apartment, but was finding that, because it was peak season, there was very little choice left. Finally he put the phone back on the charger and announced.

"Get your Stetsons out boys, we're eating with the cowboys tonight. I've got us a table for four at 7:00 in the American place two streets down. It's less than half a mile, so we'll walk. OK? Right then we'll need to be ready to leave at 6:45."

"Now you two, what plans have you got for this afternoon? I'd like to see you both unpacked and all your gear stowed away, before you do anything else. There's loads of storage in that room you're in. You should then still have more than two hours before we need to be ready to leave for dinner."

"No real plans for today dad," replied JB, "Is it OK if we go out and explore the streets around here?"

Rob looked at Phil for agreement and Phil nodded. He then looked straight at the boys and said, "That's OK, providing you stay together and don't go too far. While you're out, can you pick up an evening paper and we'll see if there's any shows on that you might like to see?"

JB smiled and taking the £10 note his father was holding out said, "Thanks dad. We will. Come on Jake, let's go!"

When they had arrived, they had entered the building via the car park, they were leaving now through the front door. They hadn't expected, and Rob hadn't warned them to expect to see a security guard at the front door who challenged them as soon as they appeared. JB explained who they were and they were in apartment eighteen and said what his dad's car registration was. The guard was happy and pulled the door open for them. As they exited past the guard, Jake asked, "Is there somewhere around here we can get an evening paper?"

"Yes lad, three or four places, but be best for you to see the old guy on the corner, just down this way," he said pointing down the street almost opposite.

"He should have copies of the second edition by now." Jake smiled his thanks and rushed on to catch JB.

As they approached the newspaper vendor, he was clipping a fresh hand written headline on the London Press billboard. JB nudged Jake with his elbow.

"Look mate, do you see what that says?" 'Search for missing diamond— police at a loss'. "Remember that on the news in the car lunchtime on the way down?"

"There's more about it here in the Late News column on the front page," Jake, said taking up the top copy from the two foot tall pile of newspapers and at the same time fumbling in his jeans pocket for the pound coin he knew he had somewhere.

For the next hour the boys explored the neighbourhood, taking particular notice of how the price of things was so much higher than they were back at home.

As they re-entered the apartment building, the guard was there to greet them. "You found your way back then, boys," he said through a grin. "This just arrived in the post. Could you take it up for me?" He handed JB a letter addressed to R. Blackstock.

At the apartment door, they remembered that Rob hadn't yet set up security codes for them, so Jake knocked loudly on the door. A moment later Phil opened the door and let them in. JB handed Rob the letter. He opened the envelope and sat at the table to read its contents. After a couple of minutes reading then rereading the three sheets of headed notepaper, he turned to Phil with a concerned expression.

"Phil, it's from the bank, they want to see us 9:00 a week on Monday. That only gives us a week to complete our proposal and outline the business plan." He turned to the boys, and seeing an ill look in their eyes.

"Don't worry boys, we've got the weekend to be all together and see the sights of the town! Now get yourselves ready and we'll go to dinner."

Over the next two days, the boys and their fathers were out doing all of the big tourist attractions. At 10:15 on Saturday morning they were occupying a prime spot outside Buckingham Palace, to watch the changing of the guard. The crowd swelled over the next half hour until they were at the front of what was possibly the biggest crowd JB had ever been part of. The pageant began at exactly 11:00. It was always amazing to watch such a precision performance.

"No other country in the world can put on a show like this," Rob said at the height of the spectacular display.

"You're not wrong there, Rob," Phil responded. "No one does pomp like the Brits."

It was turning into a hot dusty day and it was clear that some of the soldiers were suffering from the heat. Their thick woollen uniform jackets and bearskin hats, trapped in their body heat, causing sweat to cascade down their faces. But they were so well disciplined that none of them lifted a single finger to wipe the sweat away.

The display lasted a little over three quarters of an hour. When it was over and they turned to move away, they were struck by just how busy London gets at weekends in the peak season. People were milling everywhere, heading for the tube stations or the bus stops, trying to get somewhere for lunch. Every taxi that pulled up at the curb side was immediately snapped up and arguments were brewing among those waiting as to who gets the next one.

"I hadn't bargained on transport being an issue," Rob said. "I thought we might get a bite to eat at the Slug And Lettuce next to Tower Bridge, then this afternoon visit the Tower."

That raised a broad smile of approval from both boys. He went on to suggest.

"It's too far to walk, must be over three miles. But if we go that way," he was pointing at the road that runs between Buckingham Palace and St James Park, "we can walk down towards Westminster Abbey. There are sure to be plenty of taxis in that area."

Ten minutes later they were sitting in a taxi heading for lunch.

After lunch, they had only to cross the road and walk around the Tower's outer wall to join the queue. They had to queue for over an hour for the tower and the Crown Jewels, but it was well worth the wait. They took a Beefeater tour which lasted a good hour. They joined a small group of tourists and their guide, dressed in full Yeoman Of The Guard uniform, with sergeant stripes on his arm, who showed them around every part of the complex. He was very enthusiastic about the buildings, the people of the past and of the events that have been witnessed in and around the great palace in its almost thousand year history. He brought the history to life and really gave them a better understanding of what they saw, adding genuine value to the whole experience.

He told them a little of the history of various parts of the building. Like, Traitor's Gate being the result of the King ordering a hole to be punched through the outer wall on the riverside of the fortifications, so that prisoners could be brought in by river, to avoid rescue attempts in the streets.

Then before they entered the Jewel house, Phil asked their guide.

"Are these the real Crown Jewels?"

The beefeater pulled a face and replied, "Sir when you're inside the main Jewel room you won't see much by way of security. But sir, we have here some of the world's most sophisticated security and alarm systems. The jewels are far safer here than any bank vault anywhere in the world." "How much are they worth?" JB queried.

"Well, that's impossible to answer. Because they are unique, so well-known as to have no sale value other than within the criminal world, we could say they are priceless because of that. However, if we look at the gems and the weight of precious metals then we'd be talking at somewhere between £120–150,000,000. It's believed to be the largest collection of its kind in the world. Possibly the Romanov jewels in Russia are worth more. They are a collection started by Ivan The Terrible in the sixteenth century, similar period as our crown jewels here, and added to by Katherine The Great who is said to have paid ten times her own weight in gold for the main pieces. But nothing has been seen of any of it since the revolution in 1917."

As they walked slowly through the Jewel House, both Phil and Rob looked around to see if they could spot the security measures, but apart from a number of CCTV cameras they saw nothing. JB and Jake were focused on the jewels.

By the time they said their thanks to their guide, Rob tipped him with £10 as he thanked him, it was 3:20.

"River cruise next," Rob announced.

The four of them made for the jetty by Tower Bridge and boarded a small river cruise boat, paying as they boarded. It was only a basic forty five minute cruise, but the boatman was very knowledgeable about the history of the river, right back to Roman times. What he told them about the network of tunnels under the city, built in Victorian times was of particular interest to the boys. Originally they had been built as sewage routes down to the river, but in modern times they were the homes for many of London's homeless, linking all the major parts of the city north of the river. He pointed out a couple of entry points on the river bank, hidden unless you knew what to look for.

They took a taxi back to the apartment, dropping Rob off at the Chinese to pick up something for a quick tea. The security system welcomed them home and all three had showered and changed before they heard.

"Welcome back Rob. You have two telephone messages."

Rob took the food into the kitchen and left Phil to sort it out, whilst he returned to the lounge to listen to his messages. He called Phil into the lounge and there was a brief exchange between them, before they both returned to the kitchen, where they all ate their meal in silence.

They went to see 'The Lion King' at the Lyceum Theatre in the evening. After several hours at the science museum and going up on the London Eye on Sunday, they were all too tired Sunday evening to go out. So instead ordered a pizza and played cards in the evening.

They were all relaxing after several games of cards, thinking about going to bed, when Rob said, "Phil and I have to be in the office first thing tomorrow and won't be back until six at least. We're happy you two are safe together but what are you planning to do?"

Jake looked at JB who nodded, "We thought we'd visit Madame thingy, you know, the wax place. Mr Blackstock."

Rob responded with, "Madame Tussaud's. And it's Rob, please Jake. I suggest when you go off anywhere you go by taxi. That, at least will mean you get where you want to be. If you use buses or the tube and you mistakenly get on the wrong one you might end up anywhere."

"We're not stupid dad. We can read timetables and know a bit about using public transport, but we had planned on taxis as the easiest way of getting around and quicker than having to find a bus stop, work out where and when to change and actually wait for the right one to come along. Can you give us some money?"

"You're always after money, you and your sister! Where's your allowance gone? Here's £200. Keep it safe and make sure you get a lunch and are back here by 6:00. I'll book a table somewhere for dinner at 8:00."

It was a similar pattern each day that week, as the boys worked their way through the list of things they wanted to see and do.

On the Friday when they returned home they were surprised to see Phil stood in the hallway inside the apartment door. He raised a finger to his lips to indicate that they were to stay quiet. Through the closed door they could hear raised voices.

They could make out a female voice saying, "You know how I feel about children! I'm not the motherly kind. If you can't accept it, then there's no future for us." In a low voice Phil told the boys "It's the new girlfriend, she's not happy about something and I think this is the end of things."

Then they heard, what was obviously Rob's voice say, "But Justin is thirteen and Luci fifteen, they're not kids anymore, they are almost adults."

"I'm not prepared to compete with anyone for your affection Rob. Best that we call it a day now, before we get too involved with one another and it gets harder."

At that the door opened and a very smartly dressed lady, with her blonde hair in a bun on top of her head, making her look taller than her true five foot six, crossed the hallway, placed a gold locket on the side table and left through the apartment door in silence. It was obvious to everyone, looking into her green eyes that she was struggling to hold back tears.

The three walked through to the lounge where Rob was pulling the stopper from the whisky decanter and pouring a large amount into an already wet glass, then lifting it up and taking a long swallow.

"Hi you guys. Phil, join me for one of these?" he gestured by holding his glass out in front of him. "I thought we'd try that American place again this evening. You two liked it so much the other night."

He didn't mention what had just occurred, neither did they.

As they waited for their order to arrive, they discussed how the week had gone, and all the sights the boys had seen. They passed around some of the many photos they had taken with their mobiles. Rob and Phil tried to explain what they had achieved in preparation for their visit to the bank on Monday. They tried to keep it as non-technical as possible, but several times their enthusiasm for the project ran away with them and the boys were lost in the high finances. The conclusion was that there was about a day and a half's work still to be done, so they would have to go in again on both Saturday and Sunday. They did however promise that if everything went well with the bank on Monday, they would drive down to Dover on Tuesday and go across to France for a few days. Although disappointed about the weekend, the two boys were very enthusiastic over the prospect of a trip across the Channel and fired off a whole load of question at their fathers.

"How far is it to Paris? Is it possible to get to see the Eiffel Tower in just a few days? Is there anything to see from the D-day landings?" They were still asking questions when they got back to the apartment.

Saturday began extra early, with Phil going off a 6:00 to make an extra early start on the remaining work. Rob followed as soon as he'd got the boys sorted with breakfast, once he knew what their plans were and approximately where they would be for the day.

"We thought we'd go down to the Embankment and spend the day looking around there and maybe take another river cruise," JB Said.

"Looks like being a good day for it. Have fun. I expect this will help," Rob said as he gave both the boys a £20 note. "Thanks Mr Bl— Rob."

"Thanks dad," the two friends echoed.

"We've found a really great café down that way, really superb burger chips & peas for three quid and the best ice cream ever," JB added.

"That sounds good. Have a great day. Stay safe," Rob said as he left.

Chapter 3

"What went wrong out there? No one was supposed to get hurt and now Ray is dead and we don't know where the bloody diamond is. You two had better find that girl and quick. You were supposed to pick her up after the raid. You totally messed it up. I hope for your sakes the Russians don't get their hands on it."

****

JB and Jake didn't rush their breakfast but were still down by the river before 10:00. Of course it was Saturday. On Saturdays in London, you can do the same things as you do any other day of the week, but everything runs a little later. On weekdays, by 8:00 everywhere is manic, but on Saturdays things don't really get going until after 10:00. Lack of hustle and bustle in the streets had made it easy to get a taxi and the short journey to the embankment had been a quick one, so when they got there not much was happening.

A couple of guys pushing brooms around, clearing up litter left by the Friday night crowd, that appeared after most places closed and disappeared as dawn broke. It was the same every Friday night through the summer months. Young amateur musicians and singers, with their followers getting together to entertain and party. It's always peaceful and although there are some drugs passed around, it's nothing major and the police are happy not to chase the dealers or users, providing it all stayed peaceful. Litter was always a consequence of a large gathering and every Saturday, these two guys were always on hand for the cleanup, earning enough money for drinking themselves stupid the rest of the day.

A woman, pushing a pushchair, was the only other person they saw at first. But within 5 minutes, as if a dam had burst, spilling out what it was designed to hold back, people were everywhere, coming from every direction and rushing about with great purpose. Stalls selling tourist novelties sprang up from nowhere, drawing in crowds and the boards advertising the river cruises appeared by magic.

After walking up and down, reading all the boards the boys agreed that the one that appealed the most was 'History of Thames Bridges'. They booked for the 45 minute trip departing at 11:15. The boatman took their money and handed them their tickets. He told them to be back at 11:00 ready to board. That gave them 25 minutes to browse the tourist stalls and pick up a couple of cans of drink and a Mars bar each to keep them going until lunch.

"Christ Jake! £1.50 for a can of Tango," JB said "What a rip off. We get four cans for £1 at Morrison's in York."

"I know JB," Jake replied. "Dad paid £6.50 for a pint of Bud at that American place the other night. That twenty quid your dad gave us won't go very far. At least we know lunch won't break the bank."

The crowds built rapidly. They were mostly tourists, but also a few locals looking for a bargain that they could sell on at a profit. Trade between stall holders was common, each one thinking they knew more about items than the other and ever hopeful of coming across something of real value. Generally items turned out to be worthless knock-offs, but they could always pass them off to a tourist at a profit.

The boys were the first in the queue when 11:00 arrived and grabbed two of the seats in the front of the boat. It took best part of ten minutes to get everyone seated on board and once settled the boatman read the safety instructions that every boat had to read out before all trips.

"Please check your nearest exit, it may be behind you," JB said, gesturing like an airline flight attendant.

Both boys chuckled.

As the boat pulled away, Jake turned round and saw that as far as he could see every seat was taken.

Out in the middle of the river, the boat was allowed to drift on the ebb tide from bridge to bridge, briefly stopping under each to listen to the boatman's talk on the history of that particular bridge. First up was Waterloo Bridge then Blackfriars Bridge. Next was the newish pedestrian walkway, the Millennium Bridge, closely followed by Southwark Bridge and London Bridge. JB and Jake were amused to hear that when the old London Bridge needed replacing it had been advertised for sale and been bought by an American, thinking he was buying the iconic Tower Bridge which was the next bridge they passed under and the furthest point down river that the cruise went.

As they turned and faced upstream again, progress against the current was much slower, giving the boatman more time to add to the list of historical facts about each and to point out a few places of interest on the river banks.

Passing the point where the cruise had started, they passed under Hungerford Bridge, then Golden Jubilee Bridge and finally Westminster Bridge, where the boat again turned and they drifted quickly back down river to where the cruise ended.

The boat returned on exactly the forty fifth minute. As the boys had taken the front seats they couldn't get off until most of the other passengers had disembarked. It was lunchtime, so people were thinking of where to get a meal and had taken all the taxis. The boys decided to walk, it couldn't be more than a mile and they knew exactly where to go and the quickest route to get there.

It was 12:25 when JB pushed the café door open and disturbed the bell hanging above it. The café was busy, as would be expected at this time of year. There were three seats at the first table, where a young lady sat on her own with her back to the wall. She had half a cup of coffee and a screwed up napkin on the table in front of her. The boys entering the café had startled her, but she saw that they were only boys. She looked up at them and gave them a brief smile and returned to her coffee.

Across the room, against the far wall, was an empty table for two which they claimed. They took a moment to look around the other tables and saw there were no other empty seats. It was only a small café, and the capacity was only around 40. Obviously, this was a popular place. They knew the food was good from their previous visit and it seemed that others thought so too.

Wedged between a bottle of brown sauce and a squeezy bottle of ketchup on the table, was a laminated menu. Last time the burgers had been good, so they both again chose burger chips and peas with a can of orange. Jake went over to the counter, placed their order, paid and returned to the table with the drinks and two straws.

They had to wait a long time for their meals. Just bad timing! They were last in the queue and there were at least five big orders ahead of them. While they waited, they talked about the cruise and what they could do that afternoon. All the time they were talking, JB had been looking across at the girl at the table by the door. She was slim and attractive; JB estimated her age as early to mid-twenties. She was constantly looking out into the street as if waiting for someone.

Their meals arrived and they got stuck in.

Several people finished their meals and left but no new customers came in. There was always a lull following lunch that gave the staff the opportunity to clean down tables and be ready for when people started to come in wanting afternoon tea.

JB and Jake finished their meals and were deciding what flavours of ice cream they were going to have, when the bell tinkled again. The door opened and in walked two rough looking men in dirty jeans and tee-shirts that had obviously been worn for at least a week. Seeing them, the girl took something from the screwed up napkin and put whatever it was into her mouth, forced a swallow and washed it down with what was left of her cold coffee. The first of the two newcomers jumped forward, quickly leaned over the table and grabbed the girl by the chin, forced her mouth open and looked deep into mouth. At the same time the other went around the table to block the view of the majority of the customers that remained in the café.

He lent down close to the girl and in a low voice said, "You fucking stupid bitch, what have you done with it? The Inspector won't be best pleased. You know he must have it this week. Now let's leave together, quietly." He pulled her to her feet and the two frog-marched her out into the street.

The café customers hadn't seen or heard a thing or chose not to, not wishing to get involved in what appeared to be a domestic. All that is, except for JB and Jake, who slowly rose from their seats and moved towards the door. Looking out, the girl and her abductors were not to be seen. The boys opened the door and cautiously left the café.

As they stood looking for any sign of which way they had gone, there was a crash from the alley behind the café. Jake led and they ran to the alley, almost falling over a wheelie bin that had been the source of the noise. The alley was the start of a maze of back streets and alleys passing beside and behind the shops and running down almost back to the river. Keeping an ear open for any noises that might tell them which direction to turn they followed on.

The unmistakable smells of the river were filling their nostrils, as the boys broke out into a large open area. A dozen or so large wheelie bins were overflowing in one corner. In another they saw a moped that looked to have seen much better days and against the far wall, forty feet away from the boys, the girl was being held up by the wall and the two men were leaning over her. The boys hid themselves in between the bins, hoping they had not been seen. Peering through the rubbish they had a clear view of what was happening on the other side of the clearing and were quite certain they could not themselves be seen.

The bigger of the two men was talking to someone on his mobile, only the final sentence could be heard from the bins.

"OK boss, we'll find it." He ended the call and put the phone in the back pocket of his worn jeans.

"The boss says we're to do whatever it takes to get it. The Inspector must have it this week. The boss is sending a couple of blue boys to help."

JB whispered to Jake, "What's IT? And what are blue boys?" Jake shrugged his shoulders.

The thug who had been talking on the mobile, took hold of the girl by the hair making her squeal and he lifted her head so he could look at her face to face.

"What have you done with it Becky? Where have you put it? Search her Bill!" he said.

The other thug took the girls' bag from her shoulder and tipped the contents on the ground and proceeded to kick through pile searching for something. He then ripped out the bags' lining and tore the outer layer apart. Not finding what he was looking for he threw the tattered bag on top of the pile of contents and moved back to the girl saying.

"Come on Becky, don't make this any harder than it has to be. No one wants to hurt you. But we will if you make us."

"Fuck you Billy Squire and you Jay Squire. It's somewhere where you won't find it until it's too late," She said.

Hearing her speak for the first time came as a total surprise to JB. Not the words but the accent that delivered them. It was certainly Eastern European, possibly Russian.

The thug proceeded to turn out every pocket she had. He cut the heels from her trainers still not finding what he was looking for. She looked suddenly surprised when Jay Squire ripped the dress from her to expose her small breasts and leave her standing in her lace thong. After searching the dress he tossed it onto the growing pile on the floor.

"Are you happy now Jay?" she shouted.

"We know you've got it somewhere Becky, just give it up and we'll let you go," the thug snarled.

"Well you can't have it because I swallowed it. You'll just have to wait a few days and miss your deadline," she said.

"No! Oh Becky you fucking stupid bitch! We're dead men if we don't get it to The Inspector by Tuesday, so we can't wait. I didn't want this Becky, you're a great girl but I've got no choice," said Jay moving in closer to her.

"You don't know what The Inspector is capable of. The gang members are everywhere. They would track us down and we'd be finished before the week's out if we fail to recover it," he continued.

From where they were, the two thugs were blocking the boys' view of the little almost naked Russian girl. But they did see Jay pull back his arm and deliver a punch to the girl's abdomen.

She screamed "NO JAY! NO!"

"Sorry Becky," he said as he delivered a second, third and fourth blow.

Her head slumped and she slid to the floor. The thugs stepped back to let her fall and the boys looked on in horror as a pool of blood spread out from under the girl's body and they could now see a knife in Jay's clenched hand. At that same moment two policemen appeared from the alley next to where the body lay. The younger of the two knelt to find a pulse. He looked up at his older partner and shook his head.

"You silly buggers! Why have you done this?" the older cop asked Jay and Billy.

"She said she swallowed it and I'm going to cut it out," Jay replied.

"Have you two got no brains at all? The thing is more than two inches in diameter; no way could she swallow it! She must have passed it on or stashed it somewhere. Now get rid of the body quickly before someone comes and get rid of that lot." The cop said pointing to the pile on the floor.

JB and Jake were horrified at what they had witnessed and were shaking with shock.

Jake whispered "We need to get out of here. Quick, run!"

As they climbed out from their hiding place, JB knocked one of the bins and it clattered against another. Jake pulled his friend out from the bins and they ran back into the maze of back streets. The noise alerted the thugs and they turned to see the boys running off.

"Get after them, John," the older copper shouted at the younger one. "They must 'ave seen everything. Don't let them get away!"

The young man set off as fast as his thick uniform, heavy boots and helmet allowed him to go, which was certainly not as quick as two teenage boys could run. The older copper followed and as he went shouted over his shoulder to the thugs.

"Get that mess cleared NOW, before anyone else comes through here."

The boys had a good head start and were certain to get away if they could keep going and avoided any dead ends. This wasn't the way they had come and they were totally lost. Taking a sharp left down a particularly narrow alley they ran right into two very big men in smart suits. They apologised and ran on until they broke out into a crowded street. Then they slowed to a brisk walk, knowing that their pursuers were not far behind but it would be hard to pick them out in this crowd.

As they neared the traffic lights at the end of the street, the lights phased to red and a taxi pulled up at the white line on the road. There was no one inside and Jake opened the door.

"You free mate?" he asked.

"Yes lad, hop in. Where to?"

The two quickly climbed aboard, the lights changed and the taxi moved off. JB stole a brief look out the taxis' rear window and couldn't see the policeman that had been chasing them.

"That was horrific. What have we got into Jake? Why didn't those policemen arrest those two? Something's not right. That poor girl. Do you think she was Russian? And what is it they are looking for?"

"I've got no ideas, but that policeman said something about it being two inches in diameter, too big to swallow he said. It's got to be bloody important for them to kill somebody to get it," repeated Jake.

He continued, "Blue boys must be the police. Whatever this is all about, the police are definitely involved somehow. Do you think the person they called 'The Inspector' really is a police inspector?"

Having lost sight of the two boys the policemen returned to the murder scene where the two thugs were piling rubbish into one of the bins to cover the dumped body.

"Jay, do either of you two know who the hell those kids are?" The older copper said. "Are they connected to the girl? Could they have the stone?"

"They did look familiar but I can't think where I've seen them before," came the reply. "We know Becky had the stone on her when she went into the café and those two were in there when we picked her up. They must have been working with her. Why else would they follow us here? Stands to reason she passed the stone to them."

"We have to find them and quick," said the copper.

The other thug interrupted them. "Jay could those kids be the ones from that place we delivered The Inspector's horse to last month?"

"Yes! Well done, little brother. The Blackstock racing stable North Yorkshire. Three of them. A girl, the black kid and the younger bugger. The place is run by an old guy and his missus. There are a few hired staff, old, crippled jockeys and teenagers, mostly." Jay explained to the cop.

"Right you two, get up there tonight and get us something to use as leverage. John you get back to the station and find out where this Blackstock family are staying in London. I'll brief The Inspector."

Briefing The Inspector was not as easy as it sounded. Their real identity was known by only two or three people and no one was able to contact them direct. Only a handful of people were able to speak to the Inspector and to do so they had to put up a signal and The Inspector would then ring them from a public pay phone. The older policeman, Sergeant Ken Smith of the London Metropolitan Police, was one such person and his signal was to post on the police social clubs' Facebook page that included the word UNCLE.

Twenty minutes later, the two police officers walked up the steps into their station. John Towner went off to check residential records as the first place to look for a Blackstock property. If they owned any property at all in the greater London area then he'd find them there. After about ninety minutes trawling through databases,

John had a list of over twenty properties owned or rented by Blackstocks. There were three in the list that sounded most likely and need checking out.

      William P Blackstock—Whitton Road, Twickenham.
      Stuart L Blackstock—Aberly Road, Shepherds Bush.
      Robert J Blackstock—Apt: 18, Rosebury House, Pimlico.

John lived in Twickenham so he could easily check that one out on his way home after his shift this afternoon. If need be he would have to check out the other two this evening.

Sergeant Smith had gone straight to the officer's rest area and used his phone to post a Facebook message which he signed Uncle Ken. Within just 5 minutes his phone rang and the caller ID came up with unknown.

"You had better have some good news for me, Mr Smith. Have you got it?" asked a metallic sounding voice on the other end.

"We are very close boss," Smith replied. "We know who has it and where they are. We are certain you will have it by Tuesday."

"For your sake I hope you're right. I'm booked on the Moscow flight on Tuesday afternoon I have to have that diamond with me. Sunday is our window. Miss it and there won't be another for six months." The line went dead.

John Towner found the first address on his list but instead of going up to it he walked 50 yards down the road to the corner shop, took his mobile phone out of his pocket and walked up to the counter.

"Good afternoon officer. Can I help you?" asked the middle aged woman, stood at the till.

"Good afternoon. We've had this phone handed in," John said holding up his own phone to make his story sound real. "We've traced it to someone named Blackstock living somewhere on this road. Looking at the apps on the phone we believe it to belong to a teenage boy. Do you know the Blackstock's?"

"I do but you must be mistaken. Mr Blackstock is in his eighties and lives alone. He wouldn't know one end of a phone from the other."

"Thank you, I need to report that back to the station," John said and left the shop.

"One down, two to go!" he thought.

The Squire Brothers arrived in Yorkshire just after 6:00 and parked up in a gateway with a clear view of the comings and goings at the Blackstock stables, looking for anything that would give them some sort of leverage to get the stone from the boys. Their timing could not have been better. They only had to wait thirty minutes before getting a perfect opportunity.

They saw a young woman leave the big house, walk down the drive and out onto the road heading to the village.

"That's the girl, the daughter or granddaughter, whichever, doesn't matter. If we take her we can bargain her for the stone," Jay said.

"I'm not sure it is her, but I'll go along with you. Let's drive on and get ahead of her. Looks like she's going to the village," Bill suggested.

"Good evening." Bill said to the young lady who approached him. "Is this the right way to the Blackstock stables?"

"Yes" she replied, "I'm Luci Blackstock. It's my grandfather's place just a few hundred yards up there."

As Luci turned to point in the direction of the stables she was grabbed from behind and a hand placed over her mouth prevented her screaming. A strip of tape replaced the hand and cable ties held her wrists together behind her back. More ties were used to bind her ankles and a bag was pulled over her head. The ties were tight and cut into her flesh when she struggled.

The two men lifted her up and carried her to their car and bundled her into the boot. They quickly looked around to make sure they had left no clues, before heading back to London, happy to have taken their prize so quickly and easily.

John Towner, still in uniform entered Rosebury House apartments at precisely 6:15. The security guard immediately appeared.

"Good evening," John said holding up his mobile and repeating his story about the phone being handed in.

"That sounds like young Justin," the guard replied, "He's staying with his dad for a few weeks but they left five minutes ago. Out for dinner I expect. Leave the phone with me and I'll see they get it tomorrow."

"Sorry mate, can't do that. I need the boy to ID it first. I'll come back tomorrow," John smiled, turned and left.

Sergeant Smith having reported to The Inspector picked up an internal telephone and dialled. His call was answered after just the second ring and Smith spoke just one word, "Romanov," and replaced the receiver.

He then walked along the corridor to the gents, toilets. He was followed in by DS Paul Jameson. Smith and Jameson were the only two in the room which Smith confirmed by pushing open the doors of each cubical. They stood side by side at the hand basin so as to not raise suspicion if anyone walked in on them.

"What have you got for me Ken?" Jameson asked.

"Not much Boss," Smith replied, "I've just told The Inspector that we know who has the diamond and working on locating them. I've sent the Squire boys up to Yorkshire, where these people are from, to try and get something to bargain with to exchange for the stone. I'm still confident of getting it back and to The Inspector by Tuesday."

"I wish I had your confidence, Ken," the plain clothed officer said. "It sounds to me like this has got a little out of control. There have been too many cock ups this last couple of weeks, The Inspector is not happy. Plans were made very clear to you. The Inspector flies to Moscow on Tuesday 20th and has to have the stone in place by noon on 25th. It's a very narrow window to work in. Don't ask me why. But if it's missed, the next opportunity won't be until the end of next February and we'll struggle to hold the Russians off for that long."

"I'll get the lads together first thing tomorrow and we'll lay down a plan. We'll do our best to get it back by Tuesday. I'll not let you down boss, not if I can help it." Smith dried his hands and he left in a hurry.

DS Jameson was one of the few people that knew the identity of The Inspector. They had joined the force in the same year and shared the beat on many a long cold night as PCs. It was The Inspector who'd showed Jameson how to get the little extras in life. There was always someone willing to pay for him turning a blind eye now and again, losing the odd piece of evidence or slowing down an investigation. As the years went by with promotion and increased responsibility, it got easier to cover his tracks and the scale of what he was into just grew and grew.

About three years ago The Inspector began to pull together all the so called 'rule benders' and built a team that could look after one another and together could work on larger projects. There were now ten carefully chosen Met officers in the team. All with too much to lose if they blew the whistle on the operation. Also working with them were the members of a street gang known locally as the River Gang, all hard men willing to do anything if the price is right.

The current project was the biggest imaginable and would allow The Inspector to disappear without a trace and with feet up live life to the full. Just forty years old and looking forward to a long comfortable untroubled retirement, just the two of them...

Chapter 4

"Ребекку не видели после рейда неделю назад. Мы договорились встретиться с ней в субботу в кафе, чтобы она передала бриллиант. Мы должны быть уверены, что инспекторы не понимают этого."

"Rebecca has not been seen since the raid a week ago. We have an agreement to meet her on Saturday at the café for her to hand over the diamond. We need to be sure The Inspectors people don't get it."

****

Rob and Phil finished work earlier than expected, so we're very surprised to find the boys home when they got back to the apartment. Rob put his briefcase down on the floor next to the side table in the entry hall as the lounge door was opened. Out rushed JB. He ran straight to his dad and gave him a big hug.

"Oh Dad, am I glad you're home," he said rushing his words into a continuous single sound "We've seen the most terrible thing and haven't been able to tell anyone about it."

"Slow down JB. Let's all go into the lounge, sit down and you can tell us what this is all about," Rob said calmly.

Phil asked his son "You alright, Jake?"

Jake replied, "Bit shaky dad. But otherwise okay, this isn't about something that happened to us, but something we saw happen to someone else. Go into the lounge and we'll tell you the whole story. We really need you to tell us what we should do next."

The two dads looked at one another. Neither had any idea what this was all about but both were very concerned by the worried looks on their sons' faces. They followed the boys into the lounge. Rob walked across to the drinks cabinet and poured two large whiskies. He carried the drinks to the sofa where Phil had taken a seat. He handed Phil a glass and sat down next to him. The boys settled on the floor at their fathers' feet.

"Now, what's this all about?"

JB began telling the story with Jake coming in here and there where he thought it would add clarity. They stopped at the point where they ran out into the open space where the girl died.

Rob quickly took advantage of the break to say, "What did you think you could do by following them? Do you know this girl or the two men? They were obviously having a domestic so why did you think you needed to get involved and follow them?"

"It wasn't like that dad," JB responded. "She's dead!"

"WHAT!" Rob said as he and Phil turned to one another then back to face the boys. "Are you sure? How did it happen? Was there some sort of accident?"

"No dad. She was murdered, we saw it all," JB explained. "She had something they said was theirs. No! Not theirs, it belongs to someone called The Inspector. Anyway, they took her bag and totally shredded it looking for something. Then they ripped all her clothes off and tore them apart as well. They even tore the heels off her trainers. She swore at them. She called them by name. She obviously knew them! That was the first time we heard her accent, we think she was Russian." JB looked at Jake who nodded his confirmation. "That was when they held her up against the wall and one of them stabbed her. Four times dad. Four times! At that moment two policemen turned up."

"So the thugs were arrested, or did they run?"

"No, neither. They seemed to know one another."

Jake added, "It was almost as if the two thugs worked for the policemen!"

JB continued, "The thug said that she had swallowed the thing they were looking for but the older police man said that she couldn't have done so, because it is two inches in diameter. It was about then we decided to make a run for it, but as we moved, I caught my foot on the wheel of one of the bins and it crashed into another making quite a noise. The thugs heard the crash of bins, and we were spotted. We ran as fast as we could. We knew we weren't going the way we had come but had no idea where we were. We kept running until we burst out into a busy street and got a taxi back here."

"Bloody hell boys, that's some story! You sure you haven't added anything to make it sound better?" Phil queried. "Did anyone chase after you?"

"They certainly did," Jake replied. "The younger policeman almost caught us at one point. We took a wrong turn and almost ran into two men and had to double back, but we were a lot faster than him. We were able to get in a taxi before he spotted us in the busy street."

"You were both very lucky. They could have hurt you," Rob said.

"Or worse," Phil added.

"That's right. Who knows what they would have done if they had caught you," Rob added. "Did you get any names?"

"The girl was Becky. The thug called her that several times. And she called those two Jay and Bill Squire. The way she said it makes me thing they are brothers. The older policeman called the young one John, I think, but that was as we were running away so I may be wrong about that one."

"That's a start boys," Rob announced. "Are you sure this girl is dead?"

"When the policemen arrived the young one bent over her and checked her pulse. He looked up at the older man and shook his head to say he couldn't find a pulse."

"Okay. I don't know about you Phil, but need to let all of this sink in," Rob said as if half in thought. "Earlier I booked a table for 7:00 for the four of us at the Thai restaurant over in Victoria. It's quarter to now, so we'd better get a move on and find a taxi."

They hailed a taxi and had just turned the corner at the end of the road, when P.C. Towner had arrived at the apartment block.

Phil and Jake decided to walk back, but Rob and JB took a taxi and were back at the apartment on the stroke of 9:00. JB wanted to see 'Match Of The Day' and wasn't sure what time it started. As they entered the building the security guard called out to them.

"Hi Paul. Is there something wrong?" Rob enquired.

"No, nothing is exactly wrong. But there was a policeman here earlier looking for Master Justin." The guard explained "Someone must have found his mobile phone and handed it in at the station. The police had traced it back to here and wanted Master Justin to ID it. He's coming back tomorrow." "But I've got my phone here, Dad," JB claimed.

"Thanks Paul. Did you get the copper's name?"

Paul looking puzzled said "No name, but I noted his number and wrote it down. Hang on a moment." He shuffled a few papers on his desk and came back with, "421. PC 421."

"Thanks Paul. If he or anyone else for that matter calls to see us, we're out." Rob instructed. "It's all very complicated, I'll explain it all tomorrow. Can you make sure the other guards get the same instructions. You're off at ten, yes?"

"Yes sir and back a two tomorrow afternoon. Good night sir," he said as they entered the lift.

Rob and JB had their feet up trying to forget the day's events and watching the football when Phil and Jake got back.

"Good game chaps?" Phil asked.

"A pretty dull draw," Rob answered. "Get yourselves a drink and come and put your feet up."

No one mentioned the murder and when the football had finished the boys excused themselves and went off to their beds, leaving the men to discuss what they should do.

"This is all a bit of a mess, Phil," Rob said. "That policeman coming here worries me. Are we looking at some sort of police corruption here, do you think, and if so how deep does it go?"

"Certainly looks like those two coppers that chased the boys at least are bent," Phil replied.

"But how did they track down Justin so quickly?" Rob puzzled, "almost as if they knew who they are. I don't think they followed the boys home, so they must know their names. But how?"

Rob and Phil continued pondering over the few facts they knew and trying to fill in some of the gaps for some time. They finally agreed they didn't actually have enough facts to come to any conclusion and in the morning they would need to see if the boys could add anything to their story.

Luci had been bounced around in the darkness of the car boot for what seemed like hours but was probably only a few minutes. She had given up trying to free herself from the cable ties binding her wrists and ankles. They cut into her skin every time she pulled. Reluctantly, she decided to conserve her energy so if she got an opportunity to attempt an escape she'd give herself the best possible chance of success. As she lay back she realised that the road noise had become a steady hum and the rocking and rolling motion was a lot less. She concluded they must be on a motorway.

The Squire Brothers, happy with what they had achieved and how easily they had achieved it, were now on the A1 heading back to London with their prize safely stowed in the boot. Jay was at the wheel while Bill had put his seat back and was trying to get some sleep. If they could keep up this progress they should be back at their lock-up by 11:00. They changed driver around the halfway point, giving Jay the chance to phone the boss with an update.

"We've got the boys sister tied up in the boot boss," he said. "The Blackstock's will surely want her back unharmed and quickly too, so will be more than willing to exchange her for the Diamond."

"You've done well boys!" Jameson responded. "We need it to have a big impact when we make contact with the family. We need that diamond back as soon as possible. I want you to secure the girl then take off one of her fingers and deliver it, with a note to their apartment.

The finger will show them we mean business. I'll text you the address. Set up an exchange at Speaker's Corner for Monday at 9:00 in the morning. Get that bloody stone to me by noon!" He ended the call.

"I don't like the idea of cutting the girl up, Jay," Bill said.

"No. She's only a girl. A sweet little thing really. I don't want to disfigure her either, but we don't have any choice do we?" the older brother exclaimed.

"Yes we do. We could go back to the bins and take one of Becky's fingers. No one will know and she's not going to miss it, is she." Bill suggested.

"Quite right, we'll call in there on the way back to the lock-up? It's Saturday, no bins are emptied on Saturday, so the body will still be where we left it, at least until mid-day. Bins in the tourist areas are usually emptied on Sundays to keep the rubbish cleared and stop rats getting about. Come on Billy, put your foot down."

A sleepy Rob Blackstock was woken by his phone ringing at 1:30 in the morning. The caller ID said Dad, so he quickly pressed the flashing green button and said "Dad what's the panic? You're never up at this time of night."

"Son, Luci is missing!" came the worried voice on the other end of the line. "She went out this evening to walk down to the village to meet up with her girlfriends. She didn't come in at 10:00, she's never late back, she knows we worry. When she didn't come in, your mum and me did start to get worried. At 10:30 we rang all the girls. None of them had seen her."

Rob interrupted, "But she should be camping. They weren't due home until next Tuesday."

"They came back on Friday. Apparently they got washed out last weekend but managed to stick it out. Then they had more rain Thursday which got into their food supplies and their spare clothes, so they had no option but to come home. This evening they were meeting to plan their next trip. I've walked her route down to the village making sure she hadn't fallen and was lying in a ditch along the way. There's just no sign of her anywhere. I fear she's been abducted, but who would want to harm her? Son, what are we to do?"

"OK dad. You did the right thing to call me," Rob said trying to sound calm even though he wasn't. "I think this might be linked to something that happened here today. Have you been in touch with the police?"

"No."

"Then don't," Rob continued. He then proceeded to tell his father the full account of what had occurred earlier.

"So you see, Dad, we don't know the extent of the police corruption. Better not to trust any of them until we know more about what we're dealing with. I'll get back to you just as soon as we know more. Now try not to worry and you and mum try and get some sleep. I'll be in touch. Good night."

Rob had been on the phone for almost forty five minutes and he doubted he'd get any more sleep. The next thing he was aware of was his 7:30 alarm going off. He lay without moving for a few minutes, gathering his thoughts and thinking over what they should do. Someone was on the move. He heard footsteps pass his door and now there were voices in the kitchen. He pulled on a pair of jogging trousers and an old tee-shirt and went to join whoever it was.

"Is that coffee I can smell boys? Pour me a cup please, I need it," he said as he walked through into the kitchen and saw Phil and the two boys there.

"Rough night Rob?" Phil asked.

"You don't know the half of it Phil. All of you come on into the lounge and I'll fill you in."

"We've got news too dad," JB added.

"I'll go first son," Rob cut across what JB was trying to say. "Eric rang me in the early hours. Luci has gone missing. Eric thinks she's been abducted. I can't think how but I believe this has something to do with what you two witnessed yesterday. If there is some connection, then there has to be more to all this than just covering up a murder. Boys I'd like you to take us to that café of yours at about the same time today as you were there yesterday, and retrace the whole thing."

"OK dad, but I think it might be better to start from where we got off the boat." JB suggested "Though I'm pretty sure you've heard everything, it can't do any harm, I guess. We need to be there at exactly 12:00."

"Good idea. Well, we've got a couple of hours so I'm off for a shower," Rob said as he turned and headed towards the bathroom.

"Wait up dad. You need to hear our news," JB called after him.

"OK son. Out with it."

"Well, Jake and I both thought the two thugs looked familiar but couldn't think where from. Then as we talked through a few things, it came to us." JB paused then continued, "about three weeks ago Gramps had a horse delivered to the stables. A horse called Policeman's Ball, owned by a syndicate of police officers. The head of the syndicate is a Peter Logan. We, that is, Jake, me and Luci, all helped with the transfer from the horse box to the stable. Dad, we are certain the horse box driver and the lad with him were the two thugs that killed that girl."

"Are you two absolutely certain."

"Ninety-nine per cent."

"I know Peter Logan very well. Or at least I did years ago. We roomed together at Uni for two years. Last I heard he'd made Inspector in the Met. He contacted me a few months ago to see if we would be his trainer. He and a few mates had bought their first race horse. Apparently his wife had received a large inheritance and he was looking for new interests."

"Inspector! Dad could he be the one behind all this?"

"Peter, not a chance! He's one of the most honest men I have ever known, but I agree it's a bit of a coincidence. I'll ring him tomorrow and try to meet him and ask a few questions. Now I really am going for that shower."

After crossing the M25, Billy left the A1 preferring the minor roads through north London. He knew the area well, having lived there or about all of his twenty years, so he could choose his route and avoid any hold ups. Even at night, there is always a lot of traffic in this part of town. As soon as they left the A1, they were no longer travelling at a constant speed and Luci began to be bounced around again, the bruises on her arms and back were starting to hurt from continually being knocked. Her bindings were still just as tight. Surely they would be getting her out soon. What were they going to do with her? Why her?

Eventually Billy pulled up at the side of the road near the entrance to an alley running into the maze where they had taken poor Becky earlier. Jay jumped out, turned and said, "Be back here in fifteen minutes to pick me up." Then he slammed the door and ran off down the alley.

Jay entered the square and was relieved to see the bins were as they had left them. He quickly pulled out rubbish from the top of the bin and reached in to search for Becky's hand. When his fingers found flesh he was surprised how cold it was. He took a grip of an arm to tug it out, but stiffness had begun to set in and it took all his strength to get the arm free and drag a hand over the side of the bin. He reached down to the bins wheel and pulled out the half of a house brick used to stop the bin rolling. He next took his knife from his pocket, opened the blade out and rested the cutting edge across the girls' fingers. Bringing the half brick down hard on the back of the blade he cleanly sliced off four fingers and they dropped to the floor. He retrieved them and wrapped them in a scrap of cloth from the rubbish and pushed them into his pocket. After pushing the body back down into the bin and covering it with rubbish again, he pushed all the bins back into place. As he was pushing the last bin back against the wall a couple in their early twenties walked hand in hand into the square. It was not quite midnight; Jay had been lucky no one had walked in on him earlier. When he listened, he could hear several people talking in the alleys around him. He smiled at the couple and continued pushing the last bin as if it was his job. They both smiled back and walked on unaware of what was hidden in the bin and not noticing the large stain on the floor by the far wall. As soon as they were out of sight, he made his way back to where Billy was to pick him up.

Luci felt the car come to a halt again, but this time was different. The hum of the engine stopped. They had possibly arrived at their destination. She heard her captors both leave the car, then moments later light burst in when the boot was opened. The bag was pulled off her head, catching and tugging at her ear stud and she issued a short squeal. It took her eyes a little time to adjust to the light before she could take in her surroundings. She saw that they were outside a row of sizeable garages, the sort that had large vehicle doors with a smaller pedestrian door set into them. Each door had a large white painted number on it. She could see numbers one to eight. They were parked in front of five and the security flood light above the door illuminated the car.

She said nothing and didn't struggle when she was pulled from the car and was manhandled through the small door. The brothers said nothing either. They half dragged half carried her across the floor to a small office with a half glazed door. Inside there was a desk two wooden chairs and a filing cabinet.

"Secure her to that chair Billy," Jay instructed. "I'll get the note done and pack up a finger. We'll grab a couple hours kip then we'll deliver the package to the Blackstocks."

Billy pushed Luci so that the chair caught the backs of her legs knocking her off balance and she sat down hard on the wooden seat. He cut away the ties binding her hands and bound each wrist to an arm of the chair using gaffer tape. Next, he freed her legs and used more gaffer tape to bind each of Luci's legs to a leg of the chair. Meanwhile Jay had found a child's wax crayon and written his note and pushed it into an old envelope. He pulled the rag holding the fingers from his pocket, pulled the package open, took out the smallest digit and dropped it into the envelope which he then folded down and sealed with a strip of tape.

"Right, I think we're done Billy. The boss has sent me the Blackstock's address. We'll go home first and get our heads down for a few hours, then deliver this package on the way back here. Don't worry young lady, we're leaving you here for a few hours but we'll be back with some grub for your breakfast."

The brothers left the lock-up and Luci in darkness, except for a few chinks of light coming in from the street through gaps around the door. Using the poor light that filtered in, Luci looked around where she was sitting for anything she could use to free herself. By gently rocking the chair she was able to slowly turn it and her eyes completed the search.

She had found nothing but all the rocking in the chair had weakened the arms of the chair. It was an old chair and had been badly maintained. The arms both wobbled so it shouldn't take much effort to break them. She tried working on this weakness by pushing the arms from side to side. Eventually an arm broke away and she was able use that to free the other then to remove the tape from her legs. It hadn't taken her long but it will probably be more difficult to get out of the building. "Amateurs!" she said out aloud to no one in particular.

Getting out of the building was actually far easier than expected. The large doors were bolted and padlocked and the only window at the back of the lockup was covered with a heavy gauge metal grill. That left only the small door that she'd been dragged through earlier. At a glance she could see two dead locks and a standard Yale. Perhaps there were some duplicate keys somewhere in the office but surely these people had more sense than to leave them lying around on the desk. Still it was worth a quick look.

She found the light switch and with more light she saw there was a small scrap of cloth on the desk. Opening the package she made a gruesome discovery.

Three human fingers fell to the floor at her feet. Her stomach lurched but she continued her search. She spent more time searching for keys than she really thought she should and returned to the door for closer look.

"You silly cow Luci," she said to herself. 'They haven't locked the flaming door, just left it on the Yale latch. They really are amateurs.'

Luci turned the knob to free the lock and opened it just wide enough to see that it was still dark outside, which at this time of year meant it was still sometime before 4:00am.

Everything was quiet as she moved outside. Following the line of streetlights to the end of the road she could see it joined a wider road where she could make out two buildings, one had all its windows boarded up and the other, where lights were blazing, had heavy security grills at all its windows. It looked as if it might be a twenty four hour fast food hall, but there weren't any customers waiting.

She walked to the junction and looked up at a plaque on the wall of a building on the corner that told her she had been on Burgundy Street. She still had no idea which city in UK she was in. The sky was now beginning to show a few signs of getting light. She knew she had to put more distance between her and the lockup. A million other thoughts raced through her head. She needed to contact someone, her dad or her grandad, but those two bastards had taken her phone. She thought she could remember her dad's number, so if she could find a phone, she would ring him and he would come and take her to safety. But he would need to know where to come and she still had no idea.

She kept walking and passed a bill board advertising shows on at various theatres, 'Phantom Of The Opera' at Her Majesty's Theatre, 'The Lion King' at the Lyceum Theatre, 'Les Misérables' at Queens and 'Mamma Mia' at The Novello Theatre. She recognised all these as London theatres. This must mean she was somewhere near or actually in the greater London area. She needed to make a list of street names to tell her dad and give him some clue as to where she was.

She had no money, no ID and only the clothes she stood up in. She'd had had nothing to eat or drink for twelve hours, however she was strong and fit and her regular camping trips had hardened her for outdoor living, she is a survivor. "You can do this baby," she said to herself and sat on a bench outside a bookshop, put her head back and drifted into a deep sleep.

She slept for about two hours, but she didn't own a watch and without her phone she had no way of knowing what time it was. There were a lot of people milling around, which for a Sunday meant it was probably late morning, although it could be much later. A young lady came and sat on the bench just a couple of feet away, so she asked what the time was. The lady smiled at her and with an accent that Luci couldn't place said, "No English." Luci asked again by tapping her wrist and gesturing with her hands. The young lady held out her arm so that Luci could see her watch, 9:15, not as late as she had thought. She smiled her thanks to the lady.

She still had no idea where she was so, she stood and asked the next passerby who looked at Luci, looked her up and down, then with a look of disgust on her face, walked on. Then Luci realised that everyone was giving her a wide birth as if she were a rabid dog. Looking around she caught sight of her reflection and saw why. Her shoulder length hair resembled a bird's nest, her face and hands were dirty and her jeans and tee-shirt looked like she'd worn them for a week. She looked like what she imagined a druggie would look like.

She set off walking down the street and outside a café was able to quench her thirst at a water fountain. Food was a different matter, she didn't have any money. Maybe if she could find a policeman or better still a police station she could get help. She walked on.

Two maybe three streets later she spotted a couple of Community PCs across the other side of the road. Desperate to gain their attention she waved and shouted. She looked both ways to check it was safe to cross and stepped off the pavement. In her rush she hadn't seen a delivery cyclist and she stepped into his path. He took immediate evasive action to avoid hitting her straight on. He almost avoided her completely but his thigh brushed her hip and she stumbled back, tripped over the curb and fell up against a street lamp. The cyclist kept his balance and raced off as if nothing had happened.

Luci got straight to her feet obviously shaken but unhurt. So the two PCs who had stopped and were looking across at her, seeing she was OK. Assuming her to be on a drug high, walked on not wanting to get involved and get all the paper work that would have to be done. Luci's only injury was a lump on the side of her head just above her temple. Otherwise apart from feeling a little unsteady she thought she was OK. But how had she got to be down on the ground and why was she here?

It was two minutes to mid-day when Rob and the others reached the gang plank to the Bridge's Cruise boat. So they set off for the café immediately, the two boys leading at a pace that they thought was the same as they had gone the previous day. In less than ten minutes, JB had his hand on the door handle of the café. He pushed it open and the other three followed him in. Just as it had been the day before, the café was almost full. The only free seats were the four at the table by the door. The table the Russian girl had sat at. They took the seats and browsed the drinks menu.

"We might as well eat here, like you did yesterday, and then we'll stay pretty much on the same timeline. So boys what do you recommend?"

"We've only been here twice and had the burger each time. But all the food we've seen has looked good," JB replied.

Jake added, "And a lot of the people in here now were in here yesterday, so it must be good. JB and I sat over there at that table for two where those two big guys are sitting. JB didn't we see those two somewhere yesterday as well?"

"They look like the two we almost crashed into when we were running away yesterday."

"Pass us the lunch menus, Jake so we can see what else they do, I'm not really into burgers."

"I didn't know that," Jake said as he handed one of the laminated menu sheets to his dad.

Once they all had decided what they wanted, Jake took the order to the counter and returned with 4 cans of drink.

"They've put it all on a tab so don't forget to pay before we leave," Jake said smiling at his dad and remembering when they had done exactly that about three weeks ago and had to go back several miles to own up and pay.

"So where exactly did this girl sit?" Rob asked.

"Here where I'm sitting now," Jake replied from the seat facing the door and back to the wall. "Yes, she was sitting here facing the door, chewing her gum and checking everyone who came in, looking as if she was waiting for someone. On the table in front of her was a mug of coffee, part drunk and a screwed up tissue that had something wrapped in it. When those to thugs came in she took whatever was in the tissue and popped it in her mouth and took a drink from her mug."

"One of the men tried to stop her, but was too late. Then the other one stood in the way and we couldn't see anything more until they got up and made her walk out."

"Made her?"

"That's right each had an arm and were pushing her along. That's when we decided to follow them."

"Jake. That's where we first saw those two men sitting now, where we did yesterday," JB interrupted. "They were just in the street outside coming towards the café."

"That's it JB, well done. When we got outside the two thugs and the girl had already gone into the alley and we only knew which way to go because they knocked over a bin and we heard it crash."

Their food arrived and they changed the subject and discussed the previous day's football results. There were the usual batch of unexpected score lines, as is typical for the first day of a new league season. They ate their food, paid the bill and left. The four walked on through the alleys, the boys leading the way until they arrived at the square. The bins had been emptied and stood side by side along one wall. On the floor in front of the opposite wall was a stain about eighteen inches in diameter that could have been anything but was probably blood. After looking around a little more but not discovering anything new, they headed back to the café.

"Jake you said the girl was chewing gum when you went in, but she must have got rid of the gum before swallowing whatever it was she swallowed. And what was it she swallowed? And what were they looking for? All we know is it's two inches in diameter," said Rob summing up.

"I don't know what she did with the gum Rob, maybe she put it in that tissue. Why?"

"Oh, just a thought. I need to go back into the café."

Within a few minutes they were back at the café. Rob led the way several paces ahead. When they entered they were surprised to see that the café was almost empty. The two big men were still there and there were four women around a table at the back. Rob went straight to the table by the door and sat himself on the chair facing the door. The boys joined him. Phil went to the counter and came back a couple of minutes later with two black coffees and two Tangos.

Rob took out his phone and selected an entry from his contacts. The volume was up quite high so the boys could hear the numbers click through, followed by three rings and then a voice on the other end.

"Hi Rob."

"Any news about Luci, Dad?"

"Not a thing son. Your mum's really upset, worried that something bad is going to happen to her."

"We're all worried Dad. But I'm sure the people who have her have a reason for taking her and they will be in touch soon with some demands. Try not to worry; I'm sure she'll be OK."

"OK son, we'll try."

Rob ended the call and returned his phone to his pocket then moved his hands under the table. Within seconds a broad grin crossed his face.

"I've found the girl's gum guys. She used it to stick this under the table." Rob slowly brought his hands out from under the table and opened them to reveal what he had found.

"Bloody hell Rob!" Phil gasped. "That's a hell of a big rock. Is it real?"

"Keep your voices down guys, we don't want everyone to know. I think it must be worth a tidy sum, if it's worth killing for. Come on chaps, drink up and let's get this back to the apartment and decide what's to be done."

"Christ dad, is that a diamond? Do you think that's what they were looking for?"

"It certainly looks like a diamond and it probably is what they are looking for. Do you remember on the news when we were coming down last week, about a raid on a jeweller's shop and all but one diamond was recovered. Well I may be wrong but I believe this is that diamond. I just can't figure out how it came to be in the hands of that girl."

The four women from the back of the café had left while Rob had been talking to his dad and now the two big men got up and also left, leaving Rob and the others as the only customers. The two serving girls took advantage of the lull in trade to clear and wipe down tables, in expectation of new customers coming in for afternoon tea.

The coffees were very hot so it was quite a few minutes before they were ready to leave and the two serving girls were hovering waiting to clear and wipe the last table. So as soon as the drinks were all finished, they got up and left.

There were no taxis about and no people either, not really surprising as apart from the café there was nothing to attract people to this area. It was more a place people passed though on their way from one place to another. So the four took a back street leading back to the main thoroughfare where they stood a better chance of getting a taxi. As they walked along the narrow street, a figure stepped out of the shadows and blocked their path. The light was poor in the back street and what light there was came from behind the figure making it difficult to pick out any detail. They just felt threatened by the presence and stopped in their tracks, the two fathers drawing their sons to them, instinctively to protect them.

"You have something that belongs to us and we want it back." The words came from behind them and were spoken in a heavy accent so obviously Russian. Rob and the others turned to see one of the two big men from the café blocking the street. He was holding a revolver, but it was pointing down at the ground and not threatening them.

Rob responded, "I don't know what you mean. We don't have anything of yours. We haven't met you before."

The two big men closed in and the one with the gun explained. "We were due to meet a contact yesterday who was to hand over a large gem stone that was stolen from Mother Russia more than a hundred years ago. We were delayed and she hadn't waited for us, but we saw these two boys acting suspiciously. Then again we saw you in the café today but no sign of our contact. You all left but returned again this afternoon, so we watched you very closely. We know you have it. Now quickly hand it over." He raised the gun so that it was now threatening them.

"Okay, we'll let you have the gem stone, if you tell me where you are holding my daughter."

"Daughter? We know nothing of any daughter! The diamond NOW!" The Russian said and pointed his gun.

Rob reluctantly handed the gem stone over. "If you don't have her who does?"

"Thank you gentlemen. Your daughter does not concern us but as a father I hope you find her. We wish you good day." The two Russians walked on down the street, leaving Rob and the others confused and concerned.

The Squire Brothers slept longer than they had intended and it was almost mid-day when they finally delivered a small package to Rosebury apartments. It was simply addressed to Blackstock Apt eighteen. On arriving at the building they were greeted at the front door by a security guard, who was happy to take the package and ensure that Mr Blackstock received it as soon as he returned.

Luci was in a bit of a daze. She continued to walk along the street even though she had no idea where she was going or why. She just knew she was supposed to be getting away from something dangerous. Tired and hungry she went through a gate into a small park area and sat on a bench shaking a little. She could remember nothing. For the last few minutes, she had been followed by two young ladies in their early twenties, dressed in very short skirts and boob tubes and wore shoes with staggeringly high heels. The way they looked, they might have been sisters. But one look at their faces made that seem doubtful. Plus, although they both had short hairstyles one was dark haired the other a blonde. They approached Luci and the blonde asked, "Are you okay, little girl?"

"I've got a sore head. I think I fell over and I don't know why I'm here. I'm tired and very hungry."

The two women talked to one another for a minute or two. Luci couldn't hear their conversation very clearly and the few words she did catch she couldn't understand. It sounded like they were talking in a foreign language. The blonde sat on the bench next to Luci and put her arm around her.

"My friend Eva and I would like to help you. We'd like you to come back with us to our house and let us give you some food and we have a spare bed if you'd like to rest for a while. My name is Oxsana but everybody calls me Ana."

"That's very kind of you Ana, I'd like that."

"We live just around the corner. So as soon as you feel able we'll go."

This was true, they only had to walk a hundred and fifty yards, but it wasn't a house. It was just the top floor of a large Georgian townhouse consisting of a kitchen, lounge, four bedrooms and a huge bathroom which Luci noticed had underwear hanging from every possible point.

Eva put the kettle on to make hot drinks, whilst Ana raided the fridge and put cheese and cold meats on the kitchen table with a loaf of bread, plates and knives. "I've just realised, we don't know your name," Ana said.

"Neither do I," Luci replied. "In fact I can't remember anything before the point when I was getting up off the floor."

"You poor thing. I'm sure your memories will return as soon as you've had something to eat and a good rest. You've obviously been through quite an ordeal. But you must have a name for us to call you by. Until you do remember, your name will be Emma. Emma Sunday. Yes I like that. I like that a lot and to Eva and me you look fifteen or sixteen, so let's say you are fifteen year old Emma Sunday. What do you think?"

"I like it! Thank you so much and you Eva, your kindness is making me feel so much better. I just can't thank you both enough."

"And tomorrow we'll get a photo of you on some posters and get them up around the tourist spots in town. Plus a few up around here. Someone will recognise you, we'll soon have you back with your folks."

Eva jumped in, "Ana isn't that a bit risky? If she really was running away from somebody, won't we just be telling them where to find her?"

"Not at all. If we put my mobile number on the poster, we can vet any caller and Emma can see them first before they get anywhere near her. Now let's make your name official." Ana dipped two fingers into her glass of water, walked up to Luci and made the sign of a cross on her forehead.

"In the name of the Holy Mother, that's me, and the Holy Sister, that's Eva, I baptise you Emma." They all burst out laughing.

"You're both being extremely kind. Thank you. You're not English are you? But your English is excellent."

"We are both born in the suburbs of Moscow and lived there until we were seventeen and have lived here for the last five years looking out for one another and waiting for a rich man to marry." Ana and Eva smiled at one another.

"Eva and I have to go to work later and depending on trade we may not be back until the morning. But you are more than welcome to stay."

Luci had a few hours' sleep in the spare bedroom and got up feeling much better. She went back into the lounge and found the two women listening to music and reading magazines.

"Well, hello there, you're looking a lot better isn't she Eva? How do you feel honey?"

"Tons better, thanks."

"Here, come and sit by me," Ana said and she moved a pile of magazines from the seat next to her on the sofa and threw them on the floor. It was a little after six and Luci was very thirsty.

"Can I grab a glass of water please?"

"Of course. You'll find a glass in the kitchen somewhere. Just give it a rinse first. Eva and I are a little bit lazy with washing up and the glass might still have the dregs of vodka in it."

Whilst she was in the kitchen, Luci heard the doorbell go and a moment later one of the women opened the door and let someone into the apartment. When Luci went back into the lounge, there was a very big man standing with his back to her. The two others were sat and they were talking together in what she assumed to be Russian. On hearing Luci enter behind him he turned and look Luci up and down.

"Hello. Who is this beautiful young lady?"

"We don't know her real name. She bumped her head this morning and can't remember anything at the moment so we've named her Emma. She's going to stay with us for a couple of days. Come over here Emma, this is Mikhail, he arranges work for Eva and me."

"Well, hello Emma."

His voice had a much heavier accent than the ladies and his English was not as good.

He turned back to Ana and in Russian said. "She's very pretty I've a lot of contacts who would pay big money for her."

"She's not in the business and too young anyway."

"Rubbish. The younger the better."

"No, she's too young. We've promised her we'll look after her."

"If you know what's good for you, you'll do what you're told. Prepare her for me. She can stay here but you two have a week to teach her some of your skills. I'll test her next Sunday. Now back to business. Where's Rebecca? Has she turned up yet? Her regular Saturday clients are very upset. When she eventually comes in, tell her to call me. You can also tell her we've got the diamond but we're not happy about how we found it. As for you two, you're booked in with the police inspector at 7:30. Ivan will be outside with a taxi at 7:15, don't be late." He quickly left the apartment calling back before shutting the door. "Remember. I want that girl ready by next Sunday."

Luci hadn't understood a word that had been said, but the expression on the two ladies faces was cause for concern.

"Are you okay? What's wrong Ana?" She asked.

"Nothing dear. Mikhail has a job for us. We need to shower and get dressed ready to be picked up. We'll be home for breakfast. Help yourself to anything in the kitchen."

Luci thought it strange that the two women should shower together, but didn't dwell on it. Instead she started looking through the magazines.

When the two reappeared in the lounge they were dressed alike in extremely short skirts, cut off tee-shirts that didn't quite come down low enough and the bottom of their breasts could be seen. On their feet they wore shoes with four inch heels and their faces, particularly their eyes were heavily made up.

"We're off now. See you in the morning. Sleep well."

"Thanks. See you tomorrow."

"Rob and the others were back at the apartment just after 2:30. The security guard came out to greet them."

"Mr Blackstock, I have a package for you. It was left with the guard on the previous shift. I'll go and get it for you sir."

The guard went back to his room and brought out a small package and handed it to Rob.

"Thanks Paul, I'll come back down later and bring you up to speed with everything."

They all rode the lift up to apartment eighteen. The security system greeted them all and reported no messages had been left. They went into the lounge and Rob opened the package. Something fell out onto the floor as he ripped it open. He bent and was horrified when he realised what it was. He picked the severed finger up and placed it on the table then opened and read the note written in wax crayon.

'If you want the rest of your daughter returned in one piece, bring the diamond to Speakers Corner at 9:00 tomorrow morning. Don't call the cops. We'll be watching you.'

He read the note again. This time out loud so that all could hear it.

"Is that Luci's finger?" Jake asked.

"I think it is supposed to be, but it's not," JB stated.

"How can you know that son?"

"Look at the nail Dad. For one thing Luci bites her nails and secondly Luci would never use blue nail varnish. It's definitely not Luci's finger."

"Well spotted JB, that's a relief. I suggest after the day we've had, we could do with an evening in. Maybe call for a takeaway. I need a drink. How about you Phil?"

"That sounds a grand idea. I'll get them. Scotch okay?"

After delivering the package, the brothers returned to the lock-up and discovered the door was open and the lights were on. Inside they were horrified when they found Luci to be gone.

"Don't worry, Jay. She's got no money and I've got her phone. She's not going to get very far quickly. Even though she's gone, we can still use her to bargain with tomorrow. So keep it to yourself. We don't tell the boss, right."

Chapter 5

"We need to watch that Blackstock chap. We don't know much about him. We also don't know how long those boys had been hiding amongst the bins, what they saw or what they overheard. Get our boys to get some cameras up so that we can watch them closely."

****

After finishing his drink, Rob went down to the front door to speak with Paul, the security guard, as he had promised he would. He sat with Paul for half an hour going through the events, with as much detail as he could. Talking with someone like this seemed to help Rob take a grip of the situation and to gather his thoughts on what he should be doing next. His biggest worry was Luci. It may not have been Luci's finger in that package, thank God, but it must have been some poor girl's. If the people holding her were prepared to do that, what would they do when they learnt he doesn't have the diamond?

"You need to speak with my boss, Mr B," Paul said, "she'll know exactly what to do." Before Rob could respond Paul had disappeared into the inner office. He returned several minutes later.

"Right I've spoken to her, told her some of the important parts of what you told me and she's coming over now. She'll be here in about forty five minutes. I'll send her straight up."

"That's very good of her but I don't see how the head of a security company can help."

"No, no. My job here is just a very small corner of what Williams Securities is all about. It's an international company. Susan Williams was an officer in the military police. She is an excellent detective. I'm certain she'll be able to help you with this. She's a very talented lady. One of the best in the business."

Rob thanked him and returned to the apartment to wait. He told the others what was happening, but he wasn't expecting it to be much help. The boys were looking at a takeaway menu, deciding what they would order for tea and Phil was reading through his paperwork preparing for the meeting at the bank the next day.

"Are you going to be OK at the meeting doing the presentation on your own tomorrow Phil?"

"Sure. You need to get to Speakers' Corner. Getting Luci back is more important than a meeting with the bank."

When a knock on the apartment door was heard, Rob went and opened it and was faced with a woman who looked in her mid to late 30s, stood about five foot ten with shoulder length brunette hair framing a very attractive face. She was dressed in a very smart business trouser suit with modest heeled black shoes and carried a simple handbag.

"Mr Robert Blackstock?" she asked.

Rob nodded.

"I'm Susan Williams from Williams Securities."

"Come in Susan. Please," Rob said offering out his hand to shake.

She took his hand and he was aware of her extraordinary firm grip. "Call me Sue. Do you prefer Robert, Rob or perhaps Bert?"

"Rob will be fine. Come through to the lounge and meet the others." He gestured for her to go through first and followed her in.

"Guys, this is Sue. Sue this is Phil Parsons, he manages my father's horse racing stable, but is coming to work for me on a new venture in India."

"Please to meet you, Phil."

"Likewise."

They shook hands.

"And these two are my son Justin."

"Dad! It's JB."

"Hello JB."

"And the other young man is Phil's boy, Jake."

"Pleased to meet you, Jake."

"Right gentlemen, Paul has given me a brief outline of the situation and the events of yesterday. Enough for me to be very interested! Can we all sit down now and go through everything in greater detail. You don't mind me recording all this do you?" Sue pulled an I-phone from her handbag and selected the record app, without waiting for a response.

Over the next hour they went through every little detail of their story, with Sue stopping them several times with questions.

When they had all finished, she stopped the recording and smiled.

"Well, I can certainly help you. Williams Securities is a big organisation, one of the biggest of its type in Europe. You've probably know very little about us, apart from the property security part. We deliberately want it that way. Our main client is the British Government. We provide security for a lot of politicians and members of the royal family. We were one of the companies engaged with security a Harry and Megan's wedding. There are five or six private companies like ours who work with MI-5 and MI-6, to keep the country safe. It's an arrangement that works very well. We recruit from the Military Police and the top military unit such as the SAS. We also take on top graduates from certain universities."

JB and Jake were gripped by what she was saying. Straight out of a James Bond film. She had their total attention as she continued.

"Firstly, you're right about the corrupt policemen. Have you heard of the

Anti-corruption force?"

They all looked blank.

"It's an independent arm of the police force with strong links to MI-5. Set up to investigate corruption within the police force and investigate any possible threat to national security. My company has been working with one of the units, AC-10, a small unit looking at what appears to be a well organised group in the Metropolitan force. We have identified a few of the lesser members and are closely monitoring their activities in the hope that it will lead us to identifying the leaders. I say my company, but what I should say is the company I work for. My name is Williams but it's my brother-in-law who runs the company that was originally create by my father-in-law Terry Williams. We've been in business since 1978. I met Tony, Terry's oldest son in 2001, we were both sergeants in the same MP unit. We married in 2002 but when Tony was killed in Afghanistan in 2014, I bought my way out and joined the company as task force leader." "So I was right not to involve the police?" Rob said.

"Certainly. Now we can bring them in and watch how they react. Which way they run, so to speak."

"What do you want us to do?"

"All in good time. Just let me continue then we'll sort out what's to be done as we go," she continued. "I think from your descriptions the two thugs, as you call them are the Squire Brothers, Jay and Bill, members of the River gang. Small time crooks who dabble in drugs, vice and extortion. If we can prove it and you identify them formally, we can put them away for murder. We also know the location of some of the places they hang out at, we can start looking there for your daughter. The Russians are almost certainly Mikhail Gorkov, leader of the London Russian mafia who we believe are linked to the Russian Wolves."

"Who are the Russian Wolves?"

"The Russian Wolves are an organisation that was formed in the late nineteenth century, originally as a sort of secret army to protect the royal family. But after the Bolshevik Revolution they went deep underground, but since the break-up of the Soviet Union they have surfaced, trying to undermine the governments of the former Soviet countries and re-establish Russian sovereignty. They are largely funded by trafficking Russian girls into the sex trade in Western Europe and drugs. Mikhail Gorkov is on our list of wanted, men but to date we've not been able to pin anything on him. The other Russian is probably his second in command, Ivan Relinski, also on our watch list. They are both nasty people. We're certain they run a vice ring in North London. Running over a hundred girls and supplying drugs in the same area."

"Okay Sue what should we do?"

"Firstly we need to get the boys to safety. Somewhere well away, where they won't be found. They witnessed a murder. Someone will want them silenced."

Phil immediately spoke up. "My folks have a place in North Norfolk. Really out in the wilds, miles from anywhere! Any good?"

"That sounds perfect."

"You can take my car Phil. It's what—a three-hour trip you could be there this evening."

"What about the bank tomorrow?"

"Sod the bank. It our children's lives at stake. Our priority is to see them safe."

"You're right, Rob. I'll ring my folks now. Get some things together boys, we could be away for a few days. Let's try and get away as soon as we've eaten. Come in the kitchen and we'll get a takeaway ordered."

"Don't order anything for me Phil. I'll grab something later. What else can we do Sue?"

"Several things! You can come with me to meet my grandparents. My maiden name was Kowinski, my grandparents are Jews who as teenagers were living in Astrakhan when the Nazis arrived in 1943. Almost a third of the population including my grandparents were shipped out to various concentration camps. Most ended up in the gas chambers, but my grandparents survived and were liberated at the end of 1944. Like many others, they walked across North Africa as refugees and came to England. I remember as a girl them telling me stories they had been told when they were children, about Katherine the Great hiding a great horde of jewels in a holy place in Astrakhan. I rang them before coming here and told them I'd see them at 8 this evening and they should expect me to bring you along. They live in Edgware about 30 minutes from here. My car is just round the corner."

"Right, what else can I help with?"

"I suggest you contact your parents in Yorkshire and if they can get away for a few days they should do so. But at the very least they should get some of their staff in to lessen the risk of anything happening to them."

"I can do better than that. I've currently got eighteen men and women in training at my stunt school. It's near my dad's place. I'll get my manager there to organise them into teams and have them work in shifts, keeping an eye on the place."

"What about the man Logan who you said you knew. Tomorrow, perhaps you could arrange to meet him on the pretext of registering his horse for races. I could go along as your PA. I have to admit that the connection with the Squire Brothers and his sudden wealth make me a little curious. It might be worth probing a little. I would also like you to go down the police station and ask for PC421. Say you're following up on his visit here. We'll see what cages that rattles. And finally Speakers' Corner. You have to be there. Best if you come clean and tell them the Russians have the diamond and see how they respond. They'll have nothing to gain from harming your daughter. They may just let her go, but more likely they'll hold on to her and tell you to get the diamond back."

"I hope you're right."

Phil came through from the kitchen. "Norfolk is arranged, the Chinese will be here any minute. As soon as we've eaten, we'll be off. If we're taking your car Rob, what will you do for transport?"

"The Ducati down in the garage is mine. I'll be fine with that. It's actually better for getting around in town."

There was a knock on the door and Phil went to answer it. He came back through the lounge carrying the takeaway and went straight through to the kitchen. Twenty minutes later they were all packed and ready to leave. Rob told them to ring when they got to their destination. He handed Phil the car keys saying, "Look after one another guys. Have a good trip; I'll see you in a few days. Take care of them Phil. I'll ring you later with an update."

"We should be making a move too. But first I need to take that finger back to my office for our lab to process and try for a fingerprint or DNA match. The office is more or less on our route. Also, I'm concerned about your safety. I don't have anyone I can spare to be with you overnight, so I'll stay." Sue said.

"Star treatment. I'm ready let's go."

D.S. Jameson was on the phone when a new case folder was handed to him by his chief. He quickly ended the call saying he would ring back later.

"What's this then chief?"

"A naked, mutilated body has been found at Brentwood refuse transfer station. Get yourself down there this evening and start the investigation."

Jameson was fully aware of how a body ended up at Brentwood but he couldn't say anything to the chief, he just had to go along with the pretence. At least he would be able to ensure nothing would come back to him, or anyone else, in The Inspector's little band. When he arrived at the transfer station the CSIs were inspecting the body. The senior CSI officer saw him approach and stood to receive him.

"What have you got for me Dick?" Jameson asked.

"Not much sir. My preliminary report is she died from blood loss from multiple stab wounds to the abdomen."

Rob stayed in the car while Susan went into her office. When she returned she was carrying a small holdall which she dropped into the boot.

"Just my overnight bag," she said as she got back into the car.

Mr Kowinski opened the front door of the town house he and his wife of 50 years owned and lived in. Sue and Rob had left Sue's car down the road because there were no spaces closer.

"Hello grandad, this is Rob Blackstock. He's interested in learning about the Russian Rocks."

"You'd better both come in. Your grandmother is out at bingo."

"Good evening Mr Kowinski. So good of you to see me."

"Go through to the front room," the old man gestured towards a door next to the bottom of the stairs.

"Now what is it you want to know?"

"Do you remember when I was a little girl, you used to tell me the legend of the Russian Rocks. Well I think one of them has turned up here in London. Rob here has seen it. I can only remember a few bits of the story. Can you remember the full story."

"I'll do my best luv. The legend really starts with Ivan the Terrible, who was the first Tzar of all Russia. History tells us he married eight times and each time the bride came with a very large dowry, making him a very rich man. During his forty year reign he was ruthless in taxing, adding to his growing wealth. When his health began to fail, he ordered the building of an extension to the chapel at Astrakhan. The chapel extension is said to contain a secret vault where Ivan hid his wealth. Ever since Ivan's death people have searched for the vault and the hoard of riches it contains, including the Tzar's crown jewels, but no one has ever found anything. Even with today's marvellous machines, no one has been able to locate it. The legend says that the vault can only be opened by a shaft of sunlight directed through a large diamond. There were three large gems cut as the keys which were named: The Russian Eye, a diamond with a hint of blue that the legend says was sent to the Vatican, but never appears on any Vatican documentation. Official papers make no mention of it.

"The Russian Sunflower has a hint of yellow and was placed in the care of the head of the Russian church. Historical records don't specifically mention the diamond but there are records telling of a large diamond being broken up in to smaller stones which were sold off to fund church repairs all over the known Jewish world. The final diamond, The Russian Rose or the Rose Of Russia, as it has been recently called, with a hint of pink was kept by Ivan and passed down the line of Tzars. In the chapel extension there are nine locks, holes in the stonewall, that any of the diamonds will fit." The old man paused his story.

"Sorry I haven't offered either of you a drink."

"That's alright grandad we're fine. Please continue."

"Okay. The legend says that to open the vault one of the diamonds must be placed in the right lock at the right time on the right day of the year for the angle of the sun to trigger the mechanism. For nine valid diamond and lock combinations there are two days each year when the sun is at the right angle for the diamond to bend the sun light onto the correct spot to trigger the opening. Those days are 6 months apart."

"Sue, the boys heard those thugs say something about The Inspector needing to have the diamond no later than Tuesday. If this diamond is really one of the three then the day when it will open the vault must be soon."

"It certainly looks that way."

The old man continued, "Each 6 months the diamond will work for three consecutive days each day in a different lock."

"This all sounds like that Harrison Ford film, 'The Lost Ark', where the hero let sunlight though a stone to show where to find the treasure," Rob said.

"It does sound like fiction. Maybe time has coloured the legend a little. Any idea of the value in the hoard, Grandad?"

"Well, it started with a large sum from Ivan. Catherine The Great is said to have added several times her weight in gold and there is some evidence to say Nicholas II added the substantial Romanov jewels to the pot shortly before the revolution. It's highly likely that every Tzar made a contribution."

"That vault must be massive. So why has no-one discovered it? If it exists it must be worth a fortune."

"My countrymen say there is more treasure than ten people can carry and it is worth 50,000 million Roubles which at today's rates is a little over £500 million."

"So, if one person found it they could possible walk away with £50 million in a single visit. But they would need a small lorry to get it all."

"Thank you grandad, that has been very useful. We'll leave you to go back to watching the TV now."

"Don't leave it so long before you visit again Susan. Your grandmother will be sorry not to have seen you. Good evening Mr Blackstock."

The summer sunlight was fading as they walked back to Sue's car, thinking over the story they had just been told.

"I don't really believe any of this, Sue," Rob suddenly said. "It's all too much of a fairy tale. Yes I believe that there must have been a lot of wealth accumulated over the centuries. What royal family doesn't have priceless crown jewels etcetera? But all this nonsense about hiding a horde of valuables in a chapel, behind a lock that can only be opened by sunlight shining through a diamond,

I'm sorry Sue it all sounds too childish to be true."

"I agree, Rob. As the story is told now it does sound a bit unbelievable," Sue replied. "But all legends have some truth that they are based on, like Robin Hood and King Arthur. As a history project at school I once studied the life of Joseph Stalin. Historical records show that when the Russian palaces were stormed by the Bolsheviks in 1917 and the Romanov family were all murdered, no crown jewels were found. There is evidence that some of the royals had been tortured and the palaces chapel being totally ripped apart. In later years when Stalin was President, he set up a government department to search religious buildings and liberate their non-religious valuables. It doesn't mean he was looking for the jewels, but it is possible."

"OK! Maybe some of it has some validity. But why hide the jewels in a chapel in a small remote town like Astrakhan, when there are massive religious buildings in Moscow that you could hide a house in?"

"From what I know about Russian history," Sue replied. "Before Ivan the Terrible, Moscow was just a trading city. Rather like London was before William the Conqueror. When Ivan conquered and unified all the Soviet states, he made Moscow his capital and the construction of all the buildings we see today was started by him. Exactly as William did in London with The Tower, Westminster Abbey and others. Ivan married eight times but his real only love was his first wife, who was by his side for more than 30 years and gave him eleven children. He married her in the Chapel at Astrakhan. She is allegedly buried there too."

She unlocked the car and continued discussing the Russian treasure as they drove back to the apartment.

"£500 million is quite a sum to most people. I can understand why someone would murder for it," Rob said.

"Yes, and to an organisation like The Russian Wolves it would fund a small revolution. But a sum like that to the Russian Government would hardly be noticed. It's nothing compared with their defence budget," Sue added.

"Who do you think has the legal claim on it all?"

"Without doubt, the Russian Government but that won't stop the Wolves or this Inspector person trying to get their hands on it."

"It's getting late Sue and we've not eaten. Shall I order some Chinese to be delivered."

"Good idea. I missed lunch as well. I could eat a horse."

"Not one of mine you don't." They both laughed.

They parked the car in Rob's bay and took the lift up to the apartment. Rob entered the code to open the door.

"Welcome home Rob. You have no new messages. You had one visit to the door at 8:34pm."

"Come on in, Sue."

"Welcome back. Please give me your name."

"Susan Williams."

"Welcome Susan."

"That's a very sophisticated system you have there," she said as she went through to the lounge.

"It's very unusual for Paul to let strangers through. I'll just nip down and have a word with him."

Rob crashed back through the door just 5 minutes later. Sue rushed out of the lounge to investigate the commotion. To Rob's shock she was holding a pistol in front of her. Rob was struggling, half carrying, half dragging a semi-conscious security guard. He took Paul through to the lounge and sat him on the sofa.

"What happened Paul? Take your time."

"Sorry boss, sorry Mr B. There must have been two of them. One came in acting like a drunk. While I was trying to get rid of him, I heard someone else come in behind me. As I turned I was hit over the head and must have gone out like a light, until you woke me a few minutes ago."

"Nothing to be sorry about Paul. Rob has a very good security system here so no one got in. Ray will be coming on in ten minutes for his shift, so as soon as you feel you are able, get off home."

"Thanks Boss." He quickly recovered and left once he had convinced Sue he was okay again.

"What's with the gun Sue?"

"It's alright Rob, I'm licensed for it."

The takeaway arrived and Rob opened a bottle of wine for them to share. Sue declined a second glass saying she needed to stay sharp. As they ate they told one another a little about themselves. They both found themselves at ease with each other and the conversation flowed until Rob touched on his daughter and stopped mid-sentence and excused himself to go to the bathroom.

Sue put the dirty dishes and the wine glasses in the kitchen while Rob composed himself. He came out of with an armful of bed linen.

"You might as well use the single room. I'll just change the bed."

"I can do that. You get off to bed. You've had an exhausting day and we've got an early start in the morning."

The Squire Brothers were in the back of a transit van parked in a street less than a hundred yards from the apartment block. Lying beside them was a monitor showing two small images and a small pile of food scraps and wrappers showing they had been there several hours.

Jay felt the vibration of his phone ringing. He took it out and read the one word on the screen, 'Romanov'. He pressed the green button and put the phone to his ear.

"Right Squire, what have you got to update me with?"

"Well sir. The boys have been taken away by the black fella using Blackstock's car. We had already put a tracer on that and we know exactly where he is. Looks like now the boys are gone Blackstock has moved his girlfriend in. Bill and me put a camera watching the front door and another watching the car park. We saw the two of them come back in her car earlier and she had her bag with her. It looks like she's staying the night with him."

Chapter 6

"I know she's young but so were we when we first got into this business. Now look at us we have a good life together and in a couple of years, we'll have enough money to get out of here. Not like Rebecca. She's really got herself in a mess and where the hell has, she been since last Friday?"

****

Rob was awake early, but when he came out of his bedroom Sue was already dressed and was sitting in the lounge drinking coffee. She looked totally different this morning. Gone was the business suit and the formal image. Now she wore skin tight jeans topped by a white shirt knotted at the front and buttoned up just far enough to keep her decent, but show a little of the white lace material of her bra. She was a very attractive lady, about the same age as Jayne would have been. She had her hair tied up in the same way that Jayne used to fix hers. In many ways she reminded him of his wife but she was so totally different.

"We must go separately to Speakers' Corner. We'll each have to get a taxi, parking would be impossible. I'll go first and sight myself somewhere where I can see the whole area. I've arranged for two members of my team to also be there. They don't know what you look like, but they are familiar with the Squire Brothers, so will be able to follow them after your meeting. When you tell them you don't have the diamond, they will want to get instructions from further up the food chain. If we get lucky we could identify further members of their team. Don't worry Rob, I'm sure they won't harm Luci. It's not in their interest to do so."

"I wish I could be so certain."

When he arrived at Speakers' Corner there was already quite a crowd building. He stood at the edge of the crowd looking around for anyone who vaguely fitted the description the boys had given of the brothers, but no one did. He checked his watch 9:02.

"Mr Blackstock, good to see you here on time." The words came from behind Rob's left ear, not loud enough to be overheard. "No don't turn round or do anything stupid, my knife is pointing at your ribs. It would be the easiest thing in the world for me to stick you with it and I'd walk away with nobody any the wiser."

Sue signalled her two team members to keep a close watch and be ready to follow. She had spotted Jay Squires as he had approached Rob, but looking all around she couldn't see his young brother.

"You know what I'm after, so let's get the business done as quickly as we can, shall we. Hand over the rock."

"I haven't got it."

"What do you mean you haven't got it? Have you left it at home, or handed it in to the authorities?"

"I mean I haven't got it. I did have it for a short while but a couple of Russians took it away from me at gun point yesterday afternoon."

"My boss is not going to be happy to hear that. We've gone to a lot of trouble to get that rock and you just give it away."

"I hardly gave it away."

"It doesn't matter how you lost it. You lost it. You'd better think how you're going to get it back."

"Where is my daughter?"

"You won't see her until my boss has the rock to hold. I'll be generous I'll give you twenty four hours. Come back here same time tomorrow with the rock and we won't harm her any more, but if you fail she will suffer."

"I'm warning you if my daughter suffers in any way, you'll all pay."

There was no answer and Rob was aware that whoever had been behind his left shoulder was no longer pressing up against him. He turned to find who ever had been there had gone. He hoped Sue's team were on the ball.

"That was all very quick."

"He's given me twenty four hours to get the diamond back. If I fail he's threatening to harm Luci. I'm to be here same time tomorrow."

"Think about it Rob, what would they gain from harming her. Believe me she's safe. How about a coffee? You look like you need one. There's a place just around the corner."

"That a very good idea. Then I'll try the cop shop after that to see what PC421 has to say for himself."

"You also need to get to see Inspector Peter Logan."

"I'd forgotten that. I'll try ringing him while we have coffee. Where did you say the coffee shop is?"

"Only around the corner! This way." Sue said as she took his arm and led him off in the direction she had pointed.

"I'm not complaining about having an attractive lady on my arm, but I must ask do you get this close to all your clients?"

"No, not normally. But we're being watched and I don't want anyone suspecting you to have engaged help. Just act naturally. Did you notice the camera overlooking your front door or the one overlooking your parking space in the garage?"

"No!"

"I think they must have installed them after knocking Paul out. We must do whatever we can to convince them that I'm your girlfriend and offer no threat. There's the coffee shop over the road. I used to use it a lot but I've not been in there for almost a year so I hope the coffee is still as good."

The lights on the crossing changed and the green man lit up. They crossed the road holding hands and entered the coffee shop.

"What are you having Sue?" Rob said grabbing a tray from the end of the counter and joining the short queue waiting for coffee.

"Latte please Rob with a shot of caramel. There's a table over in the corner

I'll go and claim it."

Rob joined her at the table with two coffees and two Chelsea buns.

"Hope you like Chelsea buns. I can't resist them."

"Personally I can't pass chocolate and not be tempted. You must ring Logan, here's the number for the police switchboard."

Rob dialled the number Sue had handed him. It rang twice and then Rob heard a recorded message say 'You have reached the switchboard of the Metropolitan Police. All our operators are busy at the moment. Please hold the line, an operator will be with you soon.' While he was on hold he listened to a series of short passages of classical music. A full ten minutes he waited.

"Metropolitan Police switchboard. Thank you for waiting. How may I help you?"

"Can you put me through to Inspector Peter Logan please."

"Sorry sir we have no inspector Logan. Could it be you mean Assistant Commissioner Logan."

Rob thought for a moment before replying.

"Yes, put me through please."

"Whom may I say is calling please caller." "Robert Blackstock."

"Thank you sir, putting you through now."

The phone rang several times before it was answered.

"Hello Rob. Nothing wrong with my horse I hope."

"Congratulations on your promotion. No your horse is fine. We, that is my father, is looking ahead to getting your horse into some races so he can start earning his keep. I need to meet with you to go through some papers to get the horse formally registered. It should only take an hour or so."

"Sorry Rob that's going to be very difficult this week. I've got an evening meeting with the Home Secretary this evening and tomorrow I fly to Moscow for an Interpol Conference. Pauline is coming with me and we're going to have a couple of days sightseeing after the conference. Not home again until Wednesday next week. Perhaps we can have dinner one evening when I get back. Include the wives maybe. You are married Rob?"

"My wife died several years ago. Car accident."

"I'm sorry about that Rob. Listen, I've got a meeting now so I must go. I'll pass you to my secretary and she'll sort something out for next week. Nice speaking with you, catch you soon, bye."

Rob heard the phone click, go silent for a moment then click again.

"Hello Mr Blackstock I'm Faye, Assistant Commissioner Logan's secretary. He has asked me to arrange for a dinner for two next Thursday or Friday is that correct."

"That is correct Faye but I can't make either of those days. I'll ring him at the end of next week to arrange something when we both are less busy. Thanks." He ended the call before she had a chance to respond.

"He can't meet me because he's flying to Russia tomorrow. The boys said they heard those bent coppers say The Inspector needed the diamond by Tuesday because he was booked on a flight to Russia."

"Don't jump too quickly Rob. It could just be a coincidence. We don't have any real evidence. We need to tell AC-10 what we know. But before we do that you'll need to sign the Official Secrets Act because you may see or hear confidential material. We can do that on the way to the police station. Let's get back to your apartment and get my car."

As D.S. Jameson's boss passed his desk he said "Jameson, my office now. Update me on the mutilated body case."

Jameson followed his boss into the small side office. "Not much to say really boss. We know who she is, Rebecca Stanslic, age twenty seven, Russian, been in UK for six years, picked up three times for prostitution, stabbed four times in the low stomach, died between 12:00 and 3:00 Saturday afternoon from blood loss. We have a last known address. I'm off to check it out this afternoon."

"We don't need to spend too much time on it then. Probably a falling out with her pimp. Do what you need to do and get it filed as quickly as you can."

Luci had slept well after her exhausting day but her lost memory was a big worry to her. It was almost 9:30 when she woke. She could hear someone at the front door and held herself absolutely dead still, frightened of being discovered if she made a sound.

"Emma dear we're home. Are you awake yet honey?"

"I'm just getting some clothes on. Be out in a moment."

She jumped out of bed and pulled her nightshirt over her head when there was a knock on the door and without waiting for a response Ana walked in. Luci instantly pulled the nightshirt up in front of herself attempting to cover her breasts and pubic area. Ana laughed.

"No need to be shy with us Emma, we're all girls here. We're all the same under our clothes. All our bits are the same. Maybe a different shape or size but basically the same. As you're naked why not have a bath and freshen up. It will help you relax. Eva run Emma a bath please lover."

Ana sat herself down on the edge of the bed and they heard water start to run. Luci began to allow the nightshirt to slip away but pulled it back to cover herself when Eva appeared at the door. The two girls both laughed then Luci began to laugh as well and the nightshirt fell to the floor. When she turned to see the two women together she saw Ana in a green short skirt and Eva in a blue one. She was sure that when they left last night Ana was in the blue one. Her memory was obviously still playing games.

Eva turned to Ana and gave her a strange look.

"Yes I had noticed Eva. We'll see to getting that trimmed later. Right young lady that bath should be ready, go and climb in I'll bring in some towels in a minute or two."

Luci hadn't really taken notice of the bath before when she had been in the bathroom but now as she stepped up onto the plinth it was mounted in and climbed down into the oversized oval corner bath she realised how big it was. She turned off the tap and sank back into the water resting her head on the edge and breathing in the herbal scents rising from the water. She was almost asleep when the door opened and the two girls walked in totally naked and carrying a bundle of towels.

"Move up young lady there's room in there for us. We need to get the oils and other stuff off our bodies before they soak in."

Luci sat up and moved forward. Eva climbed in behind her and sat with a leg either side of Luci's hips then Ana climbed in behind Eva. All three then lay back and allowed the scented water to cover their bodies. Luci thought 'what would the girls back home think of her lying here with her head resting in between Eva's breast and Eva gently rubbing soap over her own shoulders and breasts. It felt so good, like nothing she had experienced before. It was making her nipples as hard as bullets and now Eva started pulling on them. Another new feeling.'

Suddenly she sat up quickly in the bath and said out aloud. "What girls back home? Where's home?"

"What's wrong little one?"

"I don't know. I thought I remembered something but now I'm not sure.

Perhaps it was just a small part of who I am. It's so horrible just not knowing."

"Lie back again and relax. Maybe more memories will come back to you."

"No thanks I'm ready to get myself dry and dressed." She climbed out of the water, wrapped herself in a large fluffy towel and went back to her bedroom closing the door behind her. She dressed, pulled her bed straight and headed for the kitchen. As she passed the bathroom door she could hear a lot of splashing and giggling.

In the kitchen she found coffee in a cupboard. She wasn't keen on coffee but needed something to wake her up. She switched the kettle on and quickly washed one of the many mugs she found on the counter. She couldn't find a teaspoon, so she tipped a little from the jar into the mug and poured on the hot water and went to the fridge for milk. With her hand on the fridge door, she stopped dead. How did she know she wasn't keen on coffee? Her memory was coming back hopefully something important would come back next.

"Good girl. Coffee. Two black and no sugar, please." Eva and Ana entered the kitchen in short floral silk wraps, Luci assumed them to be naked beneath as neither had taken clothes into the bathroom.

"Bring them through to the lounge please, honey."

Luci carried two mugs through and set them down on the coffee table in front of the girls who were lay back together on the sofa. Ana had her bag on her lap and was searching through it. Eva had her arm around Ana's shoulders and had her hand inside her wrap. Luci fetched her own coffee and set it down on the other side of the table and sat herself opposite the two girls.

"What do you do to earn money? Where did you go last night to work? The clothes you went out in last night were not what I would expect a waitress or shop girl to wear."

"We were working at a private party in North London. The clothes are a sort of uniform for what we do."

"Are you prostitutes? Is that guy... Boris, no Mikhail. Is Mikhail your pimp?"

Ana was quick to respond "We are not prostitutes and Mikhail is not our pimp. He does find work for us but we are dancers. Erotic dancers. People pay to watch us dance and perform. We perform in private homes, in clubs and pubs and occasionally on a big stage. We do not have sex with our customers only with each other. People pay a lot of money to watch us. A lot take pictures and videos and we had a lot of fun doing a scene for a movie."

"You have sex in front of an audience?"

"It's not an issue once you've done it the first time. We love one another's bodies and it's great to be paid for something you enjoy doing anyway."

"Are you lesbians?"

"No, we both like boys as well. We are just lovers who enjoy one another and get paid well for it. Look." And she pulled a bundle of notes held in a money clip, from the bag on her lap. "For last night we were paid £300 and picked up almost another £300 in tips and that was just a private party. At bigger events we can make three or four times that amount for exactly the same amount of effort. Typically we earn about £10,000 per month. It's not cheap living here. Rent for this apartment is £1,600 a month. We need to appear in new clothes so budget £500 a month for that and as you know we're not good in the kitchen so we eat out often. We are saving as much as we can so that we can buy our own place and get out of this business."

"That is a lot of money."

"We're very good at what we do. We thought of our act when we first came to London. We were already lovers, had been since we were fifteen. We knew we would get dragged into the sex business in order to survive and this act of ours works and is very popular. Besides parties like last night's are fun."

Eva joined in. "Yes. A ladies only night and didn't they like us. Did you see that Faye and our hostess going at it?"

"Yes. That Faye really is something. Someone told me that she works with the hostesses' husband, he's a very lucky man. Something in the police. Now Emma what are we going to do with you? Mikhail likes the look of you and says he has many people who would pay big money for you. Of course he means selling you for sex. If you want to stay away from that we can try teaching you what we do."

"Is there something else I could do?"

"Well, you could become a stripper but that's the seedy side of thing. It's real hard work and there's very little money in it. Because you have no ID and don't actually know who you are, you don't have a lot of option."

"I guess not. Perhaps I should take your advice."

"Before you decide you should see our act. We have a few copies of videos that have been taken. We'll get them out for you to watch, they are all loaded on my laptop. You can borrow it if you like."

Rob and Sue took a taxi back to the apartment block and as they rode the lift up to apartment eighteen Sue said. "Rob, in your left hand jacket pocket you'll find a small black plastic cube, about the size of a sugar cube. Jay Squire put it there before he left you. It's a tracker."

"Thanks, I never felt a thing. I'll leave it in the apartment."

"No don't do that. They are watching us come and go from here anyway and I assume they've got people following us most of the time. Now that they have planted the tracker on you the ones following us will back off and mostly stay out of sight relying on the tracker. I suspect they've also put one on my car whilst we were out this morning."

"It's not easy to get into the garage."

"For you maybe not, but don't forget these guys are professionals. Remember they were able to get at least two cameras installed yesterday evening, so having seen my car park in your space when we got back from my grandparents place and seeing us both leave this morning, why not get in again this morning and put a tracker on the car. I know I would."

"Yes, I can see the logic in that."

"So let's work on the assumption that there is a tracker and use it to our advantage. My office and AC-10's office are about 1 mile apart, slightly off a line between the two offices is a large shopping mall. So what we'll do is this…" And she went on to talk Rob though her plan.

In the apartment Sue made a few phone calls and Rob gave Phil a ring. At first he couldn't get a response so he sent a short message 'All okay?' About five minutes later the phone rang the ID said Phil Parker.

"Hi Rob, have you been trying to ring me, only the signal up here is practically non-existent. I've had to come down the lane to get even two bars." His words were all broken by the poor service and Rod had difficulty piecing together what he was saying, but finally got the message that everyone was OK.

"Right Sue I've checked on the boys and now I feel a bit peckish. Can I make you an omelette for brunch, then we'll get off to the police station."

"That sounds lovely Rob, thank you. I've made an appointment with the guys at AC-10 for three this afternoon so that should give us plenty of time to call into my office on the way."

Rob enjoyed cooking, he always had when Jayne was alive. Once a month he would plan and cook a special meal just for the two of them, served with a bottle of good wine. It allowed them both to relax.

Fortunately he had a good selection of vegetables in the freezer so he was able to show off a little and take his mind off everything that was happening.

DS Jameson's desk phone rang. Caller ID said Unknown, so he answered it cautiously and a rough sounding voice at the other end said.

"It's me, Jay Squire."

"What the fuck are you doing using my desk phone. For god's sake this can be traced. Use my mobile." He hung up and went and stood outside to wait for the call.

"Squire, update me quickly."

"This morning, they went off in different directions by taxi, so Billy went in to plant a tracker on her car."

"What about the meeting? Did you get the diamond?"

"He said the Russians took it from him yesterday. So, I told him he had 24 hours to get it back before we start hurting his daughter. Before I left him, I dropped another tracker in his pocket so we should be able to follow them anywhere."

"That's not good enough. The Inspector must have it tomorrow. Cut off her hand and deliver it to him to show we mean business. I'll do the meeting tomorrow. Call me when you have news. Let the Inspector down and you'll regret it."

John Towner had been stood near Jameson's desk with an armful of paperwork related to several cases the detective was investigating. He only heard the one side of the conversation but he worked out that the Russians somehow had taken the diamond. He knew that if that was truly the situation then it would almost certainly be in the hands of Mikhail Gorkov and from what he'd heard about the Russian hard man, it would be on his person at all times. Towner knew the inspector would not be happy about the way he had gone about tracking down the Blackstocks but if only he could track down Gorkov and get the diamond back he would be back in the Inspector's good books.

The apartment phone rang with caller ID showing 'Unknown'. Rob answered it with a single work "Blackstock."

"Rob its Phil. The boys and I are in the pub, we've just had lunch and I saw this public phone so thought I'd ring for an update. How's things?"

"I'm worried about Luci, those thugs are threatening to hurt her if I don't get that diamond back for them by tomorrow morning. Other than that we have made a little progress. We've found out that Peter Logan is flying to Russia late tomorrow. Suggesting further that he is The Inspector. Remember the boys saying they heard that The Inspector is on a flight to Russia on Tuesday so must have the stone before then."

"Sounds like you may be right. Well, the boys are happy and well."

"Phil, the bad guys have installed a couple of cameras and we suspect they have placed a tracker on Sue's car. We think we're being continually watched. I'm a bit concerned that they may have placed a tracker on my car and know where you and the boys are."

"They did Rob. You know how mad Jake is about engines, well he was keen to look under the bonnet of the Jag and did so when we stopped at the services near Stanstead. While he was looking it over he spotted a tracker fixed to one of the engine mounts. We removed it and fixed it to a coach in the car park that is taking some pensioners to Skegness for a holiday."

"Well spotted Jake. That will certainly spoil someone's fun."

"That's what we thought. That's why I say the boys are safe and well. I'd better get back to them now. I left them playing pool. I'll try and ring again tomorrow."

"Thanks Phil."

"Phil and the boys found a tracker on my car and have sent it off to Skegness so they should be safe where they are in Norfolk. We'd better get going Sue."

Chapter 7

"The Inspector was very specific when ordering that everything we do must tie back to police activity. No one should do anything that has no connection to a case. There is no case that supports your story about going to the Blackstock place. You invented a good story but if any one checks at the station there is no record of a phone being handed in. You've opened yourself up for investigation and put the organisation at risk. There will be a price to pay."

****

"Well, let us see how professional whoever is watching us really is." Sue said as she drove out of the underground car park. "Watch that blue transit we just passed if I'm right we'll see it again soon after we stop."

She drove into the carpark of the large shopping mall near her office. They parked close to the stairwell. As they walked towards the stairs they looked out over the open parking area and saw a blue transit being manoeuvred into a parking space. For the next part of their plan they needed a member of staff coming on duty to cross their path. Rob took the tracker from his jacket pocket and passed it to Sue as they walked towards a paper shop. Coming out as they were going in was a young woman obviously late for her shift she was pulling on her security over jacket as she rushed. Sue deliberately bumped up against her as they passed in the doorway and Rob watched her rush on towards her job.

"That was easy. Now the tracker will stay in the mall long enough for us to do what we need to and will be continuously moving around the place as if we were browsing the shops."

"You mean you planted it on her."

"I did, but I'm not sure how we'll get it back. But our guardians won't follow us in here. They'll be happy to watch their monitors. Now let's find the back door to this place and get to my office."

Fifteen minutes later Sue was swiping her security card through the lock so they could enter her office building. They took the lift to the sixth floor and walked the length of the floor to a door bearing the name Susan Williams. On the desk were a number of hand written notices.

"First things first let's get you signed up on the Official Secrets act. Here read this and sign it." She pulled a form from her desk draw and handed it and a pen to Rob. Then she started to read the notices on her desk.

"Fantastic, the techies have identified who's finger you were sent. I've got her last known address here. If you're okay with doing the police station on your own I'll go to this address and see what I can find out about her. Apparently the police are looking at the rest of her body. I assume they'll have someone going round there as well. D.S. Jameson is heading the investigation into her death."

"I'm impressed. So much information from one finger so quickly. Yes, I'm okay doing the police station."

"Great, then I'll meet you at AC-10. We're seeing James Moore at three.

You've got an hour and a half don't be late I'll text you the address."

They left together. Each hailing a taxi and going off in different directions.

The doorbell rang and Eva answered the door to a tall thin man standing outside. She pulled her wrap tight around her naked body.

"I'm D.S. Jameson." He said showing her his warrant card at the same time. "Is this the home of Rebecca Stanslic?"

"Yes. But she's not here at the moment. I don't know where she is. Is she in trouble?"

"I'm afraid I have some bad news for you. May I come in?"

"Ana come out here please. There is a policeman with news of Becky." Eva called as she opened the door wider and allowed the detective to step into the entrance hall.

"Do you both live here and share with Miss Stanslic?"

"We do."

"Well I regret to inform you that Miss Stanslic was found dead yesterday evening. We suspect she was murdered."

Both girls gasped and put hands to their mouths in shock. Then they hugged one another for support as tears began to well up.

"Do you know if she had any enemies or anyone who might want to hurt her?"

"No—she is…. She was a very quiet girl, never got on the wrong side of anyone. How did she die?"

"She was stabbed I'm told."

The girls' facial expressions showed they were horrified.

"That's horrible but I don't think we can help you officer, sorry."

"Thanks for your time, ladies. I don't suppose you know of anyone we should contact. A relative perhaps."

"Sorry no. We didn't have a lot to do with her really she's not been here long." They lied; they had all lived in that apartment for over three years.

"We'll go through her things for you if you like and ring you if we find anything."

"That would help very much thank you. Here's my card. You can leave a message anytime." He thanked them again and walked back to his car. As he walked, he passed a good looking lady, so good looking in fact that he turned for a second look before getting into his car. He was happy that he had made a show at investigating the murder and could say he had no leads as to who the murderer might be. In truth he knew exactly who it was and why but that would not be in his report.

Sue recognised Jameson as he passed her in the street. He was already on her list of known members of the group of bent coppers. She had been told he was heading the investigation into Rebecca's murder and he had obviously just been visiting her apartment to speak to her flat mates, therefore it would be wrong to do it now. Maybe in a day or two, she could claim to be following up on the case.

It only took Rob a few minutes to get to the police station. After paying the taxi what seemed like a huge amount for such a short journey he climbed the three or four steps and entered. Inside he joined a short queue waiting to see the duty sergeant at the desk.

"Next. How can I help you sir?"

"Good afternoon sergeant. Would it be possible to speak with PC 421 please?"

"Will, is John Towner about today?"

"No sergeant. He's on a split shift, went off at 12:00, back on at 6:00."

"Sorry sir, he's not here at the moment. He went off duty over an hour ago.

Can I ask what this is about perhaps someone else can help."

"PC 421 came to my apartment yesterday with a mobile phone that had been handed in here and traced back to my son. He said he needed my son to verify it was his in order to get it back."

"That doesn't sound right at all. PC 421 is PC John Towner who was off duty yesterday. Will, do you know anything about a mobile phone being handed in?" "Not had one in for a couple of weeks sergeant."

"You heard that sir, so I don't know what this is all about. Can I get PC Towner to ring you?"

"No it's okay, the phone isn't my sons—I'll leave it."

PC Towner was actually out on the streets looking for Mikhail Gorkov. He'd searched through records in vice and compiled a list of girls he pimped. His plan now was simple but would demand a lot of his free time. He would actually visit each of the girls and enquire if they knew of Gorkov's whereabouts. He had called on twelve girls on his day off and today on his way to the next girl when he actually saw Gorkov on the step of a town house waiting for the door to be opened. Towner checked his list and saw that in the top flat lived Rebecca Stanslic, Eva Andelova and Oxsana Kolanski all on the list. He watched as Gorkov was invited into the house then stood a little way off waiting for him to come out again.

He waited almost fifteen minutes before he did come out. John watched the Russian walk about a hundred yards then stepped out to follow him unaware that he himself was being observed and followed by Ivan Relinski, Gorkov's bodyguard.

The Inspector was on edge and was beginning to think that the big prize was slipping away and the plans for making their fortune would have to be postponed for six months. Secrecy would be critical, they couldn't let it be known that the 'Rose Of Russia' had been discovered by a Jew in London after being lost for more than a century. There had been only three or four people knew of the find, far more knew now. The Inspector was one of those, because of advice given about special new security measures the jeweller wanted to install. There would be far too many people interested in it not just for its own value but for its link with the legend of the Romanov treasure.

A lot of effort had gone into planning this project and it wasn't going to be abandoned just because one or two things had not gone to plan. The Romanov treasure was the subject of legends but the facts were proving the legend to be accurate. Finding the diamond was only part of The Inspector's quest of more than twenty years. It was of little use without knowing which of the chapel locks it should be placed in and on which day and time. All this had been documented on a parchment obtained by an ancestor of The Inspector who had been a military advisor in Russia at the time of the revolution. Its significance at the time was probably not known. It was simply a piece of pre-revolution history and not much of that was being preserved. Twenty years ago it had been found by The Inspector, then a student at Oxford University, studying European History, when cataloguing the books in the family library. It had been tucked into a copy of the Russian Orthodox Bible. Years of research had followed to realise its real significance and to follow countless trails looking for the Russian Rocks all eventually leading to dead ends. But The Inspector did conclude that there was no actual evidence to be certain that any of the diamonds had been destroyed. The discovery of the Rose of Russia was a dream come true.

Sergeant Ken Smith posted a message on the police social Facebook page "Uncle Tom is coming to see me so I won't be at the darts match."

It was a good twenty minutes before his phone rang and a metallic voice said

"Have you recovered that stone for me yet?"

"I'm afraid we've run into some difficulties and the Russians now have it."

"Damn you Smith. You have to get it back no matter what. Understand me?"

"Yes boss. There is some good news though we've been able to put trackers on Blackstock and his vehicles. Plus get cameras set up so we can watch their movements. We've already tracked the boys to their Skegness hideout. We're now able to follow Blackstock wherever he goes."

"You were very quick finding the Blackstock home. How did you do it?"

"It was actually an ingenious move by Towner. He used the computers to narrow down the search to a few possibilities, then visited each claiming to return a phone that had been handed in."

"And had a phone been handed in."

"Well…. No Boss."

"I specifically gave instructions that every move had to be as part of a legitimate police action. If anyone follows up on this and finds it all to be fake, then questions will be asked. AC-10 are already too close. This could undermine our entire organisation. Anything else I should know about?"

"No Boss." The phone went dead before another word could be added.

The Inspector immediately called Sergeant Derek Drayton of the firearms unit.

"Derek are you aware that PC Towner has been compromising the organisation. We need him out of the way before AC-10 start questioning him. I don't care how it's done but he must be separated from us quickly."

"I'll speak to the River Gang straight away. Leave it to me boss. Good as done."

Ana and Eva watched the detective go off down the street then closed the door. They weren't unduly upset, after all in three years they hadn't really got to know her at all. They shared a kitchen and bathroom when she was there, which was not very often. She never used the lounge, she had the largest bedroom in the apartment and when she was at home that's where she spent her time. The only thing she had in common with them was her age. Even though she was also Russian she was from a totally different part of the country. The girls said nothing, just turned and returned to Luci who was still watching videos of their performances on Ana's laptop.

"Well, do you like what you've seen, Emma?"

"Your act is far more explicit than I expected. You don't hold anything back, do you? I don't think I could do anything like that."

"Sure you could. It's just a matter of ignoring where you are, who's watching you and what they are doing, just focus on what you are doing and you'll find you can do anything you want. Was there anything that particularly got you excited?"

"Well..." she replied rather shyly. "I did enjoy the scene where you shaved each other."

"Gosh that's an old one. I remember that one. Do you remember it, Ana?"

"I certainly do," she replied "That was the first time we saw Faye get it together with Mrs Logan."

"OK Emma, I'm going to put some music on, and we want you to dance for us. Get us excited like you've seen us do." The two girls quickly pushed the furniture back against the walls to give Luci room to perform. The effort in doing so made their wraps come loose but they made no attempt to cover up as they sat on the sofa in anticipation.

Luci felt very embarrassed but as she moved to the music she began to relax and after a while started to seductively shed her clothes in the same style, she had seen Ana and Eva do in the videos. She was totally lost in her actions and only vaguely aware of Eva applauding and Ana's words of encouragement. Her thong was the last item to be removed leaving her totally exposed. She momentarily came to enough to see the two girls smiling. She slowly at first began to caress her breasts and for the second time that day her nipples were as hard as bullets. Her hands travelled across her stomach, her hips and outer thighs before moving inward. That's where she stopped. "Eva, will you shave me please?"

"Yes, if you really want me to."

"I do, I like the way you two look and I want to look the same."

"I'll go and get the things then we can both do it." Said Ana heading towards the bathroom.

"Does your mother shave?"

"My mother died when I was seven. I live with my grandparents."

"Has anyone talked to you about sex at all?"

"My gran explained about periods when I had my first bleed, and our housekeeper has told me what to expect from boys. But I've seen in your videos that there is more to it than that."

"Well done, Emma. Do you realise that you've just been telling me about your past? Your memory is coming back."

Jameson had returned to his desk at the station, wrote up a few notes from his meeting with the two Russian girls adding it to the case folder. He was now standing outside with a cigarette when he was joined by Derek Drayton. After checking that no one could overhear them he spoke quietly to Jameson. "This project isn't going to plan Paul, too many things going wrong I've got a bad feeling. The Inspector has just asked me to do something about Towner."

"And Ray Watts getting shot dead by the police at the raid on the jewellers is a mess. What went wrong there?"

"New kid in the team we initially thought had been a little too eager but when we watched the videos Ray had actually raised his gun towards the public and anyone in the team would have similarly seen it as a threat to human life and taken him out. I hear you're leading the investigation into the little Russian girl's murder."

"That one's down to that crazy bastard Jay Squire getting carried away with his job. Complete nutter that one. Let's hope things go a bit smoother from here on in."

"Don't count on it. See you around." He turned and went back indoors.

Rob and Sue arrived at the AC-10 office block at the same time so entered the building together. They reported to the reception desk and Sue told the guard the purpose of their meeting. The guard made a phone call then said, "Please take the lift to the tenth floor where someone will meet you and show you to Mr Moore's office."

They moved to the body scanner, which to Rob looked a lot more complicated than the ones at airports. Sue handed a guard her handbag for inspection. The guard pulled out her gun and a clip of ammunition saying it must be left here and collected when they left. They then passed through the body scanner.

When they reached the tenth floor, they were met by a very young Asian looking secretarial type of girl who showed them to James Moore's office.

"Good afternoon to the two of you. Come on in. Pull up a chair."

"Thank you James. Good of you to see us so quickly. This is Rob Blackstock."

"On the contrary, from your call you are most certainly dealing with a group we are closely monitoring. Please tell me your story. Don't leave anything out however insignificant you may think it is, it might be important to us." Rob talked James through the events of the last three days.

"Thank you Rob. Nothing new there although it does provide more evidence against two or three in the group. You will stand in court with this won't you Rob?"

"More than happy to do so."

"Good man. Now let's try and lay out all the pieces and see what we've got."

First of all; The Inspector, no one, even members of the team, knows the real identity of The Inspector. Evidence is pointing us very strongly towards it being Assistant Commissioner Logan. We then have D.S. Jameson who we've watched for almost 2 years. We have evidence of tampering with evidence and altering case notes. He is certain to know more about your little Russian girl's murder than he is filing in the case notes. Sergeant Derek Drayton, actual name Robin Yates. He's one of mine who we got into the group about 18 months ago. He leads a team from the Armed Unit. We're pretty certain there is a woman near the top. Faye Mason fits the bill but we don't have any firm evidence. Sergeant Ken Smith and PC John Towner who fit as the couple at the murder witnessed by your son and you've had further dealings with Towner Rob. Smith and Towner are certainly guilty of giving false evidence in court and making evidence disappear. PC Janet North known to us for several years, following a cover-up of a couple of major fraud cases. Then there is PC John Lowe who has covered up at least one gangland murder. We believe there are at least two others who we haven't been able to identify.

Each of these had a folder with their name and their photograph on the front. Inside there were more copies of the photograph plus a diary of evidence held and a collection of documents, each summarising, one of the pieces of evidence. Some folders were thicker than others and a few had a reference number instead of a name. As James went through each folder he took a photograph from each and gave them to Rob. Rob was quite shocked when he saw Peter Logan's photograph. This was the image of a person who every inch looked like a police commissioner not the person he had shared rooms with at university. The person he knew then was loud mouthed and un-kept, a typical student. They had drifted apart when Pauline came on the scene. She was a little rich girl on the same course. Within a month of getting together he had moved in with her. Rob had heard they had married but he had seen neither of them since their graduation.

"If you have firm evidence against some of these why are they not behind bars?" Rob enquired.

"It's all about the ones at the top who we don't know. They are the ones with the power that we have no control over. The others that we can name we can control and ensure they don't do any damage. Whilst they are still out there, there is always a chance they will lead us to the big players. We have also identified that there is a close link to the River Gang who are mostly small time apart from a couple of real hard-nosed criminals who have both done time for manslaughter. You've already met Jay Squire, he's the worst of the bunch. But AC10 is interested in the police officers. Anything we can hang on the gang we'll pass to the main force."

"I see. So how can I help?"

"Quite simply keep eyes and ears open and pass on anything you find out. I'll give you the number of a direct line to my team before you leave."

James asked Rob a few questions about his story but they left the building before 4:30 and walked back to the shopping mall.

"Now we've got to find that female security person and recover the tracker. When we find her,- you distract her for a moment so I can recover it." Sue said and Rob nodded a reply.

They found her directing an elderly couple to the toilets. Rob moved in to distracter her while Sue came up behind her.

"Excuse me love. I'm a little lost. Can I get to the car park from this floor?" he asked.

"Yes sir. That way." She said pointing. "Go left at the end there and the exit to the car park will be on your right."

Sue pushed forward bumping quite hard into the security guard.

"Oh sorry love. Caught my toe on the step and almost fell. Well John did you find the way back to the car."

"Yes dear. Thank you for your help." He gave the guard a quick smile and they walked towards the car park exit.

"Did you get it?"

"Of course!" she replied. "Exactly where I left it."

As they walked back to the car, they looked over the wall and saw the blue transit was still there.

"We've supposedly been shopping for three hours Sue and we don't have any bags of shopping. Don't you think that will look a bit odd?"

"I'd already thought of that. I want you to take the car and drive around for an hour. Make sure they don't get too close. Meanwhile I'll get a taxi back to my place. I'll pack some fresh clothes into a few shopping bags and get a taxi back to your apartment building and I'll meet you just inside the carpark door, well away from the camera. We can put the bags in the boot and then park in your spot. When we get the bags out of the boot it will look exactly like we've had an expensive afternoon. I'll call you when I get to the apartment block. I should be there around 6:15. Now get going."

Chapter 8

"We have to tell the boss that the girl has got away before he finds out from someone else. He won't be happy and when it gets back to The Inspector there will be hell to pay. But it will be worse for us if we don't get in first."

****

"What made you put two trackers on Blackstock's car, Bill?" Jay asked while he drove the van following the girlfriend's car on a route that seemed to be following a sight-seeing route of all London's land marks.

"It wasn't really my idea. I copied the idea from one of those American cop shows. They put one somewhere where it would be difficult to find and a second somewhere where it would easily be seen so that if someone suspected they were being followed and looked for a tracker, they'd find it, get rid of it and think they were off the hook. I've put two on the girlfriend's car as well."

"Okay, they obviously found one and off-loaded it on another vehicle and assuming they didn't find the second one they are in one of two places, Skegness, or the backwaters of north Norfolk."

"My money is on Norfolk, Jay. The one in Skegness has been moving around all day today but the other one has not moved. To me that one is someone trying not to be noticed."

"The boss has lost interest in the boys but if they go to the cops they can identify us and pin us with doing Becky. If I go down for murder with my history I'll be in for life. So as soon as we get back to Blackstock's apartment we'll get Pete and Harry to take over the babysitting duty and we'll get off to Norfolk."

"Well that all appears to have gone well." Rob said to Sue as they travelled up in the lift.

"Certainly the trick with the tracker worked but I had hoped we would have made some progress towards getting your daughter back and we're actually no closer to that than we were this time yesterday."

"And we're no closer to getting that diamond back. So come 9:00 tomorrow morning Luci is going to be in even more danger."

"Try not to worry about it Rob. I know it will be difficult, but worrying won't help and you need to stay focussed. Right if we're going out to eat, I need a shower so if you'll excuse me, I'll only be a few minutes."

Phil and the boys had an evening out. They borrowed Phil's dad's ancient Range Rover and drove into Cromer. Just twelve miles but it took over forty minutes on the narrow Norfolk roads. After a burger at McDonalds they found the cinema for the 7:00 showing of the new 'Mission Impossible' movie. They didn't get back to the Range Rover until after 9:30 and with the combination of unfamiliar car, narrow roads and night time the journey back was even slower and they were in the middle of nowhere when the 10:00 news came on the radio.

"This is the news at exactly 10:02 on BBC radio 2. The Metropolitan police have released the name of the policeman found shot dead in his home earlier this evening as PC John Towner…"

"Christ dad, that's the copper who chased me and JB down the back streets on Saturday. One of the two coppers at that girls murder."

"We need to talk to Rob. We can't do it tonight it'll be too late when we get back, but we'll do it first thing tomorrow," Phil said, now finding it even harder to concentrate on driving.

As Sue emerged from the bathroom wrapped in a bath towel she called "Bathrooms free."

Rob appeared at his own bedroom door, "Well you look gorgeous. Is that what you're wearing to go out to dinner?"

Sue just smiled and walked into her bedroom.

"While you were in the shower I managed to get us a table at Petrus for 8:00, they'd had a late cancellation. So we've got about forty five minutes to get ready. I'm off to the shower."

"Petrus. Isn't that Gordon Ramsey's French Restaurant?"

"It is. Now I really am going for a shower."

Ten minutes later the bathroom door opened and Rob appeared out of the cloud of steam with a towel around his waist. He immediately spotted Sue in just her underwear sitting on the edge of the sofa with a foot up on the coffee table painting her toenails. It was the sort of thing that Jayne would be doing and for a moment he was lost in his thoughts.

"Well you brush up well. Is that what you're wearing to go out to dinner?"

"Ha bloody ha." Said Rob as he stood and stared at Sue. They both went into their bedrooms to dress.

Sue came out wearing a skin tight pale blue off the shoulder dress that showed off her very shapely long legs.

"This isn't my first choice, but my little black number has got what looks like baby dribble on the shoulder. Last time I wore it was to my nephew's christening. It's a good job I packed this one. At least my boobs don't sag. I didn't pack a strapless bra and I hate seeing straps showing."

"I think your boobs are lovely."

"You men, you're all the same. You only think of what's under the wrappers and not how good the wrapped package looks like."

The Squire Brothers were well onto the M11 heading North when Jay rang Jameson.

"Well, what news have you got for me? It had better be good."

"I'm afraid not boss. We've lost the girl. She got out and we haven't been able to find her."

"You pair are fucking useless. Can you do anything right?"

"We've found the boys and we're off to get them now Boss. One kid is as good as the other for what we want. Aye Boss."

"Just get on with it and let me know when you have him."

Rob and Sue were shown to a table in a quiet alcove. They browsed the menu and ordered a starter and main plus a wine recommended by the wine waiter to complement their meals.

While they were waiting Rob asked, "Can you ride a horse?"

"My dad was a council road worker. We lived in a high rise. What do you think?"

"I guess that's a no then. Well you'll have your first lesson tomorrow. I've got over fifty horses in Hyde Park this week. We're providing the horses for a new movie, a prequel to Dunkirk. The scene being filmed is showing the drills and parades of the cavalry units before they ship out as part of the Expeditionary Force. Crazy to think we sent horses to fight the might of the German tank units. I'm sure I can take a couple of horses out for an hour or so tomorrow afternoon."

"I'm not sure about that Rob. I'm a city girl; I've not had much to do with animals."

"You'll be fine. These horses are so well trained all you need to do is sit on its back. It will give us chance to relax."

As they ate their meal Rob continued to put Sue at ease about riding. As their plates were being cleared Sue's phone rang. She quickly checked the screen and immediately pressed the green button.

"What's up James?"

"John Towner has been found shot dead. Initial thinking is he was executed. He was shot in the head at short range. These people are serious about keeping their identity a secret. I thought you should be told as soon as I heard so you can be alert to all dangers."

"Thanks James, I'll keep in touch as we go on. Good night."

"Was that James Moore?"

"Yeh. John Towner has been murdered. Probably the gang trying to cover their tracks! They've raised the bar a bit so we'll have to respond to stay ahead of them. We need to let Phil know and tell him to be extra careful and I'll send two of my men up to your folks in Yorkshire. But that's for tomorrow morning. We can't do anything about it tonight, so let's relax."

"Easier said than done!"

Quite late in the evening The Inspector called Faye Mason. "Hi Faye I'm just doing a final check on everything for the flight tomorrow. We have to be at

Heathrow by 3:15. Correct?"

"That's right I've packaged up all the paperwork for the conference and that will go with your luggage. I take it there's still no word about the diamond."

"No and I really need it by 2:00 tomorrow at the very latest. Everything else is organised, we're just waiting for that bloody rock."

"What if I brought it with me on Thursday when I come to assist with the presentation? That will give the lads an extra twenty four hours to get it back."

"Are you willing to risk carrying it through customs? It might save the day if you did."

"A smart girl like me can find many ways for getting that sort of thing through customs. It will be no problem. It's what I'm getting the big bucks for." "Thanks Faye. I'll let Jameson know when I speak to him in the morning.

Thanks again and good night."

It was beginning to get dark when Jay and Bill arrived in North Norfolk. Once they had left the A11 at Thetford they were on single carriageway roads and their progress slowed. Jay used his iPhone to book a room at a travel lodge on the out-skirts of Kings Lynn. There was no way they were going to get to the boys' hideout before dark and as they didn't know the terrain it made sense to wait until morning before making their move. On the map it looked less than twenty miles they would have to go. Should only take half an hour from the hotel to the remote village where the tracker was and where they hoped they would find the boys.

Luci was becoming an emotional wreck. Why couldn't she remember who she was? She was regaining odd snippets but nothing she could piece together. She had remembered that she lived with her grandparents but couldn't remember where. She remembered something about some girls but couldn't remember anything about them. Were they her friends or even her sisters? Worse of all what was she doing in London on her own?

"You all right Emma love." Ana asked "You look a little pale. Eva's gone to put the kettle on. You really danced well for a beginner with no training. You must have studied those videos very closely. It won't take long to get you ready to go public."

"I'm still not sure I can take my clothes off in front of strangers."

"You'll be fine. We'll start you off with small groups, perhaps four or five mixed ladies and gents and build it up from that."

"Okay. If you're sure."

"What we need to do next is sort out what you can do once you've got your kit off. Any thoughts Eva?"

"Not at the moment. Why don't we leave it for now, get out a bottle of wine and have an evening in-front of the TV. Watch a DVD or two. Tomorrow we'll try a few make-up and hair styles and sort out some working clothes. You can borrow from us until you can afford your own. That way that might help the thinking about the act."

Luci nodded her acceptance of the idea. "I just need to go and clean up. I need to get rid of the odd bits of shaving foam that have dried."

"Fine love, we'll pour you a glass. Don't be long."

Rob and Sue got back to the apartment at around 10:30. As he opened the door Rob turned towards Sue and kissed her full on the lips. She responded eagerly. They broke and walked inside closing the door behind them.

Sue faced Rob, smiled and said. "That was for the benefit of our babysitters wasn't it? Just continuing the pretence that we're a couple."

"That's all it was, honestly Sue. Can I get you a night cap?"

"What I'd really like is a cup of cocoa. I need to stay alert tonight."

"Your right. Two cups of hot cocoa coming up. I've got a machine in the kitchen that is supposed to make anything."

Sue followed him into the kitchen. "I'll have to get the instruction booklet out. I've only ever made coffee."

"Typical man. Out of my way." Sue turned a couple of dials. Pressed a few buttons and liquid started to flow into the waiting mug.

The two of them moved back into the lounge and sat side by side on the sofa.

"I love all these pictures you have around the apartment. Is film memorabilia a hobby of yours?"

"Sort of! But they are actually all from films my company has worked on since my great grandfather started it a hundred years ago. We always get the star of the movie to sign it. I've got hundreds of them in storage." Sue stood and walked around the room.

"Stagecoach starring John Wayne. He looks very young in that?" she said and moved to the next. "Vikings with Tony Curtis, Errol Flynn as Robin Hood, Elizabeth Taylor in National Velvet and who's that Charlton Heston as Ben Hur. Christ Rob, these are all great movies. You must be a big name in the business. I see you also did Bonanza and The Lone Ranger for TV."

"We've done quite a few TV shows. They were big business in the fifties and sixties when westerns were so popular. Currently we are actually the biggest and trying to get bigger by opening another centre in India." He replied proudly. "Phil and I are down here to get bank finance for the Indian venture. We should have had a meeting with the bank today. You'll see some of what we do tomorrow in Hyde Park."

"Thanks for dinner Rob. I don't get much chance to get dressed up and have an evening out."

"It was my pleasure. I can't remember the last time I took a lady out and felt I didn't have to impress and flash money around. Such a pleasant change."

"I know you are rich Rob, but how rich?"

"That depends on the stock market. I can make or lose millions in a day. Let's just say it's a toss-up between me and those Russian jewels as to which is worth the most."

"Christ!" She said with a whistle.

"There's a lot, of money around in the movie world. For my team's role in the latest 'Mission Impossible' film out in cinemas at the moment I received just a little more than Tom Cruise. But I had thirty stuntmen working on that film for almost four months the stunt planning and coordination team is six people and over £750,000 of equipment and props were destroyed to create the effects needed for the film. Then there's five full time employees at the Stunt Training Academy. I provide food and accommodation for everyone and pay them big bucks for doing a dangerous job. Because it is so dangerous no insurance company will cover them against accidents that happen at work so I cover them for broken bones, loss of limb etcetera and should they be killed I will pay £1 million. Thankfully I've never had to do that. So you see I have a lot of overheads but I also admit I do quite nicely out of it."

"When you watch these movies and you take in all the action, you may wonder at the stunts and acknowledge that a stuntman has stepped in to do the dangerous bit, but you don't appreciate that there is a team behind the scenes making it all happen."

"You say you don't get chance to go out much. Does that mean you don't have friends or relatives?"

"I'm very much a loner. Especially since I lost Tony. I was seventeen or eighteen when I lost my parents. I have got a brother who I see at Christmas and christenings. As for friends I've got a couple of life long girl friends who I meet up with every three or four months but they're both married so that's difficult. Most of my friends are in the military. What about you?"

"It's amazing how many friends you have when you have money, but no real friends. I do have Luci and JB." He replied. "That's why this evening was so good for me. Thank you, Mrs Williams, for your company. Sleep well, good night."

"I won't be able to sleep. I'm dreading this horse riding you have planned," she laughed. "Good night, Rob."

Chapter 9

"She stayed the night again last night boss. The lucky bastard, she's drop dead gorgeous. They spent the evening in some foreign restaurant and came back at around 10:30 and were down one another's throats even before they got into the apartment. They haven't left since then. Jay and Bill told us when we took over from them that the two had spent the afternoon in a shopping mall and came back with several loaded shopping bags. They had no opportunity to get the diamond back."

****

"I've tried ringing Phil but there's no service so I can't get through. We'll have to hope he gets to a phone and rings us. There's coffee made. Help yourself," Rob said as Sue walked bare foot into the kitchen wearing tee-shirt and sleeping shorts.

"Sorry about this but I forgot to pack a dressing gown."

"Don't apologise. I quite like the look."

"Two of my most experienced officers left for Yorkshire ninety minutes ago with a small arms arsenal. Your grandparents will be well protected from around 10:30. I'll grab a shower now while my coffee cools. We need to leave in about forty five minutes in order to be on time at Speakers' Corner. We should be okay travelling together today. After last night's performance outside the apartment it won't look out of place."

"I've had a shave and a shower already. Just pull some clothes on and I'll be ready."

Phil had the boys up at 6:30. It was a mile to walk to the pub if they went through the woods. He knew the pub opened at 8:30 serving coffee and cake to catch the mums on the school run. Although the schools were on holiday they still had enough trade to make opening worthwhile. Phil wanted to be there when they opened so he could call Rob and update him with the news if he didn't already know. The pub was open when they got there and Phil was able to call Rob.

"Hi Rob have you heard about PC Towner."

"We got a call yesterday evening. The police are looking at it as a gang land killing and CS-10 are watching to see who is appointed to investigate the case and whether there will be an attempted cover up. CS-10 initially suspected Jay Squire as the executioner but Sue and I gave him an alibi, because at the time of the murder we saw him in a van following us. Another possibility is it was the Russians. If Towner was getting too close to them, they may well have taken him out."

"Bloody hell! You wouldn't dream anything like this could be happening in Britain. Is there anything we need to do up here?"

"No, just keep a low profile. Sue has sent two armed guards up to Yorkshire to protect mum and dad, but you should be safe."

"Will do. Is there any news of Luci?"

"No news at all."

"I'm sure she's okay. I'll try and ring again tomorrow morning."

The three of them stayed at the pub for a coffee before setting off for home. They went back through the wood even though it was slower going, it was about half a mile shorter, so the woodland route was actually quicker.

As they approached the house they first heard and then saw a car pull up in front of the house and one of the occupants got out and went to the door. Of course no one answered it because his parents were down on the south coast helping his sister who had just given birth. When he turned back towards the car he was instantly recognised.

"That's Jay Squire." JB said in a whisper.

"Keep out of sight boys. Hopefully, they won't hang around too long. How the hell did they find us?"

"Two trackers!" Jake said "They planted two trackers on the car. It's what they did in the film we saw the other night. We were so happy that we had dealt with the first one that we stopped looking."

"We must assume that the one in the car is the brother. With any luck they'll leave and come back later to see if we've returned. While they are away we'll load our things and get the hell out of here. Your dad said that armed guards were in place at the racing stables. We'll go there."

Jay walked over to Rob's Jag and rested his hand on the bonnet. There was no warmth there at all so it hadn't been used this morning and by the layer of dust he disturbed it hadn't been used since they had arrived. He went back to the house and peered in at the windows, then walked around to the back of the house to look in through the rear windows. When he re-appeared, he had his mobile phone in his hand and looking closely at the screen. He made his way back to his brother continually looking at his phone and pressing buttons. He leaned in at the open window of the car and Phil and the boys heard him complain "This really is a shit hole. There's no service on the phone. Get me back to the road and we'll try again."

Phil and the boys watched the Squire Brothers leave, then as the boys gathered their things Phil turned the car. It took Jake only a couple of minutes to locate the second tracker and he threw it as hard as he could into the woods. They were about to get into the car and make their escape when the Squire Brothers return. Coming down the long drive at speed, they raised a cloud of dust then braking hard when they saw the boys raised even more and for a moment obscured their view of the boys.

"Into the woods boys, split up. We'll all meet at the end of the drive. RUN." No one noticed Jake slide under the Jag.

As the dust settled Jay and Bill saw Phil and JB run into the woods. Jay quickly pulled out his gun and fired at the disappearing Phil with no real hope of hitting anyone.

"You go after the boy. I'll take care of the black bastard. Keep your eyes open for the coloured kid I haven't seen him."

Phil and JB were far fitter than their hunters and were soon a safe distance ahead of them. They had both been running along parallel paths leading to the village. The paths eventually merged, and Phil and JB ran on side by side.

"Where's Jake?" JB asked.

"I thought he was with you. Let's take the next intersection and make our way back to the house. If we keep low the undergrowth is thick enough to prevent them seeing us. I expect when they get to where the paths come together, they'll give up the chase and return to the house. So that should give us two minutes or so to get in the car and get away."

As they broke cover Jake was walking towards the car from the opposite side.

"Thank God son. In the car quick and we'll get out of here. What you smiling about?" Phil asked as they all climbed into the Jag and started off down the drive.

"While you two were off playing chase in the woods I was under their car cutting a hole in their radiator hose. They'll certainly be able to follow us but within minutes the coolant will start to heat up, pressure will increase, and fluid will leak out at a faster rate. I recon they'll get about ten miles at most before their engine overheats." "That's great Jake."

"I thought it better than tampering with brakes or steering. Less danger to other road users. This way they will just roll to a halt hopefully in the middle of nowhere."

"Right let's get up to Yorkshire without getting shot at again."

Keeping up the pretence of being his girlfriend, Sue held Rob's hand as they walked the short distance from Marble Arch tube station to Speakers' Corner. Travelling by tube had given Sue an opportunity to pick out anyone following them. She had spotted two likely candidates.

One she thought she recognised but just couldn't place, the other she did not know. To her experienced eye they stood out from the crowd. As did two members of her own team, who she had arranged to be present and armed. James Moore was also there mingling in the small but growing crowd, he would have at least one other member of AC-10 with him. No sign of Jay Squire yet even though it was coming up to 9:10. Then she spotted Paul Jameson making his way towards them.

"Blackstock you're late. Have you got the stone?"

"You must think I'm stupid. No, I haven't got it with me but I will tell you where it is as soon as I see my daughter and not before."

"That is not the deal we had."

"Maybe not but it's the only way it's going to be so you'd better get used to it."

"Alright it's a deal. We'll bring her to your apartment block at 11:00 this morning make sure you have the rock with you there and we'll do the exchange on the pavement outside your apartment building."

"That's more like it. I look forward to doing business with you at 11:00.

Come on Sue, my business here is done and I'm ready for a coffee." James Moore joined them in the coffee shop.

"Well that confirms Jameson is in this right up to his neck. You did recognise him both of you." They both nodded in response.

"Quite a complicated life our D.S. Jameson has had." James continued "He first came to our attention when crucial evidence went missing in an armed robbery case about seven years ago. As a result the case fell apart and the criminals got off. Their leader was Robin Gill."

"Would that be the same Robin Gill who is now running the River gang?" Sue enquired.

"Small world isn't it. Around the same time his wife walked out on him. He covered his tracks well and got promotion to D.S. Then five years ago he started visiting prostitutes and eventually met Rebecca

Stanslic. Over the last three years he's been seeing more and more of her and has been encouraging her to get out of the business. She was with him when he went to check the new security system at the jewellers where the armed robbery took place and that diamond that is causing you all these problems went missing."

Sue jumped in. "So you're assuming she carried the diamond out of the building and was supposed to get it back to Jameson."

"That's what we think happened, but the poor girl also had loyalties to the Russians. She went into hiding, literally underground. Yesterday evidence was found by us that she had spent several nights in the old Victorian tunnels. As Jameson is supposedly leading the investigation into her death, we don't expect any of this to be in his report."

"Do we know why she was also loyal to the Russians?"

"Rebecca Stanslic was born Olga Gorkov. She was Mikhail Gorkov's little sister!"

Sue went white "Shit... He'll be wanting revenge, this could be the start of gang warfare in central London."

"It's already started Sue. First of all Towner was found dead. Then about four hours ago Sergeant Ken Smith was found, shot dead, and executed in the same manner as Towner. We're certain that Towner was involved somehow in the Russian girls' murder and we assume Smith was as well because they have been patrolling together recently. I think we can assume either Smith or Towner was tortured to give the names of the others involved in the murder in which case the Squire Brothers will also be on the hit list."

"And we know the Russians were there because my boy and his mate almost knocked them over when escaping from the murder scene." Rob added.

"I think we're in for a messy few days, what with fighting over a valuable diamond and revenge killings between the same two gangs. You two take care.

When they come for that 11:00 exchange they may come mob handed, wanting to scare you off or even worse now with this recent development. How they react to that we can't possibly predict."

"I was thinking the same," Sue said. "We've also still got the problem that we don't have the diamond to make the exchange with."

"I'm sorry but you're going to have to play this by ear. Just let me know how it goes. I've got to go now and brief my boss about all this." With that he got up and left Rob and Sue looking blankly across the table at one another.

Mikhail Gorkov stood on the doorstep waiting for either Ana or Eva to answer the door. He went straight in as soon as the door was opened.

"What's up Mikhail? You never call this early. It's barely 10:00. We're only just up."

"I'm taking my son to Hyde Park this afternoon to watch them making a movie there. Something different for him to see. He's ten and likes movies. I have work for you tonight."

"So that's why you're here. We expected a couple of days off."

"It is a gentlemen's party. I have 6 other girls going and want you two to open the show and get the party moving. There's £500 in it for each of you if it goes well. Ivan will bring a taxi at 7:00. Now I must go."

"What about our new girl, Emma. We've already got her dancing and we're thinking of building an act similar to ours." Ava announced.

"That is no good for me. A single girl will need a minder and that costs me money. If you want her to dance then you add her to your act. Although I can't think how. Your act is very popular and I wouldn't like you to ruin it just to save one girl."

Jay and Bill didn't get as far as the ten miles Jake had predicted. Because they had driven from their hotel near Kings Lynn to the remote house their engine was already warm. They actually only made seven miles before being forced to stop in clouds of steam miles from anywhere. Just one farmhouse in view and that was at least a mile away across the fields.

"Bloody cars. Never work when you need them most. Thank god for mobile phones." Jay said pulling his out of his pocket. "Oh for Christ's sake, no bloody service again! How do the people in this wilderness survive? Let's head for that farm and see if we can find some wheels. There's no chance of finding those boys now because the tracker still says they're at the house. We'd best just head back to London."

Rob and Sue got back to the apartment at around 10:30. On entering the building Sue spoke with the security guard before joining Rob in the lift.

"I've got a funny feeling about this exchange Rob. Paul downstairs has agreed we can sit in his office until they bring Luci. So let's dump our stuff and get back down there."

"What about the camera outside the apartment. Won't they see us leave and then not leave the building?"

"We'll just have to take a chance that having seen us go in they won't be watching for us to come out again so quickly."

They had only just gone into Paul's small duty office when there was a commotion in the reception area, and they heard someone say. "If you don't want a beating mate stay there quite still. Don't call anyone especially the cops." Next, they heard the lift doors open and close then move off.

Sue risked a look out into reception.

Paul whispered, "three men with baseball bats. Get back, I'm OK."

Every minute they stayed hidden felt like an hour, until they heard the lift again and the same voice as before said. "Tell Blackstock and his girlfriend we called, and we'll be back for the stone later."

When they had gone Paul called Rob and Sue out.

Sue said, "I don't expect anyone to turn up at 11:00 but just in case we'll stay down here a bit longer."

At 11:15 they gave up waiting.

"As I thought Rob. The 11:00 meeting was just a means of getting you back to your apartment so that they could give you a good beating and get the diamond back at the same time."

"What about Luci? How are we going to get her back now?"

"Honestly Rob I don't think they've got her. Maybe never had her but certainly they don't have her now, which is why they resorted to rough tactics. Relax Rob, we'll find her."

When they returned to Rob's apartment they saw just how thorough the three goons had searched. Every draw had been pulled out and emptied onto the floor. Every cupboard opened and the contents pulled out. Vases had been smashed even the boys' box of cereal had been emptied onto the counter. In the lounge cushions had been ripped open and their stuffing pulled out. All the seats were turned over and the fabric ripped open, It was the same story in all of the bedrooms with pillows, duvet turned inside out and mattresses cut open.

"Sue we can't stay here. It's just not safe we need to find somewhere to hide."

"We'll go to my place. There is absolutely no way they know about that. But we must be certain they don't follow us."

"We can use my bike, the Ducati down in the garage. My wife Jayne and I used to use it to get away quickly into the country from our home in Birmingham when we could get a baby sitter. For some unknown reason I kept her leathers, they were hanging next to mine in the wardrobe so should be somewhere in the mess that was once my bedroom. You are about the same build as Jayne so they should fit. You should look good in leather."

"Down boy. I'm surprised that when trashing this place they didn't smash the security system."

"It's a very cleaver box of tricks. If the door is forced it goes into silent running, still recording everything but not giving itself away. We should be able to see the images it recorded. The black box is in a floor panel in the entry hall."

As Rob had said the system had recorded images of all three goons and Sue was able to name them as PC John Lowe, Ryan Hope & Bill Montgomery both known to be members of the River Gang and wanted for extortion and GBH.

"I'll ring James Moore later and update him. Now let's find those leathers. Before we go to my place I must speak with Rebecca's flat mates. We'll call in on our way."

Eva and Ana had been talking over what Mikhail had said. Could they, should they incorporate Emma into their act. They had already done a lot for her. Was it right to carry on this way?

"She can't be more than sixteen. Maybe not even that old, and has no memory of who she is or where she's come from. We've shown her what we do and taught her a few moves but where we go from here has to come from her. Do you agree Ana?"

"Sure, but would you be happy with her joining us."

"Well we have been talking recently about the need to update the act. This might be a good time. Whatever we do, it won't change my feelings towards you."

Luci finally made an appearance in the living room just before lunch. The two girls talked her though what Mikhail had said and their own discussion that followed. "Have you got anything to say Emma."

"I really do appreciate what you two are doing for me and what you are now offering me. But I'm feeling that things are moving too fast and I feel out of control. I think I should be trying harder to find out about myself before I decide anything."

"We're happy to slow down and give you all the time you need, aren't we Ana? We have to work tonight, and we have to agree and work out one or two small changes, so you'll be on your own most of the day. Will you be alright?"

"Don't worry about me. I'll be fine. I'll go for a walk and see if anything can trigger my memory recall. I won't be out too long. I just need to do something. See you both later."

There was no one at home when Jay and Bill reached the farm house and stealing a car was child's play. The Range Rover was unlocked and the keys were in the ignition. The owner presumably thinking that the remoteness of the farm meant it was safe to leave it like that. They drove it away unchallenged and headed south. They left the Range Rover in a railway carpark on the outskirts of London and took the underground back into town.

"Boss, we're back in town," Jay said into his phone.

"With the boys?" Jameson asked.

"Afraid not. We had 'em in our hands until the bloody car broke down on us."

"Never mind your excuses, Blackstock has the diamond and has gone missing. He's got some of his workers in Hyde Park this week filming for some movie. I want you to get over there and see if he's hiding amongst them. If he is, deal with him and bring me the stone."

Jameson ended the call and immediately it rang again. He checked the screen and pressed the green button.

The voice at the other end said. "I assume as I've heard nothing we don't have the diamond."

"Not yet Inspector but we are very close now."

"Too late for me to take it. I'm off in a few minutes. But there is now an alternative. Faye is flying out on Thursday with material for the final day of the conference. Get the diamond to her for her to bring out to me. You have twenty four hours. Get me that stone!" The call ended.

Sue and Rob were spotted as they left the building. Not as the couple to be followed but as a lucky bastard in black leather sitting astride a shiny silver Ducati Diavel 1260 and a tasty looking long legged bird with her arms around his waist.

Having got away undetected they secured the bike outside Ana and Eva's flat and removed their helmets as they waited at the door for a response to them pressing the doorbell. Eventually Eva opened the door and Sue flashed a fake warrant card in front of her.

"I'm D.C. Lucas and this is D.C. Crane. D.S. Jameson came to see you yesterday. He's sent us with a few follow-up questions if you don't mind. Can we come in?"

"Yes, Yes, certainly" Eva opened the door for them and pointed them towards the living room.

"Ana, these are two police officers with a few more questions about Becky."

"Firstly can I have your names please?"

"I'm Eva Andelova."

"and I am Oxsana Kolanski."

Rob had his phone out and was recording the conversation.

"Are you the only ones living here now?"

"Emma Sunday is staying with us for a few days but she's not here at the moment. She's only been here a couple of days and never met Becky."

"Could we possibly have a look in Miss Stansic's= room?"

"Of course. This way." Eva led them to the room and left them to look around.

"Doesn't appear to be anything out of the ordinary in here. Clothes, shoes, bags, a TV, bed and a chair. All the things you'd expect in a young lady's room," said Sue summing up the rooms content.

"No jewellery?" Rob queried.

"That's not really unusual. I only have a few pieces myself." They returned to the girls in the lounge.

"Do you know who Miss Stanslic was seeing? Did she have regular clients? Anyone in particular we should question?"

"We didn't really discuss that sort of thing." Ana replied. Eva quickly added, "But for some time we know she has been spending more and more time with one person. She called him Paul. I think he was asking her to get away from here. She never brought him home."

"When did you last see her?"

"About 2 weeks ago," Ana replied and Eva nodded in agreement. "But that's nothing new. She would quite often disappear for a week or so. We think she was staying with her man."

"Well, thank you ladies you've been most helpful. Please call the station if you remember anything that you think may be of use."

They left the flat, put on their helmets and climbed back on the bike. As they moved off Luci rounded the corner. Seeing them ride off down the street triggered a memory.

"Dad, mum," she shouted recognising the image moving away from her.

"Who was that that just left?" She asked as she entered the lounge.

"Two cops asking about Becky. No one wanting you," came the response.

"Only I thought it was my parents."

"But you said, your mum was dead."

"I did didn't I? Oh I'm so confused. The bits I remember just don't join up to make any sense."

"They will do, you poor little thing. It's only been a couple of days, give yourself some time and everything will come back to you."

Rob and Sue went straight to Sue's home, a small detached house near the rugby stadium at Twickenham with a garage to one side where Rob left the bike. Inside they put their helmets down on the table in the hallway and Rob threw his rucksack stuffed full of his clothes on the floor under the table.

"Nice place you have. Is it yours or do you rent?"

"All mine. I bought it after Tony was killed. Using money he had left me and his insurance pay-out. Gives me a place to hide away from the world when I need to."

"You mean for us to hide." He laughed. "I've been thinking about Hyde Park this afternoon. We've done well to get away from our minders and I don't want them to get attached to us again. So I thought we'd put a change of clothes in the rucksack, take the bike out to the suburbs, change our clothes, leave the leathers in left luggage and take the subway to Marble Arch. If we get spotted and followed when we're in the park there's a chance of losing them on the return tube journey, or when we're back in leathers. If none of that works we'll lose them on the bike. Shouldn't think they'll have a bike around that can tail us back to your place here."

"You've given this a lot of thought, I can see," she replied "All so you can laugh at me on a horse."

"You know you'll enjoy it. You're looking forward to it really. Last time I was at Twickenham we had some marvellous fish and chips on Twickenham
Road."

"You mean Mario's. It's still there! Are you going to treat me to lunch then?" "Well I thought I might."

"I've just got to give James a ring and update him with what happened this morning."

After speaking to James, Sue told Rob what James had told her.

"Faye Mason and Mikhail Gorkov are both on the Moscow flight Thursday afternoon. James wants us both on that same flight."

"I can understand why you should go, but why me?"

"He must think you'll be of use, or he wouldn't ask. Now I'm hungry."

The Inspector called Jameson from the airport for a final update before the plane left.

"You haven't got it yet then?"

"Not yet Boss. But I'm sure we will have it soon and I'll get it to Faye as quickly as I can. Don't worry boss we'll get it." "But I do worry." The line went dead.

Sue and Rob followed the plan and arrived at Hyde Park in time to see a rehearsal for one of the cavalry parades to be included in the movie. The horses, about fifty of them in all were smartly turned out; the riders were all dressed in replica uniforms. There were also around two hundred extras standing around in period costume waiting for direction. The production team were huddled together discussing the scene to be shot next.

Suddenly there was activity everywhere. Shouts of "Ready!" came from every corner. The movie making process was underway. There was a large crowd gathered to watch. For the moment Rob and Sue were lost in the crowd.

The parade marched by three times before the director was happy that he had all the shots he wanted.

"Would you like to go behind the scenes and watch how things work to produce what the audience sees in the final product?" Rob asked.

"Are you kidding me? Course I would, I may never get another chance."

For a time they stood and watched make-up artists change a young actor into someone at least ten years older. Several actors were practicing their lines in different tones trying to make an impression with the few words they had to say. Rob spoke to several people as they walked through. Obviously he was familiar with the environment and the people. Eventually they entered the 'Tape Room'. The place where all the film was brought to and secured ready for the editors to start their work.

"In this digital era tape and film are no longer used and this area is fed by every camera on the site, even the ones not used for this or that scene," Rob explained.

Sue stood and stared at a wall of TV monitors displaying what was being recorded by each camera, more than a dozen monitors in all. Seven or eight were showing the movie action from different angles. One of the cameras had obviously been left pointing skyward, another pointing at the ground. Three others were pointing into the large crowd. As Sue moved her focus from one monitor to the next Rob heard her take a sharp intake of breath.

"Oh my God! Mikhail Gorkov is here in the crowd watching this. Look Rob."

"It certainly looks like him, but to be honest the only time I've seen him he had a gun pointed at me. So I didn't take a lot of notice of his face."

"Well I'm certain it's him. He's got a boy of ten or eleven with him and a woman, could be his wife and son. I'll phone it in. With luck we can pick him up and with all our new evidence we should be able to hold him."

In an instant she had reported in and told Rob the back-up was on its way. "They are sending an armed response team. Now I must also call James Moore. He tried to ring me earlier, possibly when we were on the tube which is a good reason he couldn't get through."

"Okay but don't take too long. I still want to get you on a horse."

Despite Rob's comments about being quick Sue was talking to Moore for several minutes and from the changes in her facial expressions something was seriously wrong. She showed horror, concern and aggression. As the call went on Rob could see she was getting worried about something and as soon as it ended he jumped in.

"What's happened? Is it news about Luci? Sue speak to me."

"This is not being released to the public yet, so don't say a word to anyone. Four more police officers have been killed. They were found in a burnt out car in a scrap yard in Islington. The bodies were burnt beyond recognition. A provisional identification has been made from the metal officer numbers on the uniforms. They are PC Janet Downes, PC John Lowe, Sergeant Adam Blunt and PC Bob Penning. Downes and Lowe were on AC-10's list of members of the Inspector's corrupt group. We suspect the other two were members too."

"That's horrific. Not the deaths but the fact that it should happen here in

London. New York, yes, but not here."

"What makes it worse Rob is that at least two of them were shot in the head before being torched."

"Is this some sort of gang war or is the Inspector getting rid of loose ends?"

"Most likely the latter. Whoever this Inspector is, they certainly run a mean outfit."

"Now you've done your duty, we're here to relax. Come, I'll introduce you to some of my team." Rob took her hand and turned her away from the monitors.

Phil and the boys arrived at the Yorkshire stables mid-afternoon. They were stopped on the driveway by a guard in a black uniform. A hand gun was holstered at his waist and he carried an automatic short barrelled rifle. They had to be identified by Eric or Rose before being allowed to drive on to the main house.

Eric's first question was, "Any news of Luci? It's been more than twenty four hours since we last heard from Rob."

"Sorry Eric. There was no news when I spoke with Rob at 8:30."

"Sorry Phil I should have welcomed you before launching into you like that. What brings you back here and not with Rob."

They all went indoors and Phil talked them through the full sequence of events.

"Well we're totally secure here now so you can stay here. It should only be for a couple of days. Make yourself at home in the spare room Phil. We'll put a camp bed in there for Jake."

Rob walked Sue further through the maze of vehicles and caravans until they came to a row of identical articulated trailers.

"Welcome to my world," he said. "Each one of these six trailers is a mobile stable for four horses. They will stay here for the duration of the filming. Other horses are brought in by traditional horse transport as and when required."

Sue looked around and all the vehicles were marked with the same logo, the black silhouette of a prancing horse over the single word BLACKSTOCK.

"Am I supposed to be impressed, because I am," she laughed.

"Come and meet Pete Doyle. He's managing this job for me. We call it Gang Master. He works with the production team for the whole duration of the film from casting right through to premiere, advising on all stunt work and supplying all the horses as and when needed."

"Sound a big important man."

"Well I don't know about important, but he is big and he's right behind you." Sue turned and her eyes came level with a man's chest.

"Jesus Christ!" she said as she took a giant stride backwards.

All three of them laughed.

"Sue Williams meet Pete Doyle." Pete held out his hand for her to shake.

"How tall are you?"

"Seven One."

"I discovered Pete when he was playing basketball for the Sheffield Sharks and doing three part time jobs to make ends meet. He started as a stuntman and has risen through the ranks so to speak. Pete, are my horses ready for me yet?"

"Good afternoon, Mrs Williams. Yes boss, two horses ready as requested. They are tethered to trailer six."

"Nice to meet you Pete. Call me Sue, please. I do hope you've chosen a nice quiet horse for me."

"Honestly Sue, all our horses are so well trained all you need to do is sit on its back. Have fun you two."

They walked to the front of the trailers and found the horses and next to them a mounting step. Rob helped Sue up the step and onto a horse then with ease, climbed onto the other horse.

"Don't we need helmets or something?" Sue asked.

"Not with these horses. They know better than to throw their riders unless told to."

Sue turned her horse, kicked the horse's flanks and rode of at speed. Rob, taken by surprise rode hard to catch her. They both then slowed as they were reaching the far end of the park.

"You lied. You've ridden before."

"Sorry. Between finishing Uni and joining the army I had a year out working at a small stable in Herefordshire and rode in a few Point-to-point races."

"Were you any good? Did you win any races and earn any money? I hear it can be good money."

"I actually won two races. But there's no real money in it except for a very few riders who are racing at three or four meetings a week, getting fifteen or so rides and are winning maybe four races a week. Racing costs a lot of money. Well, you know how much it costs to keep a horse and transport them around the country."

"Add in the vet's bills and I agree it is very expensive. But it looks like it made you a very good rider. When all this business is over you'll have to come up to Yorkshire and I'll take you out onto the moors for some real riding."

"It's a date. Now shall we go back the other way at a slower pace?"

"Ladies first," Rob said with a wave of an arm and they began to walk their horses back, passing the horse trailer and towards the crowds watching the movie makers.

"Your police friends are taking a long time to get here. I had expected them to be keen to get Gorkov into custody."

"Oh don't worry, they have been here for some time assessing the situation, locating their target, minimising the risk to the public and deciding how to take him down. There will be six of them in plain clothes armed with hand guns. Then a further two in uniform with automatic weapons stationed at each of the park exits. Gorkov is not going anywhere. We just need to be patient and strike when the opportunity presents itself."

As they rode slowly behind the crowd Sue pointed out Derik Drayton. "Can you see him? He's the one between the teenagers in Star Wars tee shirts."

"Drayton?" Rob queried "Isn't he in with the Inspector's gang?"

"He is but he works with James Moore and has gone undercover as an ARU officer. Obviously his team were given this assignment. He's a good officer. He'll see this through alright."

Rob caught sight of Gorkov who had also just seen Drayton moving through the crowd. He turned to his wife, said something to her and kissed her. He then put a hand on the child's head said something then bent down and kissed his forehead. After a quick look again towards Drayton he began to slide towards the back of the crowd.

Sue and Rob halted their horses and were actually blocking Gorkov's chosen escape route. Seeing this he pulled out a gun and grabbed the nearest person to him as a shield and started pointing the gun all around. Several people in the crowd who were aware of what was unfolding started screaming and running leaving Gorkov and his hostage out in the open. Nothing was said and the crowd went silent as the six members of the ARU emerged from their midst and converged on their prey from three sides, Rob and Sue still blocked the fourth side.

Gorkov held his prisoner close to him. He had his back to Rob and with the young female hostage held tight into his chest, the armed offices did not have a clear, risk free shot at him. D.S. Jameson and two uniformed officers came from the crowd to join the pursuit. As senior officer present, he would normally take charge of the operation, but the ARU were already engaged so Sergeant Drayton was in charge.

"Gorkov, let that girl go and give yourself up. There are six men here with guns pointing at you. You're not going anywhere," Drayton called.

Gorkov responded by pointing his gun at Drayton and then held it at the girl's head while trying to formulate an escape route. The two on the horses didn't have guns and if he got passed them it was only a short distance to the park exit and then a quick sprint down to Marble Arch tube station where he could lose his pursuers in the migrating crowds. He had to create a distraction to gain vital seconds. There were too many people around for the six guns to fire at him. He turned and fired his gun towards the two horses some thirty five—forty metres away and instantly turned back so that the girl was again his shield.

Rob reacted instantly. He kicked his heels into his horse's flanks, crouched low across the horse's neck and raced on. After three or four strides the horse was travelling at speed towards Gorkov who was facing the opposite direction but edging backwards towards the horses. Rob took one foot out of its stirrup and brought his leg over the horse's rear so that he was hanging on to the saddle with his whole body on the horses flank with the horse between him and Gorkov. The gap closed rapidly and with just a few yards left, Rob straightened his body so that his feet hit the floor. Using the forward momentum, he bounced from the ground swinging his whole torso over the saddle to the other side of his horse with his feet out in front of him. At the very same moment, Gorkov became aware of something coming up rapidly behind him and turned to face whatever it was. With no time to avoid it, both of Rob's feet struck Gorkov squarely on the chest sending him flying to the ground and ripping the hostage from his arms. His impact with the ground was hard enough to send his gun flying and knock Gorkov unconscious.

D.S. Jameson ran to the fallen Russian and secured him with his hands behind him held by zip ties. One of the uniformed officers picked up the young hostage and checked her over. She was clearly unhurt but shaking from her ordeal. At the speed he had been travelling it took Rob time to bring his horse to a stop and he pulled up next to Derik Drayton.

"Well done mate. I'm not sure whether that was brave or fool hardy but it was certainly spectacular. Are you with the movie people?"

"I own the company that supplies the stunt men and the horse. I was actually here with a friend giving her a ride out on one of my horses. She's over there," Rob said pointing and looking back to where he'd left Sue. To his horror she was slumped forward in the saddle and a large red patch was spreading across her shirt. Rob spurred his horse forward and rushed back to her side. As he reached her she was lifting her head and pushing one handed to get her-self upright again. "Are you shot? Where are you hit?"

"I hope someone got that bastard he's ruined this shirt." She joked. "Yes I was hit when he fired at us but it almost missed me. Just nicked my upper arm as it passed by. Probably looks worse than it is."

"We'll get you checked by the medical team here then quickly off to the hospital."

"Don't be so dramatic. Honestly it's only a scratch. Just needs cleaning and a Band-Aid. We can get the horses back first."

Whilst everyone was distracted checking that all those around were OK. Jameson located Gorkov's body pouch and to his relief the diamond was inside. He quickly transferred it to his own jacket pocket.

It was twenty minutes before Gorkov came to, by which time a police Range Rover had pulled into the park and he was bundled into the back and driven away. The movie makers had hardly stopped working and the park was soon as if nothing at all had occurred.

Rob walked In front of the two horses, the reins of both in his hand, until they were back at the trailers and he handed them on to one of the stable girls then helped Sue down. She was insistent that a hospital was not necessary but agreed it would need a medic to clean the wound and dress it. When the medic cut away the shirt they could see just how lucky she had been. The bullet had only scored a furrow across her arm and hadn't passed through and the blood loss wasn't very much at all it just looked a lot because of the way the shirt had soaked it up.

"OK I agree, no hospital. Just as soon as you're fixed up I'm taking you home though."

"You're just an old mother hen Rob Blackstock," she said and leant forward and kissed his cheek.

They left the park and walked back towards Marble Arch tube station.

"Are you going to be alright on the bike with that arm?"

"How many more times do you need telling, I'm fine it's just a scratch."

Luci had a quiet afternoon. She spent a long time thinking about the two people riding away on the bike. Why did she think they were her parents if her mother was dead. Something must have triggered it, but what. The more she dwelled on it the more depressed she got so she picked up a magazine to take her mind of it.

Eva came back mid-afternoon. She'd been clothes shopping and held up a carrier in each hand.

"New clothes for the act. You'll see them later when we get ready to go to work."

Ana burst in less than five minutes later. She was very excited about something and was almost hoping from one foot to the other.

"Good news Emma I've been out calling in a few favours. Firstly Jason at the print shop. He turned that photo of you I took on my phone when you first arrived and made up a simple poster from it. It just says. 'If you know this girl ring' and then my mobile number and the picture of you. He printed two hundred for me. Then I went to see Larry Butterworth, he works for that food processing company in Watford. He delivers peeled and chipped potatoes to dozens of places all over north London every day and has promised to ask everyone on his round to put up a poster. By this time tomorrow your face will be on fifty chip shop notice boards in the area."

"Well done Ana," said Eva.

"That's not all," Ana continued. "I called in at the news agent down the road and left him about a hundred. He's going to put them in copies of today's evening news. That left thirty or so, so I've just spent the last half hour in the Tesco's car park putting them under car wipers. Now we just sit and wait."

"Thank you so much Ana," Luci said. "You both so very kind but the longer

I'm here the less I think I belong here. I pray your posters help."

Chapter 10

"So, you've finally got the diamond. Too late for the Inspector to take but I'm flying out in forty-eight hours, so you had better get it to me as soon as possible. I'll send you a text later with a time and a place for us to meet up."

****

Ana and Eva dressed as St Trinian style school girls were ready and waiting at seven o'clock but Ivan didn't arrive until a quarter past seven. He'd never been late before.

"What's wrong?" Ana asked.

"Mikhail has been taken by the police, He's going to be sent back to Russia at best he's facing murder charges here in Britain."

"That's awful. Who will run things now? Who will get us work?" asked a shocked Eva.

"Me for the next week or two, but the Wolf Pack will send someone to replace him soon." Ivan replied. "It is for certain that Mikhail will not be coming back to his wife and child."

"And he was here this morning so looking forward to a family day out taking his son to watch a movie being made. But that's how things happen sometimes. So why do you still look so worried? What are you not telling us."

"Mikhail wants revenge for the murder of his sister. He was my boss yes, but also my friend too. He has told me who he suspects. I must confirm and settle the matter for him."

"Sister, what sister? We didn't know he had a sister. And what do you mean settle the matter? Another murder?"

"I will kill for my friend. You knew his sister as well as anyone else. To you she was Rebecca Stanslic."

Both girls gasped at the news.

"Of course we knew Becky had been murdered, the police have been around here twice asking if we knew if she had enemies, anyone who may want to harm her, but we had no idea that she was Mikhail's sister."

"Come now we must go. We are already late, the taxi meter is ticking."

"Bye Emma. See you in the morning."

Luci lay back in the armchair resting her heels on the coffee table summing up all that had happened, what she had remembered of her former life and what her options were moving forward. Reality hit her hard. If her memories didn't return then this life here was possibly her only choice so she had better face the facts and put all her efforts into making it a success. After all her body in quite good shape and if people wanted to pay to look at it then why not give it a try.

"I wonder what a 3 way exotic act would be like." She said to herself.

Rob and Sue were back at Sue's house. Rob had pushed the bike up to the empty garage and Sue went inside and put the kettle on. By the time Rob came in she was out of her leathers and wrapped up in a short housecoat.

"Can I get our trick riding hero a drink? Coffee, tea or perhaps something stronger."

"I could murder a beer if you've got one. But I must ring Dad, he'll be wondering what's been happening."

"And I must contact James Moore. I expect Sergeant Drayton has told him about Gorkov already but even so I need to check in. He might have news of the Inspector." Sue levered the top off a bottle of beer and handed it to him. Rob took it and sat down on the sofa to ring his father.

"Hi dad, how are things in Yorkshire?"

"We're doing fine. The two guards you sent up are nice people and very thorough. We're feeling like royalty with our own body guards.

Phil and the boys arrived mid-day. Phil was going to ring you in an hour or so but he's here now if you want to speak to him."

"Yes please."

"Well, I'll say goodbye then and hand you over. Phil can pass on any news you have when you've finished."

"Hello Rob."

"Phil. What are you doing in Yorkshire? Why did you leave the safety of the Norfolk back waters?"

"They found us Rob. They had two trackers on the car so they had no trouble tracking us down. But we got away and lost them good and proper this time. As you said you were sending armed men here I thought it the best option. When we saw the Squire Brothers at the house I got the impression they were there to kill us."

"You're probably right Phil. They'll see the boys as a threat, witnesses to the murder of the Russian girl who incidentally was the brother of one of those big Russians that took the diamond. If the boys give evidence the brothers are certain to go down for a long stretch. You did well to get out and a wise move to go to the stables. We still don't have any more news of Luci. That's my biggest worry. Oh, I'm off to Russia to help AC-10 catch the inspector. I'm flying out Thursday afternoon."

"Bring me back a bottle of vodka. Seriously don't try being a hero, keep your head down and come home in one piece. If you need anything you can call me on my mobile again now, there's a good mobile service here. Take care. See you soon. Bye."

Sue ended her call at pretty much the same time. "James said that they have been looking through the evidence again searching for clues to the identity of the inspector. They didn't discover anything concrete but the circumstantial evidence is stacking up against Peter Logan."

"He must have changed an awful lot since our college days. I was thinking about what we're going to eat this evening."

"Ha, you won't be able to wine and dine me this evening, you can't turn up in jeans and tee-shirt or motorbike leathers to a posh restaurant and you've got nothing else here."

"I've thought about that problem too. I'm taking the bike back to the apartment."

"But they'll see you enter your apartment, or had you forgotten about the camera watching your front door."

"But I'm not going to go to my apartment. I'm going to ask Mrs Parfitt, my cleaning lady to go in and put some clothes into a bin bag and bring them down to me in the garage. I'll also ask her to make a start getting the place put back together. I know I'll need new furniture but firstly the place needs to be cleaned and tidied."

"OK, so where is my rich housemate taking me tonight?"

"All depends on who's got a free table. I'll make some call while I wait for

Mrs Parfitt to get some clothes. If I go now I should be back here by six."

It was actually ten past six when he got back. Sue was still in her short housecoat but had obviously showered and washed her hair. She was sitting in a chair with her one heel up on the edge of the seat pad painting her toe nails. As she leaned forward with the brush to apply a coat of ruby red to the waiting toe Rob was treated to a birds eye view down the front of her robe and could clearly see that the robe was the only thing she had on.

"That went well. Mrs Parfitt is a real treasure she's got her husband to help put the apartment back together and also sort out getting the furniture repaired or replaced. She says it will be back as if nothing had ever happened in two weeks."

"Well that's good news for you. Were you able to get us a table somewhere." "Yes. We have a table for two at Goodman's in Mayfair. Hope you like steak. The table is booked for 8:00 so you've got about an hour to change your knickers and make yourself decent."

"It won't take me more than ten minutes to be ready. But you need to get out of those leathers and get into the shower. I'll get on to Goodman's website and check out what the ladies wear there. I don't want to stand out. If you need a towel there are plenty on the top shelf in the cupboard next to the bathroom."

He quickly showered then went to his bedroom to sort out his clothes. Mrs Parfitt had been good enough to pack a variety of trousers, shirts, shoes, underwear and even two ties. She had carefully placed all these In a hold-all to make it easy for Rob to carry on the bike. For the benefit of anyone watching she had put the hold-all inside a black bin bag and carried it out as if it were a sack of rubbish. Rob emptied the hold-all onto the bed and selected his clothes for the evening and went into the lounge.

It was another twenty minutes until Sue's bedroom door opened and she walked into the lounge. Rob looked her up and down and she turned herself round to give him the full effect. Her makeup was perfect and made her hazel eyes shine. She had fixed her hair so that it was high on one side and hung down to her shoulder on the other. Her dress was bronze in colour and of a material that moved like silk but with a metallic look to it. There was no back to it at all from the neck right down as low as it could possibly go and remain decent. There was slightly more material at the front but not a lot. The neckline plunged to below her navel where there was diamond stud that matched her earrings and the pendant around her slender neck. Two narrow straps above and below the bust line held the dress together. The dress ended quite high on the thigh showing her shapely legs to their best. She carried a small clutch bag and wore a matching pair of sandals with 4 inch heels. She had removed the bandage from her arm and left the wound uncovered and it wasn't really noticeable. For a woman in her late thirties she was in amazing shape and the dress showed every inch.

All Rob could do was stare and say "WOW."

"I'm glad I checked the website otherwise I would have gone over dressed. Will this do. Tony used to call this my catwalk dress, because I have to walk with my shoulders back like a catwalk model to stop the dress falling off."

"You look absolutely stunning. But you'd look good in anything."

Assistant Commissioner Peter Logan and his wife Pauline landed on schedule in Moscow. They had to wait almost twenty minutes for the baggage carousel to start moving and they could collect their luggage, a suitcase of clothes each, another containing formal clothes for the conference, not just for the daily meeting but this evening there was a formal reception and then a ball on the final evening. The forth piece was a large document case carrying everything he needed for the first two days of the conference. Faye was bringing a similar case with her on Thursday with notes and handouts to support a lecture he was giving on Friday.

They were fast tracked though customs and were met at the gate by a driver arranged by the conference organisers. He took them directly to their hotel and called a porter for their luggage. Peter signed the register and they were taken to their two bedroom suit. The second bedroom was for Faye when she arrived. Peter said he needed her close so they could go through his lecture material. It was Pauline's idea to book a suite and for Faye to have the second bedroom. Peter was happy because Pauline would have someone she knew around to talk to. He was aware they were good friends because he'd seen Faye's name at the top of Pauline's list of friends to invite to her girls' night earlier in the week. A party that had cost him over £1,000 a donation to children's charity Pauline had assured him.

"We've got ninety minutes before we need to go down for the reception party so plenty of time for a bath and getting dressed up. I have to check in with Faye to make sure all the papers are finished and ready for her to bring out, so you go and have the first bath, dear."

"I've got to ring the travel company for final arrangements and vehicle details for our break after the conference but I can do that later."

Pauline had her bath and while Peter was in the bath she called about the vehicle she had ordered.

"Hello, do you speak English?"

"Yes madam. How may I help?"

"I'm Mrs Logan I have ordered a vehicle via your internet site and would like to confirm details."

"Certainly, madam. I'm just bringing your records up on my computer, it will just take a moment. This says that a vehicle has been prepared as you requested, but there is a note saying no driver has been specified."

"The driver will be Miss Mary Lancaster." Said Pauline using the name on Faye's false papers. "She will be with you to collect the vehicle on Saturday morning. She will have all the paperwork you require with her."

"That was my only query madam. Can I help you with anything else?"

"No thank you."

As Rob and Sue walked through the restaurant to their table Rob felt every male eye was watching them or rather watching Sue and she was soaking it up. When they got to their table she leaned towards him and in a low tone said "Do I look like your security guard would anyone guess I've got a loaded gun in my bag?"

Sue sat back and Rob looked hard at her and said. "Certainly no man in here is thinking that. I'll tell you what they're thinking and any one of them would swap places with me right now."

"And I know by the look on your face what you're thinking." She said smiling.

A waitress came and left them two menus. Rod asked to speak to the wine waiter who appeared within minutes.

"Mr Blackstock, it's been a long time."

"Good evening, Charles. Yes it's been a couple of months. Charles, do you still do your special bourbon soaked steaks?"

"For our special guests only, sir. Would the beautiful lady like one too?"

"The beautiful lady would like one too, both medium rare and with your special salad. A dish of oysters to start and a bottle of whatever you recommend." Thank you Charles. Good to be back.

"Thank you, sir. Leave it all to me. I'll tell chef you are here and for him to make special effort."

"What was all that about?" Sue asked.

"I've known Charles for many years. He practically runs this place. They do a few specials that are not on the menu. A particular favourite of mine are steaks cut from a large hunk of beef that has been soaking in bourbon for four weeks at least. I've ordered one for each of us. Hope that's OK."

"On this occasion. But don't make a habit of making my decisions for me. I may dress like a lady but I'm ex-army and trained to kill."

"Point taken. What have we got lined up for tomorrow?"

"I was hoping you'd take me down to the embankment and walk me through to the murder site. It will help me picture the incident and you need to get your passport from your apartment. Plus we must meet with James Moore to understand what he expects from us in Russia."

"Don't forget Luci. She's my top priority. Surly the kidnappers will be in touch again soon."

"Of course she is Rob. My team have searched all known Squire hangouts. Without finding a trace. They don't have any leads at the moment but are questioning hundreds of people in the likely spots."

"I know you are doing everything you can, but you don't have children. You can't know how I feel."

"I know exactly what you are going through. I had a child. A girl, she would have been similar age to Luci. I left her with an aunt and uncle I was very close to and went off to play at soldiers. When she was just five she was snatched by a paedophile. She was traced to a point where she had been sold by him into Eastern Europe but not until after some very nasty pictures had been published. She was eventually found in a shallow grave in Croatia three years later. She had been repeatedly raped and sodomised. She was only eight years old when she died. So I think I do know exactly what you are going through."

"Sorry, I didn't know, forgive me."

"It's all right. But I do understand."

"When we first met I thought you reminded me of Jayne but I was wrong, you actually remind me of the feelings I had for Jayne." At that moment their wine arrived.

The Squire Brothers had been in Hyde Park and seen Gorkov taken by the police. They had seen Rob Blackstock ride in on horseback and knock the Russian down then Jameson secured the felled man while he was unconscious.

"I haven't got a clue where the rock is now," Jay said to his brother. "Any one of the three could have it. One thing is certain, if Gorkov has it, Jameson will get it off him and we'll be off the hook with the Inspector. But if Blackstock has it I don't know what will happen. We need to speak to Jameson and see what happened at the meeting this morning. But I'm thinking we are out of the loop now as far as the rock is concerned. We need to think of saving ourselves now and silence those boys. They can see us put away permanently."

"But how do we find them? We've got no clue where they have gone?"

"That may be the case. But if I was that blackie and wanting to keep the boys safe, I'd know not to take them back to London but want to keep them somewhere near family. So where would I go?"

"It must be the racing stables."

"My thinking exactly little brother. So why don't we make an early start tomorrow and head back up to Yorkshire and see if we're right. That girl might have found her way back there by now and we can deal with her at the same time. At least we can sleep easy knowing the Russian is secure behind bars and no longer a threat to us."

It was close to eleven o'clock when their taxi dropped them back at Sue's house. Their evening had gone very well. They enjoyed one another's company and found it easy to talk about each other's past, their likes and their dislikes, their highlights and lowlights and their successes and their failures. Charles had brought the chef out to speak to them and Sue complemented him on possibly the best dessert she had ever tasted and also on the melt in the mouth steak. He had returned to the kitchen with the broadest possible smile.

Once again conversations paused and heads turned as Rob walked Sue back through the restaurant to the exit. As an officer she was used to have eyes stare at her but this was different. She could almost feel everyone undressing her with their eyes and had to admit to herself she got a thrill from it. A taxi was waiting for them when they reached the exit.

The evening had turned cool and Rob had put his jacket across her shoulders. He had joked that it was to stop her shivering and shaking her boobs out of the dress.

"You were never in the forces were you Rob? If you had been you would know that there is no place for modesty. If I happen to fall out of this dress then my main concern is no one is offended rather than being embarrassed. I'm sure you wouldn't be offended would you?"

"You've got totally the wrong idea about me. I was married to a film star. I know that real beauty is more than just good looks and I would call you a real beauty."

"You say all the right words."

They entered the house and Sue pressed the buttons on the alarm.

"Can I offer you a night-cap? I've got brandy and a decent malt."

"A brandy would be good, thanks."

"Do you mind getting the drinks. You'll find the bottles and glasses in the cupboard above the fridge. I need to change. I'd be totally exposed sitting around in this dress."

She went into her room to change but didn't bother to close the door which allowed Rob to ask her "What can I get you Sue?" As he asked he turned towards her room for an answer and saw her cross the room totally naked.

"Brandy please Rob."

She came out of her room in a simple tee-shirt no longer than the dress it had replaced. She went to the opposite end of the sofa from Rob with her and sat with legs folded under her.

"Thanks Rob. Spending time with you the last couple of days has reminded me I'm a woman."

"From where I'm sitting and what I'm looking at, you're all woman."

"You've been peeking again, Mr Blackstock."

"Every chance I get, Mrs Williams."

She rose from her seat, walked up to him bent and kissed his cheek.

"Goodnight Rob."

Chapter 11

"This Robert Blackstock sounds like quite a find, the sort we should be recruiting. Obviously it would help us no end if he would join us. I'd very much like to meet him James. I'll come along to your meeting with him and Miss Williams. I'd like to meet him face to face before we ask him to risk his life for his country."

****

Wednesday started early. Rob was woken by Sue shaking him gently at a few minutes after six.

"James Moore has just been on the phone."

"It's a bit early for a social call, so what's up?" Rob glanced at the clock on the bedside table.

"There's been another policeman murdered. D.S. Jameson has been found dead on Tower Bridge. Shot in the back of the head. Executed."

"This incredible, that's eight police officers murdered in two or three days. We don't normally have that many murdered in twelve months across the entire country."

"It's a nightmare. Only the first two have been made public and announced as gang land killings. We can't release the others too quickly. It could cause the public to panic, but that won't stop the investigations."

"Am I right that this D.S. Jameson is tied in with the Inspector or is that someone else?"

"He's the one. It would appear that the inspector is cleaning out the entire corrupt team, brutal, but actually doing our job for us."

"Did James say anything else?"

"He wants to see us first thing this morning. We're booked in for an 8:30 meeting in his office. You need to get dressed. The bad news is

I've got nothing in for breakfast except black coffee. But Mario's does a first class full English with toast and unlimited coffee refills. So get dressed and we'll go down there for breakfast then on to AC-10 from there. The weather forecast says we're to expect the hottest day of the year so far. It's going to be in the nineties, so you won't need a sweater."

"Sounds good. Give me five minutes."

Sue was ready first, dressed in a floral print short cotton dress with shoestring shoulder straps. She was perched on the arm of the sofa when Rob came through in pale green cotton trousers and a tee-shirt.

"You look very nice," he said.

"What's that supposed to mean? Nice. I'll have you know this dress cost me a small fortune. Do you think you could put a little of this on my shoulders please?" She asked holding out a bottle of sun cream.

Rob took the bottle from her and squeezed a little onto his hand then started to rub the lotion into her neck and shoulders while she held her hair up out of the way.

"Sorry. I really mean you look tremendous. So, as Peter Logan is now in Russia either he is not the Inspector or it's perhaps it's someone else getting rid of the opposition."

"It could be some other organisation, but I think it more likely to be the Inspector cleaning up. He may be in Russia but it's easy enough to arrange for a contract killing on the internet these days. If you don't get a move on and get ready to go to breakfast, I'll be taking out a contract on you."

"OK, I'm ready, let's go."

As soon as they stepped out of the door the heat of the day hit them. It was only 7:15 but the temperature was already in the mid-twenties. The forecast was looking right. It was going to be a real scorcher. "I'm glad we're not on the bike today." Sue commented. "Wearing those biking leathers and that helmet would have been unbearable in this heat."

"Yeh. By the end of the day we'd have been soaked through in our own sweat."

"Thank you Rob. I didn't need that image in my head."

Mario's was at least half full when they got there. "There's a table over there," Rob said pointing to a table by the window. "I didn't expect it to be this busy."

"They open at 6:00 weekdays and 7:00 on Saturdays. It's always busy and as you'll see very good value. I've been here several times."

The menu read like a 3-star hotel menu with options from kippers to eggs Benedict as well as the full English. They had hardly had time to read all that was on offer before a short, rather round young lady with pencil and notepad appeared at their table.

"Tea or coffee?" she asked.

"Coffee please," Sue replied.

"Coffee for me too, please," Rob added.

"Are you ready to order or do you need more time?" the girl asked.

"I think we're ready aren't we Sue?"

"Yes I'm ready. Can I have the full English please, but no black pudding thank you."

"Same for me please love," Rob added.

The waitress headed off through a swing door into the kitchen. A couple of minutes later she returned with a jug of coffee. Sue turned over the two cups on the table in front of them and the waitress filled them then moved around the other occupied table re-filling cups where wanted.

"This is a first for me," Rob said to Sue. "Breakfast in a chip shop."

"Yes. It's not a common thing but it seems to work for them. Six—eleven open for breakfast eleven—twelve closed for cleaning. Then 12:00 until midnight they're open as a chip shop. They appear to be well organised and it runs like two separate businesses sharing one building. You only need to look around to see that it works."

Their food arrived and they ate in silence. Their coffees were topped up and their empty plates cleared.

"Good idea coming here," Rob said. "That was first rate. A grand start to the day! How long will it take to get to James's office?"

"We've got plenty of time, it's only ten minutes by taxi, fifteen at most."

"More coffee?" said the waitress with another pot of steaming coffee in her hand.

"No thanks, love. Can we have the bill please?"

"If you just go to the counter," she pointed "they will sort you out. Just tell them table 11."

Rob went off to the counter, Sue went to the door to wait for him and the waitress moved straight in to replace the cups with clean ones and wipe a cloth over the table. As Rob turned away from the counter he was holding a poster in his hand and stared at it whilst walking to the door.

"What's up Rob? You look like you've seen a ghost."

"It's Luci. My Luci! Look," he said and handed her the poster.

"What you waiting for? Do what it says. Ring that number and find out if it really is her."

"It is her."

"Ring!"

He took out his phone, typed in the number and hit dial. As it was clicking through he put the phone on speaker so that Sue could listen in. The call was routed straight through to answer phone.

"Hello, my name is Robert Blackstock. I got your number from a poster showing the picture of a girl I believe to be my daughter, please ring me as soon as you get this message. Thank you."

"Stay positive Rob. If that is Luci in the picture she looks well and you'll know soon."

"If it is her we'll need to get her away to somewhere safe quickly. I don't want her mixed up in any more of this shit. I'm going to work on the assumption that it is Luci and I'll have her back by this afternoon. So I'll ring Phil and get him down here to take her back to Yorkshire."

"Believe me Rob she'll want some female company. We know she's been kidnapped but we don't know any details. I just hope they didn't rape her. Not that I think that likely, but it will have all been very traumatic for her and it would be easier for her to talk to another female about it."

"I understand what you're saying. She gets on very well with my parents housekeeper Madge Little. So I'll see if she will come down with Phil." Sue hailed a taxi while Rob selected Phil from the list of contacts on his phone and presses the dial button. They were in the taxi and moving off when Phil answered.

"Phil, we may have found Luci."

"That's great news, Rob, how is she?"

"We haven't actually seen or spoken to her yet." He told Phil about the poster on the counter of the chip shop and the unanswered phone call. "Sue and I have to fly to Russia tomorrow so I need someone to get her away. That is if it is her. Do you think you could drive down here, pick her up and take her back up to Yorkshire."

"No problem Rob."

"Good man. Can you also ask mum and Madge Little if they will come down with you so that Luci will have someone she can talk to about her experiences. I'll book some rooms at the travel lodge at South Mimms services, it's basic but it will do for one night and it is easy for us all to meet up."

"Sounds OK! I'll speak to Rose and Madge now, I'm sure they'll both want to come. We'll get things sorted and ready, then, if you ring back once you've confirmed it is Luci we'll get on the road. It's probably a three and a half hour journey."

"Thanks Phil. I'll be in touch soon, I hope." He ended the call and sat back in the taxi. Sue rested her hand on his leg. "I'm sure she's fine Rob, you'll have her back later today."

Fifteen minutes later they were sitting in an interview room at the AC-10 office waiting for James Moore to arrive. Sue had caused a minor disturbance in reception when she forgot to declare the gun in her bag when she passed through the body scanner on the way to the lifts. The alarms had gone off and two armed guards appeared from nowhere and held her until she was able to convince them who she was.

It was several minutes before James joined them. He entered the room carrying a bundle of folders. He was followed in by a much older man, tall, well-built and by the way he was dressed and his military like walk he had to be someone of importance.

"May I introduce Sir Bernard Howe, head of MI-6 Operations. If you're familiar with the Bond films Sir Bernard is 'M'. Sir Bernard this is Susan Williams Task Force Leader with Williams Security and Robert Blackstock whom we have been discussing."

"Miss Williams, Mr Blackstock, pleased to meet you both," said Sir Bernard holding out his hand to shake theirs.

"Pleased to meet you too Sir Bernard," Sue said as she felt his firm hand shake.

"Likewise," said Rob as he also felt Sir Bernard's firm grip.

"Let's all take a seat. I've got some coffee on its way." James gestured towards the chairs around the table.

Rob placed his phone on the table in front of him. "I'm sorry but I'm expecting an urgent call about my daughter. She was kidnapped and we have a lead on where she might be. I'm expecting a call to arrange her pick up." "That's OK Rob! Sue has kept us up to speed with everything. I've got two daughters myself. The past few days must have been awful for you."

"Indeed," Sir Bernard added. "My daughter is now in her 30s and I still worry about her. I think it's the price we pay for being a parent."

Four coffees arrived on a tray with a jug of milk and a dish of sugar cubes which was set down on the table and coffees were passed around.

James passed one of his folders to each of the others "This case is extremely complex and potentially threatens European political stability. Hence Sir Bernard joining us today! I'd just like to go over some of the facts if I may, and then we'll plan what's to be done. There is more detail in the folders.

"Firstly, we are aware of an organised gang of corrupt police officers on the Metropolitan force. Most of whom my squad have been able to identify and been observing for some weeks. This is within the remit of AC-10 and we will continue. Unfortunately we have not yet identified the leader known as the Inspector and in the last few days several members of the gang have been executed by an unknown person or group. Not knowing the full extent of the corruption is hampering the investigation into these murders, as we must be sure of getting the right result. You know we work closely with national security, MI5, they are helping us with this. Secondly, there is the matter of a diamond going missing."

"That's where MI-6 comes in," Sir Bernard claimed. "Not specifically the theft of the diamond. That is a police matter. But the impact that diamond might have in the wrong hand is of great concern. Indeed, it could lead to governments in Eastern Europe being overturned and total political upheaval in the area. Plus, with the military power held by that area there would be a significant threat to the rest of the world."

"And finally," James continued. "There is the, shall we say involvement of your family Rob. Unfortunately you seem to have been dragged into this mess like it or not. We're very pleased Sue is with you. Sir Bernard and I see your continued help would be very beneficial to both our issues. I will warn you this will be dangerous but we know you are well able to take care of yourself from what you did yesterday in Hyde Park. We'd both like the two of you on the payroll for the duration of this operation. I expect Sue has told you I'd like you both to go to Russia tomorrow to keep tabs on Peter Logan. But this is far beyond that."

"I don't know about you Sue, but I'm certainly up for it." Rob responded.

"You can count me in too, gentleman. I joined the army to see some action and if I'm truthful I miss the rush I used to get."

"Thank you both. I was hoping you would both agree," said Sir Bernard. "I wanted to be here today to meet you. First impressions for me are so important. I'll leave you with James now, but I'd like you to meet the rest of the team at 9:00 tomorrow morning for a mission briefing. Have everything you need for the trip to Russia packed and I'll have a driver pick you up at 8:15. I understand you are both staying at your house Miss Williams." "We are," she replied.

"Then I'll see you both tomorrow." He shook hand with the other three and left the room.

James followed Sir Bernard to the door then returned to the table with two other people.

"Sue and Rob. This is Zoe Crump and Glen McNab, both members of my team who will be travelling with you to Russia. We've been communicating with the Russian equivalent to our Anti-Corruption Unit for many years. They have similar problems to those we see in the UK and have given us permission to operate on Russian soil, with a few restrictions. Zoe and Glen both speak Russian and will be working closely with the local team. With luck and your help the

Inspector will finally be exposed and we can round up the rest of the gang." Greetings and hand-shakes were exchanged between the four.

"You're all booked on the Moscow flight tomorrow afternoon. On Friday morning the local team will make contact and you can agree the way forward with them. All four of you must attend Sir Bernard's briefing tomorrow. The entire operation will be led by MI-6. Good luck to you all."

Luci was in the shower when Ana and Eva got home it was just before nine thirty. Luci had not slept well. Too many thoughts going through her head! Too many questions still need answers. She heard the other two come through the front door, so got out of the shower, wrapped a towel around herself and went through to the lounge, happy that they were home and she'd have someone to talk to. Ana had picked up and was looking at her phone which she had left on the bookcase while they were out working. The light was flashing indicating a message had been left. She pressed a button and held the phone to her ear. Next she picked up a pen from the coffee table and started writing something on the back of one of the magazines.

"The posters are getting some responses. I've got five messages on here. One wants to marry you, another wants to, well he was being suggestive the other three are possibly legitimate. They all claim to be your dad. Strange they are all calls from men."

"Did any of them leave their name?" Luci asked. "One said he'd ring again later today the other two are Michael Raynor he had a strong Scottish accent and the other who sounded quite educated, said he was Robert Blackstock."

"Neither name means anything to me, so what do we do now?" Luci asked.

"Well I think we should sit down with the bits of your past that you have remembered and we make up some questions to ask. If they give the right answers we invite them here to meet you face to face."

"I'll leave you two to it," said Eva. "We're out of milk and need some fresh bread. I'll nip to the shop now then make some coffee and toast for breakfast. Don't make those calls until I get back, I want to listen in."

Eva was only gone a few minutes and found them still refining the questions so went to the kitchen and made three coffees and a plate full of toast. Ana dialled the first number, switched on the speaker and laid the phone down on the table in front of the three of them.

After a couple of rings the phone was answered by a man with a very heavy Scottish accent. "Hello." "Is that Michael Raynor?" Ana asked.

"It is." The voice replied, "Are you the person who put up the posters with my daughter's picture on.?"

"I organise the posters by we need you to answer a few questions before we can say she's your daughter."

"I understand. Ask away."

Hearing the voice Luci was shaking her head. She had a deep feeling this was not her father.

"Who bought this girl her last pair of jeans. Was it you or your wife?"

"It would have been a long time ago but my wife would have bought them, she does all that sort of thing."

"I'm sorry Mr Raynor but this is not your daughter. Our girl here lost her mum several years ago and now lives with her grandparents."

"Oh. I was sure she was my Ruth. Thank you for calling me back. Goodbye." They could hear the disappointment in his voice.

"Let's try the next one." Ana said and dialled Rob's number.

Rob still had his phone in his hand as they walked through reception and out onto the street so when his phone rang he answered it immediately. "Robert Blackstock."

"Mr Blackstock you left me a message asking me to call about the person you think is your daughter."

"That's right, she's been missing since Saturday. Where is she? Can I see her?"

"Sir, we need to ask you a few questions before you get to see her. First question: Who bought this girl her last pair of jeans? Was it you or your wife?"

"My wife was killed in a car accident some years ago. My son, Luci's twin brother died in the same accident. Luci lives with her grandparents so her grandmother will have bought her last Jeans."

Luci burst into tears and was only able to mouth a single word. "Daddy."

"Mr Blackstock I'm really happy to say we have your daughter here. She is overcome with emotion at the moment. Please give us a few minutes and we'll ring you back so that the two of you can talk."

"Don't be long."

Rob threw his arms around Sue and hugged her then his lips met hers in a kiss. Sue responded and they kissed passionately. Rob broke away and they stepped back from one another as if nothing had happened.

"She's OK Sue! I am going to get her back." He looked again at his phone studying the number of the last caller. Then he took his notebook from his pocket and turned a few pages.

"I thought I recognised that number. When we saw those two Russian girls, Rebecca's house mates. The blond one gave us her phone number. It was one of the few things I made a note of. It's the same number. Luci must be with those two girls."

"That's going to make picking her up a little difficult. We went there as two police officers following up on a murder, they are sure to remember us."

"They'll certainly remember you Sue, you did all the talking. But I was in the background, less memorable plus I was in motorbike leathers. I'm sure if I go in alone they won't recognise me."

"I hope you're right."

Rob's phone rang again and as he answered it he heard the voice at the other end say "Daddy, is that really you. Are you coming to take me home?" She was obviously crying again and a second voice said. "Mr Blackstock my friend and I found your daughter on Sunday. She had taken a blow to the head. Physically she is OK but has little memory of her past. She's a very nice girl, you can be proud of her. You must come as soon as you can to get her. You need one another."

Ana gave Rob the address, he didn't let on that he already knew it. He told her he'd be there as soon as he could. Sue had stopped a taxi and they set off.

Luci was almost in hysterics. Ana and Eva both put their arms around her to comfort her.

"I'm being flooded with memories, like a dam has been split open. My name is Luci Anne Blackstock. My birthday is January 22nd, I am sixteen years old and have a brother two years younger. We live with my grandparents at their racehorse stables in a village near Tadcaster in Yorkshire." "That's wonderful I'm so happy for you." Said Eva.

"What is the date today?" Luci asked.

"It's Wednesday 22nd August." Eva answered.

"Tomorrow I will get my GCSE results. If my grades are good enough I will be going to Sixth Form college to do my A levels, Economics, European history and Russian."

"You study Russian?" Ana queried.

"Yes but only for one year, not enough to take GCSE but I have understood some of what you and Eva have said to one another."

"If we had known we could have given you lessons."

"You've both done more than enough for me as it is. I don't know where I would have ended up if you hadn't taken me in. And now you have found my family and given me my life back. My family are extremely rich, like my dad is worth hundreds of millions. We must reward you for what you've done."

"Don't be silly we were more than happy to help."

In the taxi Rob rang Phil again who confirmed that Rose and Madge were going to travel with him. They would be leaving almost immediately and should get to South Mimms for 3:00.

When the taxi arrived at the girls' house Rob paid the taxi letting Sue climb out ahead of him. He noticed the back of her dress had damp patches where she had been pressed against the leather of the taxi seats and sweat had soaked into the dress fabric. The back of his t-shirt must be the same. He hadn't noticed until now just how hot the day was getting. The only drink they had had since breakfast was the coffee with James and he was suddenly aware that he was very thirsty. So once he'd collected Luci they must all go somewhere for a drink. The way Sue was moving it was clear to him that she was suffering too.

Sue went off a little way down the street and stood in shade waiting out of sight from the door to the flat. Although the girls' flat was on the first floor it had a front door off the street behind which was a staircase up to the flat. Rob rang the doorbell and stepped back to wait for someone to answer it.

"Mr Blackstock?" Rob nodded. "Come in. Your daughter is upstairs waiting for you!" Rob followed the young brunette up the stairs and into the lounge. As he entered the room Luci saw him and ran into his arms and hugged him.

"Daddy this is Ana and Eva they have been so kind to me these last few days. It was Ana's idea to make the posters we must reward them."

"I agree totally. Thank you both, I really would like to reward you for all you've done, I'll get my PA to get in touch with you. Sorry that's a bit impersonal but I'm flying to Russia tomorrow for a few days."

"There really is no need, anyone would have done the same."

"Maybe, but they didn't you did. Have you got anything to take with you

Luci, we must get moving."

"I must change my clothes. These I'm wearing are what Ana has leant me."

"No Emma, I mean Luci, they are yours now."

Rob hadn't noticed until now that Luci was wearing a very short, pleated skirt and a boob tube. She looked somehow very grown up, jailbait he thought.

"Thank you, Ana. I'll just get my clothes, they are all I have." She left the room and moments later returned with her jeans and t-shirt in a carrier bag which Rob took from her. Luci gave each of the girls a hug.

"Thank you again for everything."

"Stay in touch little Emma and if you need help with your Russian homework you know where we live."

Both girls went to the door with them and after final goodbyes Rob took Luci's hand and led her off in the direction Sue had walked earlier.

"Luci this is Mrs Williams. Her company supply the security for the building my apartment is in. She has also helped me find you and a few other things."

"Glad to meet you Luci. Please call me Sue. Your dad has talked a lot about you but never mentioned how pretty you are."

"Nothing to do with me," Rob said. "She gets her looks from her mother. Now, I'm sure we could all do with a drink. Sue do you know this area at all, any idea of where we can get a decent coffee?"

Five minutes later they were sitting at a table in a Costa waiting for an order of one black coffee and two diet cokes. Whilst they sat with their drinks Rob told Luci about the events of the last few days and Luci told them about being abducted and how she got away. She skimmed over most of the details of her time with Ana and Eva. She didn't feel comfortable talking about those things with her dad.

"So how does this trip to Russia you're doing fit in?" Luci asked.

"We hope it will bring an end to this whole affair and bring several crooks to justice. I'm not allowed to tell you details, It's all organised by some government department and we've been asked to help. I even had to sign the official secrets, so I can't talk about it."

"So it's both of you! What am I going to do while you're away?"

"Phil Parsons is driving down from Yorkshire this very moment. He's bringing Grandma and Madge with him. You'll all drive back to Yorkshire tomorrow. Sue's company has provided two armed guards so the stables are pretty secure and you'll be safe until this is all over. We're all meeting up later at the hotel where you'll spend the night tonight."

"I guess that'll be OK. After everything it would have been nice to spend a few more days with you. But I understand that going to Russia is important. At least we can have time together when you get back."

"I'll tell you what we'll do this afternoon. We'll go up west. I need clothes and a suitcase for this trip. You can help me choose. Your mother always said I had poor clothes sense."

"You won't need me tagging along spoiling the father daughter bonding."

"Nonsense Sue, Luci will need to have someone to talk to while I'm in the changing room."

"Yes Sue, I need you on my side when dad's picking out clothes. If we don't take charge he'll dress worse than a scarecrow."

Sue smiled. "In that case I'd be neglecting my duty as a woman if I didn't come along. But can I suggest we have lunch before we shop."

Peter Logan had a leisurely breakfast. Peter being fussy about trying new foods walked past the large bowl labelled kasha. He said looked and smelt like wall paper paste so he had just toast and coffee. Pauline was more adventurous and went for the kasha telling Peter that it was excellent porridge. The first day of the conference started with a champagne reception meet and greet session starting at 10:30 through to lunch at 12:00. Partners were invited to attend both the reception and the lunch. Pauline loved these sessions, she saw them as an opportunity to dress up and turn heads. To her it was even better than ladies' day at Royal Ascot and she made the most of the occasion, making sure as many people as possible knew who she was.

The first lecture started at 2:00 and lectures went on until 6:00. Partners were invited to attend a guided tour of the Kremlin organised by the conference committee with coach transfer from and back to the hotel. Pauline declined the tour saying she felt she was coming down with a heavy cold and was going back to her room. But instead she went to the hotel reception and ordered a taxi. She didn't return to the hotel until a little after 4:30.

The Squire Brothers reached Yorkshire late morning and parked up on the side of the road on a hill giving them a clear view down on the racing stables. They were there just in time to see Phil and the two women leave.

"There's the black fella driving two old biddies. He's probably taking them shopping. I told you he'd come back here with the boys. God its bloody hot today, is there any water left in that bottle."

"What are we going to do with them Jay? It needs to be final if we're to save our own skins."

"What we need to do is get out of this hot sun. Let's find a pub, have a pint and some lunch first then come back later to plan out what we're going to do."

Chapter 12

"You've done a great job as usual Faye. We'll have to watch Derek Drayton. Knowing he is AC-10 has proven useful for laying false trails, he can stay for now. I don't know what I'd do without you. I should never have got married. As the years go by, I've come to realise we've got nothing in common and we're drifting further and further apart. Since you came into my life five years ago, I've found out what true love really is. Our time together has become very important to me. I can't wait to see you again tomorrow and when we've completed this project we can go away and be together permanently."

****

Rob hailed a taxi and asked the driver to drop them at the Barratina restaurant in Drury Lane where they took a table out on the terrace and ordered tapas and a bottle of Chardonnay. Whilst they waited for their order Rob rang the hotel at South Mimms and booked 4 rooms although he hoped his mother would share a twin room with Luci.

Luci and Sue seemed to be getting on well together, talking about Luci's exams and her camping. Luci noticed the fresh scar on Sue's upper arm which the sun had made look angry despite the sun cream applied earlier.

"How did you do that? It looks nasty," Luci said pointing to the wound.

"I was shot at yesterday. It's nothing really, they almost missed."

"Shot at! You could have been killed. Who did it? Was dad there?"

"It was the Russian involved in this jewel thing and your dad was the hero of the day who took him down."

They continued talking whilst they ate. Sue told her about her life in the army and Luci admitted she had thought of joining up but knew her dad wouldn't like it.

"Get you're A-levels first then a good degree and you'll be able to join up as an officer. A much better life than that of a squaddie! More opportunities, better living conditions, more pay and less chance of being shot at." They both laughed.

Conversation continued all through the meal. Rob poured Sue a second glass of wine and Luci pushed her glass forward for a refill.

"I don't think so young lady. You may look over 18 with that make-up on, your hair up like that and in those clothes barely covering your body but I know how old you are, so no."

"Don't be mean to her Rob. She's been through a lot the last few days so pour the girl another glass. She looks super with that make-up and her clothes are perfect. She's a young lady not a little girl. Whoever helped with the hair and make-up did a wonderful job."

"I see, the two of you ganging up on me now," he said as he filled Luci's glass, then emptied the bottle into his own. "Mixing with those two Russian girls has taught you some bad habits."

"You don't know the half of it dad," Luci thought to herself.

"Right, you two drink up and get the bill paid." Sue said "We're only a five-minute walk away from Jones's, one of the best places in the area for designer men's wear. We should get all we need there. Then we need to get out to South Mimms to meet up with Phil."

At the racing stables the two armed guards Steven Thorne and Mary Gilbert were standing in the stable yard with racehorses being walked around them.

"Did you see that?" Mary asked.

"What, the flashes of light on the hill top?" Steven replied. "Looked like someone up there watching us through binoculars, I'll speak to Bill about sending a couple of the stunt guys up there to check it out. You'd best try and get some sleep this afternoon we could be busy tonight."

Bill Martin was Rob's Stunt Training Manager. The training academy took ordinary people and trained them in the basic skills they need: horse riding, motor bike riding on and off road, sky diving, skiing, advanced driving and many others. It was Bill's job to schedule and coordinate these activities into an eighteen—twenty three week course. Rob had asked Bill to organise some help with the protection of the stables so he had divided the twelve trainees into three shifts of four in a way that they could continue some of the skills training as well. Night time stunts were often being asked for so had to be trained for. So when Steven asked him to get the hill top checked out, he sent two of the trainees out on trail bikes whilst the other two were being taught how to jump fences on trail bikes like Steve McQueen in the movie 'The Great Escape'.

The two riders returned from the hill top and reported to Steven that it looked like it had been two men up there for some time. They had seen clear tyre tracks in the dust at the roadside and two sets of footprints. There were also two discarded empty water bottles.

"Thanks guys. Can you ask Bill to come and see me?" Bill appeared a few minutes later.

"I've got a strange feeling about this, Bill." Steven said. "Something is being planned and I don't know what. We need to be extra vigilant, especially tonight. The boys were witnesses to a murder and can identify members of three London gangs, any one of which could try and do them harm. Mary and I will both be carrying arms and will be patrolling the property tonight. I need your team upstairs in the house looking out and reporting anything they see."

"I'm sure they'll be happy to help."

"It's most important everybody stays in the house. Mary and I will be setting up a few surprises for any uninvited guests and I don't want any of our people getting hurt."

Like a lot of travel lodges the one at South Mimms had limited public space and the only source of refreshment was a vending machine. Rob pumped coins into the machine and selected two tangos and a bottle of water. He sat by the door keeping an eye open for Phil who was due anytime. On the floor beside him was a new leather holdall stuffed full with his purchases. Luci and Sue were sitting huddled close together talking too quietly for Rob to hear what they were talking about and occasionally they giggled like schoolgirls.

Luci felt very at ease with Sue, she felt she could tell her anything, so she began to talk about Ana and Eva. The fact that they were in the sex trade but had found a way not to be selling their bodies and were trying to save money. She talked about the big Russian called Mikhail. She even told Sue about the videos the girls had given her to watch. But what she stressed most of all was that the girls wanted to get out and were putting away as much money as they could so they could buy their release. They owed over £5,000 each for being brought to England, over half of which they already have saved in a bank. Luci said she wished there was something they could do to help them get out.

Luci went off to find the ladies and Sue went and sat up close side by side with Rob and rested her head on his shoulder. "You two are getting very chummy," Rob stated.

"She's a very nice girl who has done a lot of growing up in the last few days. You can certainly thank those two Russian girls for helping her through a difficult time. You possibly guessed they were in the sex trade but they are exotic dancers not prostitutes. Their pimp, for the want of a better description was Mikhail Gorkov. Small world isn't it? They are desperate to get out of the business but owe a lot of money to the people that brought them to England and got them legally accepted. Luci is hoping you can help them."

"I've had an idea, I'll talk to Luci about it."

"Talk to Luci about what?" Luci asked having returned unnoticed.

"I've been thinking of what I can do to reward your two friends. I've had a lot of my people working on filming location, complaining that there's never any cold drink when needed or the hot food option is cold. We've tried to address this by recruiting locals to keep fridges topped up and keep food in right conditions, but it's not working out well at all. So I'm looking to take on some permanent staff to ensure that everything delivered by our suppliers is available to our people in good condition whenever and wherever it is needed. Pay will only be a basic rate but accommodation and food will be provided free plus all the other bits that come with permanent employment. I could also see about loaning them the money, at a reasonable rate of interest, for them to pay off their debts. Do you think they would be interested?"

"Let me use your phone and I'll ask them right now."

"Two attractive girls like them would give the blokes in the team something to look at and would give the females a new topic to bitch about."

"That's a great offer Rob. Your dad's a clever man Luci."

"Luci took Rob's phone and moved into a quiet corner to make a call. She returned with a smile stretching from ear to ear."

"When can they start dad?"

"I'll ring Pete Doyle. He's my Operations Manager and is working in Hyde Park. He can get things moving today. He should be able to move the girls out of that flat within a couple of days and train them up for the job his team needs filling. He can also arrange for a personal loan to the girls. Give me my phone back and I'll ring him."

"Let me just give Ana a ring back and let them know what's going to happen. They were so worried that with Mikhail being arrested they would not get any work."

"Phil has just pulled into the car park," Sue announced.

Jay and Bill had driven down the hill into the village of Carlton Miniott and were sitting in the shade of large beer advertising umbrella outside the Dog and Gun with the second pints of cold lager. Their order of Giant Burger Special with side portion of chips arrived and they attacked the food as if they hadn't eaten for a week.

"What's your plan then, Jay?"

"Keep your voice down little brother, we need to be very careful. We know someone is thinning out the team and I don't want to be next. It might be the

Russians. It may equally be orders from the Inspector."

"We need to get this done quickly, then get away and lay low for a time."

"Spot on brother. What we'll do is rest up this afternoon. Have a few more of these maybe," Jay lifted his glass and took a sip. "Then later we'll go back and watch the stables to make sure those boys are there. Then once it gets dark, really dark, around 11.30 we'll make our move. Do you remember when we delivered that horse up here. Around the end of the stable block is a large heating oil tank servicing the stable accommodation and the main house. There are horses so there must be loads of buckets lying around. We collect up half a dozen of those buckets, cut the outlet pipe from the oil tank and fill the buckets. We then make a trail of oil from the tank to the house and throw the oil in the buckets up the house wall so that it gets a good soaking. Then from a safe distance we throw a Molotov cocktail into that oil. They've had no rain up here for a couple of days so everywhere is bone dry and the fire should spread too quickly for anyone to get out. The oil tank will go up like an atom bomb. It will all be such a mess that no one will think it's anything other than a tragic accident caused by a leaky oil tank."

"That's brilliant Jay."

"Luci!" Rose shouted when she saw her granddaughter run out into the car park. "We've all been so worried about you. Are you alright?" "I'm fine gran. It's good to see you too. You as well Madge." "Have you eaten?" Rob asked.

"We stopped at Peterborough for a toilet break and picked up a snack then," Phil replied.

"Well it's coming up to 4:00 and it's been a long hot day for us all. Your rooms should be ready so why don't you go and get booked in, dump your bags in the rooms, have a shower or whatever and then we'll go down into the village of South Mimms to the White Hart. It's a pleasant little pub where we can have a drink and some food in comfort. This place is OK for a bed for the night but that's about all."

"Robert, are you going to introduce us to your young lady."

"Oh sorry mum! This is Mrs Susan Williams. Sue this is my mother Rose Blackstock. Sue works for Williams Security who provide the security for the building my apartment is in. She has also helped me find Luci. It's her company that provided the two guards for the stables."

"Sorry Sue, I had assumed you were my son's latest girlfriend. He's had so many recently it was only natural to think you were one."

"That's alright, Mrs. Blackstock. He is a very handsome man!"

"Sue Williams of Williams Security. Is that a coincidence of is it a family business? You look too young for it to be your company," enquired Rose.

"My brother-in-law runs the company. I'm just an employee."

"A very attractive employee if I may say so. Shame she's married aye Robert."

"Widowed actually Mrs Blackstock," responded Sue.

"Stop digging mum and go and take a shower. I don't want to be too late eating Sue and I have some packing to do for our trip tomorrow. We'll be off quite early in the morning."

"I would have thought spending time with your children more important than a business jolly after what they've been through in the past few days."

"No mum, this is not up for discussion. I've explained to Luci, she understands and will explain to Justin. So leave it."

Phil got the bags in from the car whilst Rob organised registration. Luci was happy to share with her grandmother, she didn't really want to be on her own.

Madge took Luci to one side for a quiet word.

"Are you alright young 'un?"

"I am now, but from Sunday until this morning when I saw dad, I didn't know who I was or where I came from. I'd had a bump on my head which caused me to forget everything. It's a long story and when we get home I'll come and see you and tell you all about it. Thank you for coming to collect me. It's so nice to have a family again."

The sun was still very hot at 5:00 when the six of them squeezed into Rob's car which Phil had driven down in. Luci was sitting on Sue's knee but it was only for about a mile so they managed. Rose wasn't too happy about eating outdoors so they found a quiet corner with a couple of tables that they pushed together so that six could sit round it to eat.

Steven and Mary spent time in the afternoon sorting through things in the barn used for storage and doubled as a workshop. They uncovered a large blacksmith's anvil that the two of them needed help to manoeuvre to where they wanted it. They looked for rope but only found a few short lengths that used as halters on the horses. But they did find several spools of barbed wire which would be better than rope for what they were planning. Now they only had to agree where best to site their defences. JB and Jake were fascinated watching everything come together like something from the A-team.

Steven was concerned that they may still be being watched so did very little actually building of the defences. But he and Mary talked through what was needed to be done as soon as light began to fade and they were both confident everything would be ready before it was completely dark. Because of the secrecy that always surrounded racing stables the perimeter of the property was secured by a six foot high electrified fence topped with razor wire. So they were satisfied that if anyone were to come on to the property they would do so via the main gate. That made deciding defence placement quite simple and they were quite certain they could hold off a small force. If more than 3 or 4 tried to get in they might have to use their weapons and it would be worth checking what Eric had in his gun cabinet.

Sue and Rob left the others in the bar with another round of drinks ordered. Rose who didn't drink had agreed to drive them back to the travel lodge so Phil was enjoying another drink.

Rob had promised he would call them every day with an update and Sue had said she would ensure he did so. With his holdall full of new clothes Rob climbed into the taxi while Sue gave the driver the address.

On the journey back to Sue's house they discussed the day, both satisfied with the outcome.

"I like your mum Rob, and Luci is very much like her. Very honest and straight forward. Very likable."

The roads were exceptionally busy with people out enjoying the end of a beautiful summer's day. So it took a long time to get back to Sue's house. Rob paid off the taxi while Sue unlocked the front door and Rob followed her indoors and closed the door behind him.

As she walked into the living room Sue said "I've had enough of this dress it stinks of sweat and I'm all sticky!" With that she slipped the straps from her shoulders and allowed the dress fall to the floor. She stepped out of it and left her shoes behind at the same time, leaving her stood with her back to Rob in just a white lace thong. She next put a thumb under the fabric on either hip and eased the thong down until it dropped to the floor.

"I need a shower. Are you coming Mr Blackstock?"

The hot sun and the alcohol had an impact on Bill and Jay and they were not as sharp as would normally be. Jay drove their car back to their observation spot on the hill top and the sat watching the evening activity below them in the stables. The horses were stabled one by one and there was a lot of activity going on cleaning the yard after a busy day. They saw JB and Jake with yard brooms helping to sweep up. So they would execute their plan as soon as it went dark. There was very little cloud about but the moon was showing a small sliver. So there should be enough light for them to see where they were going, but not enough for them to be seen.

They gave it until mid-night before moving their car closer to the property gates and made their way towards the back of the house, being careful not to make noise on the gravel driveway.

Jay felt something crush under his foot as he set it down. Something grabbed his leg and he was thrown up into the air. There was a tremendous crashing noise as something heavy fell to the ground followed by an ear piercing scream of agony from Jay.

Shocked that something serious had happened, Bill turned towards his brother's screams not seeing a trip wire until too late. His foot pulled the wire and a coil of barbed wire uncoiled itself from both sides and wrapped around Bill gripping him ever tighter the more he struggled. The noise outside alerted the household, several outside spotlights came on and Steven and Mary walk round the corner from the rear of the building followed by Eric Blackstock.

"Eric can you ring 999 and get the police and ambulance out here as quickly as possible. We'll need some help to rescue these two."

Bill had given up struggling in the wire that wrapped him. Jay was in a far worse position. He was hanging upside down a yard off the ground, held by a loop of barbed wire wrapped around his ankle and over a pulley on the end of the building and down to the blacksmith anvil that had fallen from its high perch. His struggle had caused the barbed wire to rip deep into his leg and blood was beginning to stain his trousers. His gun had fallen from his pocket and lay on the ground beneath him. Steven picked up the gun using a plastic bag to preserve it for evidence. He then cut the wire from the anvil and Jay fell into the tangle of wire that was holding Bill.

Mary stood guard with rifle in her hand. She was licensed as an armed guard so it was OK for her to do so. Meanwhile Steven rang his Task Manager with his incident report.

Sue's phone rang on the bedside table and she answered it on its third ring. Steven was somewhat surprised at how quickly his boss had answered and thought she sounded a little out of breath. He gave her his verbal incident report and she told him to get it all down on paper plus a report from Mary and any statement from anyone who was witness to what happened. One copy for her, one for the police and he should retain one.

She thanked him for his actions, ended the call and turned to Rob who lay beside her.

"My team have both the Squire Brothers in custody and they will be handed over to the Yorkshire police. We have our own evidence against them so there is no danger they will get off. It's been a good day for your family, they are all now safe again. Now what were you going to do when the phone interrupted us?"

Chapter 13

"Good morning Prime Minister. Bernard Howe here. You asked me to keep you updated on the Russian matter I briefed you on a couple of days ago. Well, I'm pleased to say we have apprehended Mikhail Gorkov the leader of the UK faction of the Russian Wolves. We are holding him on charges of murder and attempted murder, but he is wanted by the Russians for at least eight murders that they have hard evidence on plus another nineteen others he's probably responsible for. So, we've agreed to send him back under armed guard on the Moscow flight this afternoon. In exchange the Russians have agreed to fully cooperate with and work alongside my team who are following the jewels. I have a team of six of our best people flying out later today."

****

Sue woke Rob early with a kiss. While Rob shaved she showered then made coffee while he showered. They dressed and did their packing. There was no time for breakfast, just as well because she still had no food in. The car from MI6 arrived at exactly 8:15 and took then directly to the MI-6 offices. At reception they had their photographs taken and had to wait while laminated security passes were produced.

The guard handed them their passes, and said "These passes will allow you into the common areas only, that's ground floor and floor one. Your meeting today is on the eighth floor so you'll need to wait for someone to come down and collect you. Please hand your passes in when you leave the building."

They waited some time to be collected and taken to a meeting room on the eighth floor. Zoe Crump and Glen McNab from MI-5 were already there and greeted them as they entered. They were followed into the room by Sir Bernard Howe and two others.

"Good morning everyone, thank you for coming in this morning. Can I introduce you to Mark Trett and your mission leader Tony Bates? I'm going to leave you with Tony who will fully brief you about the mission and get you to complete some necessary paperwork. But before I go, can I thank you on behalf of Her Majesties Government for volunteering for this mission? Good luck team. I'll see you again when you return."

"Good morning everybody," Tony began. "I'm Tony Bates and as you heard Sir Bernard say, I'm the Mission Leader. It's not my first time as leader, more like my twenty first. Being Team Leader means I am the decision maker and link back to our mission control. Should something happen to me, Mark will take over. Firstly this is an MI-6 mission but it is nothing like you've seen in Bond films. We are not individuals, we will succeed only if we work as a team. We need to rely on everybody pulling their weight. The purpose of the session this morning is to get to know one another. There is some paperwork that has to be done but that won't take long. Let's us start with a chat over a cup of coffee."

After coffee Tony explained to the team the particular skill set which each of them would bring to the team and why they were chosen. "As I have said, I am the team leader, the decision maker. Mark is my number two on this mission. He is also an explosives expert. Glen is a marks-man, a former SAS snipper. Zoe is a research and technology specialist. Sue is a security expert and an experienced investigator as well as being a crack shot. That leaves Rob." "I'm just an observer." Interrupted Rob.

"Not at all Rob, I've seen your profile. Peter Logan is our prime suspect and you were once quite close and perhaps able to understand his actions. But personally it is your driving skills that I see as being of value. Ladies and Gentlemen may I introduce the former under eighteen British Rally Champion:

Mr Rob Blackstock."

"That was a lot of years ago, Tony," Rob added.

"Maybe it was, but I understand that from time to time you keep your hand in by teaching advanced driving skills to students at your Stunt Training Academy. Welcome to the team everyone."

The paperwork included a new diplomatic passport for each of them, which gave them diplomatic immunity against prosecution in foreign countries.

The morning slipped away quickly but they were all happy that they knew what each member brought to the team and they chatted during the morning to get to know one another. At the end of the session Sir Bernard joined them for lunch and to see them off.

Two taxis picked them up at 2:45 and took them to Heathrow. They checked in at the VIP desk and were fast tracked through to the VIP lounge. Also in the VIP lounge waiting for the flight was Mikhail Gorkov with a security guard handcuffed to him on either side.

They were allowed to board the aircraft at 3:30, the plane had about thirty five rows of seats. Each row having three seats either side of an aisle. As Rob walked down the aisle he saw Gorkov sitting between his minders. The three seats in front and behind were not occupied and obviously were not going to be, as they had been filled with blankets, pillows & magazines.

Rob also saw Faye Mason sitting towards the back of the plane. He recognised her from the photo James Moore had shown them at their first meeting.

He stood back and allowed Sue to squeeze through to the window seat. He took the centre seat and Zoe took the aisle seat. Tony Mark and Glen took the three seats behind them.

The second day of the international police conference was scheduled to be a morning of lectures, the highlight being what the Russian police had learnt from the problems seen at the World cup in Brazil in 2014 and what changes they had made to make the recent world cup in Russia such a success. Then in the afternoon session there would be one further lecture followed by a debate on policing poor neighbourhoods. Peter Logan planned to attend all the lectures today. He was not only interested in the subjects but wanted to see the standard of the presentation delivery. 38 countries had delegates at the conference and Peter Logan felt honoured to have been asked to deliver the final lecture of the event. His subject was 'What can be done to combat the growth of crime within schools'.

Peter knew the subject inside out, it had been one of his interests for several years and what earned him his latest promotion. However due to pressure of work he had struggled to complete the paperwork and projector slides to support the presentation in time for this conference and had to rely on Faye to put the finishing touches to it from his rough notes. Fortunately she had agreed to travel to Russia with copies of the papers today. She wouldn't arrive until late but at least they would have time in the morning to rehearse. There hadn't been a chance to get all the projector slides spliced together so Peter would be relying on Faye and her laptop showing his slides in the correct order. If he needed to, Peter was prepared to miss the Friday morning lectures in order to get his own presentation to a good enough standard.

The conference organisers had arranged a behind the scenes trip to the Bolshoi Theatre for the partners of the delegates. Pauline left a message with reception saying she was too ill to attend.

Aeroflot flight 2573 departing Heathrow at 6:10 was on schedule to land at Moscow Sheremetyevo at 22:50. The team of six should be met by a driver and taken to the Moss Boutique Hotel, the same hotel that was hosting the International police conference and where the delegates for that conference were staying.

While waiting in the queue to register, Rob saw Faye Mason enter a lift with Peter Logan. He hadn't seen her register or collect a key. He noticed the lift stopped at floor six then return to the ground floor. When he reached the front of the queue, he asked which room Faye Mason was in and was told no one of that name was registered or expected. It was late, he was tired, he could have been wrong and when he spoke to Sue, she'd seen nothing.

Breakfast for the team was taken late. They were to be collected at 10:30 to be taken to meet the Russian officers assigned to the mission. Rob had not had chance to speak to Sue since they went to their separate rooms last night, but they did manage a smile over breakfast. With true military efficiency the car for them arrived at exactly 10:30 and they were driven in a police MPV to what looked like ex-barrack building. Once inside they were taken straight to a large first floor room, empty apart from a small folding table in the centre of the room and two wooden church pew like benches set against the wall opposite the door. A bare light bulb hanging from the centre of the ceiling provider the only light in the room, as there were no windows.

They were soon joined by a man and a woman both in high ranking military uniforms.

"All of you sit." The man barked order like. "My name is Major Alexei Yusupov and my colleague is Captain Irina Bakunin. We are both military officers seconded to the Politsiya. I have been ordered to assist your team on its mission. I am told you plan to intercept a person or persons attempting to steal Russian artefacts namely the mythical

Romanov jewels. I say mythical because there is no evidence they exist. The chapel in Astrakhan has been torn apart over the many years and nothing has ever been found. It is a myth. There are no jewels."

"Does that mean that Russia will not support our mission?" Tony enquired.

"If you English fools want to waste time and money running around our country, you are welcome to do so. I believe you are following someone you suspect as being the leader of a gang of corrupt London police officers, who may also be in my country with the illusion that they will find these jewels that don't exist. Your mission is to gain evidence that will expose this person. Am I right?"

"Not quite but close enough!"

"The person you are looking for is known as the Inspector. Yes?"

"That is right?"

"You suspect Assistant Commissioner Logan but have absolutely no evidence. What if I told you that until 5 years ago Mikhail Gorkov was an inspector in the Politsiya, as well as being wanted for numerous murders. He is the known leader of a gang of corrupt officers within the Politsiya. I don't think you need look further, do you?"

Tony and his team all looked shocked by this news.

"In my opinion this mission has achieved its goals and I have reported that to my superiors, who have agreed and the Captain and I have already been reassigned to a new case. Effectively you and your team are now tourists. You are welcome to stay a few days but you must leave this country by noon Tuesday and I must ask you to hand over your weapons now. They will be returned to your office in London via our London embassy."

"We've got no choice guys. Do as he says and hand over your weapons," instructed Tony reluctantly.

"My driver will of course take you back to your hotel. Please wait for him here. I hope you have a pleasant stay in my country and now I wish you good day." The Major turned and left the room followed by the Captain who had not spoken a single word to anyone.

"So much for full Russian cooperation," Sue said. "I don't actually believe any of what he said. How would Gorkov get officers in the Met to work for him. One or two he could possibly blackmail but what could he possibly have over so many. It just doesn't ring true. Secondly, tell me of any legend that doesn't have some fact it is based on. I admit the stories of there being three diamonds and a number of possibilities sound beyond reality, but it is very possible that when the sun is at the correct angle light can be refracted though a diamond onto another surface. Zoe, you and I need to do some research this afternoon to find out more about Mikhail Gorkov and dig deeper into the Legend of the Russian Rocks. Rob it might be useful if you helped us."

"That's a fine idea Sue." Tony responded. "The rest of us can plan what we can do next, see what help if any we can get from the British embassy here and get hold of some transport. I'll also brief Sir Bernard on these developments." Their driver opened the door and beckoned them all to follow him.

"OK everyone let's get back to the hotel and grab a bite of lunch. We've got a busy afternoon ahead of us."

Peter Logan had missed the first lecture of the third and final day of the conference. He had been up since 5:30 working on his presentation with Faye. Pauline had reluctantly acted as his audience. The first run through had one or two minor glitches but the second run was just about as good as he could want it to be and he left Faye to pack everything up and rushed off to catch the start of the 11:00 presentation. Pauline was happy to have missed today's outing for partners, which was starting at the Red Square then on to St Basil's Cathedral. Not really her thing. Last year's conference in Las Vegas was far more interesting for her.

The team were dropped outside the hotel and headed straight for the restaurant, except for Tony who said, "Go ahead and order. I just need to call in at reception."

He joined them just a few minutes later. The waiter was still taking the order from the others. After a quick scrolling glance down the menu he added his own order. "I've spoken to the embassy and someone will join us in about an hour. I've also arranged with the hotel for us to use one of their meeting rooms for the rest of the day. So let's get lunch over with and get to work."

They were just finishing their lunch when a boy came to the table and handed Tony at note. "Hurry up guys. Our man from the embassy is here already." Final mouthfuls were taken and they left the table and went out to reception where two men stood at the desk with a large holdall at their feet.

The older looking man took a step forward and held out his hand. "Tony Bates?" he asked.

"That's me!" Tony said, taking the strangers hand and shaking it.

"Richard White Embassy Comms Officer and this is my colleague Ned White, no relation. Do you have a room we can use?"

"We do, on the first floor. This way please."

As they left reception the conference delegates were leaving the conference room and moving into a side room for their buffet lunch. Rob spotted Peter Logan. He was deep in conversation with another delegate and didn't see Rob.

Sue and Zoe went off to their rooms to get their lap tops. The rest of the team entered their assigned room and Ned set the holdall on the floor, took something out and handed it to his namesake. It was a small radio that blasted out loud local music.

Richard held a finger to his mouth indicating they should stay silent. "Just sweeping for surveillance devices."

Ned waved a locator around the walls and few items of furniture. When he'd finished he held up three fingers to indicate three devices found. He moved a flip-chart easel in front of a picture of the Red Square and Richard moved a dial on the radio and it went silent.

"Sorry about that but I guess you don't want anyone seeing or hearing what we're up to. Two microphones, this little gizmo will jam their signal and a camera hidden in the picture now showing a close-up of the easel." Sue and Zoe entered the room.

"Now that the ladies have returned, can I introduce the team? Zoe intel and comms, Sue investigations, Glen arms, Rob transport and Mark explosives."

"Pleased to meet you all. We've assigned Ned here to assist you. He's familiar with the districts you want to travel in, so will be your guide. Now let's get down to business. Ned let's open Santa's sack."

Out of the holdall were pulled three short barrelled automatic rifles and six hand guns.

"We're guessing you had to hand your weapons over to the Russians. That is what usually happens."

The team settled down to their various tasks. Sue, Rob and Zoe moved to one end of the table, fired up the laptops and started work. Glen, Mark and Ned checked over the weapons and some miscellaneous explosive still in the bag.

Richard told Tony that there was a car and two bikes waiting for them in the garage beneath the embassy. He also gave him a list of contact numbers to be used in an emergency. Richard wished the team good luck and after a quiet word with Ned, he left to return to the embassy.

After a couple of hours, Tony rang reception and had some coffee brought in. Zoe and Sue were browsing the notes they had taken and Sue told Tony they had found some interesting facts about both the Inspector and the Russian Rocks Legend and she was just about ready to present to the team.

The team gathered around the table with their coffee to listen to what Sue and Zoe had discovered.

"Firstly, we heard this morning that the Russians believe Mikhail Gorkov is the Inspector based on their evidence. He held a similar role in the Russian police. Well, I think we have proof that is not the case. From what Zoe has uncovered he led a gang of around twelve to fifteen corrupt officers in the force from 2008 to 2013 when he disappeared. He didn't reappear until he was seen in Paris in October 2015, he was next seen in London in December of that year as the leader of the London faction of the Russian Wolves. Since then he has been closely monitored. MI-5's first reference to the Inspector was in 2012, the year that Peter Logan was promoted to Inspector. There is in my opinion nothing to support the Russians claim that Gorkov is the Inspector."

"But another pointer to Peter Logan," Rob added.

Sue continued, "We now have an alternative possibility, Faye Mason. Miss Mason is personal assistant to Peter Logan and to his predecessor since 2012 the year reference to the inspector was first recorded. In her job she has access to all police records and personnel files. In 2010 Fay's father committed suicide after being investigated by Internal Affairs for corruption. Faye spent eighteen months fighting to have her father's name cleared. She spent a small fortune on legal costs. Her father whom she obviously idolised was an inspector."

"So we have two suspects to watch, Peter Logan and Faye Mason," Tony summarised. "I agree Mikhail Gorkov is out of the frame. Now what have you found out about the jewels?"

"They do exist. Nicholas II wore the crown Jewels at his coronation in May 1896. At the same time Jews from Astrakhan did an inventory and a valuation of the entire pot. They valued it, including the crown jewels at £50m. That was in

1896. At today's values that would be in excess of £500m." "Good work, ladies," praised Tony.

"There's more. In 1927 Stalin ordered a search of the chapel at Astrakhan and all buildings within half a kilometre of the chapel. Nothing was found but the documentation produced included detailed drawings of the inside of the chapel. These drawings include an enlarged drawing of an ornate plaster moulding above the alter that has an odd shaped hole five centimetres in diameter. The drawing shows the moulding bathed in sun-light."

Rob interrupted. "Five centimetres. Two inches. My son said he heard the cops at the murder scene last Saturday say the diamond was two inches in diameter."

"Hang on, we've still got more," Sue continued. "Another drawing shows the ceiling of the chapel where there is a map painted marking the ancient religious cities of Russia. 1954 Stalin's troubled successor Gregory Malenkov, desperate for funds to support his political ambitions, believed that when the diamond of the legends was fitted into the moulding, sunlight would be focused onto one of the cities shown on the map. He ordered that all religious buildings in each of the cities on the map be searched. Buildings in twelve cities were reportedly ransacked but nothing was found. Finally, August 25th is the anniversary of the birth of Ivan The Terrible whom is reported to have had the hiding place built. It's logical that his birthday and two or three days either side are the days when the sun in the right position." "That's fantastic work Sue," Tony said.

"It's all down to Zoe. She's a real wiz. Whatever the language there's no stopping her! She's in like a ferret."

"Well done Zoe. Now we need to locate Logan and Mason."

"That's easy," Rob said. "When I nipped out for a pee, I saw them both going into the conference room with bundles of papers and a laptop. The schedule board has Logan presenting to the conference from three until four thirty. Faye is probably assisting."

"Right Glen and Sue watch them when they leave the conference. Rob, Zoe and Mark get reception to call you a taxi and get down to the embassy. Richard said there's a car and two bikes in the garage there which we can use. Collect them and bring them back here. Ned, sort out somewhere to park our transport. I'm going back to my room to call Sir Bernard. We'll meet in my room at seven thirty."

Tony checked his watch. 5:10. It would be 2:10 in London. On a Friday most offices will be winding down for the weekend so he wasted no time in ringing Sir Bernard.

His call was answered with a single word. "Howe."

"Sir Bernard, this is Tony Bates."

"Tony, why have you rung me and not your mission coordinator?"

"We have a problem that only you can possibly help us with, sir. The Russians have walked away from the mission. They have said Gorkov is the Inspector. Apparently he was an inspector in the Russian police and ran a ring of corrupt officers. So they are convinced he is the Inspector. They also dismiss the jewels as a myth with no evidence to support it and the Chapel has been searched many times with nothing found. They are arguing therefore that our mission goals have been met. They have taken our weapons and told us to leave the country by noon Tuesday."

"Who has said all this?" Sir Bernard asked.

"He says he is an officer seconded to the police his name is Major Alexei Yusupov."

"I know of him, former KGB. A nasty piece of work by all accounts! Leave this with me. I take it you are continuing your mission without the Russians help."

"We are, sir."

"Good man Tony. Carry on and good luck."

Sue and Glen saw no point hanging around outside the room. If Logan or Mason were going to go anywhere they would have to pass through reception so they stationed themselves in comfortable chairs to one side of reception.

Rob and the others had no problems bringing the transport back to the hotel and parked in spaces allocated at Ned's request.

On entering the hotel Rob saw Sue and Glen in reception. He agreed with Glen to take his place. Now that he had a moment to relax

Rob checked a message on his phone. He had felt it vibrate in his pocket while he was driving.

It simply read '7As + 5A*'.

A broad smile crossed his face.

"Have you won the lottery Rob? You look like the cat that's had the cream," Sue said.

"As good as," he replied "Its Luci's exam results. She got all A's and five are A star."

"That's fantastic news. You must be so proud."

"It's mid-afternoon back home, so I'll ring them now."

Rose eventually answered the phone after it had been ringing for some time. "Hello love. Are things going well? I tell you it has been a real mad house here, not a moment free to draw a breath. But Phil is here so I'll let him fill you in. I'm in the middle of washing up and no one else will finish it for me. Bye for now."

"Hi Rob." Phil started. "How are things?"

"Two steps forward, one step back as you might expect. The Russians are trying everything they can to slow us down. But I hear things have been happening your end."

"Well, where shall I start? I'll begin with our trip back from London yesterday. We left South Mimms around 10:00, and were doing well until about ten miles north of Newark we picked up a puncture and modern cars don't carry a spare, do they? So, I rang Eric, and he sent one of his lads down to where we were, but of course he had to go down to the next junction and come back up to get to us. He took the tyre and got it fixed but had the long route to get back to us again. It was half past five when we got back here. Luci was upset because by that time the school was closed for the day, and she couldn't get her results."

"Why didn't she ring the school?"

"She did but they wouldn't let her have them because they didn't recognise the number she rang on which is fair enough. You don't want to give results out to anyone who asks. They only have a record of your phone and hers, which of course she lost when she was abducted. You've heard that Sue's people captured the Squire Brothers haven't you?"

"Not the details but it was good to hear. You can all relax again now. Is Luci around?"

"She's not, I'm afraid. She's down in the village with her girlfriends planning their next camping trip. They want to try and get away before school starts again. Eric has volunteered to drive them."

"He may never recover! I'm not sure where I'll be or what I'm doing over the next few days, so not sure when I'll have chance to ring again. Say hi to everyone for me. Bye for now."

For the first time since they got off the plane Rob and Sue had an opportunity to get together without drawing attention to themselves. They touched hands allowing their fingers entwine. There was no need for them to speak, the touch said everything.

Peter's presentation went very smoothly, the rehearsals had been well worth it. He had a few questions fired at him when he'd finished and when he finally left the raised platform the chairman of the organisers took his place. He thanked the delegates for attending and all the presenters for sharing their work with the group. He concluded by introducing his successor John Wade of the Royal Canadian Mounted Police. Vancouver was to host next year's conference. His final words were to hope everyone enjoys the end of conference ball and to wish them all a safe journey home.

Peter Logan and Faye Mason walked out of the conference room together chatting and smiling at one another. Sue, leaving Rob in reception, shared a lift with them and discretely followed them until they entered a room together. She saw nothing to suggest they were anything other than what they claimed to be. She returned to reception and asked the receptionist which room Faye Mason was in. The receptionist tapped away on her computer and reported that no one of that name was staying at the hotel.

Chapter 14

"The plan is coming together well now Faye. I've spoken with reception and extended the room booking through to Tuesday. I've told them that someone in the room has a very heavy cold and will be in bed for a couple of days, so housekeeping are not to enter. It will be Tuesday mid-morning before the body is found. The poison given to me by the Wolves is very slow working but they say completely undetectable. The Wolves will be blamed for the murder and it will be assumed that I have been taken to be ransomed later.

"I've had the tickets for the flight down to Astrakhan changed from Peter and Pauline Logan to our new identities. The flight leaves at ten, so I've booked a taxi for seven thirty. We'll change to our new identities once we get to the airport. We need to be in the chapel by three with the diamond. Find the jewels, take pictures of everything and get out as quickly as we can. We'll drive an hour north to Volgograd find the jewels and drive south again, crossing the border into Azerbaijan and on to Baku where we meet up with the Wolves, exchange the pictures and the diamond for the £7m. We dump the vehicle and pick-up a car for the drive down to Turkey and the villa in the mountains where we can be together for the rest of our days."

****

7:30 and everyone was in Tony's room to hear about the next moves. There was a knock on the door and Tony was surprised when he opened it to see Captain Irina Bakunin standing in the hallway.

"It would appear your Sir Bernard and my chief commissioner are good friends. I have been ordered to give you full cooperation with your work."

"Well, you had better come in. Have you got transport?"

"Yes I have a car. It is parked in the hotel carpark."

"Good, that will prove useful in what I have got planned for the team. Right, everyone Captain Bakunin has been assigned to us, so let's get down to business. We know that sometime soon we're going to need to be in Astrakhan. It's one thousand three hundred and fifty kilometres from Moscow, that's about eight hundred and fifty miles. Anyone wanting to quickly travel between the two cities would normally fly. The next flight is 10:00 tomorrow. Peter and Pauline Logan are listed as passengers. I have booked myself on that flight and will observe and follow them both. As roads in this part of the world go, I have been told the road between Moscow and Astrakhan is superior. Zoe and Glen get together what you need for a couple of days and take the bikes and get on the road as soon you can. I'd like you in Astrakhan by noon tomorrow. It's a tough ask but if you ride through the night, you should make it with time to spare. When you get there locate the Chapel, familiarise yourselves with the layout and set up cameras to watch the inside. Find somewhere where you can observe the comings and goings unnoticed. The rest of us will get there as soon as possible"

"We'll do our best sir," Zoe said as they left the room.

"Sue, Rob and Ned I want you down there quickly as well. Take the car. It won't travel as fast as the bikes but if the three of you spell the driving you should get down there by mid-afternoon. When you get there find Glen and Zoe and assist them in the surveillance. If the flight is on schedule I should arrive at a similar time."

Mark, Captain Bakunin I'd like you two here with me to react to whatever our suspects do. I don't expect anything to happen this evening and tomorrow we'll probably see Logan and his wife leave for the airport early for their flight to Astrakhan and Mason will leave later and return to London. Once you've see her on her way I want you both on the road south to Astrakhan.

The car had only sufficient fuel for a hundred miles so Rob's first task was to find a petrol station. After thirty miles they were finally able to fill the tank. They would need at least one more tank full before they reached Astrakhan, two refills was probably more likely. He made a mental note to start looking for petrol after another three hundred miles. As they drove away from Moscow the road became noticeably less well maintained. There were numerous potholes and grooves formed by the repeated pounding of heavy vehicles. Any speed above fifty mph was uncomfortable and getting to Astrakhan by mid-afternoon might prove difficult.

"I hope Glen and Zoe are doing better than this," Sue said.

"They are on trail bikes, designed for rough terrain they will cope well on this surface. So long as they avoid the biggest potholes and can stay awake they should be there before mid-day."

To celebrate Peter's presentation, Pauline had ordered Champagne for when they got back to the room. They sat and enjoyed their drink and general conversation until it was time to get changed for the ball. Pauline said her cold was better but it had left her quite washed out, she felt she couldn't face a ball.

"Faye, you go with Peter."

"I've got nothing suitable to wear." Faye responded.

"We're the same size. You can borrow my dress. No arguments. You deserve a night out. Now get yourself dressed and be off the pair of you. Leave me to rest."

Peter and Faye followed the outgoing chairman into the ballroom. When he looked back and saw who was behind him the chairman turned and congratulated Peter on his presentation once again.

"It was interesting to hear how you British are tackling the problem. We have very little crime in Russian schools but you have given us something to think about should that change."

"That's good to hear and thank you," Peter replied, but he was thinking

"That's because at thirteen the trouble makers join the gangs and leave school."

Champagne flowed freely and the buffet was consumed quickly. Peter joked with Faye. "It would be shandy and Sainsbury's sandwiches in London. All expenses are met by the host country."

The buffet remains were cleared away and the music began. Faye was immediately asked to dance by several of the younger men in the room. Her background had provided her with sufficient skill to manage most dances. After an hour or so she returned to Peter at the table.

"Not dancing Peter?"

"Not really my thing. You go and enjoy yourself."

"Are you alright? You're looking a little out of it."

"I do feel a bit odd. I think I should lie down."

"Come on, I'm taking you back to the room." She helped him up onto his unsteady feet. Then supported him as he slowly moved to the lift then again as they walked from the lift to their room.

Pauline let them in. "It's working quicker than I expected. I thought it would be a slow overnight death."

"Whatever, it's working! Now let's get the room so that it looks like there has been a struggle. I didn't use my bed so we can get that room so that it looks like it's not been occupied and if you put everything you need to take with you in my bag we'll take that and no one will know I've been here. Don't pack makeup or wash-bag, it will look odd if they're missing, kidnappers wouldn't take them."

"But you've been seen around the hotel. At the conference and again at the ball this evening."

"Don't worry, you and I have not been seen together and everyone has assumed that I have been you. At the ball guys were calling me Mrs Logan and I didn't correct any of them. Let's try and get a few hours' sleep, we've got a busy couple of days ahead."

Captain Bakunin was back at the hotel at 7:00 and Rob met her in reception. Together they watched for their prey to leave. Mark joined them at 7:15 with a tray of coffee. At 7:25 a scruffy taxi driver came into reception and said something to the receptionist who made a call. A few minutes later two women came out of the lift gave their one bag to the taxi driver and followed him outside.

"That's a surprise. That was Pauline Logan and Faye Mason where is Peter Logan? I hope we haven't missed him. Quick, upstairs we need to check his room."

Captain Bakunin went to the reception desk and got a pass key and the three rode the lift then ran along the corridor to the Logan's room. The Do Not Disturb sign was hanging from the door handle. Ignoring it the Captain opened the door with the pass key. Lying on the bed in front of them, still fully dressed was Peter Logan. Tony rushed to the bedside and checked for a pulse.

"He's alive but barely. We need an ambulance quickly. It looks like a heart attack." Captain Bakunin used her mobile to request and ambulance and police to attend.

"The ambulance will be five minutes. He is not having a heart attack. I have seen this many times. It is a slow reacting poison based on spider venom. It causes heart failure in fifteen to twenty hours and is undetectable after forty eight hours. It is a particular favourite of the Wolf packs."

"Christ. Another copper dead, or nearly dead," Tony said "You two stay here and get things sorted I must leave and get on that plane. Get yourselves down to

Astrakhan as soon as you can."

Zoe and Glen parked their bikes in the chapel car park just as the chapel clock chimed twelve o'clock.

"All the talk about a chapel, I imagined a tiny place like those in the Welsh mountain villages. But this is bloody massive." Said Zoe. "Just look at the size of this car park. Easy get a hundred cars parked in here."

"Like you Zoe, I imagined something much smaller and been wondering how you'd hide all those jewels in a small building."

They entered the building and wandered around. There were around 20 people inside. Cleaners, flower arrangers and clergy, but as time drifted past noon they all left for their lunches leaving Glen to set up the cameras while Zoe networked them to her laptop and tested she had control of all directional movement and zoom. They then moved outside and found a neglected rooftop garden at a derelict house across the street which allowed them a clear view of the street, in particular the chapel door. They weren't overlooked and well hidden from street level. They sat back and waited.

Tony was late getting to the airport check-in desk but showed his diplomatic passport and was fast routed through to the plane. Logan and Mason were sitting about a dozen rows ahead of him. When they landed he let them off before he moved then followed them through arrivals but then things went wrong for him. Unknowingly he walked past a body scanner and his gun triggered the alarms. Security staff seemed to appear out of the woodwork and he was bundled to the ground and his hands secured behind his back with a cable tie. His gun was taken and he was dragged into a side room. Little notice was taken of his diplomatic passport, except to allow him to make one phone call. He used it to call Captain Bakunin. He explained his dilemma and she immediately rang her Chief Commissioner who in turn rang the airport. Tony was freed but he had lost an hour. He rang Sue.

"Hi Sue, what progress are you making?"

"Hi Tony, we're just entering the city suburbs about two miles from the airport. Where are you?"

"I'm actually still at the airport. Can you detour and pick me up?"

"Sure. See you in five minutes."

They were actually ten minutes but found him easily and he climbed in the back.

"You were right to warn us about the state of the roads Tony, Diabolical in places! That's why we're a little late. Certain stretches we were only able to do forty mph."

"However," Interrupted Sue, time has not been wasted. "I know who the

Inspector is."

Tony responded, "I do as well. It's Faye Mason."

"Sorry Tony you're wrong! It's Pauline Logan."

"Explain your reasoning. I need to be convinced."

"While Rob and Ned have been avoiding potholes I've been researching. Pauline and Faye were at a convent school in Reading together and were both expelled when they were fifteen. For conduct not acceptable at the school. They were discovered pleasuring each other in the gymnasium changing rooms. They were allowed to go back to sit there exams, but that's all. Pauline was then home tutored and Faye sat her A-levels at a comprehensive schools 6th form in Croydon then on to secretarial college. Qualified she took a job in the office of an escort agency. She soon found out that she could earn much more as a high class escort.

Pauline went on to Oxford where she studied Russian History. As part of her degree course she spent eleven months working in the city museum in Astrakhan. With her first class degree she was able to enrol in officer training with the Met. She rose steadily through the ranks and married Peter. She resigned in 2012 after being passed over for Inspector 3 times.

Meanwhile Faye had been introduced to Duncan Harris, Peter Logan's predecessor as Assistant Commissioner. She became a regular partner to Harris. Regularly they were seen at public events and private parties. Harris was investigated for corruption on two occasions and proven innocent both times. Harris introduced Faye to Mikhail Gorkov during a cultural exchange with Russia. They had a brief affair. When Harris made AC he arranged for Faye to be recruited as his PA. In that job she soon discovered how much money could be made from tampering with cases and Gorkov taught her how to cover her tracks. When Harris was forced to resign following a heart attack and Logan replaced him he kept Faye on as his PA.

Logan bought a flat in London for convenience to save the journey back to their home in Surrey, when working late. It happened to be in the same block as Faye's flat and Pauline stayed there increasingly more often over the years. It was Faye that introduced Pauline to Gorkov.

There is also evidence that she has also been researching the jewels.

We learnt earlier that there is a valid theory about the jewels being hidden somewhere other than in the chapel and the map on the chapel wall shows where that place is. All the places on the map are religious centres dating back to Ivan The Terrible. The hub of all this religious activity was Volgograd, formerly known as Stalingrad and before 1925 as Tsaritsyn. Tsaritsyn was granted its citizen status by Ivan The Terrible and he ordered a great cathedral be built on the most religious site of all. St Nicholas Cathedral stands above land riddled by lava tunnels extending for miles under the city. These were formed millions of years ago as the landscape was being formed. Ever since Christianity first came to Russia and up until a couple of centuries ago, these tunnels were used as the final resting place for all of Russia's religious leaders. Their bishops. Now, what if the places named on the map on the Chapel Wall are not pointing us to the cities but to the bishops of those cities."

"You mean if the diamond lights up St Petersburg the jewels will be located where ever the bishops of St Petersburg are buried?" Tony summarised.

"That's exactly it. Once someone knew the location they would be able to visit as often as they liked but could never pass the secret on. Probably only the Tzar and the head of the church knew the location and the diamond arrangement in the chapel merely a back-up. With both the Tzar and the head of the church both being lost in the revolution this back-up has become significant."

"What led you to this theory, Sue?"

"I discovered that last year Pauline Logan spent a month in Volgograd working on the cathedral archives. Then one thing led to another."

"So we're expecting Logan and Mason to be going to Volgograd once they've been to the chapel. I'll contact Captain Bakunin and divert them to Volgograd to set up surveillance at the cathedral. Fantastic work Sue. Sir Bernard told me you were a great investigator. He was right."

Rob drove the car through the city to the chapel, there was panic in the streets all around, with people running in every direction. Tony looked to the roof tops opposite the chapel main entrance and saw Zoe beckoning him to go up. When he got there Zoe was applying a field dressing to Greg's wounded shoulder. His shirt was soaked in blood and Zoe herself had a cut across her cheek plus several scratches across her face.

"What's happened?" Tony asked.

"The two women arrived at about quarter to three and went straight inside. Two men who we'd seen loitering around the car park for some time followed them to the door but did not follow them in. We watched inside via the cameras. As we expected they had the diamond and fitted it into a hole in the plaster moulding. It took several attempts to get it round the right way. Nothing happened until three o'clock then suddenly the diamond lit up as the sun light through the window hit it. The diamond emitted a beam of light like a laser. It highlighted the city of Kaluga. The light only shone for a minute or two. Logan said something to Mason, retrieved the diamond and they left the building. The two men didn't follow them back to the car park but instead they went off down the street. The next thing we knew was something being thrown onto this roof top. It was some sort of explosive device. Thankfully only the detonator went off but it totally destroyed the laptop, a piece of which is imbedded in Greg's shoulder."

"Is the wound serious?"

"Not overly. I don't think anything major has been hit, but the shrapnel needs to come out as soon as possible."

"What happened to the device that failed to go off?"

"I'm not sure. I think it must have gone over the edge."

"OK, I'll get Sue and Rob to look for it and clear away this scrap. You both have had a lucky escape but we do need to get you to hospital, I'll make a couple of calls then I'll drive you there."

Rob reported to Tony. "Sue and I searched the street below the roof top and eventually found the device which wasn't actually an explosive but a small box of nails. It was obviously intended that the detonator exploding would shoot nails a few feet in all directions. Thankfully the box and the detonator must have separated when the device landed."

"Could have been nasty!" Tony said "Zoe is helping Glen down off the roof top. Here are the keys to the bikes. Get Zoe to show you where the surveillance cameras are so you can retrieve them. Then get that junk down off the rooftop and into a bins when you've done that get after those two women. They've got about a thirty minute lead over you but they are driving a Toyota Land Cruiser and on the bikes you should catch them with no trouble. Check with Zoe and Glen to get a description and registration of the vehicle. Don't get too close, just follow them and take care. The attack on Zoe and Glen was probably by members of the Wolves. It's their style. I'm guessing they are looking out for the two women. I just don't know why."

"Could it be like us they are waiting for the women to find the jewels then they'll just step in and take the jewels?" Rob suggested.

"Somehow we've got to stop that happening and without help from the Russian forces we will be hopelessly outnumbered by the Wolves. Right you two get going, Ned and I will take Zoe and Glen to the hospital then ring the embassy and get someone down here to take them back to Moscow. Soon as that's done

I'll be heading for Volgograd. Stay in touch."

Chapter 15

"We are quite safe Faye. When Mikhail and I planned this job and he and I were going to split the money 50:50 he gave me a list of the Wolves most senior members. Many of them respectable members of governments, for me to have as security. I've told the Wolf leaders that the list is sealed in an envelope with instruction that should anything happen to me it would be sent to MI-6. Then a few months ago Mikhail had a change of heart and decided to cut me out and get the diamond for the Wolves and I was warned that if the list was made public, I would be eliminated. Mikhail is now out of the picture so the £7m payment from the Wolves is all ours."

****

"Well that was quite simple wasn't it?" Pauline said as she unlocked the Land Cruiser's driver's door.

"Quite amazing that something a technical as that could be designed and built as long ago as the sixteenth century." Faye replied and climbed in next to Pauline. "What do you think those two men were up to? Did you see them in the car park when we got here and they followed us to the chapel door. I thought they were going to follow us in but they didn't. They were still at the door when we left and then walked off in the opposite direction."

"You sound very nervous all of a sudden. Seeing trouble around every corner! Relax!"

"Sorry. I guess it's because I'm short of sleep and probable still a bit jet lagged."

"You're probably right. But we've done the bit that had to be done in a very narrow time slot. If we hadn't got here on time today then tomorrow would have been the last time the sun would reach the right angle for it all to work. Miss that and it would be six months until the next window. So far everything has gone to plan. Nothing now is time critical, so I think we should rest-up tonight. It's a long eight hour drive up to Volgograd on some really grotty roads and there is no point rushing to get there because the cathedral will be busy tomorrow. It's Sunday and there will be services all day. Better to get in there on Monday when there are less people to interrupt us. We don't what anyone checking up on us."

"I thought you had a cover story ready to explain our presence."

"I have but it's a bit thin. It relies on people remembering me from my visit last year and us being back to follow up on the work I did then. Its 3:30 now so why don't we try and get a room at the airport hotel, have a meal, get a good night's sleep and head off for Volgograd refreshed in the morning. We can take it steady, we've got all day."

Pauline heard a sudden noise.

"What was that?" She said "Sounded like some sort of explosion!" Looking up at the rooftops opposite the Chapel she saw a thin trail of black smoke rising. The two men reappeared and walked towards them.

"I don't like the look of them." Pauline said turning the key to fire up the engine.

The two men stopped, and one waved his arm across his chest gesturing her to move on. As he bent and turned, they could see an automatic rifle slung across his back. The other man simply took a step back and waved as if he was waving his mother off on holiday. Pauline slipped the car into gear and moved away quickly, heading back to the airport.

"Wolf Pack men, I'm guessing," Pauline said as she pulled the lever into second gear. "I'm pretty certain they'll do us no harm. That explosion may well have been them seeing off someone who interfere."

Faye put her hand in her handbag for a reassuring touch of her gun.

"It doesn't look much like a laptop anymore," Rob said as he started to gather up the pieces on the roof top.

"Yes, but just imagine the mess up here if that device had stayed in one piece." Sue replied. "It's a warning and a reminder of just how dangerous this mission is, especially without Russian cooperation."

"I was shocked by that," Rob replied. "After all Russia has got as much, if not more to lose if that loot gets into Wolf hands and funds the start of a political uprising. Who knows where or what it might lead to."

"Don't be so sure that the Russians have abandoned the mission. Just because they are not supporting us, doesn't mean they are not watching our every move." "Do you really think so? Well if they followed us down that grotty road I hope they are as tired as I am. The thought of another seven or eight hour drive now doesn't have too much appeal."

"You should have let me and Ned do more of the driving."

"No, you were busy researching. I'll survive. Come on let's get it done. At least we know what to expect and it should be a lot easier on the bikes."

"I'll just get my rucksack and laptop out of the car before Tony goes off with them. Then I'll be ready."

They set off side by side on the bikes retracing the route through the city back to the airport, where they stopped to refuel the bikes. They went into the kiosk to pay for the fuel and pick up some water.

"Rob look over there. In the hotel car park, there's a Land Cruiser in the right hand corner. Not too many of them about. I don't suppose it's the one we want. What did Glen say about it?"

"He said the radio aerial had been snapped off about a quarter of the way up."

"That's it then. It's them. I'll ring Tony."

"Sue! What's wrong?"

"Nothing's wrong Tony, we've found Logan and Mason. They are parked up at the airport hotel. Looks like they are here for the night! Rob and I stopped to refuel the bikes and spotted the car just by chance."

"Maybe they're as knackered as the rest of us and need some sleep. We're about twenty minutes away from the hospital. Give us an hour and a half or two hours and we'll join you. Until we arrive, keep your heads down, the last thing we want is for them to think they are being followed."

"Tony says were to stay here and he'll join us in a couple of hours." "Maybe then we will get some sleep tonight," Rob concluded.

"Tony, Mark here. We've got a bit of a problem."

"What?"

"We're about a hundred miles south of Moscow and Captain Bakunin's car has broken down. Look like the timing belt has broken. Anyway it's terminal. The Captain is on the phone at the moment talking to her superiors, trying to get another car sent out to us. But even if they do that it will be at least another three hours before we get moving again."

"OK, can't be helped. Keep me informed as to progress. At the moment it looks like the two women are spending the night in Astrakhan so it will be late Sunday before they get there. We'll be a short distance behind them. It's an eight hour drive from here to Volgograd so there is still a good chance you'll arrive first."

"OK Tony, we'll press on as soon as we get a new vehicle."

Rob made use of the time they spent waiting for Tony to call home.

"Hi dad how's things."

"You may well ask son." Eric replied. "We've had the police here most of the morning. Two lots of them! One lot taking statements from Justin and Jake about what they saw of the murder of that Russian Girl. They then interviewed Luci about her kidnapping. I sat in on all those. I was asked to because they are all under age. I must say from what I heard your children say to the police I'm worried now about what you've got yourself mixed up in."

"Don't worry dad, I've got one of the best watching my back," he winked at Sue.

"That wouldn't be that Mrs Williams that your mum has been talking about, by any chance, would it?"

"It might be. Anyway, what did the other police want?"

"Oh there were several of them, eight or nine. Some in white coats looking over the exact spot where Steven trapped those buggers. Others were interviewing your people from the Stunt School that were here that night and two plain clothes female officers were interviewing Steven and Mary, wanting to check their weapons and their licences. They seemed happy enough."

"Who are Steven and Mary?"

"They are the two armed guards your friend sent up here to babysit us. Both of them very nice young people and very resourceful. It was so simple the way they trapped those two. I'm not too sure it was legal, but the police seemed happy after they had spoken to them."

"Anything else exciting been happening then?"

"Not really. It's been good having your stunt students around and seeing what you put them through in training. One of the girls broke her leg this morning falling of a horse. The other thing is on Wednesday Luci and her mates are off camping. Your mother volunteered me to be their driver etcetera. What am I going to do with four teenage girls for three days?"

"Take a good book and some ear plugs with you dad. I'm sure you'll survive. You might even enjoy it."

"It will certainly be an experience alright."

"I've got no idea when I'll be home or when I will be able to ring again. Give my love to everyone and enjoy your camping." Ha laughed and ended the call.

Tony and Ned got to them soon after six.

"How are they both?" Sue enquired.

"Well, Glen is doing well. His injuries look worse than they are. But Zoe appears to have been hit in the chest by the force. By the time we got to the hospital she was having trouble breathing. They had to treat her for a collapsed lung while I was there. She was stable when we left. The embassy said they would be flying someone down in a private plane to see they both get all the treatment they need and to get them home."

"Poor Zoe. Nice girl too and such a whizz on the computer," Sue added. "We've seen no sign of the two women since we got here."

"I think it is now safe to assume they're staying the night. In which case I don't see why Her Majesty's Government can't stretch the budget for us to have a meal and a good night's sleep. Will either of you two be recognised by either of them?"

"I've never met Faye and it's a lot of years since I last saw Pauline. We were students together but in those days I had dreadlocks and a beard. I'm certain she wouldn't recognise me," Rob said.

"Nor I," Sue added.

"Even so, we'll steer clear. If we watch from a distance we should get through the night without issue and we'll set our alarms early so that we're ready to follow as soon as they make their move. Come on, let's get signed in. Do you two want two singles or a double?"

"Two singles of course." Sue jumped in.

"Sorry I must be misreading the signs."

Pauline and Faye had booked a twin room and an early morning call for 7:00. They stopped off at the bar for a large gin and tonic before going to their room. They showered together then lay on the beds together wrapped in towels and discussing what they needed to do next and over the days to come. Their next priority was food. They had gone all day on just a packet of biscuits. So at 7:15 they headed for the restaurant for a steak and a good bottle of red.

Tony, Rob and Sue also showered before meeting in the bar prior to going into the restaurant. Ned was outside placing a tracker onto the Land Cruiser. He didn't join them as he had a family crisis at home he was trying to sort out over the phone. They avoided walking past the table where Pauline and Faye were eating which wasn't difficult because the restaurant was quite full. Tony smiled when without hesitation Sue chose to sit next to Rob. From where he sat Tony had a clear view of Pauline and Faye at their table. He noted that they only ate a main course with a bottle of wine and left their table before eight. He made an excuse of needing the toilet and left the table to follow the two women, expecting to see them head for either the lounge of the bar for the rest of the evening. But they did neither. He got to reception just in time to see them getting into the lift, so he returned to the table.

"They're heading back to their room," he reported.

"I expect they want an early night, I know I could do with one," Rob said.

"Then we'd better get on and order some food."

Mikhail Gorkov had been held in the cells at Moscow's central police station since he had been flown back to Russia on Thursday. He had been intensely interrogated all day Friday and all morning today, giving up nothing that incriminated him or connected him to any of the people he had being accused of murdering. Tomorrow he would be handed over to homeland security for further interrogation. He'd been through all this once before and survived, he could do so again. The important thing was to keep his strength up. He needed to take every opportunity now to sleep. There would be very few chances in the next few days.

"Wake up, Mikhail. Quickly, you're getting out of here."

"Good grief Ivan what are you doing back in Russia? I thought I ordered you to hold the fort in London until my replacement was installed."

"Your wife sent me. She wants you home Mikhail. Now hurry we've not got long."

Ivan Relinski had flown in on the same flight as Gorkov was on. He had boarded early and sat at the back of the plane and recognised Rob and his girlfriend and made sure that they did not see him. He had used his contact to find where Gorkov was being held and now in the uniform of a Major from Homeland Security with false papers including an authorisation to move Gorkov to Homeland Security cell block. As it was Saturday night, it would take time to locate any senior police officer, should anyone at the central police station want to challenge his paperwork. As a major he would almost certainly outrank everyone at the station. So he simply walked in, showed the transfer order to the duty officer and walked out with the prisoner in handcuffs to a plain black car waiting in the street. It was all over before anyone at the station could contact their senior officer.

"Faye Mason and the Logan woman are both here boss. They are in Astrakhan this evening. Just like you said they would be." Ivan reported.

"Did they get to the chapel for the 3:00 showing." Mikhail asked.

"Yes, boss and the report say they came out smiling so we can assume they were successful. However, the report also said that they had been watched by a pair of professionals, but the local team dealt with them."

"So Ivan you are taking me to Volgograd to meet up with the team?"

"I am, but I must also tell you that Blackstock and his girlfriend were on the plane. We don't know why and they haven't been seen since you landed."

"We need to watch out for that one. He is a complete unknown and the way he took me down in London, he could be dangerous if he's here to oppose us."

Tony, Ned, Sue and Rob all met in reception as planned at seven next morning.

"Hope you both slept well," Tony said in greeting to Sue and Rob who arrived just seconds behind him and Ned. "Shall we go straight in to breakfast? We can plan our day while we eat."

A waitress met them at the door and they followed her to a table at the back of the restaurant. The same table they had used the evening before. As soon as they were seated a second waitress appeared with a pot of coffee and said something in Russian and pointed at the pot in her hand. Tony and Rob both smiled and nodded to her but Sue spoke something back to her and she poured four black Russian coffees. She then said something directly to Sue. Sue's response made her laugh before she turned and walked away.

"What was that about?" Rob asked.

"Well," Sue replied, "she said someone will be over in a few minutes to take our orders and I said to her that men don't have enough brain cells to learn to speak Russian."

The menus were in Russian, French and English. The three men gave their choices to Sue and when the waitress came, she gave her four orders and asked for orange juice and toast as well.

"I'm glad you're here Sue," Tony said. "Else we'd be down to pointing at the menu and hoping we get what we think we ordered. Anyway, the plan for today is for you two to get up to Volgograd at a steady speed and make contact with Mark. He sent me a message over night; they were on the move again around mid-night and expect to be in Volgograd before noon. I've instructed them to secure somewhere from where we can observe the front of the cathedral and use as a base for our surveillance. I told him to expect you mid-afternoon which should give you plenty of time on the bikes. Take all the cameras with you. We'll need your laptop Sue to link to the cameras. Ned and I will stay here until the women leave then follow them up to Volgograd."

"Why don't we just wait for those two in the car park and arrest them and go home. Save all this running around the country?" Rob asked.

"There are three very sound reasons not to Rob." Tony replied. "One; I'm not a cop I'm MI-6. Two; if I were a police officer I would not have jurisdiction here to make an arrest. Three; what grounds do we have to make an arrest. We believe that Logan is responsible for several murders but she didn't commit those crimes even though she undoubtedly ordered them. We don't actually have any hard evidence.

So far they have not been seen committing any crime in Russia for the authorities to pick them up. So our brief here is to follow these two and collect evidence against them. We are also tasked with preventing the theft of Russian property, namely the jewels. Once the women remove the jewels the Russians can pick them up for grand theft. Britain can then ask that they be extradited to face multiple counts of murder and preventing the true course of justice."

Mark and Captain Bakunin arrived at Volgograd's St Nicholas cathedral at 11:00. After checking out several alternatives they setup base in a hotel room from where they could at least see the whole of the front of the cathedral.

Rob and Sue stopped to refuel the bikes on the outskirts of Volgograd. While they were stopped, Sue rang Mark to get the exact location of where they were and any suggestions as to where they could leave the bikes. He gave her directions to where he had left their vehicle and said he would meet them there. Half an hour later Rob and Sue were stood in a car park next to a row of Russian built cars.

"It's that big blue monster to your left," came a voice from behind them.

Sue turned to see Mark pointing at a Marussia SUV.

"Big isn't she. Made for these roads. We came down here at a hundred kph this morning. Hang on I'll drop the tailgate and we'll get the bikes in the back."

Even with the tailgate down the bikes had to be lifted at least three feet off the ground to get them onto the flatbed which formed the back half of the vehicle. But the vehicle was so big that once up there the two bikes could be laid down side by side. Mark pulled a tarpaulin over them and pushed up the tailgate. As they walked away Rob turned to look back and was happy that the bikes couldn't be seen.

"I pushed those bins into that spot there," Mark said pointing at the two large wheelie bins occupying a parking space three along from the vehicle they had just loaded. "Trying to reserve it for Tony. Thought it might prove useful to have the vehicles close together."

Sue nodded her agreement.

It was only a short walk to the hotel and they were all soon at the window of the hotel room looking down at the main door of St Nicholas Cathedral and the paved square in front of it.

"It's very busy down there," she said. "People going in and out all the time."

"Yes! It's been like that since before nine this morning and likely to stay like it until the last service turns out at ten this evening," replied Mark.

"We're not going to get much chance to get the cameras set up before it gets too dark to see. We can at least link them up to my laptop whilst we wait."

Tony and Ned finally joined them around 8:30. After an update from Ned and a quiet word with Captain Bakunin he and Sue took the cameras in a rucksack down to the cathedral door and entered with a dozen or so going in for the late evening service.

"This is a lot bigger than I had expected. Five cameras are not going to help very much, so let's make the most of what we've got," Tony said quietly to Sue. "One for monitoring this side of the main door, one for each of the three main aisles and the final one looking into the altar area. I'll keep lookout while you install them as high as you can get. If anyone asks what we are doing, we are installing the first part of a new security system."

No one did ask and they were quite pleased with what they had set up. Even more so when they checked the monitor back in the hotel room and practiced zooming and rotating to the point where they could count the money on the collection plate at the end of the service.

It was a long uncomfortable night. Six of them in one room in a very basic hotel. They had running water, but the toilet was at the end of the corridor. Tony woke at 6:30 and saw Captain Bakunin stood at the window looking down at the cathedral. He walked across the crowded floor and stood beside the Russian.

"I have an uneasy feeling about today. I am unusually nervous," Bakunin told Tony.

"We're all going to be fine. Why don't you go and track down breakfast for us all while I wake these snoring animals."

One by one he woke his team and they were all glad to see Bakunin when she returned with a large jug of coffee, a bag of pastries and hanging out of her jacket pocket, a tube of disposable coffee cups.

"The cathedral had been locked at 10:00 and would be unlocked at 8 o'clock Monday morning when an army of cleaners would move in plus a few local worshippers."

"Right guys we need to get organised!" Tony commanded. "Rob, I want you up here in front of the monitor, you know most of the faces better than the rest of us. Sue can you stay with him to keep your laptop running and Irina we don't want your uniform frightening anyone away. I need eyes inside as well, the cameras don't cover everywhere. Ned can you cover that? That leaves Mark and myself to watch any entrance on the sides and rear of the place. If everyone is happy, turn your comms on and we'll be off. Everybody stay in touch with regular updates even if you've got nothing to report. At least then I'll know you're still awake."

At around 10:15 Logan and Mason turned up. Tony spotted them first and reported seeing them enter by the door on the north side. Ned then reported seeing them on the inside of that door and moments later Rob saw in the camera's frame that they were making their way towards the altar and he turned the camera to follow them.

He reported, "I have them on camera three. They appear to be making for the altar. Yes I can now see them on camera five. They are definitely heading for the altar. They are there now. Going behind it. They've gone! Looked like they went down some steps or something. They just went down out of sight." "Ned, can you check it out?" asked Tony.

"I'm almost there," he replied. "Yes. I can see a stone staircase down into some sort of cellar. There's a light on down there. Do you want to go down?"

"No wait for me and Mark to join you!" Tony ordered. "Mark come round this side. We'll go in via this north door."

Sue joined the conversation. "I don't recall seeing any record saying there was a cellar under the altar. I suspect it is the entrance to the tunnels."

"Looks like you could be right, Sue." Tony was now at the top of the staircase looking down. "These stairs are easily wide enough to carry a body down."

We're going down. "Keep a sharp lookout up top for us."

For a second night Pauline and Faye had shared a bed together trying to relax in each other's arms. This was an important day for them. The jewels had not been seen for over a century. If her research was correct, they were only hours from being very rich. If she was wrong or if someone else had beaten to their goal they at least had the diamond to fund their future together.

There was no need to rush, so after showering together they dressed and went down for a light breakfast. The cathedral was just a five minute walk away.

"The cathedral cleaners finish at 10:00 and for the fifteen minutes after that there's a lot of coming and going while the cleaners put their equipment away and leave. It should allow us to get in unnoticed," Pauline told Faye.

"Do you actually know what we're looking for?"

"I think we can go straight to our prize. At least we can go directly to the right chamber. When I was here last year I spent some time browsing the documents cataloguing the burial chambers. They are large. For fifty generations bishops were buried in these chambers. There are sixteen chambers in all. Our first job is to find the chamber where the bishops of Kaluga are buried then we search for the jewels."

"Will the bodies be in coffins?" Faye asked sheepishly.

"More likely they will be wrapped like Egyptian mummies and laid on shelves. We're looking for something that perhaps looks out of place or is different in some way. We'll recognise it when we see it, I guess. We'd better get packed up and check-out."

Once they had descended the stairs behind the altar Pauline tugged on a pull cord and lights came on. They were in a room approximately forty feet square. It was more of a cave really. The ceiling and walls were bare rough rock painted white and the floor had been chiselled out to be almost level. There was row after row of filing cabinets and a desk in the corner.

"All these cabinets contain the national archives. It's a sort of historical record of all events in the country. It's what I was working on during my visit last year. We need to go down that passageway there." Pauline pointed at a passage to their left. "There are no lights from here on so we'll use the torches down here. Then when we get to the next level and the burial chambers, we'll use the glow sticks."

Faye took two torches out of her rucksack and they walked the length of the passage and came out into another large cavern off which ran several more passages, possibly twenty or more. It was difficult to count in the poor light from the torches. But the torches did show up that above each passage was plaque with a city name carved into it.

"Here we are, Kaluga, down this one," called Pauline, as the light of her torch showed a passage disappearing steeply downhill. "Careful! It is quite steep in places."

Faye followed a few yards behind with her torch angled down showing the uneven passage floor. Finally they broke out into another cavern. This one was not as rough as the previous ones that they had just walked down. There was only one other passage leading from this cavern. Pauline snapped one of the glow sticks and the cavern was filled with a pale green light. They could clearly see that against the two side walls were large wooden structures, like bottle racks in a wine cellar but on a much larger scale, each space being about two feet square. In each space they could see what looked like a body wrapped just like Pauline had expected them to, Egyptian mummies lay on their backs with the head pointing towards the entrance. Above each body was an inscription bearing the bishop's name and the date of his death.

"This reminds me of those body fridges in hospital morgues. All that's missing are doors and the sexy doctors," Faye whispered.

"Why are you whispering?" Pauline asked. "And less talk of sexy doctors. Male or female. You're mine now. All mine." She moved closer to Faye and kissed her. "We had better begin our search. We've only got enough glow sticks to give us about an hour. Then we're torches only and I don't fancy finding my way out of here in the dark."

Still whispering Faye replied, "I thought everyone whispered in church. Isn't that an altar over there? It's got a cross on it with candle sticks either side."

Pauline looked to where Faye was pointing. "Looks like it could be. I expect they held a service for each bishop as he was interned. Now get searching!"

Tony and Mark descended the stairs down into the cavern like vault leaving Ned up top as look out. As they neared the bottom of the staircase they carefully looked around for Pauline and Faye. Happy that they were not there they moved on.

"What do you think is in all these filing cabinets, Tony?"

"Sue says that this cathedral houses possibly the world's largest collection of reports of historical events, going back about three thousand years. She said that Logan was here last summer helping to kick off a project to get them all on computer. My guess is that these cabinets hold all those papers."

They checked some of the cabinets and found documents written on many different materials. Some were parchment scrolls that looked too old and fragile to touch. Some wax tablets. Others in the style a monk would produce with elaborate art work. They even found notes written in a crude form of shorthand obviously using a biro.

"I wish I could read Russian," Mark said. "There must be some really fascinating stuff in here."

"Maybe once it's on computer we'll all get access!" Tony suggested.

They walked around the wall of the cavern. "There are three passages leading out of here Mark. Logan and Mason could have gone down any one of them. We don't have any chance of following them. We don't know where any of these passages lead, they're dark and we don't have a torch. We may as well go back up and sit and wait for them to come back out."

Having searched both body racks and found nothing, Pauline and Faye came together in the centre of the chamber and gave each other a hug.

"Well if it was here, it ain't now." Faye proclaimed.

"I just don't understand it." Pauline said with doubt in her voice. "In all the years I've spent researching this I have never come across anything that hinted that it had already been discovered and robbed away."

"Well, we've been very thorough. We looked into every last cell in each of these structures and there's just no sign of anything other than bags of bones," Faye added. "Either it's been robbed away, was never here or simply we're looking in the wrong place."

"I'm sure this is the right place, I was so certain. All the clues have led us here. I'm really frustrated, pissed off and upset." Pauline exclaimed with tears coming.

Faye put her arms around her partner to console her.

"I'm alright Faye. We had better pack all our rubbish away and get out of here." As she said it she dropped her rucksack onto the alter to put the rubbish in.

"Did you hear that Faye?" she said. "The altar made a strange noise when I dropped my bag on it. Get the other end and we'll see if we can look inside, it looks as if the top lifts off."

With a bit of a struggle they managed to lift the top off.

"Bloody hell, Pauline you were right! Just take a look at all those gems. Can I have one? Just one as a souvenir. Please."

"Just one small one. I'm sure amongst this lot one missing won't be noticed." Pauline opened her rucksack and took out her camera and proceeded to take photographs of the jewels from every possible angle.

"Can we try and get the lid back on now. We don't want anyone coming in here and nicking it all."

Getting it back was far more difficult than taking it off. It was heavy and a very tight fit so it was all about getting it lined up perfectly before setting it down. There were only a few glow sticks left as they made their way back up the passage to the next cavern.

"You know Faye this is truly unbelievable to think that once upon a time these tunnels and caves were carved out of solid rock by molten lava. Hot enough to cut through the rock like a hot knife through butter." "Do you know how far they reach?" Faye asked.

"Many miles I believe. Some people say that they run all the way into the high lands of Afghanistan."

Rob was stood at the window rubbing his eyes, sore from hours of staring at the tiny images on the laptop screen.

"Oh shit. It can't be him! Sue come over here and tell me that is not Mikhail Gorkov!"

"I'm pretty certain it is him and that looks like Ivan Relinski is with him," Sue agreed.

"I agree it is Gorkov. I must ring my office to find out what has happened," said Irina now standing looking over Rob's shoulder. "As she spoke on the phone she paced the room."

"Tony can you hear me?" Sue asked.

"Loud and clear Sue. What's up?" He whispered back.

"We've just spotted Mikhail Gorkov and one of his lieutenants. They are standing still at the moment but look to be heading for the main door."

"If he's coming in through the front door then we're leaving by the North door! Mark, Ned, out through the North door NOW!"

As they turned for the exit Tony saw the light downstairs go out. Was this Logan and Mason coming out. He hung back in the shadows to be certain and waited.

Sure enough it was them, but there was no sign of any treasure. Could this mean they couldn't find it or there isn't any? He had always thought the stories about the jewels were exactly that, stories, added to over time and if by chance they did once exist, they would surely have been robbed away before now.

Chapter 16

"Good morning Sir Bernard, things have moved on a little. Unfortunately we have lost Zoe and Greg. They were both injured in an attack, we assume by the Wolves. Their injuries are not serious and the embassy is arranging to get them home. We are now convinced that Pauline Logan is the Inspector. Peter Logan is in intensive care at the hospital having been poisoned. Doctors say he has only a thirty percent chance of recovery. Pauline Logan is the prime suspect. She and Faye Mason have visited the chapel in Astrakhan and are now in Volgograd. We believe they are very close to discovering the jewels.

Mikhail Gorkov is at large again and has turned up in Volgograd. We're not sure yet if they know that Logan is here or even if they are connected to her activities in any way. We're going forward with the assumption that they are. Captain Bakunin has requested back-up to apprehend Gorkov. They will be here soon."

****

Mikhail and Ivan stood in the street talking for well over twenty mins. While they were talking they were constantly looking around them. Not just at the growing number of people milling around the streets but also up at the buildings too. They weren't hiding the fact that they were looking. In fact at one point Ivan raised his hand to shade his eyes as he looked up a one of the buildings.

The sun was directly behind the hotel Rob and Sue were in and the hotel cast its shadow almost to Gorkov's feet. Rob's attention was caught by a flash of light across his eyes. Looking across the street he saw several open windows and he assumed the flash had come from one of those being opened.

Irina finally finished on the phone. She'd been on it for twenty minutes. At times she had periods of long silence, when she was by her expression, listening hard and at other times her voice was raised as if trying to convince whoever was on the end of the call about something she felt was important. She had ended the call and placed the phone back in her uniform jacket pocket and pulled on the side tabs of her body armour vest to tighten it before she spoke.

"My commander is sending officers from the local force to support me in arresting Gorkov and getting him back to Moscow. This means I will be leaving you when they arrive. My commander will request that one of the local officers replaces me to support your mission."

"You'd better bring Tony up to speed. Do it now over the comms rather than waiting until he gets back here," Sue suggested. "How long before your support arrives and where are you meeting them."

"I've said they are to approach through the streets behind the hotel and I'll meet them at the back door in thirty minutes. I need to plan how to approach Gorkov without making him run."

"To be honest, you are probably best off getting him to run but have your team behind him to trap him."

"That's a very good idea Sue, thank you. I'll call Tony now and explain what is happening."

Mikhail and Ivan eventually moved towards the cathedral main door but did not enter instead they sat on a bench outside.

"They're definitely waiting for someone," Rob said.

Sue went back to her laptop and moved the angle of the cameras to try and establish what was happening inside the cathedral. She eventually saw Logan and Mason standing by the altar. Three men were marching down the central aisle towards them and there was a look of alarm on the women's faces. As the men got closer to the altar Sue could see the men talking to the women. The women started to walk down the aisle towards the main door and the three men fell in behind them. Sue told Rob what she saw. "The two women are being escorted out of the front door by three men."

From where he was stood at the window Rob saw the cathedral main door being pulled open from inside. "I see them coming out now. They are outside now and going over to Gorkov who is talking to them and waving his arms around."

Irina had slipped out of the hotel room un-noticed and made her way down to the back door to meet her back-up team. When she got there she found six armed officers already waiting for her. She quickly outlined her plan. She sent four of them off to circle around to the streets behind the cathedral. They were to be the net into which she would drive the prey. She gave them five minutes to get into position.

"Hello Pauline, Faye. You are both looking well. Russian air must suit you both," Mikhail said. "Ivan told me you would be here this morning."

"Good morning, Mikhail." Pauline responded. "How are you? You look a little tired. Didn't you sleep well in prison?"

"I slept well enough, thank you but it has been a hard week. What about you ladies? Have you had a good week? Have you found the jewels?"

"Yes. Only a few minutes ago we were taking pictures of them."

Mikhail gave a signal to one of the three men who tore Pauline's rucksack from her shoulders and passed it to him. He opened it and pulled the camera out. Looked closely at it and turned on the viewer. He quickly browsed the thirty or so pictures. Then returned the camera to the bag and handed it back to Pauline.

"Very impressive!" he said. "Well done. I was never convinced that they existed. But you've proved me wrong. What is your plan now?"

"We drive south as far as Baku. There we will show the pictures to your leaders and tell them exactly where they are and how to get to them. He will pay us and we will continue south into Turkey."

"Ah yes, one our leaders. Mr Romanov is a very good friend of mine. The distant grandson of Tzar Nicolas and whom himself will soon be crowned Tzar Nicolas III of all Russia, now that we can finance the revolution. You say you are driving to Baku. That is more than a days' drive, the roads are not good. You will be driving across the vast salt flats of Southern Russia. All too easy to get sun blindness and get lost. You have a strong vehicle and have arranged sleeping quarters for the trip? I expect you will have to sleep two nights on the journey and food, have you got food and plenty of water?"

"We have a Land Cruiser and camping equipment, we'll be sleeping at the road side and we have more than enough food and water."

"That is very good. A Land Cruiser! Good choice. Very suitable! I will come with you. If you have any problems, a puncture or a breakdown perhaps, you will need help."

His attention was snatched away as a figure step out of the shadows the other side of the square and start walking towards him. Now fully out in daylight he could clearly see it was a female police officer in high ranking uniform. She stopped twenty yards away from him. He noticed she had an officer ten yards either side and slightly behind her.

Rob, again stood at the window, watched Irina emerge from the shadows beneath him and start to cross the square. She stopped a few yards short of Gorkov. Rob once again caught a flash of light from the building across the square. He looked across to check it out and could see a wide open window with someone pointing a rifle down into the square.

"Christ, she's walking into a trap!" he shouted and started banging on the window. "Irina! Irina, it's a trap get out!"

Sue rushed to his side to see what was happening.

Irina took her gun from its holster and levelled it at Gorkov and said. "Mikhail Gorkov I'm taking you in. Come quietly with me now and no one will get hurt. I don't want to shoot you, but I will if I have to."

Mikhail rose from the bench he had been sitting on just as a rifle shot was heard. A red star appeared on Irina's forehead. With her eyes wide open she sank to her knees and then fell forward on to her face. It was clear to everyone she was dead, there was a hole the size of a fist in the back of her head, where the bullet had ripped through throwing blood, bone and brain matter across the square.

Both Sue and Rob turned away in horror. The two officers that had been with Irina dived for what little cover there was. One behind a table and chairs the other behind the waste bins. Everywhere people were screaming and running in all directions. When Sue looked back Gorkov and everybody with him had gone. In all the confusion caused by the gunshot, they had made their escape.

"What the hell is going on out there?" Tony said as he burst into the room followed by Mark and Ned.

"Irina has been shot!" Sue explained.

"Is she badly hurt?"

"She's dead! Shot in the head by a sniper," Sue added.

"And Gorkov, where is he now? Did Logan and Mason meet up with him?"

"Logan and Morgan were with him, they looked like they may have been arguing about something then a camera was pulled out of Logan's rucksack and Gorkov appeared to look at some pictures on it then gave it back. In the confusion of the gun shot they all slipped away. They may have gone into the cathedral we just don't know. The cameras don't give full coverage they could easily be in there and we just can't see them. We just don't know."

"We have to know! Ned you're not known to them. Get into the cathedral and check it out. Carry a broom or something so you look like a cleaner. Get in look around and get back here quickly. Rob get back on the monitors watch for any indicator that they are there."

Tony walked across the room to the window and looked down on Irina's body. One of her back-up team had found an old coat and was covering the top half of her body with it.

"She told me this morning that she was uneasy about today. She felt something bad was going to happen. Have you got the surveillance tracker on your phone! Sue? The only one the embassy could let us have only has an effective range of around fifteen miles. If they're on the move then we'll have to get after them pretty smartish."

"I've got it on my laptop, I'll Bluetooth it across to my phone. It'll take fifteen to twenty minutes. I'll get onto it straight away but we'll lose the camera monitors for a few minutes."

"If that's the case get on as quickly as you can. Ned's eyes will have to do until you get the monitors back."

Rob went back to the window and relived the shooting. Then to nobody in particular he said. "They knew we were here! Gorkov was out there as bait to draw us out. Irina wasn't the target she just happened to be the one out there at the wrong time. Gorkov just wanted a distraction so that he could get Logan and

Mason away without us following them. It worked didn't it? And Irina is dead."

"You knew these were not nice people Rob," Sue replied. "You want them to answer for their crimes. You want to save your family from harm. You want justice. You volunteered because of this, knowing the risk we're all taking. Irina's death, Zoe and Glen's injuries are all unfortunate. It means we have to be even sharper and watch out for one another. We will win Rob, we have to. If we don't believe that then we may as well go home now."

"You're right Sue. Thanks."

"The app is loaded and it's showing that the car is on the move heading south on the E119."

"OK!" Tony said as he thought about what action they needed to take. "Let's not rush things here. Let's think about things for a minute or two. The Wolves have obviously been watching Logan and Mason and were at Astrakhan when the women were in the chapel. They will have seen Zoe and Glen which is why they tried to take them out with that crude nail bomb. They will also have seen me and you three arrive in the car. Then they will have seen you two leave on the bikes and Ned and me in the car. If they were really good they will have seen me plant the tracker on the women's Land Cruiser. What they probably won't know is about Irina and Mark with the second vehicle. If that's the case they may think that Irina was part of the local force and not connected to us at all. So the car starting to move off might just be the Wolves trying to distract us and split our forces by getting us to follow them. But I'm going to gamble that they're not aware that there is a tracker on the Land Cruiser and it's the two women in the car. Gorkov may or may not be with them. That camera intrigues me I don't think it was holiday snaps. And why, if they found the jewels, didn't they stuff as much into their rucksacks as they could carry?"

"I'm surprised you haven't worked it out by now Tony." Rob said. "They obviously found the jewels, photographed them and are now doing a deal to sell information on how to find them. Maybe they are selling to Gorkov."

"You could well be right, Rob. It would fit what we've seen. But if that is the case they are taking an awful risk as soon as they give over the information. What's to stop whoever it is killing them rather than paying?"

"They must have some kind of hold over this unknown. Perhaps some incriminating information that would be made public if anything happens to them," Sue surmised.

"Whichever way this is going we have to stop it. We can't let those jewels get into the hands of anyone other than the Russian government. It would have been nice to find them ourselves and hand them over, but if they were down in those tunnels somewhere we could search for years and not get a sniff. Not only do we not know where they are but we don't know what we would be looking for. I mean, are they in some sort of crate or a bag or something? I wouldn't think they are just lying in a heap on the floor. No, our only course of action is to get the information we need from those two women and pass it on to the Russian government so that they can retrieve the treasure. Our reward will be taking the Inspector back to England to face multiple charges. But first we need to get hold of those two women. I'll be needed here to sort out Irina's body with the local forces, bound to be masses of paperwork. Ned as a member of the embassy staff you had better stay as well. So, Mark take Rob as your driver and Sue with her tracker and get after them as quickly as you can. We've wasted enough time, they'll be out of the range of the tracker soon. I just don't understand why they are going south. Surely their buyer would not be anywhere too remote I would have expected them to go north."

"You don't think they might be heading for Afghanistan do you Tony?" asked Rob.

"I hope not," Sue said. "If the Taliban get hold of that sort of money, I hate to think what sort of weapons they might buy. That war has gone on for long enough without more fuel being thrown on the fire. We can't let that happen, we've lost too many of our boys over there already." Tears ran into her eyes as she remembered her own husband being blown up by a Taliban IED and only being able to take half his body back home because that's all that could be found of him. Rob moved in close to comfort her.

"I'm alright thanks, Rob," she said, shaking his arm off her shoulders. "I'm OK. Really!"

"If we can't get hold of the women then I've been authorised by Sir Bernard to eliminate them rather than let the wrong people get rich. So the Taliban won't get them if we do our job properly. Now you three go. Keep me informed of your progress." Tony waved a hand towards the door.

Rob grabbed the keys off the table as he left the room.

They walked briskly out of the hotel and to the car park but when Rob came to open the car he couldn't.

"Sod it! I'll have to go back, I've got the wrong set of keys. These are for Irina's vehicle." He said.

"So we'll take Irina's vehicle instead," Mark replied. "It's probably better suited for these roads anyway. Besides that way we're pretty certain that the Wolves have not identified it as one of our vehicles, so that could be to our advantage as well."

Sue interrupted them. "Hey guys we've just lost the tracker signal."

Mark responded, "Well we know which road they were on and that for at least the first 50 miles there are no side road off it and it's not the sort of countryside to go far off road. So let's get in and get after them quickly. We need to get back in range before we lose them totally. For the next ten minutes at least we're going to be on city roads and they will be out on the open road getting even further ahead of us."

Although Rob tried to get out of the city quickly, he was hampered by pedestrian spilling from the crowded pavements and stepping out into his path. Twice had to brake hard it avoid hitting someone. For several minutes he wasn't able to get the car beyond second gear. When they did break through and out onto clear roads, he ignored the speed limit and put his foot down as much as the road conditions would allow him to.

Mark and Ned packed the equipment into a couple of rucksacks, cleared the room of rubbish and went out into the square to where Irina's body lay.

Standing around the body were four members of the back-up team standing with their backs to the body, their hands clasped in front of them and their heads hung low. The other two were on the far side of the square dragging a man, assumedly one of the wolves, across the square towards them. One of the officers was carrying a snipper's rifle. The captive had his hands secured behind his back and his face looked bruised. Tony thought to himself, 'That poor bugger can forget his human rights. He's going to carry the can for killing Irina, whether he did it or not.'

With Ned as his interpreter Tony move towards Irina's body. One of the officers standing guard bore the stripes of sergeant on his sleeves. Presuming that he was in charge of the unit Tony walked up to him, but was challenged before he got too close. With Ned's help Tony was able to introduce himself as the leader of a task force and that Irina had been assigned to assist them. When Gorkov appeared, she had to step back from supporting the task force in order to apprehend the escaped prisoner. The officer said he was full aware of the Captain's assignment which had brought her to Volgograd and thanked Tony for making himself known to them.

Through Ned's interpretation Tony asked, "What will happen to Irina's body?"

The officer replied. "Firstly she will be taken to Volgograd's mortuary to await transportation back to Moscow. A military aircraft will carry her there probably tomorrow. Then in a few days she will be given a hero's funeral. She showed no fear in coming out here, leading from the front. Such a shame for her to die like this. She was a role model to all female officers in the force and had quite a reputation earned over several years of exceptional service. She will be greatly missed."

"I only met her a few days ago but struck me as being exceptionally good at what she did and must have been well regarded by her superiors, because anything she asked for they gave to her."

"Yes, she was certainly heading for a long and very successful future in the service."

"Do you need anything from me sergeant? I'd rather like to follow the rest of my team on the road heading south."

"No, you may go. I have five reliable witnesses in my fellow officers here, we won't need anything further."

They shook hands and Tony and Ned turned and walked away, heading for the car park.

On reaching the car park they located the embassy car and wasted no time getting out on the south road but soon became aware that the vehicle was not suited to these roads and their progress was quite slow.

"I don't know how Rob was able to drive this car on this road in the dark.

It's as much as I can do to do it in daylight," Tony said.

"There are roads far worse than this further south," Ned replied.

"Thanks for that. Let's hope we don't have to go that far."

Chapter 17

"Aleksei my friend I give you an update on progress in obtaining the jewels. The two English women have proven that their theories about the location were correct. They have shown me pictures of the jewels and I am happy they are genuine pictures. They show the treasure to be far more than we expected. We got away from Volgograd without being followed and are now nearly a hundred kilometres south of there. We should be with you in Baku by Wednesday or perhaps early Thursday."

****

Thirty miles south of Volgograd Sue finally picked up a signal on the tracker. It showed the other car to be approximately twelve miles ahead.

"We caught them just in time," Sue said. "They've just turned off this road and are now on the R221. It's a turning on the right in about nine miles."

"We should stay back a good distance so that they don't see us following them. Just close the gap to about a mile Rob, then hold back," Mark instructed.

Rob kept the speed up as much as he could and they continued to close the gap rapidly. "I think I'd better ease off a little now. We're creating a cloud of dust that can be seen for miles. We don't want them seeing it thinking that someone is after them at speed."

"You're right Rob. If we can match their speed and are still producing so much dust they'll reckon we're just another road user, probably a lorry as that seems to be the only type of vehicle using this road this afternoon."

Mark contacted Tony to update him and was told that he and Ned were in the car just leaving Volgograd suburbs. Mark told him that they had got a firm signal on the Land Cruise and were only a few minutes behind. He also told him about the junction they were coming up to. After the call he repeated what Tony had told him about what would be done with Irina's body and they were to proceed with extreme caution.

"They've stopped. It looks like they're on the edge of the town of Tsatsa. We're about six miles behind them," Sue announced.

"They probably need fuel. We're getting low and could do with a drop soon," Rob said.

"We can't risk getting too close yet, guys. If Gorkov is with them he'll recognise Rob and me from earlier in the week, when we were involved in his arrest."

"Yes, but this is an excellent opportunity to find out who exactly is in that car," Mark replied.

Rob jumped in with the solution. "Mark, you're not known by any of them and they don't know this vehicle, so if Sue and I get out a short distance before the fuel station and you drive in and get our tank filled. You should get there before they drive off and be able to see exactly who we are following. Sue and I will make sure we're not spotted. Then, once they have moved on, we'll come and re-join you."

"That sounds good to me. Let's do it."

So as they approached the fuel station Sue confirmed they were still there, so she and Rob got out and Mark climbed into the driving seat and drove up to the fuel pumps. As he climbed out and turned to close the door. He saw one of the women climb into the front passenger seat of the Land Cruiser. The other woman was behind the wheel and in the back seat leaning forward was the shape of a third larger than average person. They were gone down the road before Mark had started the fuel pump. Sue and Rob crossed the forecourt and took their places in the vehicle while Mark finished the re-fuelling and went over to the kiosk and paid. He returned to the vehicle and told them what he had seen.

"I didn't get a look at the man's face, so can't be a hundred percent certain but it was most likely Gorkov in the back. The two women were in front. Logan was driving. I picked up some bread, cheese and local sausage while I was in there. There's a half dozen bottles of water in there too," he said as he handed a weighty carrier bag across the seat.

Rob took over the diving again while Mark talked to Tony to confirm Gorkov and the two women were in the car.

Tony ended the call to Mark and turned to Ned who was driving. "Mark has confirmed that Gorkov is in the Land Cruiser. Stop the car and I'll take over driving again. I'd like you to contact Richard White at the embassy. Bring him up to date with everything, especially Irina's murder. Ask him to get onto the Russian police and kick their arses into action. He's to tell them Gorkov is undoubtedly responsible for Irina's death, even if he didn't pull the trigger himself. Tell them also that we are tracking them travelling south and give them my number so I can update them directly."

They swapped drivers and Ned made the call. "Richard said he's already heard from the Russian police. He said the Russians are blaming you for allowing Irina to get killed."

"Tell him what really did happen. Tell him if we don't get help down here pretty soon, Gorkov will get away and the Wolves will get very rich because the jewels do exist. Pauline Logan has photographed them and is about to sell information to the Wolves."

"He said he'll get on to it right away but because it's gone 5:00 it may take a little longer."

"Christ, is it really gone five? Another couple of hours and it will be getting dark and there's no way I'd want to be driving these roads in the dark. Plus we haven't eaten anything since those pastries Irina scavenged for us at breakfast and we need more water. Check the map will you please, Ned, it looks like they're heading for Elista next. Two hours should get us as far as Elista. We can pick something up there and maybe find somewhere to spend tonight."

"We're just a little under five miles behind them," Sue said as the passed the first building of Elista. "I don't think they stopped at all. They've just turned left onto the R216 heading for Yashkul. The junction is just at the south side of the town."

"How far is it to Yashkul?" Rob asked.

"About 90 minutes at this speed. It will be beginning to get dark soon after that. At Yashkul they will most probably turn south again towards the Metletinsky National Park then on to Artezian where they could pick up the E119, which goes all the way down the coast of the Caspian Sea into Iran. It all depends on where they are trying to get to."

"I was just thinking that if they are trying to get out of the country then Georgia or Azerbaijan borders are by far the closest but a good day's drive away. So they'll need a place to spend the night. By the time we get to Yashkul light will be starting to fade so they may stop there for tonight," Rob suggested. "Adyk is only another thirty minutes further on. They could try to reach there," Sue suggested.

"Yes, either of those is possible." Rob concluded.

"Or neither," Mark interrupted. "Three of them in the car they could keep changing driver and go through the night. It would be slow going on these roads but they could still make two hundred to two hundred and fifty miles." "I'll keep a careful watch on the tracker," Sue concluded.

They kept up a steady speed along a mainly primarily straight road maintaining a five to six mile gap between them and the other vehicle. They travelled in silence apart from the road noise for more than forty five minutes.

Rob broke the silence. "Have you two noticed how few vehicles there are on this road? Apart from us they all seen to be heavy trucks. I've passed an empty wagon on this side of the road about every five miles for the past half hour. The same numbers are going by on the other side, but they are fully loaded."

"It's salt being moved from the great salt works north to be loaded on a train. They'll probably be running all night. Salt is a major export from this part of the world. And are you surprised there are no cars. Look around there is absolutely nothing here. You'll be hard pressed to see a tree let alone a house. The salt content in the soil prevent almost everything from growing. There is just the odd salt works building."

"You're certainly not going to annoy the neighbours by playing loud music.

That's for sure."

"Did anyone catch what that road sign said?" Rob asked.

"It said Yashkul thirty kilometres Rob," Sue replied.

"In that case Mark, I'm going to ask you to take over the driving so that I can relax a little, just in case you're right and we have to drive through the night."

Mark wasn't as good behind the wheel as Rob and although he kept pace with the Land Cruiser he would have struggled to close the gap quickly. The relentless heat of the day was beginning to fade as the sun slowly dropped towards the horizon. It was sliding away so quickly now that Mark was finding that in the failing light he must slow down to stay safe. They were still five miles behind the Land Cruiser, which must by now be entering Yashkul.

"They're not stopping here guys," Sue announced. "They are almost through the town now and have just turned right on to the road heading towards Adyk. We're beginning to get into the dead country now, where the salt is so concentrated that nothing will grow. The few towns that we're seeing are in small pockets of ground slightly higher than the rest and not so salty and small communities can survive. As we go further south the concentrated salt is so strong that it can burn human flesh if in contact for any length of time."

"Thanks Sue," Mark said. "I assume that the glow we're seeing ahead is the lights of Yashkul."

"You're a real fountain of knowledge this afternoon Sue," Rob said. "You should write a tourist guide."

Pauline was still driving but was now beginning to struggle because of the failing light. "I think we should stop soon. It's getting a bit too dark to drive on these roads. We could hit one of those pot holes and damage a wheel," she said.

"You won't be able to use your tent anywhere along here," Mikhail said. "All around this area the ground is highly toxic. There is so much raw salt in the soil that it will burn your flesh within minutes. It would melt your groundsheet if you were to put your tent up. If you are tired, I suggest we get off the road where we can and we'll rest up for a couple of hours, get whatever sleep we can. Then we'll wait for one of the empty salt lorries to come along. They run all night returning to the large salt factories down south. They only travel at about forty kph at night. If we pull out behind it we can follow in its tracks and reduce the risk of hitting a pot hole. We should be able to get two hundred kilometres further on. We can share the driving. Do you drive Faye?"

"I'm afraid not," Faye answered.

"So it's down to the two of us then, Pauline. Perhaps we try half hour spells. We can stop regularly there will always be lorries we can slot in behind."

"OK, I'll look out for somewhere to stop. I just hope it's not too long before we find a suitable place," Pauline said.

"This is the junction we need, Mark," Sue said "We'll be out of the town in a minute or two. The Land Cruiser is now approximately ten miles ahead and appears to have stopped."

"Right! Are they at a hotel or something?" Mark asked.

"I don't think so. It looks like open country."

"It will be very cosy, three of them in that Land Cruiser trying to sleep if that is in fact why they have stopped," Mark surmised.

Rob suggested, "It's only half past eight. That's a bit early to be settling down for the night."

Mark responded, "You might be happy driving in the dark on these roads but I know I'm not and I'm guessing they are the same. I expect they'll have something to eat, get whatever sleep they can and be ready to move on at first light around five thirty tomorrow. We should plan to do the same."

"Three of us in just these three seats are going to be even cosier. At least they've got five seats," Sue commented.

"I've got a solution for that problem," Rob answered. "If we pull off the road in one of these tarmacked lay-by type pull-ins. We can offload the bikes from the back, they will be safe providing we can stand them on tarmac. Mark and I can then sleep in the back and you can have the cab to yourself."

"But the temperature drops to freezing out here at night," Sue replied.

"There's a whole pile of blankets under that tarpaulin and we can throw the tarpaulin over the whole thing."

"I'm happy with that. I can keep going for a few more miles. We'll close the gap a little, five or six miles should do. Then we'll stop at the first pull-in we find."

Tony and Ned were struggling. They were twenty five miles behind and only travelling at about thirty five mph. When they closed on one of the returning salt lorries with three or four other vehicles behind it, no one was prepared to pass the lorry. Tony decided to contact Mark to see what was happening, now that darkness was on them.

"Mark, how are you doing?" Mark told Tony that they would soon be stopping and that their prey was about 5 miles ahead. He also gave him enough detail as he thought necessary for him to be able to find them.

When they eventually they reached the junction in Yashkul the vehicles between them and the lorry all went straight on, only the lorry and Tony turned right. As they moved away from the junction Tony took advantage of the better quality town roads and the slow acceleration of the lorry and put his foot down to pass the lorry. Soon after leaving the last of the town buildings behind them, the road deteriorated again. The last twelve miles to the lay-by where Mark had pulled in took thirty minutes.

The parking area was only twenty metres long and only just off the carriageway, so both vehicles shook every time a lorry passed them. Mark got out and walked back to the other vehicle to talk to Tony. After several minutes Mark came back and said, "They haven't got any food or water so bring that bag and we'll all sit in the car and share our stuff with them."

The only light now came from the few stars that were visible between the drifting cloud and the headlights of the passing lorries traveling in both directions. During their meal they went through the events of the day, spending a long time on what had happened to Irina, concluding that there was nothing they could have done to prevent her being killed. It was all very unfortunate but no one could have predicted it.

Sue was again reunited with her laptop and fired up the tracker app. Once loaded she located the Land Cruiser and confirmed it hadn't moved. Rob and Mark lifted the bikes down from the back of the Russian vehicle and stood them beside it away from the passing lorries.

"It will start getting light soon after five tomorrow morning," Tony said. "So we need to be awake and ready to move by then."

He was interrupted by his phone ringing. He answered it and the others could only hear one side of the conversation, but it was clear that the caller was a Russian official, hopefully telling Tony that support was on the way. When Tony ended the call he briefed the team on what he'd been told.

"The Russians are sending a military police task force of two helicopters and twenty crack officers. They will leave their base near Moscow at first light tomorrow morning. They should be with us by 8:00. They want us to continue tracking them until the task force arrives. They will land in front of the fugitives and create a roadblock. They intend capturing all three and taking them straight back to Moscow. Gorkov will be taken to a high security facility to await trial.

The women will be handed over to the police for interrogation about the jewels."

"So we won't be involved in catching them?" Rob said. "And are they flying us back to Moscow?"

"They didn't say, but I'm expecting we'll have to make our own way. Anyway that's tomorrow. We need to get some sleep now and be bright for a 5:00 start in the morning." He checked his watch. "It's coming up to 10:00, so let's get sorted."

"It was early evening in Yorkshire. JB was out with Jake and Phil working in the stables, getting things ready for a busy few days with the Doncaster three day festival starting on Thursday. Four horses were racing on the first day. They had been checked over by the vet earlier in the day and all given the OK to race. The horse boxes had all been cleaned and fresh straw spread on the floors. The boys were just going through the checklist for a fourth time."

Luci was down in the village with her girl-friends planning for their last camping trip of the summer holidays starting tomorrow. Eric had insisted on taking her down to the village and had arranged to pick her up at 10:00. Since getting home he and Rose had been sitting together at the kitchen table with a cup of tea.

"That girl has suddenly grown up," he said. "She is no longer a girl. She has become a woman and isn't she like her mother?"

"Yes. It will take a very strong man to get the better of her," Rose replied. "She's determined and intelligent, what she's been through in the last few days has, in some strange way, built her character. She has tremendous self-belief. She's going to really make something of herself and she seems to be carrying her friends along with her. She and I had a long chat this morning while you were dealing with the horses. Those two girls that took her in, have been a great influence. They've taught her how to discover her-self and to believe she can do whatever she has a mind to do and how to succeed. They may be in the sex business but they are both something special and I know they will stay in touch with Luci. You know they've already spoken to all Luci's friends. They all had a conference call yesterday morning, Luci is trying to get them to join them camping tomorrow."

"What do you mean? They are in the sex business. Are they strippers?"

"Worse than that dear! But they are not prostitutes! Luci has talked to me in some detail about what they do and how they are trying to make a better life. Thankfully, Robert has given them a way out. He certainly sees some good in them."

"Are you telling me, not only will I be camping with four teenage girls, there will also be two sex workers there as well. If this gets out I won't be able to show my face down the Dog And Gun ever again!"

"Don't be silly Eric. From what Luci has told me Ana and Eva sound like really nice girls. They wouldn't be in the sex business if they had a choice but she says they owe an awful lot of money to the people that brought them into the country and arranged their papers."

"Well, I still want it on record that I'm not happy about this trip tomorrow."

"Oh stop whinging you silly old fool. Take some books with you and relax, no one's going to think you're a pervert or even a dirty old man."

Gorkov allowed Pauline and Faye almost four hours sleep. It had been a struggle for them to get to sleep, what with thinking about events of the last couple of days, the rumbling road noise and the shaking of the vehicle every time a lorry went by. Worst of all no bathroom facilities, squatting by the car did not appeal to either Pauline or Faye, but there was simply no alternative. It was just after midnight. He woke Pauline who was to be taking the first spell of driving.

"Are you going to be awake enough to drive?" he asked.

"Just give me a minute to wake properly and I'll be fine," she replied. "Christ! I don't think I've ever been anywhere this dark, there's no light coming from anywhere. The cloud cover was now complete no star and moon light was not getting through. Then as a lorry passed they were momentarily bathed in light. She turned to Faye in the passenger seat and gently shook her shoulder and then lent over and kissed her on the lips."

"Good morning sleepy head. It's time for us to get moving. Do you need a pee before we set off?"

"No thanks, I'm fine. What time is it?"

"It's a little after midnight!" came a voice from the back seat. "Now watch your mirror for the next lorry and be prepared to move off as soon as it passes. You need to be about thirty yards behind it and try to keep your wheels in the same line as the truck."

Sure enough a lorry appeared within five minutes. As soon as she saw its headlights in her mirror, Pauline started the engine. Then just as the lorry passed them she lifted the clutch. Quickly moving through the gears she soon got to approximately thirty yards behind the lorry. This was much easier than she had found driving earlier. All she had to do was follow the lorry and let the lorry driver worry about looking into the distance and watching for and avoiding potholes.

Mikhail's phone rang. He answered it quickly and there was a short conversation in Russian. As soon as he had ended the call, he lent over from the back seat and said. "It seems we are being followed. One of the lorry drivers has radioed in to say there are two vehicles parked up about five kilometres before the point we've just left. One of the vehicles matches the description of the car the English agents were seen in yesterday. They must have put a tracker on this car otherwise they would need to be a lot closer. We're heading into barren county now, but by the time it gets light we'll be in some really wild terrain.

That's where my people will set up an ambush and take them out."

"You say English agents. Do you know who they are?" Pauline asked.

"MI-6," he replied. "For now we keep moving. You're doing well. I'll take over in thirty minutes."

Something disturbed Sue enough to wake her. Outside was totally black and she could see nothing. She felt around in the foot well for her phone to check the time. It was still running the tracker app and she could see the Land Cruiser was on the move and was close on fifteen miles ahead of them. She rubbed her eyes to clear her sleepy vision and checked again. Sure enough it was fifteen minutes passed midnight and they were now sixteen miles ahead. Quickly she climbed out of the vehicle and using the light on her phone moved to the back and banged loudly on the side panel to wake Rob and Mark. She then moved to the other car and banged on the side windows to wake Tony and Ned. Tony opened the window and before he could say a word, Sue spoke out loud enough for everyone to hear. Mark and Rob had thrown off the tarpaulin and were sitting up to hear her. "They're on the move again we've almost at the point of being out of range of the tracker."

"Shit!" Tony responded as he pulled himself out from the backseat of the car and pulled on his jacket as protection against the cold. "We must not let them get away. Ned you and I will get after them on the bikes and Rob it's time for you to show us just how good a rally driver you are, with Sue and Mark take the SUV and get after us at best speed. We'll leave the car. It's not suited to these roads. Let's go guys!"

Tony and Ned were on the bikes and away instantly. Rob and Mark shut up the back of the SUV and climbed into the cab, one either side of Sue. Within seconds they too were away. Rob moved off smoothly and fast, the headlights shining forward but failing to pick out the bikes, they were travelling at a much faster speed. As he became more familiar with the light Rob was able to increase the speed. He was comfortable at sixty to sixty five kph his experience as a former rally driver and his incredible speed of reaction kept them away from the worst potholes, giving them a fairly smooth ride.

Sue's app on her phone still wasn't picking up the car they were chasing but her map showed there were no roads leaving this one for the next thirty five miles and with Rob driving like this they would surely be in range soon.

Tony and Ned kept to the centre of the carriageway where the surface was smooth and not broken up by the continuous pounding of the salt lorries. After about fifteen minutes they could see a set of car tail lights ahead of them. They were completely different from the tail lights on the lorries, so they were confident they had found the land cruiser. Tony reported it back to Mark and eased up a little so that they didn't close the gap too much and cause their prey to take some sort of evasive action.

With Rob doing the speed he was, it wasn't long before Sue was saying the tracker was back in range and they were closing rapidly. They passed empty salt lorries every few miles and after about forty five minutes they could see the lights of the bikes ahead of them. Rob was really enjoying this challenge, he hadn't felt the adrenalin rush that driving on the edge like this gave him for too many years. He was sorry that he would have to slow up once they caught up with the bikes. Forty kph was far less of a rush for Rob and they no longer caught lorries as they all seemed to be travelling at forty kph as well.

Mikhail was now driving and was quick to spot the headlights of a vehicle that didn't look like a lorry in the mirror. He watched them carefully until he was certain that they weren't closing the gap on him. He just had to maintain this speed and let the miles slide by. In another two and a half hours it would begin to get light and in three hours they would be close to where his men would spring the ambush. But why were these English agents holding back and not trying to catch and stop them. Then he spotted more lights. Now there were four headlights together. Probably two vehicles, ten agents at most. His men at the ambush would be at least twice that number.

Chapter 18

"He'll be fine Sue, you'll see. Just look at him go, he's really at one with that bike. He'll ride the big Russian into the ground without breaking a sweet. Before you know it he'll come riding back down the road demanding another kiss."

****

The two bikes in line with the Russian SUV tucked in behind stayed a mile or so behind the Land Cruiser and the miles ticked by. The lights ahead of them began to lose their brilliance as the sky brightened with the mornings rising son. The unwelcoming terrain they were passing through seemed never ending. They had passed through a few small towns and villages all tucked up and asleep, but they were now entering some really wild countryside. They could easily have been on the surface of the noon. No sign of human life and no vegetation of any kind not a dessert because of a high annual rainfall but the high salt content made it impossible to support any form of life.

Suddenly Rob threw himself hard against the back of his seat. His hands left the steering wheel as he raised them to his chest and the SUV left the road, one of the front wheels hit a rock causing the vehicle to flip over onto the passenger door and slide to a halt. At almost the same instant Ned flew backwards off his bike, the bike continuing on for some distance before toppling over. Realising something was seriously wrong Tony threw his bike on its side throwing his body well away from the machine. He had only been travelling at 40kph so did himself very little damage apart from skinning his elbows and ripping open the leg of his trousers. His bullet proof vest had the fabric ripped off it across his shoulder blades. He had slid across the road and was only a few feet short of a rocky outcrop that he quickly crawled towards as he heard two bullets hit the ground just inches away from him.

Safe for the moment at least Tony looked around. His bike was 10 yards away in the centre of the road. He could see his phone lying next to it having fallen from the ripped pocket of his trousers. He checked his other hip, his gun was still there. He drew it out and cautiously peered round the rocky outcrop gun in hand but quickly drew back when he heard another gun shot.

Looking across the road he could see the other bike at least 50 yards ahead. Ned had been only a few feet ahead of him but he was now not in sight. Tony assumed he was the other side of the road. He didn't know whether Ned was hurt or not. He called out to him but there was no reply.

Looking back at the SVU he could see the three occupants hanging in their seat belts. Sue and Mark were struggling to free themselves but Rob hung there motion less. He watched Sue climb out of her seat and stand with Mark on the passenger door and reach up towards Rob still hanging motionless. Then he noticed the bullet hole in the windscreen in front of where Rob had been sat.

"Rob, are you hurt. Rob! Rob!" Sue called out. "Mark, help me get him out."

Between them they managed to free him from his seat belt, they had to move his hands from his chest to get the belt off and Sue could clearly see a bullet hole in his shirt in line with his heart. "There's no blood!" Sue said in a surprised tone.

"There bloody well should be. It bloody well hurts like hell." Came Rob's first words as he came to and opened his eyes.

"Oh Rob. You're OK. I thought you were dead." Sue said and she hugged him the reached up and kissed him.

Mark kicked out the windshield and they climbed out. The SUV had turned so they were not facing their attackers and they were able to slide around the wreckage and put the vehicle between them and the gunmen.

"I'm OK but I don't think this will work again." Rob said pulling his buckled phone from his breast pocket and holding it up for inspection.

The flattened bullet had pushed the battery through the phone casing.

"That bullet must have been slowed down as it went through the toughened windscreen or it would have pushed that battery into your chest. Even so it would have still killed you if not for your phone. You were extremely lucky." Sue hugged him again.

We will be Tony could feel the chemicals starting to burn his skin and he had no choice other than more soon. He raised himself up into a crouched position. It was only 15 yards to the wrecked SUV but it was totally exposed. Keeping as low as he could he zig zagged back to join the others. Several shots winged by him but he wasn't hit.

"What weapons have we got Mark?" He asked.

"We've each got our hand guns and there's a box of ammo in the cab plus a pump action shotgun and a short automatic rifle with a box of ammo for each. About 150 rounds in total."

"Can you get it all? We'll need to watch those rocks ahead of us closely. I don't think they'll try and flank us, the toxic ground should save us from that. But they may try and rush us. It depends how many of them there are. The task force should arrive in about an hour the trouble is my phone is lying out there on the road so they can't talk to us."

Mark scrambled back out of the cab with shotgun and rifle over his shoulder and three boxes of ammo tucked under his arm. The sun was well up in the sky now and looking back along the road Rob could just make out two empty salt lorries pulled up about a quarter of a mile from where they stood.

"We're not going to be safe here for very long. If they've got anything more powerfully than a hunting rifle they will use it soon against us here and force us out in the open. There is no cover so I think our only option is to surrender. Our only hope is that task force. Mark at the front and Rob at the rear of the SUV were watching for movement in the rocks on either side of the road. Rob had the best view down the road and could see an open backed lorry that he assumed their attackers had arrived in. It was large enough for around 20 men but he could only make out three on the side of the road. Further down the road he could see a salt lorry pulled up on the side of the road not wanting to be involved in and troubles. As he was looking at the lorry he saw the Land Cruiser slowly drive past it coming back towards them and eventually pull in beside the open backed lorry."

"Gorkov has just shown up." He announced to the others. "Come to see the kill." Sue suggested.

From his end of the SVU Mark could only see the right hand edge of the road but he could see Ned lying quite still just of the edge of the Tarmac on the gravel verge.

"Ned looks to be in a bad way. I can't see any movement, he's just lay on his back about 40 or 50 yards down the road. His bike is about the same distance further on."

He lifted his view to the rocks further on and counted eight men each with a rifle in their hands. Not modern weapons but still deadly enough at that sort of range.

"How are you feeling now Rob?" Sue enquirer.

"Rather sore across my chest. I think I may have at least one broken rib. But another kiss would make the pain more bearable." He cheekily replied.

"I think I can manage that." She said and wrapped her arms around Rob's neck and placed her lips on his.

"Gorkov and six of his men are making a move heading this way." Mark said in an urgent tone.

"Hold your fire until you've got a certain target we can't afford to waste our ammo." Tony ordered.

"And here comes the heavies." Rob added. "They're just unloading some sort of rocket launcher off their lorry."

"Keep your eye on that Rob. It will take them a couple of minutes to get it ready to launch." Tony said.

"Quiet everybody, listen." Sue instructed. "Can anyone else hear that? It sounds like helicopters."

"I think you're right." Tony said as he searched the sky where he thought the noise was coming from.

"The opposition have heard it too, four of them have turned back to find cover. Gorkov and two others are still coming, they're about 100 yards off us now."

"Get ready to see them off." Tony ordered.

"It's two military helicopter gunships flying one behind the other." Sue said excitedly. "They've seen us and have turned towards us."

"The rocket launcher is ready." Rob announced. "But we're not there target. They are aiming high. They could be aiming at the helicopters."

Moments later they watched a rocket pass over then heading skywards towards the helicopters which took immediate evasive action. One diving to its left and the other climbing to the right. The rocket passed harmless between the two gunships that were now closing rapidly. The one that had climbed right now turned to the rocky outcrop, hovered then opened fire with heavy machine guns. One or two of the men on the ground tried to shoot back with their rifles but we're cut down by the relentless killing guns. The second helicopter had landed and the troops were spreading out and advancing on the remaining ambushers.

Mikhail was cut off from his main force. He was between the troops on the ground and agents behind the SUV. The two men with him had thrown down their weapons and sat on the road with their hands on their heads. There was no way Mikhail was going to surrender. He rushed the short distance to Ned's bike lying on the road. He picked it up, threw his leg over, started it up and raced away across the salt pans avoiding gunfire from Tony, Mark and one of the troopers.

Rob rushed out from behind the SUV shouting. "Leave him to me he's mine." He picked up Tony's abandoned bike and raced off chasing the big Russian.

Sue shouted after him. "Take care. I'd like you back in one piece." She and Tony rushed to where Ned was lay. He still wasn't moving and Sue feared he was dead. Tony put his fingers on Ned's neck to feel for signs of life. "He's got a strong pulse." He told Sue. "But he's out cold."

Sue checked his chest and found his bulletproof vest had been hit directly over his breast bone. "He was hit in the chest and that must have thrown him backwards off the bike." She told Tony. He responded by saying. "He must have hit his head when he landed, there's a lot of blood here."

"Don't move him until he's been seen by a medic. A head injury can be major and there might be some spinal damage."

"Who is Mr Tony Bates?" Came a voice from behind them in perfect English but with a strong Russian accent.

"Over here." Tony called raising his hand.

"Captain Yuri Kossov of the Police Tactical Support." Said the tall officer. "We appear to have arrived at a good time for you."

"Yes. Thank you."

"Do your people need any help?"

"This man here needs medical help quite urgently."

"We have a medical officer on the other helicopter. I will call for him to come now. He must also look at some of the prisoners but they must wait."

The second helicopter had landed and the medic was called across. He quickly assessed Ned's injuries and said something in Russian that Sue and Tony couldn't understand but when he pulled a neck brace from his bag and carefully put it around Ned's neck they guessed that he said he was worried about possible spine injuries.

"He says this man needs urgent hospital help. There is head trauma and there could be some brain damage. He's going to call for immediate medical evacuation by helicopter." The captain translated.

"How many prisoners have you taken?" Tony enquired.

"9 are dead, 9 others are injured 3 of who are unlikely to survive and the two here are unharmed. We have also found two English ladies in a car. Am I correct in assuming these are the ladies connected to the search for the mythical treasure?"

"Yes two ladies hold the secret to the treasure which is no longer a myth but a fact and they have proof. Your government will want to interrogate them thoroughly to find out what they know. Then the British police want them in connection with several murders. Mikhail Gorkov was travelling with them. He has escaped on a motorcycle heading south west." Tony said.

Sue added. "He's being chased by one of our agents."

"I'll get a helicopter in the air and go after them."

Mikhail was weaving back and forth avoiding large rocks but travelling very quickly. After about 1200 yards he hit a minor road heading to the town of Dagestanskiy on the shore of the Caspian sea approximately twenty miles ahead of him to the east. From there he could head south by boat for the border with Azerbaijan where the Russian troops could not follow. When Rob reached the road he was at least 400 yards behind his prey, but the bikes were identical and Rob being by far the lighter man so would have a slight advantage. They raced along the road Rob closing the gap only slightly. They were climbing all the time and when they reached the crest they looked down on the town of Dagestanskiy with houses cut into the hillside and the road snaking down the steep slope between the houses.

Mikhail followed the road twisted and turned down the hill. But Rob was really at home on a bike. He trained stuntmen to do various tricks and he himself had performed several motor bike stunts in some big box office movies. So instead of following the road he went straight down the hill. He skimmed over the tiled roof of a small cottage cut into the hillside, jumping off the front of the building and landing on a car roof, down onto the bonnet and onto the road. Across the road and between two cottages crashing through the fence at the bottom of the garden of one of the cottages. He was now out on a flat roof still travelling at speed he jumped to a second flat roof and then a third. The jump from the flat roof to the ground jarred his ribs and the pain made him gasp loudly.

He saw the big Russian swing his bike around the next corner just 50 yards ahead of him and gave chase. He was much better on the corners than the heavier man and by the time they reached the bottom of the hill Rob was just 20 yards behind.

Mikhail glanced behind to check how close Rob was and when he turned to look forward again there was no time to avoid what he now saw in front of him. A big Russian built tractor was pulling out of a farm yard. Mikhail had no chance of avoiding it and at speed hit it squarely on the side. Without a helmet on he stood no chance, his head hit the heavy metal of the tractor, he must have died instantly. Seeing what was happening just a fraction of a second ahead of him Rob had just one option he threw all his weight to one side of the bike and turned at the same time. The action took him past the front of the tractor but threw him off the bike. He went straight up and down landing hard on his right side in a heap rather than bounce and slide along the road surface which is what the bike did.

He lay where he landed for several minutes mentally checking him-self over bone by bone and muscle by muscle. Amazed to have survived with just a few bruises he slowly got to his feet. As he did so he was struck by the down draft of a helicopter. There was nowhere near for it to land but several ropes were lowered and six troopers descended. An officer walked towards Rob and the others went to the tractor where the driver was bent double being sick having looked at the mass broken bone, flesh, blood and brain matter that moments before had been a head.

The officer said something in Russian to Rob. Who replied saying "English! No Russian."

The officer then pointed to the body by the tractor and said. "Gorkov?"

Rob nodded and the officer smiled and indicated that Rob should follow him. The officer shouted something across to the other troopers. There was a lengthy response and the officer said something else and three of the trooper walked towards Rob and the officer. They all walked to a patch of level uncultivated land where the helicopter had landed. Rob was flown back to the site of the ambush. As he climbed out of the helicopter holding his arm across his suspected broken ribs

Sue saw him and ran towards him, she threw her arms round his neck and kissed him hard.

When they broke away Sue looked up at him and said. "You stupid bastard. What did you think you were doing chasing off like that; you could have so easily been killed? What would Luci and JB do if you were dead? What would I do?" "How is Ned?" Rob asked, changing the subject quickly.

"Not good. It looks like he hit his head when he came off the bike. He's lost quite a bit of blood and the doc is worried about spinal problems and possible brain damage. They've called for a medical evacuation. It should be hear soon. What about Gorkov where is he? Did he get away or is he under guard somewhere?"

"Neither. He's not going to pimp any more young girls." He replied and told her what had happened leaving out how his ride had ended.

"And the Russians have the women." Sue chipped in.

"So we've achieved all our mission objectives." Rob boasted.

"We have I suppose and surprise-surprise, we're all schedule to go with the medivac team when they pick up Ned. The captain is a very nice man and says that we have been in a road accident and need to be medically assessed as soon as possible. So we'll all be back in Volgograd in a couple of hours. From there we can fly to Moscow and then London.

"So can I ask you one last question?" He said quietly.

"I guess so. I'll give you the answer if I know it."

"Will you marry me?"

"That's an easy one! YES."

Chapter 19

"Aleksey, eto Ivan Relinskiy. YA rabotayu na Mikhaila Gor'kova. S sozhaleniyem soobshchayu vam, chto Mikhail byl ubit agentami anglichan. Mikhail i ya vyrosli v odnoy derevne vmeste. My byli kak brat'ya, yego bol'—moya bol', i ya dolzhen otomstit', kak ya sdelal za yego sestru, kogda on byl vzyat v plen v Londone. Zatem ya vysledil yeye ubiyts. Dvoye, s kotorymi ya imel delo, i yeshche dvoye skoro budut kazneny. No ubiytsa Mikhaila dolzhen stradat' ponemnogu, poka on ne plachet, chtoby ya prekratil yego bol'."

"Aleksei, This is Ivan Relinski. I work for Mikhail Gorkov. I regret to inform you that Mikhail has been murdered by agents of the British. Mikhail and I grew up in the same village together. We were like brothers, his pain is my pain and I must seek revenge as I did for his sister when he was captured in London. Then I hunted down her killers. Two I have dealt with and two others will be executed soon. But Mikhail's murderer must suffer bit by bit until he cries for me to end his pain."

****

The medical helicopter landed on the roof top landing platform of Volgograd hospital a little after 10:00am. A small party of doctors and nurses were waiting to rush Ned into theatre. Rob had heard the in-flight doctor discussing things over the radio and Sue had been able to translate enough of it to tell them all that the hospital was being made ready for immediate surgery if it was necessary but the doctor was hopeful that it was not as bad as first thought.

It had been a long two hour flight to the hospital. None of the Russians spoke more than a few words of English and though Sue's Russian was good it wasn't good enough for more than basic sentences. Rob's chest was beginning to hurt more and the motion of the helicopter wasn't helping. Tony's skinned elbows had been cleaned and dressed by the medic on the ground but he was obviously in some discomfort. Sue had no injuries but was absolutely drained. The combination of poor diet, very little sleep plus the mental and physical exhaustion of the last few days was catching up with her. As she sat in the helicopter holding Rob's hand, she smiled as she said to herself the words Rob had said. "Will you marry me?"

Once Ned had been taken off by the medical team, a translator came on board and told them that they would be taken to the assessment ward where they would be fully examined and given whatever treatment was necessary. They each had a blanket thrown across their shoulders and helped out of the aircraft by a team of nurses. They were escorted to the assessment ward, three floors down on the ground floor, each given a bed and told to rest.

Hot drinks and sandwiches were brought in and a nurse switched on the TV. Rob laughed when he saw what was on the screen. "It's bloody 'Bonanza'. Doesn't Hoss Cartwright sound good with a husky Russian voice."

When the scene changed to include some horse riding. Sue asked, "Are any of those yours, Rob? Do you recognise any of them?"

"How old do you think I am? I was only a kid when this was being made." "What are you two on about?" Tony asked.

Sue replied, "Rob's in the movie and TV business."

"I know that. I read his profile. He trains stuntmen."

"His company also supplies the horses and he has actually been the stuntman in a few big movies. It was Rob's dad that taught John Wayne to ride."

"Hold on Sue," Rob interrupted. "You just made that last bit up."

"Maybe, but it sounds good."

A nurse entered the room, looked around, took Rob's hand and said, "Come."

Rob followed the young blonde nurse into the examination room and the door closed behind them.

"I hope I get a full examination with that one." Mark said cheekily. "There is something about Russian girls."

"Steady on mate," Tony said. "there's a lady present."

"Oh don't mind me. I was in the army for 15 years. Nothing men say will shock me."

"What regiment?" Mark asked.

"I was a captain in the military police."

"That's funny! I had a good mate named Williams who was an MP. I lost touch with him a few years back. Tony Williams, do you know him."

"Tony was my husband. He was killed in Afghanistan in 2010."

"Sorry to hear that. At one time he and I were great mates. Went to the same school, played in the same football team, argued over girls and even joined up together. But you know how it is. Once training has finished you get posted to different places and sort of drift apart. We did bump into one another a few times and the last time he did tell me he'd got married. Now I know why he was so happy about it."

Rob returned and the nurse took Mark's hand. As he walked through the door he looked over his shoulder gave the others a smile and winked at Sue.

"How are you now, Rob?" Sue asked.

"A bit sore but they say, no broken ribs, just bruising. I must say they are very efficient. That nurse is really good, very thorough and knows what she's doing."

"I'm glad there's no broken bones but you were incredibly lucky you had your phone in your pocket, the bullet came from an old rifle and not a modern high velocity weapon."

The translator came in again and told them that Ned's injuries were not too severe. He was now conscious and talking. They just want to keep him here under close observation tonight. But he should be able to be transferred to Moscow hospital tomorrow. So the hospital will arrange accommodation for tonight and a helicopter to take them to Moscow in the morning.

"That sounds good. I really must phone home and let them know I'm OK. Can I borrow your phone please, Sue?"

He dialled the house phone at the stables where Rose was peeling potatoes for lunch.

"Hi Mum."

"Robert. It's good to hear you, we've been so worried about you."

"I'm OK, picked up a few bruises chasing the bad guys down in the south of the country. But it's all done now and we should be back in Moscow tomorrow. I'm staying on in Moscow for three or four days. One of our guys took a nasty tumble off a motor bike and he'll be in hospital for a few days. He's one of the embassy staff so he's got family here to go home to but one or two of us thought it would be nice for him if we stayed on. It's also an opportunity to do some sightseeing. I've never been to Moscow before. I'd like a quick word with Phil if he's around."

"No dear he's not. Luci is off on one of her girly camping trips this morning and they needed to take two cars to get everyone in. They haven't gone far, just down somewhere near Castleton. Rachael's family are mad on fishing and they own a stretch of land down there on the side of a river. They go there several times a year. You don't know do you? Luci's been talking with her two Russian friends. Apparently they were frightened to stay in London, something to do with someone forcing them to change their act. Anyway, Luci invited them to go camping and Phil picked them up from Leeds station yesterday evening."

"What do you make of them?"

"Absolutely wonderful. So polite. And they did all the breakfast washing up before they left. They are truly lovely young women. You father is very taken with them because they said they would supervise the girls for the three days camping, meaning he doesn't have to. He's very relieved about that. He wasn't looking forward to it at all. Talking of lovely young ladies, how is your Mrs. Williams? She rather impressed me as well."

"She's fine. Like the rest of us very tired. It's been a tough few days. Anyway, she's not going to be Mrs. Williams much longer, she's getting married very soon."

"That's nice. Give her my best wishes."

"Will do. How is Justin? Is he doing OK?"

"To tell you the truth I haven't seen much of him. He's always off with Jake from breakfast until bed time. Phil has found them work and paying them a little for what they do. He's doing great."

"That's good to hear. He's been through an awful time the last couple of weeks. I'm going to have to go now, mum. Say hi to every one for me and I'll ring again in a couple of days to let you know when I'll be home. Oh, I almost forgot. You can't ring me because I've lost my phone. Bye for now."

"Bye love, thanks for ringing."

The Russian translator returned a short while later and told them he had booked four rooms for them in a hotel near the hospital, curtesy of the Russian Police and a car was outside waiting to take them there. The hotel was basic, but they had a room each. The food was good, and the wine flowed easily. But by 8:00 the exertions of the last few days caught up with them and they retired to their rooms.

Sue woke early. A noise had disturbed her, but it wasn't there now and she couldn't actually think what it could have been. She looked at the clock next to her, 7:15, not as early as she'd thought. Not worth trying to go back to sleep, having a shower was perhaps the best option. There was the noise again. Like an animal scratching at the door to her room. Wrapping the light weight duvet around her naked body she went to investigate. She opened the door just wide enough to peep out but not enough to let anything larger than a mouse in.

"Good morning, Mrs. Williams, Rob said with a broad smile on his face."

She opened the door wider, grabbed him by the elbow, pulled him in and quietly closed the door.

"Get in here before someone sees you. You daft bugger."

"I've never seen that angry look before. I quite like it!"

"What the hell are you playing at?"

He stepped forward and kissed her gently. She kissed him back a little harder. Rob was stood on the corner of the duvet and as Sue moved back the duvet was pulled from her and she fell naked back on the bed. Rob moved towards her but she quickly moved around and stood up again beside him.

"Oh no you don't! We haven't got time and I want a shower," she said.

"I had one ten minutes ago but I think another wouldn't hurt," he replied.

"No. I need a shower. Not fun and games," she said and went through into the bathroom and started the shower. As she closed the shower cubicle door Rob came into the bathroom and sat on the toilet.

"I've been thinking," he said.

"That's dangerous!"

"We could get married in Moscow tomorrow, so I've checked with our hotel and they will arrange everything for us."

"I've told you before. Don't make my decisions for me. I don't want to marry you in Moscow. I appreciate it's a romantic gesture but there are other people to consider."

"Like who?"

"Like Luci and Justin. I'm going to be their step mum and I don't want to be resented. I need to get to know them and they need to get to know me and to trust me. To trust that I'm not coming to pinch their dad away."

"They won't do that. They know better."

"No Rob, they are your children and I want them involved in our future starting with our wedding. Your mum and dad to."

She opened the shower door and Rob handed her a large white fluffy hotel towel. She dried herself then wrapped the towel around her and tucked the corner in to hold it in place. She used a small towel to rub her hair then wrapped it around her head like a turban and went back into the bedroom to find a hair drier.

"I definitely don't want a big wedding but there are a few people, very close to you, that must be there."

"OK I give in. Close family and friends in York registry office next week."

"That's better."

Sue dressed and they went down for breakfast. At the restaurant door they stood and looked in to see if Tony and Mark had come down yet. They were surprised to see Zoe and Glen sitting with Tony and Mark. They walk over to the table and joined them.

"Hello you two, how are you both?" Sue asked and lent down to kiss Zoe's cheek.

"We're both fine now thanks, Sue," Zoe said and Glen nodded his agreement. "I thought you both would have been back in Moscow by now," Rob added.

"No. We were only discharged from the hospital this morning. We were told that there would be transport for us to Moscow, today. It seems we're all on the same flight. Tony has told us about Ned and Irina. Shame about her, she was a nice lady."

"Ned should be well enough to travel this morning and we'll all travel back to Moscow together," Tony announced. "I'm just waiting for confirmation."

They sat and waited most of the morning. Tony kept his eye on the time waiting for 9:00am London time. When the time came he rang Sir Bernard to update him. They talked for several minutes but Tony passed on nothing to the rest of the team.

Sue had earlier spoken with AC-10. James Moore was not available so it was left that he would call her when he was free. As Tony's call to Sir Bernard ended. Sue's phone rang.

"Hi Sue. James Moore here, I'm with Sir Bernard Howe at MI-6. He's been talking with Tony Bates, so we know your mission has been successful." "I know. Tony is right here with me," Sue answered.

"When I get back to the office I'll contact MI-5 and we'll start talks with Russian Police to get Logan and Mason back to Britain. Peter Logan arrived back two days ago and has spent several hours with my team. He has resigned his position as Assistant Commissioner and will take early retirement. You may also be interested that both the Squire Brothers are dead. Murdered while in remand in Leeds prison."

"Have those responsible been identified."

"Not yet. We think it's in connection with that Russian girl's murder a couple of weeks ago."

"Quite possible. She was Mikhail Gorkov's sister but he couldn't have organised it. He's been in custody since before they were captured."

"But someone may have organised it on his behalf. However, that is not your concern. The final members of the Inspector's group have been rounded up and AC-10 are now compiling a list of cases that will need re-investigating. Sir Bernard and I both thank you for your part in this mission. We'll need you both to attend a de-briefing as soon as you are back in London but for now I'll just wish you a pleasant journey home."

Sue told Rob about the brothers but he didn't react other than to say, "They deserved all they got."

Finally at 2:00 transport arrived to take them to the heliport where they met up with Ned, a heavy bandage about his head. The flight to Moscow and the transfer to the hotel were uneventful and passed quickly. An embassy car had met Ned at the airport and taken him home. The other six were taken by police cars to the hotel where they found their rooms exactly as they had left them.

"After four days in these clothes I can even smell my own stink. I'm going straight in the shower and get into fresh things," Sue said.

"I think we all feel like that. A couple of hours sleep as well would be good," said Rob.

"It's 4:45 now. Let's meet in the bar at 7:00." Tony suggested.

They all agreed and entered their rooms.

Sue showered, dressed in t-shirt and leggings then lay on the bed to try and sleep. She had only been lay down for five minutes when there was a knock on the door.

Sue opened it to see Rob standing there. She opened the door further and he walked in.

"Sue, I've just been talking with mum and she said dad has booked them both on a cruise around the med to get away from all the aggro of the past weeks." "That's a great idea. It will do them both a world of good. When do they go?"

"There's the rub. They leave on Wednesday. Which means I need to get back to UK as soon as possible to get things organised for the kids going back to school."

"That's OK, Rob. We can get the first flight home tomorrow. We can be at my house by lunch time, collect some clothes and get up to Yorkshire in my car. We should be there by early evening at the latest."

"You don't have to come with me."

"Oh yes I do. I've been promised a wedding and if you think I'm going to wait 5 weeks for your mum and dad to get back before it happens you can think again. It's going to be next Monday or Tuesday. You're the man with the money, so make it happen."

There was a loud knock on the door.

"Can you get that Rob? I need a pee."

Sue closed the bathroom door as Rob went to open the main door. As he turned the handle, the door was violently pushed open knocking Rob backwards. He lost his balance and fell onto the bed, knocking the bedside lamp to the floor with a crash. Horrified Rob watched as the tall stranger open his jacket and pull out a machete. He raised it above his head and walked towards Rob.

Rob rolled across the bed just as the stranger brought the machete down narrowly missing him. Rob grabbed a pillow to protect himself. He was now cornered down the side of the bed and against the wall. The machete came down again splitting the pillow open. Rob closed his eyes as the machete was raised high for the killer blow. Rob felt something wet hit his bare arm. It must be blood but he felt no pain. His eyes were shut so he could see nothing then he realised he could hear nothing either. Was he dead?

He felt something warm on his neck and forced his eyes open. In front of him stretched across the bed, was the tall stranger with a bullet hole in his forehead. The machete still in his hand. Rob turned his head sideways to see Sue beside him in the bathroom doorway with her gun in her hand.

"Are you OK Rob?" He didn't reply.

She turned her head towards the bed and said again, "Rob, are you OK?" "I can see you're talking but I can't hear anything," he said.

"It must be the shock wave noise from the gun it was right next to your head when I fired. Don't panic it will wear off in a few minutes," Sue told him.

The noise of the gunshot brought Tony and Mark running to Sue's door from their respective rooms. With their guns at the ready they cautiously entered the room.

"Sue what's happened? Are you and Rob OK?" Tony called when he saw Sue in Rob's arms standing over a body prone across the bed.

"Rob's temporarily deaf from the gun going off next to his head but otherwise we're fine. I recognise this guy but don't know where from."

"Well, he won't cause anyone any trouble now. I'll call my contact in the local police and get someone up here ASAP. I'll also get in touch with the embassy, we may need their assistance. Don't go too far until the local police have spoken to you."

"OK Tony, I'll take Rob along to his room and stay there until he gets his hearing back."

The Police arrived at the hotel before Sue had got Rob to his room. They were closely, followed by a medical team. Everyone was ushered downstairs into one of the hotels small function rooms and left there with a police officer stood in the room blocking the door.

While they waited, Tony made a couple of phone calls and Rob slowly regained his hearing. Sue made a call to her own office but kept her voice low and Rob couldn't hear more than the odd word.

Eventually after what seemed like several hours, but was only about forty-five minutes, the door opened, and a uniformed officer entered.

"Major Alexei Yusupov, it is good to see you again," Tony said.

"Mr Bates, I didn't expect us to meet again. At least not as soon," he replied, "Would one of you like to tell me what happened here."

"I will," said Rob. The Major turned slightly to face him. "I went to Susan's room to discuss our plans for travelling home and was just about to leave when that big guy burst through the door, thrashing about with a machete. He forced me back into a corner. That's when Sue came out of the bathroom and shot him."

"Certainly the evidence supports your story so I am happy. Do you know who the man was and why he attacked you?"

"His name was Ivan Relinski. He was Mikhail Gorkov's lieutenant in a London gang. I assume he was after revenge for the part I played in Mikhail's death."

"Ah yes, I've read a report of what has happened on the road in the south of the country. No one that matters will mourn the death of either of those two. My regret is that I failed to support you when you all arrived last week. If I had perhaps Captain Irina Bakunin would still be alive."

The Major turned to leave then turned back to face Sue. "Mrs. Williams one of my officers will help you collect your property from the room and the hotel will provide you with another room. I'm afraid we will need to keep your gun. It is evidence. If you will just follow me please. The rest of you may go now."

Everyone but Sue was in the bar at seven. Rob was a little concerned that he'd not heard from Sue since she had left with the

Major. Then to his relief she appeared. "Sorry everyone, the phone rang just when I was leaving my room. I'll tell you about the call later Rob but I'm ready for a drink. Who's buying?"

"Once everyone had a drink," Sue edged Rob to one side to talk to him about her phone call. "Before the Major, arrived I called my office and spoke to Alice, the boss's secretary and asked her to sort out our flight home. It was her ringing back that made me late. She has been able to get us two seats on tomorrows British Airways flight 236 leaving at 5:40 and arriving in London at 6:55. We should be at my house by 8:00. So as soon as we've had something to eat we'd best get our packing done. There's no point trying to get any sleep, we've got to be at the airport by 3:20."

"Before we head off to Yorkshire, I'd like to call in at my place to see how Mrs. Parfitt and her husband are doing straightening up the place. It will also give me a chance to grab some more clothes if they left me any."

Chapter 20

"Alex, this is Robert Blackstock here. I'm getting married in a few days and my wife to be is concerned about people seeing her as a gold digger and is eager to disclaim anything of mine other than that which I freely give her. With my first marriage you, as my solicitor, held a letter from my wife in her own hand-writing as a prenuptial agreement disclaiming all rights. I assume the law hasn't changed and my wife to be has done the same. I'll be in York on Friday so will bring the letter to you."

****

The girls camping were having a great time. Once they had got the tents set up they spent their time sitting around a camp fire. While lunch cooked, they talked to Eva and Ana and listening to them about life in Russia when they were young and how they came to be living in London. The two of them talked quite openly about their work and the four girls took it all in.

Being supervised by two people closer to their own age suited the four girls. It gave them more freedom and they felt easier talking about themselves and they were learning a lot about each other. They also had the freedom to do new things and a lot of the time Ana and Eva would join in. The day was getting warmer and by early afternoon it was very hot so they went down to the river to sit on the bank and cool off. But when the two Russians stripped off and jumped naked into the river the others quickly followed.

Amy was the first to comment on Luci's lack of hair. Then Rachael let it slip that her boyfriend and her had been playing around and he'd asked her to shave.

"I didn't know you had a boyfriend Rach. Are you two having sex?" Luci asked.

"No. But I hope we will soon. We're just playing around but I think it won't be long before he wants to go further."

At this point Eva jumped in. "Don't talk like that. You girls are all so young. Don't give your bodies away too soon or too easily. Don't think of it as sex but as making love. Give yourself because you want to show your emotion, to demonstrate your deepest feeling, not to satisfy any lustful urge. You can do that to yourself at home in bed. Your bodies are very precious, guard them well. Once you've committed you can't go back."

The girls all nodded to show they understood and they all started swimming and splashing about in the water again. After their evening meal Luci asked Ana and Eva if they would teach her and the other girls some Russian. They had all done some at school so knew the basics. Three of them planned to do Russian A-level so this would be a great opportunity to get ahead. Eva said they would be more than happy and the best way would to only speak Russian to one another while in camp. They said it would improve their confidence and make them use what they already learnt in different ways and they would start to think in Russian rather than translate everything. It was the way they had learnt English and they knew that they could, in the few days left, teach the girls a great deal.

Sue and Rob were both unable to sleep during the flight so to keep them going and give them a lift they stopped off for a coffee before leaving the airport. Then a taxi took them straight to Sue's house. She'd given a lot of thought to what she needed to pack for what she thought would be at least a week away. When she had spoken to the office, she had told them she was taking the leave that was owed her. Her workload had already been shifted to other task leaders because of her Russian trip and she knew the boss, her brother-in-law, would be OK about it. After all, he knew she put in more hours than anyone else and was one of the best in her field. It just meant she wouldn't be around to scope any new work.

"It will take me thirty minutes tops to pack Rob. Have you thought about what you need?"

"I've got some things in Yorkshire so it's not too critical. I've got a few bits here to take and the rest depends on what I have left at my apartment. I'll be ready as soon as you are."

"I'll be as quick as I can. Why don't you give your Mrs. Parfitt a call, see if she is going to be there. Maybe she can get some things ready for you."

"Good idea, I'll ring her now."

Sue got everything she needed into two suitcases. All of Rob's clothes went in a holdall.

"I'll need something new to wear to be married in. A simple plain summer dress would be nice. Can we stop off somewhere?"

"Why don't you and Luci go into York over the week-end. Have some girlie time together, a bit of bonding and get what you need. Because if I know women, you'll need new shoes and a bag to go with the dress," Rob replied.

"That's a very good idea, you clever man. I've actually never been to York but I expect Luci knows her way around the city. I was going to ask her to be my bridesmaid, do you think she would like that? I'm all packed and ready. Let's get this lot in the car and get over to your place."

"I'm sure she'd love to be your bridesmaid, she was quite taken with what you said about a career in the army. Let me have those bags and I'll put them in the boot."

As they pulled into the road where the apartments were, they found the road blocked by a breakdown truck. With vehicles parked either side and the breakdown truck sat at an angle, its front overhanging the central white line there wasn't enough room for Sue to squeeze through. Looking past the breakdown truck they could see the driver removing a yellow clamp from a transit van.

"They've come to tow away the Squire Brothers' van," Rob said.

"Well they don't need it anymore," replied Sue.

"It's going to take them a few minutes to get sorted, so you stay with the car and I'll go up to the apartment and get things sorted. When you can get through park in my space and come on up," Rob said as he climbed out of the car.

Rob had quite a shock when he got to his apartment. Everything was as if nothing had ever happened. Mrs. Parfitt was busy placing his clothes in piles on the sofa in the lounge.

"Mrs. Parfitt, you are incredible! This is marvellous."

"Thank you sir, but it's not all finished. Jim was able to get the furniture people to replace the bits in here. The sofa and chairs are very slightly different from the old ones but not so as you'd notice. Jim gave the walls a lick of paint while the furniture was out. We've also done the kitchen, bathroom and single bedroom. We were a little confused there sir. There appears to be both gentlemen's and ladies' clothes in that room." Rob explained why.

"There's just your room and the twin room to finish now, sir. Jim's painting those today and the new mattresses should arrive tomorrow. We should be all finished by Saturday afternoon, sir."

"Thank you so much Mrs. Parfitt and thank Jim for me please. And you've got all my clothes clean and sorted out here for me. You are an angel."

"Well, they were thrown about everywhere I thought it best to get everything cleaned. I'm afraid some have been damaged and I've got rid of them."

"Thank you again. I'm going to be up in Yorkshire for the next week or so,

I'll just pack what I need for that and leave you to get on."

He filled a case and another holdall and carried them to the lift and waited.

After waiting several minutes, Sue arrived on foot.

"You didn't give me the security code for the garage door so I'm out on the street where the transit was. I had to pay for two hours on the meter. Is this all you're taking?"

"Yeh, just these two. A lot of my stuff got slashed and Mrs. Parfitt dumped them. At least they left me one decent suit to get married in. We'll get these into the car then I just want to take you around the corner."

The two bags plus Sue's two filled the boot of Sue's small car.

"Where did you say we were going," Sue asked him.

"I didn't say. But seeing Mrs. Parfitt's hands made me think we haven't got rings for the wedding and just around the corner from here is a little shop owned by an old drinking partner, Richard Cohen, who just happens to be a jeweller. I think you will like his style. I'll be very surprised if you've ever seen anything like his things and he makes everything himself."

"That sounds expensive. I don't need anything too fancy, I'd be happy with rings from Argos."

"Don't be silly, you're marrying a very rich man. Come inside and have a look around," he said as he pushed open a door to what looked like a very ordinary London terrace house. Above the door in hand painted black letters were the words 'Cohen and Sons. Jewellers'. There were bars at the window but there were bars at the window of every house along the street. They all looked the same.

Rob closed the door behind them and Sue saw they were stood in the hallway with all the doors around them closed tight. Rob knocked on the first door on the left and they heard a noise behind the door. Sue noticed a spy hole in the door then heard bolts being drawn and the door opened.

"Blackstock, how the devil are you! What brings you to my door, I'm sure the pubs aren't open yet!" came a booming voice from just inside.

"Cohen, you look well. Dick, I'd like you to meet Sue Williams. The future Mrs. Blackstock. I've been telling her how unique your junk is and brought her along to show her. We're in need of some rings and if she sees something she likes we may do a bit of business."

"Welcome Sue. Did he really call my work junk? Let me show you a few pieces and let you decide if it's junk or not."

He guided Sue to a table in the middle of the room, flicked a switch on the wall which filled the room with bright light. Then he moved to the other side of the table and pulled out a drawer full of small velvet draw string bags with little numbered tags attached. He selected one of the bags, checked the number and emptied the contents onto a velvet lined tray. Lay there in front of Sue were a mans and a lady's wedding rings identical in all but size. The design was a plait of three strands each of a different colour gold white, yellow and red. The two ends of the plait came together in a simple flat knot to complete the circle.

"These are absolutely gorgeous. You were right Rob, I've never seen anything like this. Modern but classical at the same time." "Try it on," the jeweller said.

She did and it was a perfect fit.

"I've got the engagement ring that goes with that if you'd like to see it."

"Of course she would."

The jeweller shuffled around a few of the bags in the draw and checked a couple of their labels then finally pulled a ring from one of the bags and handed it to Sue. It was the same plait of three colours but instead of the flat knot the ends of the plait were folded out to form a six pointed crown with a large pure white diamond in its centre and 6 rubies set between the points. Sue slipped it on to her finger and slid it down to the other ring. The two nestled together as one, the crown of the engagement ring locking over the knot of the wedding ring.

Rob looked at the expression on Sue's face. "Looks like the lady likes what you've shown her."

"Perfect," she could only say one word.

"That's a sale then. That was quick. How much for the three Dick?"

"Because it's you Rob I can do you a special deal." He wrote a number on a piece of paper and showed it to Rob.

"That's very reasonable. Thank you Dick."

"Would the lady like to keep the engagement ring on. I can give you the box for it and I have a special presentation box for the wedding rings which I will give you as a wedding present."

"The lady would like to keep the engagement ring on thank you," Sue said.

"I'll also give you 3 months insurance cover," said the jeweller. "That should give you time to get them on your own policy. I'll just go out the back and get things sorted."

He put the drawer of rings back under the table before leaving the room. Sue was still looking down at her ring. When she heard the door close she lifted her head, smiled at Rob then walked over and kissed him passionately.

"My head's spinning Rob. Everything is happening so quickly and it's all just perfect. You are simply wonderful."

"You haven't seen the mess I leave the kitchen in when I cook," he said. They both laughed.

The journey to York was straight forward. Sue drove the first leg which gave Rob the opportunity to contact the Registry office in York. After a lot of raised voices he appeared to get what he wanted. They changed driver when they stopped for the toilet and pick up some sandwiches for lunch.

"What did they say?" Sue asked having waited to be told but nothing being said.

"It's all booked, 5:15 Monday. I've got to go in to do the paperwork tomorrow at 11:00."

They travelled on in silence and arrived at the stables as Rose was taking the washing in off the line.

"We didn't expect to see you until tomorrow Robert and you didn't say you were bringing Mrs. Williams with you. I would have thought she would have wanted to spend time with the man she's going to marry after being away for over a week."

"She is with the man she's going to marry," he replied as he climbed out of the car.

Sue was also out and peered out from behind Rob. "Am I to call you mum, mother-in-law, Rose or Mrs Blackstock?"

"How wonderful. What a surprise. Rose will do fine dear. Mum might get in the way of us becoming friends and I would like us to be friends and the other two are a bit formal don't you think? Yes, Rose will be fine. Come on in, I'll put the kettle on for a cup of tea. Dad will be in soon, he's just nipped over to the stables to check on the horses that are running tomorrow."

"Where's Phil? Why isn't he checking the horses?"

"Roger had a fall yesterday. Doctor said he had concussion and had to rest for a few days so Phil has had to stand in at Doncaster today, tomorrow and Saturday."

Rob explained to Sue that Roger was head lad and would normally be in charge of the horses and the grooms at events spread over several days. Horses would be coming in and out all the time and stalls would need to be cleaned etc., just like the rooms in a hotel for changing customers.

"The boys wanted to know more about it so Phil has taken them with him and if I know Phil he'll have them on the shovels right from the start. But they love him all the same."

They sat themselves at the large kitchen table and Rose filled the kettle and set it on the Aga to boil when Eric came in.

Rose called across the kitchen to her husband. "Darling look who's turned up a day earlier than we expected."

"Hi dad, can I introduce Susan Williams to you."

"Ah, the lady my granddaughter was telling me about the other day. The army police woman."

"Robert and Susan are getting married dear," Rose cut in with.

"Well, that's a turn up for the books. Never expected to see you get married again son. You must have a special hold on him, my dear. I'll wish you luck. This calls for a drink and I don't mean tea."

He left the kitchen by the door to a corridor which led to a small annex which doubled as an office and a trophy room. He returned carrying a bottle of Champagne.

"Got ten cases of this as trainer's prize for winning the Moet handicap at Chepstow last month. What do I want with one hundred and twenty bottles of Champagne, I ask you.? Get the glasses out Rose, whilst there's just the four of us."

They moved to the lounge and the bottle was soon empty.

"I wasn't expecting you until tomorrow," Rose said, and with "Luci and Justin both away I've not got anything to offer you to eat this evening."

"Don't worry mum. We'll go down the village and eat in the Dog And Gun.

None of us has had too much to drink, so we'll be OK."

Eric's phone rang and he went off towards the office as he answered it. They all heard him curse a couple of times then make two or three phone calls before returning to the living room. "Charlie Richie's had a fall at Haydock and broken his collar bone. He was down to ride Troubled Brow for me in the big race at

Doncaster on Saturday. I'm having to chase around now to find a replacement."

"Actually dad, Sue is an experienced jockey; she's even ridden a winner."

"Don't listen to him Eric. It was at a point-to-point, and it was twenty years ago. I think you should get Rob to do it."

"It may well come to that, lass."

"With Phil in Doncaster tomorrow I need some help getting the girls home. I was going to ask one of the stable boys but if you're free Rob perhaps you can help me out. They want picking up at 4:00. It's only a half hour drive."

"Sorry dad, but I've got a meeting in York tomorrow to sign some papers at the registry office plus I need to see my solicitor. I must see my insurance broker and I really must check in at the stunt farm to make sure everything is doing well.

So I've really got a full day. But I'm sure Sue will help out. Won't you darling?"

"Would you Sue? It would be a great help. You could have Luci, Ana and Eva in with you, they are all coming back here and I'll have the other three who need to be taken to their homes around the village."

"No problem Eric, I'd be happy to help. It will give me a chance to ask Luci to be my bridesmaid. Time's getting on Rob, we need to get the bags in and unpack. I'm desperate for a shower and if we're going out to eat then I'll have to decide what to wear. I need you to show me around the house, show me where everything is."

"Have you brought the Catwalk dress?"

"I don't think I'll be wearing that to a village pub, thank you very much!"

Rose volunteered to drive as she'd only had one glass of champagne and she usually only had a tonic when out for a meal. The pub was unexpectedly busy for a Thursday and Rob had great pleasure in showing off his bride to be to several locals that he knew very well. Jim Tarrot was a special friend. They had sat next to one another all through junior school.

"Are you two coming down here Saturday evening," he asked Rob, "for the landlord's wife's 50th birthday bash? Happy hour six 'til eight, free buffet and karaoke. Should be a great evening. Probably finish with a lock in until the early hours."

"To tell you the truth Jim, I don't know what our plans are. We've had a pig of a week. Only got back from Moscow this morning. Then drove up here. We could really do with some quiet time. We'll wait and see."

The menu only had a dozen or so items on it and there was a specials board with 3 or four other meals to choose from. All were typical pub grub but nicely presented, very tasty and satisfying.

They ended the evening with Malt whiskey all round when they got home. Then early to bed.

Rob was up early and left Sue to sleep on. He made a list of everything he had to do In York and checked he had everything he needed to take with him all together and ready to pick up as he left. At 8:00 he took Sue a coffee.

"Morning sleepy head." He pulled the curtain open and the bright sunshine spread across the room causing Sue to squint. "Mum's got the breakfast on. You've got twenty minutes to get yourself dressed."

"I can smell the breakfast. I'll be as quick as I can."

Breakfast was all fresh local produce and Sue was amazed how much nicer it was than what she was used to in London. As soon as they had finished, Eric went out to supervise the horses being loaded to go to Doncaster and Rob left to go to York leaving Rose and Sue to clear the table and do the washing up. Normally some think Madge Little would have done, but her daughter was ill, Madge and her husband Reg and got to look after their two small grandchildren for a few days.

"Rose, what do you think Luci and Justin will make of Rob and I getting married?"

"They have both met you and have been impressed, so I don't think there will be a problem. But I'm a bit concerned myself that you are rushing into it. You only met last week."

"I was married to Tony for seven years and in that time we barely spent seven months together. When he was killed, I grieved not just for the loss, but for the wasted time which we could have had together. That has taught me to grab every moment and not sit back and wait because it's the acceptable thing to do. I'm not gold digging. I've given Rob a letter disclaiming any rights to his wealth other than that which he freely gives. He's handing that to his solicitor today. We both knew when we first met each other that there was chemistry between us."

"Sorry love, I didn't mean to suggest any alternative motive. I completely understand what you're saying. When I first met Eric I told my best friend at the time that I was going to marry him and that was before our first date. Now let me have a closer look at the gorgeous ring on your finger."

The Russian lessons were going well. The pupils were gaining in confidence as well as expanding their vocabulary. Everything they talked about they did so in Russian. Their limited vocabulary sometimes caused them to struggle at getting their meaning across and their instructors would introduce a new word to simplify things for them. It was a great way to learn and the girls were enthusiastic. Sadly it all had to end and after Friday's lunch had been consumed they set about dismantling the camp. When Eric and Sue arrived everything was ready to go straight into the cars.

Eric explained who would be travelling in which car and why. Then as the kit and personal items were loaded, Sue took Luci to one side and told her about the wedding plans.

"That's wonderful news! I'm so happy for you both. Can I be bridesmaid and can I have a closer look at the ring. It looks superb."

"That's what I was going to ask you. I'd love you to be my bridesmaid. I also need you to show me the shops in York, sometime this week-end, to get me a new outfit to be married in and a brides maids dress for you."

"Can Ana and Eva come as well? They've got incredible dress sense and they will look at you, talk to you for a few minutes and know exactly the image they need to create."

"Alright I'm convinced. Yes they can come if they are happy to do so. Have you had a good time this week?"

"Yes thanks! Ana and Eva have been truly remarkable camp leaders. It's all over too soon and it will be back to school at the end of next week."

"I thought all schools went back on the 4th."

"No. The girls and I will be starting at 6th form college. Term starts on 11th and JB goes to a private school, as a boarder and doesn't go back until 16th. Which is strange because most schools in Scotland are already back, but for some reason his school follows the English private school term dates."

The cars were quickly loaded and they set off for home. As soon as they were moving Ana and Eva started asking Luci, who was in the front passenger seat, questions about various things they saw on the roadside as they went along. They were asking their questions in Russian and Luci was responding in Russian. One of their questions Luci didn't have an answer for and was totally surprised when Sue gave the answer in fluent Russian.

"You speak Russian, too!" Ana said in a surprised tone.

"My grandparents come from Astrakhan. My name before I married was Kowinski. I do speak a little Russian, but I don't speak it very often and I'm very rusty." Again, in Russian she said. "Luci and I need to buy some new clothes this weekend for my wedding. Luci says you two make good choices. Would you like to come with us?"

"We would be very happy to help you. Thank you for asking us."

Chapter 21

"Hello, is that the Daily Mirror society desk. I'm David Balls. I am a freelance reporter currently producing copy for the York Evening Post. I thought you may be interested that I have recently discovered that wealthy widower Robert Blackstock is getting married in York on Monday. I will be more than happy to cover the event for you and give you copies of pictures."

****

Everyone was back at the stables by 4:30. Ana and Eva went straight to their room with their bags. They had been given the use of one of the stable worker's flats above the stables as a temporary measure, until Rob could sort out something more permanent. Luci simply took her bag into the laundry room and pulled everything out and stuffed it all in the washing machine.

She then went to help Rose who was in the kitchen preparing the evening meal.

"I do love cooking for a big family, Luci. It makes me feel valued and when Madge is around, she normally takes total charge of the kitchen. Not that I'm complaining, she's a real treasure. Do you think your two friends would like to join us this evening? There's more than enough. I'm doing coq-u-vin."

"They are both terrible cooks so were planning on walking down to the village and eat in the Dog and Gun. I'm sure they would prefer your cooking to anything they could get there, gran. I'll go and ask them. What time shall I say?"

"6:30. But tell them to come when they are ready. I expect the men will want a drink before they eat."

Rob and Sue entered the lounge from one end at exactly the moment Ana and Eva entered from the other. Eric was sitting in his favourite chair reading the newspaper. Sue greeted the girls in Russian and they both responded in Russian which made Eric look up from his paper. Eva went over to him and held out a bottle of colourless liquid labelled in Russian.

"A gift for you Mr Blackstock, to thank you and your wife for your hospitality. Special Russian vodka from our village. It is very strong."

"That's not necessary, but very good of you both. Rose come and see what our guests have given us. I'll get some glasses out."

He poured six shots and handed them round. Rose sniffed at hers and headed to the kitchen to add lemonade. Ana and Eve stood up straight, shoulders back and raised their glasses and said as one "bawe xopowee 3xopoBbe," then drained their glasses in one. Sue then followed them exactly.

"They are saying 'Your good health'," Luci translated. Ana applauded and said. "Well done to our star pupil."

Rob and Eric looked at one another, raised their grasses and said, "Your good health." Then drained their glasses.

Rob picked up the bottle to inspect it. "Hey dad this fire water is 90% proof.

If you get breathalysed you'd melt the crystals."

Rose appeared in the doorway sipping her drink from a tall glass of gassy liquid. "Dinner is ready."

Over dinner they discussed the racing at Doncaster. In the first two days the stables had sent nine horses. They had had two winners and five places so the stables staff were on a high with one day still to go with three horses entered for races.

"I'll send down a case of that Champagne for the boys to celebrate with tomorrow. They've earned it. So far they've brought in close on £14,000 to the stables. Tomorrow is Ladies' Day and I'm hopeful of at least a place in each of the two big races."

"Ladies' Day. Can we go dad?"

"I've never been to a proper race meeting Rob. Can we go?" Sue added.

"Would you two like to go too?" he said directly to Eva and Ana.

"Yes if you don't mind," Ana said. "We'd love to come."

"It's ladies day so you'll all have to dress up and wear a favour," Rose said.

"A favour is a decoration you wear in your hair. A sort of pretty hat made from feathers and the like," Sue answered the unasked question.

"You'll have plenty of time tomorrow morning to make something. I've got lots of ribbon, lace and other bits you can use." Rose added.

"First race is 1:15. So we'll need to leave about 11:30," Rob declared.

The next morning after breakfast Rose showed them all some photographs of previous ladies days so that they could see the type of clothes that should be worn as well as showing a few favours.

Ana said, "These are simple. Sue and Luci bring your dresses to our room. Eva will do your make-up and I will do your hair and make your favour."

Rob had been down into the village to fill up with petrol. When he returned he pulled into the stable yard and gave a gentle toot on the horn. Sue was the first one to appear. She wore a plain scarlet sleeveless dress with a spray of flower buds on the left breast. She had on modest heeled gold shoes and carried a gold bag. Her hair was in ringlets and her favour was again a spray of flower buds down on the right hand side of her head.

"You look stunning Sue. Just amazing.!"

Luci followed Sue to the car. Her dress was a lime green silky material flared from the bust and her hair was piled high, feathers pushed through like quills and ribbons binding it all and hanging down behind her.

Rob just said, "Wow!"

Finally the two young Russians came out dressed almost identically wearing petrol blue figure hugging dresses with shoe string straps and which stopped at mid-thigh. On their feet they wore four inch heeled sandals the same colour as the dress. Their bags were the same colour as well. Their hair was the only difference between them. Ana had the left side hanging like a waterfall and the right hand side standing upright and laced with flower buds to hold it in place. Eva had her hair the same but in reverse, she had the right side hanging down.

"You must have used a year's supply of hair spray to get those styles," Rob joked.

"No just some magic gel and Lock-tight," Sue responded.

"I hope you've all put sun cream on. It's going to be a very hot sunny afternoon."

"We have," Sue replied. "Ana let us use some of her factor 30 scented lotion. So much nicer than smelling of coconut don't you think?"

Rob showed his Jockey Club card at the gate and they were waved through and he parked in one of the spaces reserved for trainers. He got out and went off in a hurry, returning moments later with a bundle of what looked like luggage labels with coloured strings.

"These are free passes you need to wear them where they can be seen. Most ladies tie them to their dress strap. They will get you into any part of the course except the jockeys' rooms and the weighing room. Food and drink you'll find in the Club room. The best toilets are there as well. Here's a programme each, enjoy your afternoon. I'm sure Luci will show you how to bet. Luci here's £30. There are six races on the card, so don't throw it all away on the first race. We'll meet back here after the last race."

Rob and Sue stood by the car and watched the three girls walk away and join the crowd.

"Put your eyeballs back in your head Blackstock," Sue said. "We can all see that Ana and Eva are drop dead gorgeous but there's no need for you to stare. You're getting married in two days. You should be looking at your daughter and being proud of the way she looks."

"Yes, she has really blossomed this summer. Suddenly she's all grown up," he proclaimed.

Sue thought to herself, 'If you knew how close she came to a whole new life, you'd think differently.'

"The three of them are really making heads turn. Both men and women. I've seen them giving you a second look as well and suspect many of the men would like to take my place."

"And the women are looking at you and wanting to swap with me," Sue said.

They walked through to the enclosures and spotted Phil in the parade ring chatting to one of the other trainers. Justin and Jake were stood next to Phil looking smart in their white sleeveless shirts with the Blackstock name and logo on the breast pocket. JB spotted Rob and waved then said something to Phil and ran over to greet his father.

"Hi dad. I knew you were here, I saw you on the big TV screen." He pointed at large five-metre TV picture showing images from around the course being taken by the dozen or so BBC cameras covering the race meeting.

"JB do you remember, Mrs. Williams."

"Yes dad. Hello again Mrs. Williams. Congratulations. I spoke with Luci on the phone last night and she told me about the wedding." "And what do you think?" Rob asked.

"I think it's great news. Hey is that Ana and Eva and who is that girl with them? She looks tasty!" He was looking up at the TV screen again.

Sue and Rob looked up and Rob said, "That's your big sister. Doesn't she clean up well and Ana and Eva are coming to work with me."

"I'll have to go dad. I told Phil I'd only be a minute. I'll see you later. Goodbye Mrs Williams."

"What's wrong Rob?" Sue asked. "You look worried."

"I am. Seeing Luci on the TV screen like that has made me realise how she might attract the wrong sort of attention. I recognised a local reporter in the pub Thursday evening. He must have overheard us talking and spread the word, because when I called in at my office yesterday they said there had been several calls, trying to find out where and when the wedding was. With Luci all dressed up as a bridesmaid she's going to draw attention and I'm afraid we'll see her photo splashed all over the tabloids and the society magazines. She's too young for that sort of publicity."

"I agree. The Blackstock name must be pretty big in these parts which makes you and what you do big news. We can't stop them and we can't hide Luci away but we can distract their attention. Look." She was pointing at the TV screen again. It was showing Ana and Eva again. Luci was still there but the camera man was obviously following the two girls in 4 inch heels and long legs showing all the way the very high hem of their skirts.

"You mean invite Ana and Eva to the wedding, as decoys, to distract the press photographers."

"That's exactly what I mean. If I brief them about what we want them to do,

I'm certain they would be happy to help."

"They are very clever girls. Luci told me how much money they were earning in London. So they know how to attract attention."

"Has she also told you, they taught the four girls Russian in the three days they were camping. Luci is now better speaking it than me and I've got Russian blood."

They bumped into Luci at the parade ring before the third race. "How are you doing girls?" Rob asked.

"No good Mr Blackstock. Ana and me have not had winner, but Luci has," Eva replied.

"I had £5 to win in the first. I liked the name, Lucky Girl. Did you see her romp home at 33-1. But lost £5 on Two Tone in the second. I'm looking at My Dreamer, the grey in the next, but think I'll only bet each way on her. I don't fancy the jockey."

"You've spent too much time with your grandfather. We'll have to watch you. We've got horses in the last three races. Grandad says they all have a very good chance. Keep your eye out for them."

They all met up again at the car after the final race. The three girls had broad smiles on their faces.

"Dad we all bet on Grandad's horse, My New Girl, in the last race. Did you see how much it won by and we got it at 12-1. Ana and Eva won back all the money they lost on the previous races and I went a bit mad and put on £50 to win. Look!" She opened her bag to show everyone a wad of £20 notes.

"Well done you. I had a bob or two on that one too. We picked up a place in the other two races so it's been a successful meet for Blackstock racing. Three winners and seven places. Not bad from twelve starters."

On the way back to the stables they decided it would be nice to end the day at the party in the pub. After all they had a few winners to celebrate. On arrival at the stables, the drive was blocked by a big black Daimler with a chauffeur wiping it over with a cloth.

"Who would be calling here in a car like that?" Rob said. "We'd better leave the car here and walk on in. It looks like being a nice evening so we'll walk down to the pub. Leave here at 7:00. Is that OK with everybody?" The girls nodded and went off to their rooms. Rob and Sue headed for the lounge.

"Sir Bernard, what brings you to the wilds of Yorkshire?"

"I was born here. About three miles away in fact. But that's not why I'm calling on you. I had hoped to see you for a debriefing in London after the mission, but understandably you didn't hang around. I hear congratulations are in order, I wish you well. I would also like on behalf of Her Majesty formally thank you for your involvement in the recent mission and it gives me great pleasure in handing you each a cheque for £10,000 for your expenses. I have also been informed this morning that the Russians have recovered the treasure and want to reward you with a finder's fee of one per cent of the value. That's approximately £5.2 million."

Rob's mouth opened but no words came forth. Sue looked shocked.

When he could eventually speak, he thanked Sir Bernard. "That's a lot of money. Can I offer you a glass of something celebrate? We've had quite a day all in all, what with backing several winners at

Doncaster and now this." He headed off to the kitchen and returned with a bottle of Champagne and a tray of glasses. "He poured the wine and passed the glasses around."

Sir Bernard thanked him and said, "I actually have an ulterior motive for coming to see you in person. I've read all the reports on the mission and spoken at length with Tony Bates. He was very impressed with the way you and Mrs. Williams handled yourselves and the skillsets you both demonstrated. We think you would be an asset to MI-6 and I would like you to both think about joining us as agents. I don't want your answers today but I'd like you to give it some thought over the next few weeks, before letting me know. Rob, I'd also like to discuss with you sometime in the near future the possibility of you setting up a training scheme on the lines of your stunt school to extend the skill sets of our agents. Maybe you could draft a few ideas of what you could offer and get back to me sometime. It would be a government contract and they pay well."

"Thank you, Sir Bernard. This has all come as a bit of a surprise. We'll certainly think it over and get back to you as soon as we can."

"I can also give you an update on Pauline Logan and Faye Mason. Apparently they were not responsible for any of the police deaths in London. They all seem to be down to the Russians. Apparently Pauline Logan had approached Mikhail Gorkov with a plan to locate the jewels and sell the location to the wolves for £7 million and the Russians were simply cutting through her team trying to get hold of the key diamond and her knowledge of where to start looking. Logan and Mason's only crimes are attempted murder of Peter Logan and possession of a stolen diamond. Charges of them conspiring and running an organised gang of corrupt police officers can't be proven because all the witnesses have been murdered by the Russians, accept for the man we had working undercover and his evidence won't be enough."

"That's amazing. With everything they've done they should get away with it!"

"Good man. I'll be on my way. You have a wedding to plan. Good day to you both."

Rob poured Sue and himself another glass of champagne and they sat for a moment speechless. Eric and Rose joined them when the saw Sir Bernard's car leave the drive. Rob didn't tell them about the offer. He only talked about the reward money coming from Russia.

"You know it's totally bizarre," he said. "Just three weeks ago I left for London to negotiate a loan of £5.2 million to set up a new company and by helping out a few people that very sum ends up in my lap. Phil will be happy!

I'll tell him as soon as he gets back. He shouldn't be much longer."

Eric and Rose decided not to go to the pub but JB thought it a good idea. The free buffet being of special interest. So six of them set off to walk the half mile down to the village having swapped their race going clothes for casual jeans and t-shirts. Ana and Eva of course looking stunning in three-quarter length jeans that looked as if they had been sprayed on, and off the shoulder loose t-shirts.

Rob walked with his two children giving them some of the details of his adventure in Russia. Sue walked behind with Ana and Eva and talked to them about Luci and Rob's fear.

"Don't worry, Susan. Eva and I will give the photographer something to hold their attention away from Luci. You and Mr Blackstock just enjoy your day on Monday and tomorrow we help you find very special dress."

Sue wasn't sure what to make of Ana's comment about giving something to hold their attention. Knowing their background it could mean anything.

The Dog And Gun was already busy when they arrived. They found a table for four and on the next table two lads were more than happy to let Eva and Ana have their seats, because it gave them an opening to talk to them. Rob got everybody a drink and people continued to pour in through the door and there was now quite a crowd at the bar. The staff were struggling to keep up with orders. Once the buffet was opened the crowd thinned a little.

At the end of the bar, furthest away from Rob and Sue was a small stage where the karaoke machine had been set up. It was only playing a selection of popular music as background at the moment. Eva and Ana walked up to the stage followed by dozens of pairs of eyes. They flicked through the digital song book and pressed a button on the consul. Within seconds the familiar opening bars of an Abba song turned head towards the stage and the girls began singing 'Mamma Mia'. The whole pub was stunned by the polished performance and showed their appreciation with loud applause when the song ended. Another button pushed and another Abba song began and the girls sang 'Dancing Queen' to the delight of the audience. Rob noticed the local reporter taking great interest in the performance. The girls certainly had his attention. The opening bars of the third song, 'Fernando', brought appreciative applause. People liked what they heard and when the finished there were cries of 'More'. Ana flicked through the digital track list as Eva left the stage and grabbed Sue's hand with her right and Luci's with her left and dragged them up onto the stage.

"Don't worry Ana and I will take the lead you just join in where you can and follow our moves."

Ana pressed the button and the Spice Girls song 'I want to be your lover' began to play. Sue and Luci did very well keeping up with Ana and Eva and by the end of the second track, 'Wannabe' they were well into the moves and they positively glowed as they left the stage to even louder applause.

There was quite a buzz in the crowd and offers to buy them drinks came flooding in. They did perform one more Abba track before calling it a day at 11:00 and walking home. From the stage they announced that they dedicated their final track to their good friend Emma Sunday. Money, Money, Money. Luci smiled at them, but no one else had heard of Emma Sunday.

Sue and Luci set off mid-morning with Ana and Eva in the back seat of Rob's car. They were heading for Monk's Park shopping centre in

York. According to Luci it was the best place around for the latest fashions. Before they left, Rob had given Sue an envelope. She knew it was full of money because he had taken out thirty £20 notes before handing it to her.

"I put £100 to win on 'My New Girl' in the last race yesterday. Get whatever you need," he said.

They were home by mid-afternoon laughing and giggling like school girls.

"Ana says I can spend the night with them tonight so that we don't see each other tomorrow before the wedding. We're going to have a girlie night in, have a face mask, a drink or two and watch a DVD. So I'll see you at the registry office at 5:15 tomorrow. Eric and Rose are taking me and Luci. You are taking Justin, Ana and Eva." She blew him a kiss turned and followed the other three through the archway to the stable block accommodation, all four of them loaded with shopping bags.

Ana and Eva knocked on the door at 3:30 as agreed to allow plenty of time to get to the registry office. When he opened the door Rob was speechless. The girls were certain to attract attention. They had made every effort to make their make-up and hair perfect and wore very simple plain pastel green and blue summer dresses, very short of course. White open toed sandals with heels that were possibly more than four inches with a white clutch bag to finish the look.

"Come in and take a seat, we've got a few minutes before we have to go."

They went through to the living room and sat with JB who was playing a game on his phone. Rob was checking a street map of York to find a suitable car park, he had only been able to reserve one for the bridal car at the registry office. Eric and Rose came downstairs, Eric having made a special effort because Sue had asked him to walk her in.

"Are you ready then, Son?" Eric asked.

"Just about," Rob replied "I'll get my jacket on and we'll be off. We've got a good five-minute walk from the car park."

Rob was right about the press photographers. There were eight or nine of them snapping away as he approached the registry office but they weren't focussed on him as much as on the mystery girls with him and the girls played their part posing for the cameras together and singly.

Rob stood waiting at the desk in the ceremony room. Justin stood beside him with the rings tightly pressed in his hand. They heard the door behind them open and turned to see Sue framed by the doorway wearing a pure white silk dress cut to mid-thigh length over which was a floating silk jacket finishing mid-calf. Her shoes were also white with a silk finish and she had white flower buds woven in her hair and carried a single red rose. As she walked towards him on Eric's arm, he could see Luci coming behind her in an identical outfit minus the over jacket and the rose. When she reached her position next to Rob, she turned to Luci, handed her the rose and smiled at her.

The service was a blur to her almost as if she wasn't there. Her responses were automatic until she heard the words. "Do you, Susan Elizabeth, take this man Robert George as your lawful husband?"

"I do…"

Printed in Great Britain
by Amazon